THE WARRIOR GENE

Neil Staley

Paperback edition January 2023
Book design by Nada Orlic

ISBN: 979-8-218-10075-9

For Dad

You are my greatest inspiration while I make toast.

Contents

Chapter One

It didn't take long to work out why the two men had found the only open parking space on the entire street. The orange hue of the sodium street light flickered incessantly in time with the *plink, plink, zzzz, plink* of the bulb, and cast an inconsistent jittery tangerine glow around the town car. They sat inside, wearing heavy overcoats, accustomed to the practice of a nightly vigil inside a car with the engine switched off and subzero temperatures pressing against the windows. Apex Laboratories was renowned in the private security sector for its fastidiousness in recruiting its personnel, and treated them with a sort of surprising degree of professionalism not usually found outside the inner circles of government security.

Agent Reginald Thompson still held the faintest tinge of a Barbados accent that clung onto his rumbling baritone words even after four decades of life in Washington DC, most of which had been spent in the employ of the United States Treasury. His partner of four years, Harry Caine, couldn't have been a more polar opposite. Tall, pale and gaunt, he passed the time obsessively filing and polishing his nails and working over a piece of nicotine gum with a slow, rolling chew that reminded Reg of a lazy Californian cow on its last piece of succulent cud.

"Well, you really know how to pick a spot," Reg said, reaching forward to turn up the football game on the radio and trying to ignore the constant flicker of the street light through the windshield. The Redskins were playing the Cowboys and he wasn't about to let the hours of uninterrupted silence go to waste.

"What can I say," Harry replied in a drawn out southern drawl that was as slow and lazy as his chewing. "It takes a natural. You wouldn't have found this spot if there was a sign in flashing lights with your name on it."

Reg chuckled, a deep rumbling sound that always reminded Harry of some evil cartoon sorcerer. "That's because I wouldn't have parked in a spot under the only God damned broken light on the street that's gonna give you and me a seizure before our shift is out."

A pair of car headlights appeared farther along the street. Harry stopped filing his pinky nail and looked up. The vintage Camaro pulled up to the curb just shy of the entrance to the apartment building on the other side of the street. The young man who climbed out shot them a look before rounding the car and disappearing inside.

"That's a helluva ride," Harry said, admiring the pristine Camaro before returning to his manicure.

"Do you think he has any idea how important he is?" Reg said, keeping his eyes fixed on the building until he saw the lights go on in the seventh floor windows, high above.

"Nope," Harry said. "Not a clue. I'm surprised that they let him out of there at all."

Reg nodded. "Well, let's make sure he gets back in one piece. I don't want to be handing out my resume to the Downtown mall if I can help it."

The game kicked off, the thin, rasping sounds of the cheering crowd seeping through the town car's cheap speakers like a distant echoing static.

Deep into the fourth quarter, the Redskins were handing it to the Cowboys, up by thirteen going into the final four minutes. Reg sipped on a thermos of coffee, content with the progress of his team and the fact that the coffee was still satisfyingly hot. Harry carefully wrapped the used nicotine gum in a wrapper and placed it into the clean ashtray, before immediately unwrapping a new piece and slipping it delicately into his mouth.

"So how come you don't like football?" Reg said, screwing the thermos lid back on and reaching around Harry's seat to put it back into his holdall.

"It's not that I don't like it," Harry replied, eyeing up some unseen imperfection in one of his nails. "I just didn't take the time to..."

Tap, tap, tap.

Harry snapped his head around to stare out of the driver's window. A gloved hand appeared, holding a set of car keys. It rapped on the window a second time. _Tap, tap, tap._ Both agents had their hands on their guns, adrenaline flooding their systems.

"Step back from the vehicle!" Harry said, all trace of laziness dispelled from his voice as he barked the order through the glass.

The gloved hands raised, palms out and the figure moved back.

"Who are you?" Harry snapped, his fingers tightening around the grip of his pistol. From the passenger seat, Reg could only see the figure from the chest down. A heavy black or navy overcoat and red scarf, folded neatly over a bright white shirt collar.

"Roll the window down, Harry," Reg said, twisting slightly in his seat so that he could free his weapon hand more easily. Harry pressed the window button on the door and the window whirred down. An invisible breeze pushed inside the car, icy cold and full of foreboding.

"I have identification," the figure said smoothly. "I'm going to reach into my coat for it. I'll move slowly."

Harry said nothing and the pair watched, rigid with tension as the figure unbuttoned his coat and pulled it open, slowly reaching a gloved hand toward an inside pocket.

"Nice and easy, partner," Harry said.

The gloved hand didn't pause, dipped into the inside pocket and drew out a small black wallet. It moved closer as the figure held it out toward the window, and then fell open, twelve inches from Harry's face, revealing an ID card with a photo.

"FBI?" Harry said after a moment, relaxing a little. "And you're Agent..." he looked at the card again. "Smith?"

"*Special* Agent," the figure said. "Would you like to examine my credentials?"

Harry turned to look at Reg, who nodded, hand still on his weapon, tucked neatly inside his coat. Harry turned back to the window, the ID card still hanging in the air a few inches away. "Sure," he said, reaching out for the wallet. "Stay right there for me. This'll just take a moment."

"Take your time," the figure said, stepping back slightly and buttoning his coat. On the radio, the Redskin's quarterback threw an interception and the Cowboys took the game to within six with two and a half minutes remaining.

Reg opened the glove box and drew out a small scanning unit, about the size of an old CD player. He opened the lid, removed the ID card from the wallet and placed it face down on the glass plate inside the scanner. He activated it and glanced out of the window. The figure was standing back, gloved hands clasped in front of him. As the scanner hummed on his lap, Harry pulled open the small display on the rear of the unit and waited for it to flicker to life. A thumb print and password later and the screen showed an image of the ID, a slowly turning ‚wait‘ icon hovering in front of it.

Reg didn‘t take his eyes from the figure‘s gloved hands as Harry waited for the scanner to complete its cycle. A moment later, the wait icon was replaced by a green ‚cleared‘ and Harry stared at the screen.

“Hologram checks,” he said. “It‘s legit.”

Reg nodded. “Ok, give it back to him and find out what this guy wants. It‘s freezing in here.”

Harry handed the card and wallet back to the figure.

“Thank you,” he said, stowing the wallet back into his overcoat. “So what brings Apex Labs out here?”

Harry and Reg exchanged glances.

“Babysitting detail,” Harry said, but I‘m guessing you know that.

The figure stepped forward and leaned down, peering into the car with a smile. “I‘m coming by out of professional courtesy. We‘re setting up a sting operation two blocks over. Narcotics bust with the DEA. One of our spotters called you in. You‘re far enough away so that I can let you stay here and see out your shift, but I‘d appreciate it if you let your superiors know to contact our field office before sending someone out to relieve you.”

Harry nodded. “Oh, there won‘t be anyone else coming out. Just need to make sure that our guy gets into work on time in the morning.”

The figure nodded and reached his left hand into the car toward Reg. “Special Agent Joshua Smith,” he said, grinning as Reg took his gun hand from within his coat and reached out.

“Reg Thompson. Thanks for the heads up.”

Smith pulled a compact, pistol-like weapon from a pocket as Reg took his hand.

Snick.

Harry‘s head tilted to one side slightly as the needle bolt shot through his ear and into his brain, killing him instantly. His head righted itself, dead eyes staring blankly forward through the windshield. Before Reg could let go, a pair of bright headlights suddenly appeared directly in front of the car. He turned to look, squinting into the blinding light.

Snick.

“Thank you,” Smith said, stowing the sleek weapon back into his coat pocket and letting Reg‘s hand drop limply into his lap. He opened the car door, pressed the button to close the window and reached inside, stowing the ID scanner back in the glove box. Another man opened Reg's door and shifted him in his seat with gloved hands so that he, like Harry, was sitting perfectly straight, staring unblinking out through the windshield. The two men disappeared in the haze of bright headlights and the car pulled smoothly away a moment later.

Reg was spared a hard Redskins loss as the Cowboys turned the game around with a touchdown in the dying seconds. The street light flickered unsympathetically above.

Plink, plink, zzzz, plink.

Chapter Two

No amount of rummaging around in pockets or rifling through his messenger bag yielded the card key needed to gain access to the Hub, the innermost lab within the Ark complex of Apex Laboratories. Dr. Alexander Bishop patted his jacket pockets one more time and then returned to scratching his head and staring at the pile of bag entrails spread on the pristine hallway floor. He made a mental note to file the coffee receipt that was laying half under an old scientific calculator, next to a handful of paper clips and a dried out Sharpie. He could see his taser in the bag, his initials etched messily into the yellow pistol grip.

With a sigh, he bent to pick up the clutter, and paused. The coffee receipt. Coffee cup. The car! In his mind's eye he could see the blue thermal cup beside the card key, sitting on the roof of his car, parked clear across the lot on 4C, the level reserved for members of the Hub lab team.

The blurred, glass-like shimmer of the Potomac added to the icy feel of the early November morning. Despite the early hour, the lab complex was bustling with activity, as guard watches changed and the early shift alert was heightened. He pulled his ID from the warmth of his parka pocket four times on the three hundred yard walk to the parking structure. With every sector on the complex bordered with razor wire-topped fences, checkpoints and armed guards, the security was no joke. It was also a huge pain in the ass. The return trip to the lab would yield the same four ID card inspections with the added bonus of a cup of cold coffee in one frozen hand and a very runny nose.

He cursed, remembering that his tissues were among the messenger bag debris back in the lab lunchroom and reluctantly used the sleeve of his coat instead. They wanted him for his top one percent genetics brain, though, right? Not his short term memory or lack of organizational skills. Still, he felt like the bungling, nerdy doctor instead of a world leading—albeit completely anonymous—geneticist, working inhuman hours at a beyond top secret laboratory fortress and guarded by the military's finest weapon-toting killjoys.

"ID please, sir."

Alex stepped up to the small pedestrian gate and pulled the card from his pocket, immediately dropping it to the wet asphalt. The soldier was clearly unimpressed. "Take your time, sir."

He didn't offer to help as Alex bent to pick up the card, wiping it on his pants before handing it over. The soldier examined it, glancing up to compare features between photo and person. It was the third time they had crossed paths this morning and over a year since Alex had started showing him his ID, crossing this particular checkpoint on his way to work. The soldier, Pietersen, his name badge read, handed the ID back. "Have a good day, sir," he said, before disappearing back inside the security hut without another word.

It took eleven more frigid minutes to get to the Hub door, and another ninety-seconds spent warming his coffee in the lunchroom microwave. Pulling the card out once more, he slid it through the reader with a satisfying *swish*. The coffee was burning his hand. The fingerprint scanner was being temperamental again and it took two swipes and two palm-presses before the vault-like door hissed open. Drexler was waiting for him on the other side.

"You look like you just ran a mile, Alex," he said dryly, turning away and stepping into the first test room, holding the door open for Alex as he followed, sweating now in the heavy coat. Drexler was a straight shooter and a detail freak, but never usually this surly, even at this time of the morning. Something was up. He leaned over the console and hit the space bar, sparking the screen to life before punching in his user ID and password. "There's something in batch DD-401A that I want you to take a look at."

Alex shrugged off the coat and laid it over the back of the work chair. A moment later it slid to the floor in a heap. Alex didn't appear to notice. Drexler looked from Alex to coat, back to Alex, and paused. When Alex didn't respond, his gaze fixed intently on the glowing display, he turned slowly back to the monitor and navigated through a number of screens until he reached a page with a list of code numbers, each attached to a file folder.

"This was just rewritten yesterday," Alex said, leaning in to squint at the rows of numbers. "There were no anomalies. I embedded them myself. All standard protocols applied. There was nothing worth…"

"I'm not seeing any anomalies, Dr. Bishop." Drexler navigated to a nest of folders on the screen, exploding with a technical animation to show a tree of codes. One was steadily blinking, red to grey. "I'm seeing a partial code with incomplete data security profiles. *That* is what I'm seeing." He straightened, with a sense of 'I win, you lose' and Alex clicked on the blinking file. An error code flashed up on the screen, with the words *Incomplete data utility.*

"Shit."

"Shit, exactly," Drexler said. Shifting his weight, he sat on the edge of the desk and sighed, his tone softening. "I know you've been pushing hard these past couple of weeks, Alex. And there's no one in here I trust more with this stuff, but it's the simple, through-the-cracks, mistakes like this that have my boss leaving wolf-sized teeth marks in my ass, which I then feel duly obliged to pass on to you. It happens so rarely with you that if any one of the other white coats around here screwed up this badly ten times as often, I wouldn't be half as pissed off."

Alex was nodding, working back in his mind to how he might have missed adding a simple security protocol to a single code file. Drexler leaned in. "And now that this one file is corrupted, you'll need…"

"To root out the whole batch and reassign sec tags to them, I know."

Drexler straightened and moved away from the workstation. Stepping toward the door, he ran his finger along the surface of the glass worktop. Looking at it, he smirked. "And if the other coats would just keep their labs half as clean as you do yours, I'll die a happy man. See if you can get those recoded today, ok?"

Alex was already sitting, skipping through pages of code and typing protocols as the glass door wafted silently closed behind Drexler. Everything in the Hub was glass, the doors, the walls, the work surfaces, all industrial duty hyperplex. Crystal clear, soundproofed and damned near indestructible. It was possible to see from the main outer wall all the way through the labs and offices to the far back wall, with only heavy concrete support columns blocking a perfect panoramic view. A *ding* from his computer and an intrusive pop-up window on his work screen broke Alex's flow. It was an e-chat from Audrey Nielsen, another geneticist whose lab was directly across the hallway from his. He looked up. She was smiling at him, gesturing with 'I'm typing in mid air' fingers, waiting for a response. He looked at the message.

Break room at 9:00. I want to hear about the date.

Alex reluctantly typed back. *I'm busy. Maybe later.* Audrey typed an *ok*, followed by a sad face. He didn't look up. He could imagine her imitating the expression clearly enough.

Drexler exited the elevator four levels above the Hub and walked toward his office, stopping to flash his ID at the armed soldier at the check-in podium. There were only a half dozen offices on the entire floor and more armed guards than throughout the labs downstairs. Mahogany-lined walls replaced glass and his desk was an old leather-topped affair, reeking of old politics and law.

"How is our star pupil?" A grey-haired, older man in an expensive navy blue suit was sitting on the plush leather couch, opposite Drexler's desk.

"Busy," Drexler said, hiding his surprise at the unexpected visitor. "Though he will undoubtedly plough through that batch of errors again in half the time I asked him to do it."

The man stared at Drexler. "Our timetable has been altered. We are pushing up initiation of Phase One, full body trials, to the 30th. That's twenty-two days from now."

Drexler stiffened slightly. "You know what you're asking. Three weeks doesn't give us a reasonable pool testing window, let alone a full body trial test." He stood up and walked around the desk, a low mahogany coffee table between them. "I know what you are looking for, what you are looking to achieve. But it needs to be done *perfectly*. There simply cannot be any room for the smallest error. Rushing this will not help to avoid that."

The man sat forward, placing a small wood carving of an apple onto the coffee table. "I know what I'm asking, Henry. My question to you is; do you think he will find it? Is he good enough?"

"He is good enough half asleep. You should take my word for it some time. You've seen the ratings on him for two years. He's aced every test, every scenario and every type of examination we've thrown at him since we had him pulled from the MIT program. That's something they are still very much pissed over, by the way, in the same way the Bulls would've been pissed if we'd spirited away Michael Jordan right after the world had just recognized his true potential. He is intuitive in a way that makes me think he's already seen all the answers. His error rate is zero. *Zero.* I've been doing this a long time, Charles, and I'm not blowing smoke up my own ass when

I say that there aren't many in the field that don't look up to my knowledge and expertise."

"What's your point, Henry?"

Drexler paused, irritated. "I am struggling to keep up with this kid, just in order to write *mistakes* for him to find and rectify. It's quite staggering really. I keep having to come up with increasingly complex scenarios just to be sure he won't assume these mistakes are being manufactured. Hell, I'm not sure he doesn't already know that."

"Would he come to you if he thought they were?"

Drexler pondered that for a moment, uncertain. "Yes, I believe he would."

"Good." The man stood suddenly, having heard everything he needed to hear, and made for the door. "She will be pleased to hear that." He opened the door and then paused, turning to Drexler. "I appreciate what you've done with him thus far, Henry. Bring him on board. Let's see if he's as good as you say he is. For your sake, I hope he is."

The lab lunchroom was busy by the Hub's standards. Six of the eleven scientists who worked on Alex's floor were scattered about the room at the various tables, some eating pre-made lunches and others with styrofoam plates of food from the Hub's staff kitchen. 'It's not great, but it's free' was the standard rib poker. Alex sat down at a table by the window. It was the only table he ever sat at. Everyone knew this and so it was always open.

The window overlooked the front courtyard and the river beyond. Alex liked the scene. It helped to clear his mind, or at least reduce the static. He'd even tried to paint it once, from memory, in his apartment. The result wasn't half bad, but it was only deemed good enough to hang in the spare bedroom. He'd try again, when he could drum up the enthusiasm and make the time. Besides, he wanted to wait for the snow. It would arrive any day now. As he watched, hands moving automatically to open the Tupperware container holding his sandwich, a flock of geese flew overhead and out toward the river. The sparkling of the water was so bright that it left dark pinprick stars in his vision and he had to blink them away before squinting out once more, looking for the fleeing birds.

"So tell me how it went!"

Alex was startled out of his calm as Audrey scraped the chair out noisily from the table and sat down, thumping her elbows on the tabletop. She was an energetic girl in her late-twenties, with wide, bright blue eyes and thick, wavy dark red hair that cascaded down over the shoulders of her lab coat. The freckles that formed a band across her cheeks and nose seemed too ordered, and Alex had previously wondered if she painted them on somehow. She liked her appearance and aside from almost living at the gym, she spent a lot of time exploring hair color and makeup products. Half of the other guys in the Hub wanted to take her to bed, but despite her easily judged appearance, he thought she was basically a sweet girl who was at the front of the line when they were handing out enthusiasm. She was even marrying an accountant. He drove one of those small electric cars that you wished they would just make cooler looking.

"You'd better spill those beans right now, and they had better be tasty!"

He couldn't help but smile, taking a bite out of the sandwich. The roasted turkey was perfect, but the lettuce was a little too crunchy today, bitter.

"The date lasted longer than I expected," he said, covering his mouth as he spoke through a mouthful of food. Audrey slumped slightly and she tilted her head to one side in a disappointed 'are you kidding me?' sort of way. "She is, surprisingly, a very nice girl. I would think that there's a pretty good chance of getting together again at some point."

Audrey sat back and crossed her arms over her chest. "You've used those exact words on each of the previous four occasions that you've kicked one of my friends to the curb, Alex. You need some new lines. What exacting requirement didn't she meet this time? Was her hair the wrong shade of brown? Did she chew on the wrong side of her mouth? Or maybe she was just too perfect for you, Alex. Which is it?"

She sat impatiently, waiting for an honest answer. Alex looked at the table for a moment. He had the words, all chambered and ready to fire. He just didn't want to hurt Audrey's friend's feelings, especially hearing it from Audrey. He couldn't, therefore, tell her that Nikki, although very sweet, in a needy, whimsical sort of way, had a fingernails-on-chalkboard laugh, a lazy left eye that had constantly made Alex want to reach over and push it open with his finger, and to cap it off, and this was the deal breaker, a ridiculous lack of perceived intelligence and common sense. She was beautiful, fit, generally very attractive, but that was it. When they had been talking about traveling and some of the places Alex had seen during his year break before joining MIT, he had asked Nikki what country in South America she would most like to visit. When she had bitten her bottom lip, cast her eyes skyward in genuine deep thought, and said, "Florida", the camel's back had snapped.

"We just don't share the same core interests, Audrey," Alex said, not meeting her gaze until she didn't reply. When he did look up she was squinting at him, her face a mask of suspicion. He considered adding further explanation, but quickly thought better of it.

"What does that even *mean,* Alex? The same core interests. Really, Alex, what the fuck? Is that what I'm supposed to take back to her? Goddamn core interests?"

Alex finished chewing and looked outside again as Audrey huffed. A small convoy of black SUVs was pulling up to the main entrance. He wiped the corners of his mouth with a napkin as a group of men in identical dark suits got out of the vehicles and made their way to the main doors with choreographed, flock-of-birds-like precision. Two of the men carried briefcases, chained to their wrists, and all were armed, six with automatic weapons, poorly concealed beneath their jackets. A blue Charger pulled up and two uniformed men got out, saluted rigidly by the soldier who waited to take their car. They strode into the building behind the suits.

Alex took his Hub-com from his pocket and put it on the table, turning the alert volume up.

"I'm not going anywhere, Alex," Audrey said, refolding her arms defiantly.

"She is nice, Audrey," Alex said quietly, looking at the Hub-com while his hands moved automatically to clean up his unfinished lunch. "Maybe it's just too soon, you know? Maybe I just need to really relax into who I am now, without…" He trailed off and his hands stopped moving.

He thought about Rachel, his ex-wife, and the weight of not being part of that unit suddenly hit him, the awareness of being outside the circle. There was no way back, especially seeing that Rachel was now Mrs. Leoni and not Mrs. Bishop, and they had moved to San Diego last spring. The warmth of Audrey's hand on his wrist made him look up. Her expression was one of caring support and sympathy. She squeezed his arm, then rubbed it, just how a grandmother might squeeze and rub the arm of her grandson when he tells her that he's just been dumped by his first girlfriend and love of his life.

"And I keep pushing all of these blind dates on you like some meat market mercenary." She leaned back. "I'm sorry I made you try, Alex. It's not up to me when you're ready. I'm just trying to be a good friend. Get you moving again. Shake off the rust. Know what I mean? You can't turn into some hermit who only has his work, a gloomy apartment and that ridiculously ancient car of yours."

Audrey liked to think that she knew everything about everyone on their team, but Alex didn't share much, with her or anyone else. Even here, among the best and the brightest, he was an outsider. Not quite understood, not quite accepted. He did care about what other people thought of him, and he did embellish the persona of the work-obsessed introvert who was, perhaps, just a little touched in the head. It kept the vultures from circling and generally meant that he was free from the ball and chain of relationships he simply didn't care to nurture. A diagnosis of Asperger Syndrome when he was eight allowed him play a number of cards when the need arose; The 'Ah, so that's why he's socially awkward and has no friends', and 'Poor guy, but that's obviously why he's so brilliant' hands. It even worked with the girls, if he spun it the right way.

"Thanks, Audrey." He smiled briefly and nodded. "I do appreciate you trying to help me. No one really wants to be lonely—" (card #1) "—and when I'm really ready, maybe you can help me with it, seeing as I'm such an awkward fuck up."

With card #2 in play, the reaction was just as he knew it would be. She leaned forward again and took his hand.

"Awww, Alex. Come on now. You are not some lost cause! Not while Audrey 'The fixer' Neilsen is on your case! We will find someone for you. Someone perfect. I promise, ok?"

Alex glanced at the Hub-com, mentally ticking off the seconds since the men in suits had entered the building. "Ok," he said, "You promised."

She smiled, standing. "I'll leave you alone for a bit, ok, love? Just don't think I won't be doing the necessary research into finding your perfect soul mate."

She released his hand and sauntered away from the table. Alex was irked that she had left the chair pulled out. He stood and rounded the table, pushing the chair in and reaching out for the Hub-com, his hand hovering over the pager-sized communications device. A few seconds later, the screen lit up and the unit vibrated noisily on the table surface. Alex snatched it up as he walked from the lunchroom and started down the hall.

He was halfway to the elevators when he glanced at the screen. The message read; *Conference Code 02. Level 4. STAT.*

Chapter Three

The elevator opened to the backs of two uniformed soldiers, rifles held in front of their chests. They turned in unison as the doors slid open, keeping the weapons close, but not lowering them to point anywhere besides the ceiling, for now.

"Ah, Alex!" Drexler turned and raised an arm. "Let him through. Alex, come this way. Let him through!"

"ID please, sir." The nearest soldier stepped in front of him. Alex was already taking his ID card from the clip on his lab coat pocket. The soldier looked it over and nodded. "Thank you, sir."

He stepped aside as Drexler reached them, stretching out an arm and guiding Alex past the guards. "This way, Alex. We're about to get started."

He strayed toward a woman holding a note pad and spoke something softly in her ear. She nodded and made for the elevators, but she didn't push the call button. She drew a key card out of her pocket and inserted it into a metal panel in the wall. A steel panel slid in front of the elevator doors, sealing the room. Likewise, another barrier slid into place in front of a single doorway near the front wall. The stairwell exit. Drexler touched Alex's arm and then led him down a wood paneled hallway to an office door with a large brass plaque on it.

Henry Drexler. Director of Operations

It was a stark contrast to the hyper clean, glass-lined labs of the Hub. The floors were carpeted; there was wood on the walls, even on the ceiling. Alex took a seat in a chair against the far wall, where he had a good view of the rest of the room. As he watched, six of the suited men entered, including the two carrying briefcases. An Army Colonel walked in, followed by two more men in dark suits and standard issue aviator sunglasses. There were no visible earpiece wires on any of the obvious agency men in the room, but he knew that they were all wired for comms.

When every available seat was taken and everyone else had settled into a standing position, mostly behind the couch, Drexler sat on the edge of his desk and folded his arms. "We are waiting for one more," he said.

A few moments later the door opened and an older man in an expensive-looking dark grey suit entered. Immediately, the man seated in the armchair to the left of the couch stood and stepped aside, vacating his seat, which the older man took without a word. He nodded slightly at Drexler, who stepped forward to speak.

"Gentlemen, this is a day of two hands. On the one hand, it is a day that has been long anticipated and we are very excited and proud to see finally arrive. On the other, it is a day that brings with it an immense weight of responsibility and the promise of some very challenging times ahead. Make no mistake, for what we are about to embark upon is an endeavor of the utmost delicacy, that could, if not guided correctly, shred the very fabric of society, both domestically and around the world. If we succeed, as I am entirely confident we will, the world will change forever, and there will be no going back."

He paused, letting the vagueness of his statement spawn the multitude of questions now swimming in everyone's heads. He turned to pick up a small remote from the desk and pressed a button. A soft hum came from the opposite wall. A section of the wood paneling slid aside to reveal a large screen, upon which the word *Icarus* appeared, glowing brightly like a Hollywood movie credit.

The word faded and an image of a monkey in a glass cage appeared. It was atop a workbench in a lab similar to those downstairs. The monkey sat fidgeting in the cage, its head turning in quick, snappy movements, curious eyes darting left and right as various white coats walked about in the background.

"This is IC-044/A. Otherwise known as Jimmy. As you can see, Jimmy is behaving very typically. In a few moments, Jimmy will be the only rhesus of his kind on the planet, and it is his very existence today that has made this meeting, and this project, possible."

The image shifted to a technical slide and Drexler continued to talk while Alex began to study the people in the room. He concluded, after a few minutes, that at least half of them were military, and most of the other half were 'off the books' government types. Probably from various covert science divisions. The kind that are funded by twenty-thousand-dollar toilet seats.

It was the older man in the armchair that intrigued him the most, mainly because he was obviously the most powerful man in the room and he couldn't get a read on him. That fact alone was concerning, because this very facility was so high up the food chain that anyone throwing that much weight around in here was quite the deal on the outside too. Suddenly, the man turned to look right at him. His icy blue eyes locked on his and Alex found himself smiling thinly and nodding an awkward acknowledgement.

The man stared for a moment before turning back to the video, where Jimmy's cage was being moved to butt up against another identical glass case, which held two other monkeys. The sidewall divider of Jimmy's case lifted, transforming the two cases into one larger one.

"This brings us to the tip of the spear," Drexler went on. "You see that, initially, Jimmy's interaction with the other two subjects is uneventful. Besides some minor acknowledgements they almost appear to be ignoring one another at this point." The right side of the TV screen slid inwards, showing a spectrum equalizer type graph, displaying Jimmy's vital functions and brainwave type activity. "And this, gentlemen, is where we change the world."

Another pop-up window appeared, showing a DNA strand, rotating in a 3D view. The screen was split between the DNA pop-up and the view of Jimmy with his new friends.

"Over the past five years, our teams of geneticists have painstakingly developed a serum that analyzes and modifies targeted DNA strands within an individual host."

Two pairs of gloved hands reached into view and held Jimmy against the wall of the cage. Another pair of hands appeared, one holding a syringe filled with bright green liquid. It took some visible effort, but Jimmy was held steady as the fluid was quickly injected into the back of his neck.

"And so," Drexler continued, stepping away from the desk, "Jimmy is now carrying the Icarus particle. In a few very short minutes, the chosen DNA strand we have targeted will be read and analyzed, and will then begin to react to the Icarus serum."

Alex glanced across the room as the Colonel leaned in toward the older man and asked if they were watching a recording. He had called him Charles.

"No, it's a live feed," Charles replied. "From inside our Drayton lab. This test has been performed dozens of times, with the same result. You'll see in a moment."

The Colonel nodded and returned to viewing the screen, now showing an increasingly agitated Jimmy. He began to twitch, and then began to move erratically, as if being consistently shocked with electricity. There were a few murmurs in the room. Drexler spoke up. "Now, don't forget, this is an experimental evaluation. Our purpose here is to show you how far we've come and where the project is at this moment in time, as well as introducing you to the next phase of the project."

Jimmy was scaring the other monkeys in the cage. There was no audio on the video, but it was clear that the monkeys were making a lot of noise. Suddenly, Jimmy leapt on the nearest rhesus and started biting and tearing ferociously, clawing its belly with hind legs while he bit and gnawed at the other monkey's face and head. Within a few seconds, he had killed, no, *destroyed* the other monkey and turned immediately toward the second, before a glass partition was lowered into the cage, separating a now ferociously wild Jimmy from the other, terrified, rhesus. The video was paused and everyone turned. The frozen image showed a blurred and demonic-looking Jimmy mid-screech as he scratched furiously at the partition.

"This is where we are at," Drexler said. "We have the ability to re-write a DNA code in order to change behavior at the conscious and instinctive level. The magic ingredient here is that we can just about do it in a live host *instantaneously.*"

He let that sink in while he walked back around his desk. Alex latched onto the 'just about' part. "As you can see," Drexler continued, "The current protocol is flawed. Our aim is to have total control of the process of DNA reautomation, as well as the *degree* of reautomation."

He sat down and Charles stood up slowly. "We have never been as close as we are now," he said, "to rewriting human DNA and managing behavior at the genetic level in a living subject. I want to put it to you this way, before I outline the steps we have in place for the next phase of project Icarus."

Charles stood very still, hands in pockets, looking more like a fatherly boss reassuring concerned employees than a man of great power, who likely gave two hoots about everyone else in the room. "Just imagine for a moment, a world without hatred, without greed, without violence. These are simple words. They are easy to say. The vision is almost unfathomable, almost too out of reach to even comprehend. And yet, we are on the verge of being able to bring that impossibility into the realm of reality."

He nodded to one of the men holding a briefcase. The man walked over to Drexler's desk, opened the case and withdrew something before laying it on the desk top and retreating back to his spot by the wall. Charles walked over to Drexler's desk and picked up the glossy black file. Turning, he held it up for everyone to see. "This is my life's work. It will be my legacy, and it will change the world as we know it, for the better. What I need now, is your expertise in perfecting a process that, until now, has frustrated our best and brightest. We hit the same wall over and over again and yet are positive the solution is only just out of reach."

He dropped the file onto the coffee table. It was unmarked. Alex could see a smudged thumbprint on the cover. "This room constitutes the very finest minds that the United States government has to offer. You represent our best hope of success in a time when it is becoming more and more critical that an answer is found as soon as possible; for humanity's sake." He gestured to random people around the room. "The Harvard Science Laboratory, NASA, The CDC, DARPA, Berkeley Scientific Research Division, Gentex Labs, US RoboGene Industries, and our very own Apex Labs senior geneticist, Alex Bishop."

He stopped his gesturing with an outstretched arm, pointing in Alex's direction and then put his hand back in his pocket. He was immensely calm and Alex's gut told him that he could not be trusted with a dime. But then, in this business, who could?

"Gentlemen," Drexler spoke from behind his desk. "You will be individually briefed on the current project segment assigned to you and your division. None of you will be made aware of any of the other teams' assigned project or progress. Any and all communication regarding this project will be directed to your assigned project liaison and *no one* else. Am I clear?"

There were murmured affirmations and nods throughout the room. The door abruptly opened and Drexler's assistant stepped inside. "Gentlemen, if you would accompany me to the conference rooms, we will begin the project briefing process."

Alex watched as the room slowly emptied, until only a handful of bodies were left shuffling out the door. He stood and made his way to follow when Drexler leaned forward. "Dr. Bishop, stay for a few minutes, if you would."

Alex looked at the door as it closed behind the last man, leaving one of the stone-faced security suits standing by it, and the Colonel, Charles and Drexler in the room with him.

"Have a seat, son." It was the Colonel who spoke first. "This'll take a few minutes."

Alex sat in the armchair opposite Charles, with the Colonel seated in the center of the couch on his left. Drexler maintained his distance at his desk. The expression on his face was one of nervous anticipation, like that of a father about to watch his son fight in his first ever boxing match. Alex hoped he wasn't about to get pummeled.

"There are only five people in the world who know what I'm about to tell you, including you. And there are two reasons that I'm telling you at all. Firstly, you come as highly recommended as anyone I've ever had recommended to me. Secondly, we are at an impasse and have brought this team together to find a solution. We feel that if you, Dr. Bishop, can't do what we need you to do, the whole project goes up in smoke and we leave the field with a big, fat *one* in the loss column."

"What about everyone else who is working on the project?" Alex asked. "Will you be telling them the same thing when we're done here? There are more than one or two incredibly intelligent and talented individuals involved here, Colonel. Why should the buck stop with me, when there are so many to share the burden of blame when we find that, after all, the code can't be broken? Share and share alike."

The Colonel glanced at Drexler. Charles stood impassively, hands still in pants pockets.

"Despite the secrecy involved here, Dr. Bishop," the Colonel went on, "There are certain layers of the onion we should share amongst the higher levels of the government, the military and select private organizations, in the name of... calmer seas, shall we say. Maintaining the status quo, at this point, is essential if we are to be afforded the latitude and resources to see this through. As we begin this next phase of the project, it would be unrealistic for us to assume that we could maintain airtight secrecy at any kind of viable level. When you're dealing with humans, secrets and safe are two words that are never in the same sentence."

Alex thought back to the meeting with Drexler earlier in the day. The error codes. How he had supposedly made a mistake that even one of the mid-level coats wouldn't have made. "You were testing me," he said, looking at the wooden apple on the coffee table. Drexler looked at Charles. Alex went on. "You should have made those errors a little more obscure, Dr. Drexler. They were just enough to make me doubt my process, but, really, I wouldn't have come close to making mistakes like that. Any of them."

"I told you," Drexler said, looking at Charles, who simply nodded approvingly. "Simple enough," Charles said. "Really this is all child's play to you, isn't that right, Dr. Bishop? You are way ahead of us already. Your muddy, ambiguous exterior, that thing you rely on to keep the ripples down, to keep from drawing too much attention, is very effective. But we all know you're as sharp as a scalpel. That's why you're here. Drop your veil, or do not, it's up to you. I am not interested in how you portray yourself to others, or what your ulterior motives surrounding this 'game face' of yours are. What interests me are your unmatched abilities in the field of genetic decoding, reconstruction and functional bio coding and DNA research."

He stepped closer, stopping eighteen inches away from the chair, and leaned forward, looking down into Alex's face. "There is no accepting or declining this offer, Alex. There is only success or failure, and failure is not an option we will entertain."

He looked at the Colonel and nodded, turning back to face Drexler while the Colonel spoke.

"Son, we are having all of your lab equipment and notes moved from your home lab and installed at your new facility, here at the Ark. Dr. Drexler will show you to your new home. I promise you, we have spared no expense. You will be given everything you need and, as of this moment, your salary just quadrupled. There will also be a bonus that you can retire on should you come through on time. Do you have any questions for me that you feel Dr. Drexler cannot answer for you?"

Alex smiled at the delicately put question. "No, Colonel. I'm sure Dr. Drexler can clarify anything I may be unsure on."

With just a curt nod, the Colonel stood and made to leave. The security man stepped aside, opened the door and the Colonel walked from the room. Charles followed and turned as the Colonel disappeared into the hallway. "Good luck, Alex. I'll be expecting daily updates." He nodded at Drexler and stepped outside. The security man left, closing the door behind him, leaving Alex and Drexler alone in an uncomfortable silence.

"Am I free to go home at all?" Alex asked finally.

Drexler paused for a moment. "To say that our window of opportunity is small would be an understatement, Alex."

He bent and picked up the wooden apple, turning it over in his hand. Alex noticed that the tip of his ring finger was missing. He hadn't noticed it before. The scarring around the edge of the stub was not precise. That was the second scar he had noticed on Drexler, and was equally as intriguing as the first.

"Ok," Drexler said finally. "Get out of here, gather anything you think you may not be able to live without for a couple of weeks, sleep in your own bed tonight and report back at 06:00 tomorrow. I'll hold the Colonel off. And yes, he'll know. He knows how many steps you take from your bed to the pisser."

Alex looked up at him, a look of stubborn disappointment clouding his features.

"Look, you're not being held captive, Alex, either here or at home. I'm supposed to brief you on operational details, but it's safer not to until you check back in tomorrow. The less you know and all that."

"But what if I want to go home? What if I want to leave? Clear my head? This isn't exactly arts and crafts in here, Dr. Drexler."

"And you can leave whenever you want, go anywhere you want, after the project is complete." He tossed the apple to Alex. "Just think of it as overtime, for a solid two weeks."

Chapter Four

The market was a bustling, dusty sun trap, sprawling throughout the lower courtyard and some of the wider arches and sidewalks that hugged the fortress's outer walls. The swirling moat, fed from an underground spring that also supplied the fortress with fresh water, carried the scent of something dying, and on this day, one of the hottest of the summer, the stench was, to some, an unbearable blight on an otherwise majestic and awe-inspiring place.

Aaron Bashir weaved his way through the throng of market customers, his arms wrapped around a leather bundled object, clutched tightly to his chest. His robes enveloped his body and the heat crushed him from the inside and out, but he paid no attention. He was focused entirely on making his way to the Dawn Gate, beneath the southern most stone access bridge on the east wall of the fortress. His heart beat furiously in his chest as he carried the weight of his task heavily inside, yet was outwardly as calm and unhurried as all of his many years of meditation were allowing him to be. He knew that he was far from safe, even in this busy place, full of people and tourists, covering their mouths and noses with handkerchiefs and the shemaghs they had been almost forcefully convinced to buy from the multitude of aggressive vendors on the causeway leading into the market.

They were serving their purpose well, however, and Aaron spared a thought for a particularly sunburned tourist as he brushed by, his white button up shirt plastered with sweat to his pale, muscle-bound body. Aaron ignored the flies that darted about his face as he walked and did not see the pale tourist turn to follow him with his gaze as he continued on through the crowd.

A few minutes later, he approached the Dawn Gate, a dark iron door set back in the wall directly beneath the causeway above. He knocked twice, and then three more times, as instructed, and then waited, blissfully out of the blistering heat in the shade of the causeway. The wrenching of old bolts and locks drew his attention to the door and he scanned the walkway up and down the wall before stepping closer. It swung inward, revealing cool darkness beyond.

From the deep shadows of the entryway, a man appeared. He was tall and lean, and immediately imposing and he glared down at Aaron with an intensity that almost made the younger man look away. His white tunic looked immaculate in the dust-filled doorway, and a large curved sword was pushed through a red sash wrapped about his waist, the tasseled ends hanging down past his knee.

Aaron stepped inside and the man closed the door behind him before turning away, nodding for Aaron to follow. He led the way through several more heavy doors and along a series of corridors, taking Aaron deeper into the fortress. The hallways were well lit by shafts of bright sunlight, punctuating the gloom through high openings in the sandstone walls.

Aaron's grip on the bundle at his chest did not lessen, and he was shown into a large room, a solitary old table at its center. He stepped through the door and his guide closed it silently behind him. No words were spoken and he waited in silence to be beckoned forward.

The man sitting at the table was poring over what looked like stacks of papers and rolled up scrolls, inspecting them with an ancient-looking, hand-held magnifying glass. He appeared old, bent forward, with a mass of graying dark hair and a thick beard about his face. Aaron could see that he was, on closer inspection, well groomed and younger than he had thought. He saw the oil on his beard, the neat trim lines around his temples and neck, and his skin was smoother than he had first assumed.

"I am not what you expected," the older man said, without looking up from his papers. "Why are you here, Aaron? What drove you to this place? To this time?"

Aaron looked down, frowning at the awkwardness of the questions, then back up at the older man. "I… I do not understand. What do you mean? Was I not ordered here? Was this not the right time? I… thought that this was the moment that I had been called for. I…"

"Yes, yes." The older man dropped the lens to the table with a *thud*. "You were told to come here, to bring this item with you. Your instructions were quite specific, I know." He raised his gaze, staring straight ahead. "Would you not have come still, had you not been told to? When did you feel that the time was right to make the journey here, to me, today?"

Aaron's gaze softened as he recalled the waking dream, three nights ago; the illusion of his mother, dead these past three years, holding out the pewter cross and his hand reaching out to take it as it turned into the shimmering, hand-beaten tip of an ancient spear. The impulse to leave his home and make the journey to the fortress had been instant and powerful. It was only later that morning that his uncle had taken him aside and handed him the package and spoken to him of a quest of the utmost importance.

"Yes, yes," the old man said, closing his eyes and nodding as if in some kind of secret agreement with his inner voice. "You knew to come here, and you would have been able to make the journey even without a single word of guidance. Yes, these are things that we knew would come to pass." He stood suddenly. "This is not a test, Aaron, although you are now in the time where all harmful things will reach out for you. Your journey here has put you before the eyes of many perils." He walked over and took Aaron by the shoulders. "But now you are here, and you bring with you The Word. That is all that is important."

"The Word?"

The older man led Aaron toward a door on the far side of the room. "The Word, Aaron, the most powerful word in all of history. The Word that will change the lives of every man, woman and child on this planet, forever." He tapped the package, held tightly in Aaron's arms. "And you've had it with you all along."

Outside, the sun was sliding along a smooth downward arc across the November sky. It was later in the afternoon and the market was thinning out as the vendors began to pack up their stalls for the day. They would be back before sunrise to repeat the process over, each day, every day. Some of the elders, those whom, over the years, had grown to command the most desirable spots in the courtyard, had been peddling their goods for six or seven decades, their humble businesses and coveted spots of precious square footage handed down from father to son for generation after generation since before the fortress was even built, at the beginning of the second century.

It was the central focus of a generally overlooked, and otherwise nondescript, village in the middle of lush palm groves, west of Palmyra, deep in the Syrian desert. The ancient Roman fortress had briefly served a key strategic role along the only road from Damascus, through the desert and across the Euphrates River into Mesopotamia. A standalone outpost, it had been home to seventy-five restless Romans, surrounded by some of the most unforgiving terrain on earth. It was solitary, overbuilt and under manned and during the final throes of the Empire had been overrun by local tribes who had banded together to oust the Romans only to fall apart and decimate one another once the fortress had been won.

They had all died over the same, deep seated blood feuds they had fought over for so long that no one was alive that truly knew the original offense that had been committed, or by whom. Local mythology, built upon the curses of slaughtered Roman soldiers and murdered Muslim warriors, had kept anyone from daring to occupy the sacred structure, until a caravan of charismatic and mysterious travelers–The Lost Ones, as the local tribes called them, for they appeared over the shimmering horizon and brought with them wisdom, wealth and secrets as deep as the desert itself–took up residence and claimed the fortress as their own.

For seventeen hundred years, the Lost Ones held the Fortress of Sands, and sway over the surrounding desert, from the northern region of the Syrian/Turkish border, to the southern plains into Jordan and Israel, and out to the east, to the shores of the Euphrates at Al Mayadin.

Over time, their ranks swelled, their presence spread across the globe and the importance of their role, the role they had been cast from the desert to fill, became all-encompassing, imprinted from birth and carried like the weight of the world until death. For each day that passes brings them closer to fulfilling their destiny; to extinguish the evil that is spreading throughout humanity like a cancer; cold, relentless, and hungry for souls.

Professor Marco Salomon opened the ancient book before him, stirring a small cloud of dust almost as old as the pages themselves. He referred to a small, well worn note book before carefully turning the oversized, hand crafted parchment pages, as the sparkling, swirling dust motes drifted lazily in the shaft of sunlight that cut across the left third of the table.

Aaron stood close by, watching the professor as he moved the pages, oh-so-slowly for fear that the ancient paper would crumble to dust between his fingers. He had been shown through a heavy black door and through a very narrow corridor, dusty and filled with the pungent smell of incense. There were carved inscriptions on the walls and floor but they shuffled along, shoulders brushing the sandstone walls, too fast for him to make any of them out. They had ducked through a small doorway and into the round chamber he now stood in. The low, domed ceiling had a trio of small openings that spilled shafts of bright sunlight onto hand beaten silver mirrors to light the room with ancient ingenuity. Three similar doorways were set into the walls, evenly spaced around the room.

He knew that they were underground, somewhere beneath the center of the fortress. Beyond that, he was lost, shuffled and shunted from room to room through a subterranean maze of hallways and antechambers that could've spat him right back out into the marketplace where he started from this very room for all he knew.

Salomon continued to carefully turn the pages of the old book and then consult his notebook, moving swiftly until his fingers touched the old parchment, when his movements instantly became as slow and deliberate as a surgeon's, moving over a piece of the most delicate tissue. Aaron watched the shafts of light shift slightly as the sun moved across the sky somewhere above. Eventually, the mirrors became virtually ineffective as the light faded and dusk approached. Professor Salomon hissed quietly and Aaron's attention was snapped back to the professor, now standing, hunched over a page, illuminated by the yellow glow of a pair of candles and what little light there was left in the room. He did not move, for what seemed like minutes, and remained fixed, staring through the lens, with its chipped edges and dusty surface.

"There are six ways to tell a fool," Salomon said quietly, breaking the heavy silence in the room. He was still closely studying a particular page in the old book but had put the lens aside. "Anger without cause, speech without profit, change without progress, inquiry without object, putting trust in a stranger, and mistaking foes for friends." He looked up. "You've heard of this proverb, yes?"

Aaron nodded. "I have, professor."

"And can you say which of these might tell me that you have acted as a fool, Aaron?"

Aaron thought for a moment, startled by the question. As he pondered, the three doors opened and three red-cloaked men stepped silently into the room. All three were armed with scimitar swords at their hips, and all wore veil masks over their faces. He stepped back without thinking and Salomon held up a hand. Aaron noticed the red and orange woven bracelet he wore around his wrist, with three small silver beads dangling against his tanned skin.

Salomon smiled. "Calm yourself, young one," he continued. "Stay close to me. These men are here for our protection, nothing more. They are Mamluk; once rulers of Egypt and Syria and the protectors of the desert. They live only to defend the keepers of The Word. They, and we, are *The Overwatch*. These Mamluk, you and I in this place, your teachers and family, your future guardians and closest allies." He paused, his expression tightening as if he had picked up an unfamiliar scent on the wind. "We must move The Word. Even as we speak, there are forces moving against us, outside, here, now."

Aaron frowned, shaking his head slightly. "But I saw no one," he said, almost imploringly. "I was not followed, nor did anyone spy upon me. I made sure. I used the old ways that my father taught me. I was…"

"Careful. Yes, I know," Salomon said soothingly. "You were not to know. You were outwitted by an evil far older and wiser than your tender years, Aaron, and you have still lessons to learn."

Salomon signaled to one of the cloaked Mamluks who immediately moved away from the shadows by the wall. Aaron was astounded at the perfectly silent approach the man made, despite his obvious size and strength. Salomon began to bundle the book tightly in the leather wrap once more, securing it with a thong before hoisting it under an arm. The cloaked man moved beside Aaron and guided him gently toward one of the far doorways, the professor just ahead of them. One of the other Mamluks opened the heavy door and stepped through.

"So I am a fool?" Aaron asked as he approached the doorway. "How did I fail you?"

Salomon stepped through, then paused, waiting for Aaron to follow. "The big man you spared a prayer for in the courtyard," he said, walking few steps ahead, "He was no friend."

Aaron was about to reply when a distant *boom* rattled the air around them. Salomon paused and then gestured to two of the Mamluks who set off, back across the room and through the far door. They shut and bolted it. The Mamluk still with them closed and locked their door and they began to make their way along another, slightly inclined passageway, lit only by small sconces close to the ceiling. Another *boom* barely a few minutes later and Aaron looked behind him, his view blocked by the Mamluk, whose large frame filled the entire hall space. Another sound followed, the *rat-tat-tat* of automatic gunfire, though Aaron couldn't tell from where. He hoped it was behind them and whispered a small prayer as he pushed on, following Salomon.

"We will have only a short time once we get to the road," Salomon said, hurrying ahead of them, the book tucked tightly beneath his arm. "Karesh will accompany you across the sands and onwards to Damascus. Our people there will meet you. They will make arrangements for you to leave the country."

After several turns and half a dozen heavy doors, they emerged outside in the shadow of the fortress walls, beneath a stone access ramp. The air was stifling and Aaron immediately missed the cool air inside the passageways. Karesh stepped out from beneath the ramp and looked up, nodding to the professor before climbing up to the roadway above. Salomon walked out and along the side of the ramp with Aaron following close behind. As they walked, the level of the ramp dropping below eye level, Aaron saw the Land Rover, sitting atop the ramp and surrounded by several armed Mamluks, this time with assault rifles instead of swords.

The Rover was dusty and well used, but looked sturdy with its crash bars and thick, sand crusted tires. There were several gasoline cans on the roof rack and a long antenna bent over the roof from the hood, tied down to the rear bumper. Salomon motioned for Aaron to follow as Karesh walked to the driver's door. A large Mamluk with a red sash opened the door for him and he climbed in. Salomon stopped and turned suddenly, the ramp at waist height beside them, and Aaron almost bundled into him.

"Aaron, I am sorry that we have had only moments. You know nothing of what lies ahead, and of the great responsibility that is being laid upon your shoulders. For that, I am truly sorry. Trust in The Word, as I do in you, and in your instincts to do what needs to be done. Never hesitate, and remember the six tells of a fool. The whole world will know you, my son." He raised his hand and removed the woven bracelet, handing it to Aaron, pressing it into his palm and closing his fist around it. "It is from the market outside. One of my dearest friends. He makes every one by hand. This is the only place in the world you can acquire one. Perhaps it will serve as a happy memento of this place, instead of what is to come." Then, reaching up, he touched Aaron's cheek. "Your father would be very proud, my son."

As Aaron smiled weakly at the old man, he heard a sudden *zip* sound, followed by a wet *thud* as Salomon's head exploded over his face and chest in a warm mist of blood and brain matter. He stood frozen, covered in sticky, warm blood as someone crashed into him, taking him to the ground beside the ramp and barking orders to take cover.

Karesh leapt out of the truck as the red sashed Mamluk turned, raising his weapon, and then fell back against the truck as he was hit in the chest by a high-velocity round. Sprinting around the truck, he leapt from the ramp, tackling Aaron to the sand and down into the shadows below. He pulled out a radio and spoke rapidly, barking orders as more gunfire opened up above them, his men returning fire. A loud *crack* beside his head showered his face in shards of stone and he flattened himself on the sand.

Aaron stared wide-eyed at the sand a few feet in front of his face as Karesh's weight kept him pinned to the ground. His terror was matched only by his desperate desire to push Karesh away so that he could flee back into the safety of the fortress.

"What... what's happening!" Aaron screamed. "Where's the professor?" His words kicked up the sand in front of his lips and he felt the harshness of the grains digging into his cheek.

"Stay down," Karesh said, a hand pushing Aaron's face into the sand. "Help is on the way."

Chapter Five

He was a little insulted. They weren't even trying to hide. Alex reached up to adjust the rearview mirror. He wanted to let them know he could see them, too, though they were making no efforts at all to conceal the fact that they were tailing him. The shaky image of the blue town car filled his vision for a second and he was left with the mental imprint of two expressionless faces with the same suits and the same sunglasses. He couldn't quite see if anyone was in the back seat or not.

The roads were slick with icy water and he felt the back end of the Camaro slip out when he turned a corner. The radio said they were headed for record lows for November and that the national weather center had issued a severe weather warning from New Hampshire down to Delaware. He decided that the garage might be the best place for the car if the weather really did turn. He could always cab it back to the complex in the morning if he had to. It wasn't late, but he knew he would have to stay up late to steam wash her chassis before he turned in. The salt grit on the roads at this time of year was not a welcome thing for car drivers, especially those with something a little more classic.

He pulled into the small market parking lot at the corner of the block, down the street from his apartment building. As he locked his car door he could see the town car parked a little way back, by the side of the road. He resisted a wave. The market was compact and filled with crates overflowing with fruit and vegetables, locally grown in allotments on the outskirts of the city. Brian Childs, the owner since Alex could remember, was a strong supporter of small businesses and encouraged local vendors with a genuine sense of pride. He was also very adept at certain black market dealings, wearing his heart of 'free trade' very much on his sleeve. If there was something, or someone, that you wanted found, Childs was the man to find it.

"How's the magic potion stuff coming along, Harry?" Brian said, looking up from a stack of boxes in one of the narrow aisles. They said 'Local produce for local Americans' on the side.

"Oh, you know, spells and potions, Mr. Childs. Spells and potions."

Childs had begun to call him Harry ever since his granddaughter had sat him down to watch Harry Potter one weekend a few years back. Alex hadn't heard the last of it since. Brian had told him that not only did he resemble the fictional sorcerer, but that he was a genuine magic worker in the scientific arts. Alex didn't mind the comparison, or the description of his work, however far off the mark it was. He had met Sadie one afternoon while she helped Brian stack shelves and sweep the floor. She was sweet and bubbly, and a very precocious seven. She also knew every last detail, quote and character from the movie series and professed with absolute certainty that he was Harry 'all grown up'.

"If you're looking for it, you won't find it out on the floor," Childs said from behind the boxes.

He stood up, dusted himself down, and walked over to the register. He was a burly man, mid sixties, with a thick head of steel gray hair and a mustache to match. He reminded Alex of Santa's ornery lumberjack cousin. Alex glanced around the market, more out of habit than anything. There was a flickering fluro tube above the door and the *tinkle-tinkle* whirring of the small warm air fan beside the soda fridge. It was the same old, but neatly kept, store he'd been in and out of almost every day for the past two years.

"I wasn't even thinking about that, believe it or not," Alex said, stepping up to the counter and shrugging his parka tighter about his shoulders. There was a stiff breeze pushing in through the slightly ajar front door. The fan's valiant efforts were in vain. "To be honest, I wasn't even sure you'd find it, ever, let alone within a month." He smiled, but Brian saw the uncertainty there, Alex's brain working overtime as if he had been suddenly confronted by an impossible problem to solve. "I'm making the assumption that you have found it," Alex said after a moment, his hands balled into fists inside his coat pockets.

Brian reached under the counter and pulled out a package about the size of a large cigar box, wrapped in wrinkled brown paper. There were no stamps or markings and it was secured with a length of twine, tied clumsily in a triple knot, on the top.

He paused before he took his hand away. "This may not have taken that long to find, but it was way harder to find than I figured," Brian said, scratching his chin through a thin layer of white stubble. "You didn't exactly give me a lot to go on, and the fact that there might only be one of these around, well, sometimes that can help, and other times it only makes it harder. These things, these commemorative *rewards*, so to speak, are very often one-offs, and this definitely falls into the 'rare' category. So, you typically go to the people who are commissioned to make them. Like, I know the guy who used to make all the nickel plated 1911 forty-fives they handed out to retiring Generals and the likes. Not a one of em knew anything about this. Led me a merry chase, this one. Not knowing what to look for was actually what helped me to find it. One of your dad's old 'Nam buddies, stationed in Da Nang through seventy-three. He helped me put it together." He paused, looking down at the box. "Strangest thing, that."

"What strangest thing?" Alex asked quietly. The noises in the store suddenly seemed to fade.

"When I finally tracked it down, I went back, you know, to thank him, tell him I got it. I knew he'd be happy that you would have it and that it'd help you find your dad, but…"

Alex leaned forward and put one hand on the counter. "But what?"

Brian looked up. "He was dead." He shook his head slowly, closing his eyes for a moment. "I just spoke to him a couple of weeks ago. Died in his chair, in front of the TV. Just… sitting there. It's just not right, ya know?"

Alex looked down at the box, then reached out slowly to pull it across the counter toward him, his fingers resting lightly on the paper wrapping. Brian produced a folding knife and slid it carefully under the twine to cut it. He didn't try to assist any further. Alex was enjoying the unwrapping like a child on Christmas morning opening his must-have present. Brian just stood back and took it in. Alex stared at the wrapping for a moment, his fingers hovering over the open flap of paper. "I was thinking about waiting until I get home," he said. "Put it straight into the safe. Go from there."

Brian shrugged, grinning beneath his mustache. "Hey, it's your pony, Harry. I hope it helps you find him. I really do. And be sure to let me know if I can help any more." He frowned, coughing to clear his throat. "Harry, do you know what it is?"

Alex said nothing for a moment and then suddenly looked up, a faint smile on his lips. "You know what? I don't really care what it is, Mister Childs. Not yet anyway."

Brian nodded. "Like I said, it's your pony, Harry."

Alex glanced up at the small television set, hanging above the cash register. There was a faded, dog-eared Redskins ticket wedged into the bracket on the side. A news helicopter was filming what looked like a raid on a large house, capturing the swarming, ordered breach of SWAT team members as they poured in through the front door like tiny, determined ants. The ticker tape at the bottom of the screen was bullet pointing a raid on a religious sect's location after an anonymous tip off about rape and murder in the upscale neighborhood. The image switched to a news anchor, interviewing an FBI agent on the ground, and Alex stepped closer, staring at the screen.

"*I'm standing here with Special Agent Gabby Morgane of the FBI's special task force. Agent Morgane, what can you tell us about what you've found inside after this rather large-scale operation.*"

The camera zoomed in on the agent, her blonde ponytail being whipped by the breeze and her light complexion blown out by the camera light.

"*As of right now, all I can tell you is that we have the situation well in hand. No one, either present inside the house, or law enforcement, has been injured, and we expect to be extracting a number of individuals we hope will help us continue our investigation of this matter.*"

The anchor prodded. "*Have there been any deaths, murders or rapes inside this house, that you know of, as emerging information might suggest?*"

Gabby nodded, acknowledging the question. "*As I said, we hope to have the assistance of a number of individuals we will be extracting from the house to further our investigation. I have no other information outside of that at the moment. Thank you.*"

With that, Gabby turned and strode off, shrinking from view behind a police cordon and disappearing into the front door of the house.

"*So, no new developments here, but what we do know is that a number of reports from different sources have told us that at least one murder has been committed in the house behind me, along with other crimes. The FBI were called in and have raided the house in what has turned out to be a successful operation with no injuries. More information as we get it. Reporting live, this is Ellie Carter, Channel Six News.*"

Brian reached up and turned the volume down on the TV. "Those neighborhoods sure ain't what they used to be." He looked at Alex. "You ok, Harry? Look like you've seen a ghost."

Alex was still looking at the TV. A weather report showing lots of snow. It looked like a giant blanket of marshmallow on the TV graphic.

"Harry?"

Alex snapped back to the present. "Uh, yeah, I'm all good, Mr. Childs. Just reminded me to call someone I haven't talked to in a while."

He began to turn away, and then paused, his free hand reaching to touch the package under his arm.

Brian watched him silently. He felt sorry for the kid. Who wouldn't?

"I was wondering," Alex said, stepping back up to the counter. "Would you keep it for me?" He put the package back on the counter and slid it forward a few inches, almost reluctantly. "I have this project, and, well, it'll keep me busy at work for a while. It just doesn't seem right to leave it at my place." He looked up, smiling awkwardly. Brian picked up the box. "Well, sure, Harry. I'll keep it safe for as long as you need. You just come on by any time and it'll be here." He slid it back out of sight, under the counter, and Alex reached out a hand. Brian took it and Alex nodded. "Thank you, Mr. Childs. For everything."

Brian turned, untying his apron and hanging it on a hook next to the television bracket. "Don't mention it, son. Whatever I can do. Ya know, I wouldn't mind betting that..."

But Alex had left, disappearing into the cold night, the door hissing mostly closed behind him. Brian walked around to the door, turning the sign in the window to 'Closed', and watched him walk to his car. Pulling the door closed, he turned the lock and walked back to the register, pulling Alex's package out and placing it back on the counter top. He regarded it for a moment before reaching back under the counter. The hip flask still had a good tug or two of Jim Beam. He hadn't opened the damned thing for a week. Not since Parker's body had been found in his living room chair. He unscrewed the silver top and took a long pull, slamming the flask on the counter in defeat. He looked back up at the TV. The headline read: *Satanic Horror in D.C. neighborhood.*

"Good luck, Alex. Something tells me you're gonna need it."

It took a few minutes for the interior of the Camaro to warm back up, but when it did, it was like the inside of an oven. Hot, oppressive air blew out of the dash vents and Alex immediately regretted keeping his coat on. Finessing the heater was one of the lower items on the Camaro to-do list, but he would get to it eventually. Most likely during the summer, when the heater was the last thing that would need fixing. The town car was no longer in his rearview, though Alex had seen them pull away from the curb when he had left the market. During the four minutes it took him to get to his apartment building, he saw no sign of them. He was pondering what had called them off when he turned the corner on his street and saw the town car parked across from the entrance to his building. They were waiting for him and they even knew a short cut. Maybe he should ask them.

Everything used a card key for entry these days. The main entrance to his apartment building, and the apartment itself, was no different. He pushed into the downstairs lobby, checked his mail and took the elevator up seven levels to his floor. Mrs. C, the widow and ex-socialite in the adjoining apartment, was standing just inside her doorway as he stepped out of the elevator, her Pekinese tucked under one arm, and weighed down by enough gold jewelry to open her own pawn shop. She always knew when he was about to come home. Without fail.

As always, she ducked away inside and closed the door before Alex could say hello. He could hear her talking to the dog as she walked away. Smiling, he shook his head and walked down to his door, card-swiped and stepped inside.

Dropping his car keys in the glass valet, Alex brushed his hand along the perfectly smooth ash counter top and entered the kitchen. A modern, spacious apartment in a respectable neighborhood, he had lived here for a little over two years. The place still looked like a show home. Laying his coat over the back of a dining chair, he walked to the window; his heels knocking on the flawless, dust-free wood flooring. The floor to ceiling windows appeared ink black as the night pressed against the glass. Only a solitary streetlight broke the illusion and Alex saw the town car with the two agents inside, half illuminated by the soft yellow light below.

Taking his cell phone to the couch, he sat in the gloom and opened his contacts, scrolling to 'G'. Gabby's number was highlighted with a green star, indicating that it was already in his favorites list. He never used the favorites list. It was full of numbers he had consciously saved there, only never to return to use them. Her voicemail message was the same as it had been since she had given him the number of her new phone. Short, direct, yet polite and welcoming, her voice played like comforting music in his ear and he realized, as he did more often than he liked, that he didn't speak to his best friend nearly as often as he should. He hung up before the beep and placed the phone on the glass coffee table, silently promising himself that he would try again later.

Alex opened the refrigerator with a *clink* of rattling bottles in the door, cold light spilling across the floor and breaking the gloom in the unlit kitchen. The bottle of bourbon was as he left it, frosted and half full, on the middle shelf. His hand left a smudged print in the condensation as he set it on the coffee table having poured a generous couple of fingers into the heavy tumbler, a gift from Gabby that he had found on his door mat last Christmas. The entire apartment was lit only by a small table lamp in the far corner, next to the TV stand. He had it sitting on the floor because he liked how the light played through the furniture and up the walls. Two sips of the fiery liquid and he leaned back on the couch, staring at the black television screen and thinking about how dusty it would look when he got back from the lab in two weeks' time. He forced the thought from his mind. He really didn't need to sleep on that kind of anxiety, and Dr. Harrick would tell him not to dwell on those kinds of thoughts if he knew they would make him anxious. Doctor Harrick made him anxious. He was in control of his thoughts, apparently. He could feel himself dozing and reached forward to put the tumbler on the table. The couch felt like the most comfortable couch in the world. His eyes were closing. He was very tired.

Knock, knock, knock. Alex opened his eyes and refocused on the far wall. There was a framed poster to the left of the TV. A vintage Star Wars one sheet. It was dog eared and creased but that only added to its authenticity. He had had it framed behind museum glass, to prevent further damage from the light. When Han Solo's face snapped into sharp focus, he huffed and sat forward on the edge of the couch. *Knock, knock.*

"All right then, all right," he said, getting up and turning for the door. "A one second nap is better than no nap at all, I guess."

His phone was still sitting on the coffee table, silent and dark, and he thought about calling Gabby again. *Just after I see who's at the door.* He reached for the handle just as another knock echoed through the wood, pulled the door open. "Okay, okay, I'm…"

The woman was as tall as he was, had piercing green eyes and was lean, chiseled even. Her honey blonde ponytail hung over the collar of her standard issue FBI windbreaker.

"Hello Alex," Gabby said, her flawless face distorting as she smiled, revealing a row of perfectly white teeth.

"You got your teeth whitened?" Alex asked.

Gabby snorted a laugh and pushed past him into the apartment.

"When did you get your teeth whitened?"

Gabby stepped into the living room, taking her jacket off and folding it neatly on the armchair by the window. "No, Alex, I did not get my teeth whitened. These are my teeth and they are straight and white because I endured three years of braces and follow a strict flossing regimen." She sat on the couch. "And I don't drink coffee."

Alex walked away from the door and it swung shut with a solid *thunk*. He was probably feeling the effects of being startled awake, just as he was about to fall asleep, because he couldn't remember Gabby smiling so much. And she was just sitting there, legs crossed, looking at him. He sat in the armchair, being careful not to crush her neatly folded jacket.

"How did you know I was home? I was about to call you again. I don't like to leave messages."

He was feeling a little anxious and he could see Gabby frown slightly, tilting her head the way she did when she was trying to figure something out.

"Well, you called me a few hours ago, and so I came over. You never call me from the lab, so…" She leaned forward, looking more serious than before. "Are you ok, Alex? You look like you've had a few too many shots. Should I get you something?"

Alex frowned, running his hands through his hair and tried to shake the fog from his mind. He felt exhausted then, and wanted nothing more than to sleep the night away until his alarm woke him at precisely 5:04 am. He never set alarms on the hour, always a few minutes before or after. He had no idea why.

"Wait, what did you say? A few hours ago? What time is it?"

He reached forward for his phone, but Gabby beat him too it, scooping it up and turning it on so that it displayed the current time.

"Four thirty-seven," she said. "I came as soon as I could. I guess I should apologize for waking you. I know you have to get up early."

She stood and walked into the kitchen. Alex heard the refrigerator door open and then the sound of something being poured into a glass. A few moments later she reappeared with a glass of water. She held it out, looking down at him. "This'll help with the headache," She said, as Alex reached up to take it. "You're tired, mentally drained, and I'm pretty sure dehydrated. The bourbon won't have helped with that."

She nudged the bottle on the table and Alex cursed inwardly at having forgotten to put it back in the fridge. The water was cold and he sighed as the chill flowed down his throat. A few seconds later he had drained the glass and Gabby was on her feet, holding out her hand. He handed her the glass and she went to get a refill.

"Thanks," he said, and stood up, following her into the kitchen. He flicked on the counter top lamp and shadows were banished. "I wanted to call you because I have to be at the lab the next couple of weeks, and I know it's been awhile."

"The lab? For two weeks? Must be important. Drexler must *love* you. Don't tell me; you're working on a hair replacement compound to turn him back into Tom Jones."

Drexler's nickname around the Ark was Tom Jones because in his youth he had sported a thick head of curly dark hair and vaguely resembled the famous Welsh singer. Now, though, his hair was far shorter and a hell of a lot thinner. He had never struck Alex as the vain type.

"How did you know?" Alex joked, sipping more water.

Gabby smiled, folding her arms and leaning on the island counter. "Well, I *am* in the FBI, you know."

Alex held up his glass in a silent toast to her status and walked back into the living room. "I saw you on TV," he said, taking a seat, almost on top of Gabby's jacket. "You been practicing in the bathroom mirror with your hairbrush?"

"Whatever, Doctor Bishop," Gabby replied, falling onto the couch. "While I admit that I may have run through a couple of answers in my mind before talking to that news person, I feel that I have a certain natural flair in front of camera." She tossed her ponytail dramatically. "I'm expecting a call from Steven Spielberg any day now."

They both laughed and Alex felt a sense of relief that he hadn't felt in a very long time. He'd missed his best friend. She stood up and walked over to him, sitting next to him on the arm of the chair. "I always used to make it a personal mission of mine to make you laugh every day," She said, smiling. "You don't do it enough, Alex."

"I don't laugh enough? Well, not having many sources of easily attainable humor could be a contributory cause, I suppose, though I do have that mental image of you practicing your television interviews in the bathroom mirror with a hairbrush."

She tapped him upside the back of the head and then proceeded to pretend to throttle him as he struggled to put the glass on the table without spilling. "I should have you arrested for that kind of treasonous remark!" she joked, pulling his hair and poking his ribs. He struggled to fend her off as she dodged his parries and poked and jabbed at his torso at will, occasionally tapping his forehead as he laughed. She grabbed his face suddenly and spun over him, straddling him on the chair.

"Doctor Alex Bishop, I am placing you…" *jab, jab, poke,* "…under arrest, for the excessive teasing and fun poking of a federal agent…" *poke, slap, jab.*

Alex was struggling to catch his breath in between jerking away from Gabby's incessant finger poking assault and sheer, guttural laughter. She held his face and then stopped suddenly, breathing heavily, her face inches from his, grinning hard. He opened his eyes and looked at her and his stomach started to slide south when he saw her expression change and her eyes drop from his eyes to his mouth.

Her lips were pressed against his before he could react. She still had a hold of his face and chin with her hand, while the other grasped the back of his neck. Her lips were warm and soft and inviting. Panic rose in him like a hot, red tide. He stiffened, trying to somehow back away, deeper into the chair. Gabby's jacket was going to be a crumpled, creased mess and she would not be happy about it. He mumbled a protest from beneath the firm pressing of her lips on his as she turned her head and kissed him again. He felt her tongue inside his mouth and his eyes widened. He realized his hands were on her ribs and he was pushing her away. She leaned back a few inches. "Don't you want to?" she said, still holding on to his face and neck. "I want to. Don't you want to?"

He could feel the heat of her as she sat astride him and turned his head as she moved in again.

"Gabby," he gasped, before she could plant her lips once more. "Please."

She tried to pull his face to hers and he struggled, pushing her ribs and twisting his head.

"Gabby, please!"

She continued to struggle, squeezing his hips with her thighs and pulling him closer. She snaked one hand down to his pants and deftly unbuckled his belt. He thrashed, pushing hard and forcing his face to one side as she fought to kiss him, licking at his lips and breathing in short, shallow gasps.

"*Gabby!*"

She stopped suddenly and literally leapt backwards to stand a few feet in front of him, shoulders heaving. There was a scratch mark on her left cheek. Had he done that? How had he done that? He immediately fumbled with his belt, re-buckling it and pulling his shirt down as he sat up, pushing himself back into the chair. There was silence for a moment and then he heard a low chuckling. He looked up and saw Gabby grinning at him. Her face half in gloom and half highlighted by the sodium street light outside.

"Don't you want to?" She said again, her face stretched by a very intense grin that pushed Alex's panic level up another notch. "I want to."

She moved forward, put her hands on the arms of the chair and leaned in close. Alex pushed his head into the back of the chair. "You need it, Alex. You need me to do it."

She suddenly grasped his face in her hands. They felt very cool to the touch. He nearly whimpered. Her voice changed, grew deeper, more resonant, powerful.

"You... *need*... me..."

Her eyes were glowing. A soft, warm amber that actually looked somewhat soothing. Alex couldn't help but relax a little, still acutely aware of the sheer terror that had complete control of his body. She drew away slowly and stood. "You *need* me, Alex." She was not herself, not at all. "To protect you."

She moved back and the room grew darker before his eyes. She was swallowed by a deep shadow that spread across the walls and floor toward him, stopping as it cut across the coffee table. Only her glowing eyes and the fading echo of her words remained. Alex was rooted to the chair, unable to move. Without warning, a blast of air hit him, out of nowhere, and he struggled to keep his eyes open as it pummeled his face and body. Alex felt himself stand, drawn through the storm toward a now swirling black hole of infinite darkness in the center of the room, those glowing eyes at its core.

A shadowy face began to emerge, eyes alight with amber fire. Alex watched as Gabby stepped forward, her clothes tattered and singed, yet unaffected by the steadily dying wind. Slowly, the shadows receded, moving away in the background, the black hole shrinking to nothing until only the gloom from before remained. She stopped in front of him, appearing much taller now, and he heard himself ask, "Protect me from what?"

She touched his face and turned his head toward the window. The night was gone, replaced by a maelstrom of chaos, a world being blown and torn asunder by winds, lightning, fire and unseen forces. Trees were uprooted, buildings blown away, their bricks flying into the fiery air as if ripped from their walls by an unseen tornado.

Then he saw the people, thousands of them, down on the streets, in the windows, in cars and trucks, walking, running and screaming as they caught fire and burst into explosive flame or were hauled from the streets by black silhouetted creatures that screeched and swooped down from a sky that literally burned with clouds of roiling fire.

It was the end of the world, the great slaughter. Alex wanted to scream but the sound was stuck in his throat like a horse pill, and he was choking on it. Gabby turned his face to look at him. "You need me to protect you from yourself, Alex."

"What?" Alex felt his face burning, the window was beginning to buckle and vibrate.

"Well, long tall Sally, she's built for speed. She got everything that uncle John need."

Alex frowned. "What?"

Gabby just stared at him impassively, the words dead pan and emotionless. "Oh baby, yes, baby. Ooh baby, havin' me some fun tonight, yeah. We're gonna have some fun tonight, yeah."

CRASH! The living room window imploded in a roar of flying glass, debris and fire. Alex turned, instinctively throwing up an arm to shield his face.

He woke up with a start, his knee knocking the coffee table and spilling the bourbon on the glass top. His phone alarm was going off, playing a loop of a Little Richard song. *We're gonna have some fun tonight. We're gonna have some fun tonight, yeah.*

Gasping and startled, he reached out and silenced the phone. The time said 1:57 am. Typically, that was when he needed reminding to put down the book, turn off the computer or stop what he was doing and go to bed, or else he would stay up until sunrise and would be unemployed, without a fridge or the bourbon to put in it. Breathless from the visceral nightmare, he took a breath to reset.

A moment's disappointment at Gabby not calling back, or stopping by, was consciously replaced by a feeling of acceptance of a friend who was dealing with some hefty professional issues. *I'm sure she'll call back. She always does.* He wasn't comforted by the fact that, sometimes, that meant in a couple of weeks, at which point, every conversation he wanted to have with her would be very old news indeed.

The coffee table took half a dozen paper towels and a good amount of Windex to get clean. The last drops of bourbon were returned to the bottle in the fridge; too warm to drink and too precious to pour out. Alex wondered by what percentage it would taste better by the time he got back from the lab. Something told him he would notice the difference. He expected that no one would believe that.

Looking out the window, he could see the town car, with its two official occupants, on the street below. He gazed out into the inky night, recalling the dream of a burning sky, furnace-like tornados and those shadowy, swooping winged creatures. He could picture it all clearly, overlaying it in his mind on top of the real sight before him. He shuddered slightly. The screams. They still echoed around that scene and he cursed the flawless clarity of his eternal memory.

Ding, ding. His phone chimed from his pocket with an incoming text message. He looked and saw Gabby's name beside a small thumbnail image of her pulling a goofy face.

Super busy. Can't talk right now. All ok? Tomorrow?

Alex smiled, flicking his thumb across the keypad in reply. *No can do. Working at the Ark for the next few weeks. Will be out of comms. Just wanted to touch base. You seem busy.*

He waited, damp paper towels in one hand, his glowing phone in the other, as the flashing icon next to her name told him she was writing back.

Big case. Getting bigger. No details. Sorry. I'm about to fly out to NY. Sorry I couldn't make it over. We'll make up for it when you're back. Exciting project? Alex typed back, walking slowly into the kitchen and tossing the towels into the recycling trashcan.

Big project. Top secret. No details. Sorry. :) I saw you on the news. You should be on TV. He stood in the gloom, the cell phone casting ghostly light on his downturned face, and watched the pulsing icon as his friend replied.

I know. I'm a natural. I'm expecting a call from Steven Spielberg any day now.

Alex froze, the breath caught in his rapidly tightening throat. He stared at the glowing letters on the screen, recalling the moment when Gabby had said those very same words to him in his dream.

Ok, gotta go. Boarding. Call when you're back. We'll catch up. Dexter's on me. Alex hesitated, knowing that she would be waiting for his farewell response. He could picture her standing on the tarmac of some airfield, waiting to walk up the ramp of a C-130 or climb into a private government jet.

Deal. Have a safe flight. Then she was gone and Alex was alone again, standing in his dark kitchen, with only the deflating proposition of a handful of restless hours of sleep to look forward to and the knowledge that he would not be able to bring himself to delete that last text, no matter how much it fried his noodle to read it.

It took him precisely ninety seconds to fall asleep after his head hit the pillow. He didn't move an inch and Armageddon; a terrifying apparition of an otherworldly friend or any other traumatic event didn't wake him. Little Richard managed that less than three hours later.

Chapter Six

Alex looked at his watch for the tenth time since he'd brushed his teeth. It was five in the morning. He was ready to set off for the Arc complex, but wanted to stay for every available minute before leaving for the fishbowl-like confines of the lab. He puttered around the kitchen, moving containers and towel holders so that they all lined up perfectly straight on the spotless counter tops. He made sure that the fridge door was fingerprint free and that the magnets were all aligned, and that anything that would spoil was in a trash bag ready to take out on his way to the car. Finally, there was nothing left to do, no more time to kill. He would arrive early. Maybe Drexler would be extra impressed, as if Alex cared about impressing Drexler.

It was colder than he expected and his breath plumed around his head in a warm mist as he walked down the building's front steps to the sidewalk. The town car was still parked up the street under the light and he gave the two figures in the front seats a wave with his coffee cup as he rounded the Camaro to the driver's side door. Of course, there was no response. They appeared, from this distance, to be just sitting there, watching him impassively.

"Yeah, I'd rather have my job," He mumbled, sliding into the driver's seat and putting the coffee cup in the custom holder attached to the center console.

She started, as always, on the first turn. Never a complaint or a whine, the Camaro was the most reliable thing in his life. A six-year project, restored from the chassis up, he'd gathered as many original parts as possible, though he'd had to reluctantly compromise here and there. Still, it was as close to pristine as you were ever likely to see and he got more thumbs up from other drivers than he could count.

He pulled a U-turn and headed out of the neighborhood, casting a single glance in the rearview to see if the town car was following. Not yet. Maybe they were sleeping on the job. The thought gave him a small chuckle and he wondered what a disciplinary panel would make of a pair of stakeout professionals committing the cardinal sin of falling asleep on watch. He was distracted by another flock of geese, flying noisily overhead as he made his way onto the parkway.

Alex pulled up to the main gate at the Ark complex, ID card at the ready. He noticed right away that there were extra guards on duty, all armed, none of whom he recognized. A soldier walked in front of the car, hand raised in a 'stop' gesture, while another stepped to the driver's window. "Card please, sir."

By the time he got to the Hub, he was actually about on time. Each and every checkpoint had been that much more diligent and thorough, chipping into his early arrival kudos with every extended glance at his photo and car walk around. His card key didn't work. He was already frustrated, so when he saw Drexler approaching the door, he was relieved. He didn't need to start the week with a funky card key. Drexler keyed an entry code onto the keypad on the other side of the door and it unlocked with the *thunk* of magnetic bolts. Drexler pushed the door open and Alex stepped through, dragging his bag with him.

"You've noticed the heightened security," Drexler said. "We've upgraded all over the complex. New personnel, upgraded cameras and security locks, and…" he held out a new card key. Alex could see his photo on it. "New access protocols."

Alex stood at the door to his lab, noticing the new card lock set into the glass. "You move fast. You did this overnight?"

"Most of the systems have been in place for over a month now, just a few additional units here and there. It was easier to bring in new doors with the locks already fitted. And as for the military personnel, well, you say move, they move."

Alex pressed the card against the small black reader on the lock. A *beep* and *snap* later and his door opened silently.

"You changed my table," Alex said, stepping over to touch the spotless glass surface. He heard Drexler snort behind him.

"That's not all we changed." He walked to the grey paneled wall and pushed a small square glass pad. The entire wall slid away, revealing a completely new room, twice the size of Alex's lab, with two worktops and various equipment, pristine and top of the line, filling the space.

"It's everything you will need for the project, and beyond," Drexler said proudly, stepping into the new lab. "We want to make sure you have everything you need. Lack of necessary equipment will not be a factor should this project fail."

Alex put his bag on his old chair and surveyed the new room. "What makes you think I will fail? You've tested me since I started here. You realize that there is no one else even close to being as capable as I am of getting this done." He sat on the edge of one of the glass worktops. "I am not prone to bouts of arrogance, and my ego is in a permanent state of hibernation, so you know that I'm being nothing but pragmatic when I say that. And while Charles probably still has reservations, I have complete faith in my abilities, simply because they are unmatched. If they were not so, I'd have been reassigned, shipped out and forgotten about by now, not offered four times my already excessive salary and a bag load of bonuses. I'm aware of my worth, just as you are aware of it. If I can't find the answers you're looking for, then no one can."

Drexler was a little taken aback. In the two years he had been working with Alex, he had never heard such a tone before. He didn't know whether to be pleasantly surprised or a little concerned. Charles would not like the thought of a loose cannon on the team. He liked things ordered, efficient and controlled, by him.

"You're right about almost everything," he said. "If I felt you were not the right person for this project, we would've hired someone else. It's very simple. Set yourself up and head over to conference B at 08:00." He walked toward the door.

"You said *almost* everything," Alex said, stopping Drexler at the door. "What am I wrong about?"

Drexler turned. "We don't believe in faith. We believe in ability, in talent, in skills. We believe in science. Faith doesn't come into the equation. It is an overused, outmoded cliché employed as a get out clause when someone feels like they're in over their head and don't have the abilities to get through it. Use your abilities, Alex. Use your skills. Let's see where your limits are."

He left the room and Alex watched him walk along the corridor toward the elevator. The trio of armed soldiers stood by, one duly checking his ID, and he stood motionless until the elevator arrived, head slightly bowed, right hand in his lab coat pocket. Alex watched him as he stepped in and waited for the doors to slide closed. He noticed then that the other labs on this level were all deserted. As he looked around at all of the glass walled rooms around his lab, he saw not a single soul. As far as the Hub was concerned, he was its soul occupant. He had but three armed guards for company, and that fact offered nothing in the way of comfort. It was as if he had been the soul-surviving member of a lab team cull, decimated by budget cut layoffs, and was about to begin a week where everyone else's work burden would suddenly become his.

"Day one," he said to himself, turning back to the expanded room that was his new domain.

*   *   *

Gabby sat in the back seat of the armored black SUV, staring at the small screen set into the passenger seat headrest. The satellite feed, broadcast in crystal clear HD, showed the inside of the Tactical Operations Center in the Washington field office. The concerned face of her operational chief, Dennis Sorano, filled most of the screen but Gabby could see the hustle of agents on high alert scuttling about in the background. To the far right, she could see half of the main view screen. The picture was an aerial view of a city street, centered on a silver gray town car, surrounded by SWAT and local PD. As the image slowly rotated—no doubt one of the several Zion class surveillance drones that were currently deployed over the city—she could see a police officer cordoning off the street with yellow tape as a small crowd of onlookers began to gather.

"…And we have minimal leads at this point to even begin an investigation," Sorano was saying. He turned as someone stepped next to him and handed him a data pad. He glanced at it for a moment before looking up once more. "DCPD just found two more bodies, in a dumpster half a block north of the scene. Locals, by the look of it. Male and female; both early twenties, gunshot wounds to the head. The male had a bag of canine treats in his pocket. Looks like they were out walking the dog. No sign of the animal though. No IDs either. They're pushing for info."

"What do we know about the agents? You mentioned GSW to the head—both ears—but the windows are intact and there's no sign of struggle, no sign of an ambush, or even a diversion. To propose that whoever took them out is a professional would be a gross understatement."

Sorano nodded. "I'll have any evaluation you provide forwarded to the Op Center on-scene. McCarthy is heading up the field crew. I'm sure he'll appreciate anything you can give him."

Gabby paused. McCarthy was an old school, hard-nosed field agent who had worked with her father in the military back in the day. A lot of what she knew she owed to him, but now, today, she couldn't even look him in the eye for fear that she'd shoot him in the face. Sorano knew it, everyone knew it. They just didn't talk about it anymore. So, they just got on with it, business as usual, and hoped that another bullet would be dodged.

"Give me ten, Chief. I need to chew this over."

"You've got five. Contact me here. I'll relay to the field unit." He terminated the connection and his image on the screen was replaced by a graphic of the FBI seal. She looked out of the heavily tinted window at the passing cars. They were heading out of JFK. A two-vehicle convoy headed for the New York field office and the center for New Religious and Extremist Cult investigation. She had no call to make. Mention of McCarthy had thrown her off and she needed to collect her thoughts before calling Sorano back.

"Jerry, what's our ETA?"

The agent glanced at the screen in the center console. It showed a map with their position displayed as a blue arrow moving along the North Service Road toward the Belt Parkway. "Forty-five minutes, give or take," he said. 'Traffic looks ok and no detours. We should be good on the primary."

"Thanks, Jerry. Do me a favor and take Route Bravo. I'm enjoying the scenery back here."

Jerry nodded and eased the SUV over one lane, slowing slightly. After working on Gabby's team for almost two years, he knew when she needed to think. She could be blunt, hell, she could be downright rude, but the results far outweighed the price of a few dented egos. Five minutes later, she keyed in a code on the display keypad and Sorano's image filled the screen.

"Tell McCarthy to check Alex Bishop's apartment. Whoever hit the agents did their best to avoid leaving a message at the scene, but maybe they weren't there for them."

Sorano simply nodded. "I'll update you as I get it."

For the rest of the drive to the office, Gabby thought about her friend, Alex. On the eve of his biggest ever career challenge at Apex Labs, in a field that had the highest number of secret, government funded projects outside of military defense, the two agents assigned to watch over him are slain, right outside his apartment. She cursed beneath her breath. Her focus had shifted now, and it would take all of her to maintain discipline and continue pursuing her current case with the attention and focus it deserved.

"Everything ok, boss?" Jerry said, negotiating around an erratic bike messenger. She looked up and saw his dark aviators peering at her in the rear view. She realized that her foot was tapping and she was biting at the nails on her left hand absentmindedly.

"Yeah. There may be a break in the other case in Washington."

"The one with the two agents? Sorano will be under a lot of pressure to figure this thing out, and fast."

Gabby nodded, her thoughts drifting back to Alex, his apartment, the project, the Lab. She shook her head. "Something is coming," she whispered. "Alex, what are you into?"

Jerry looked back at her again as she stared out of the window, the SUV gliding along a busy street, skyscrapers on all sides. The city was moving by outside, living and breathing, but she didn't even notice.

Less than an hour later, Gabby, Jerry and two other agents in her field team, were shown into a conference room on the eleventh floor of the FBI building at Federal Plaza. Foley Square was bustling with the clean up from a charity concert the night before and Gabby had noticed the extra police on Lafayette when they had been dropped off at the steps to the main entrance. They all took seats near one end of the giant conference table, surrounded by at least thirty leather chairs, close to a laptop that sat open beside a coffee thermos and shrink-wrapped chicken club sandwiches.

"Director Cole will be with you in a moment. I'll have someone come up with some refreshments for you." Their liaison smiled before leaving the room and closing the door behind her.

"I hope they don't have that ridiculous coffee cake like last time," Special Agent Danny Forkes said, swaying left to right in his chair and making himself at home.

"You mean ridiculously terrible?" Jerry chirped from the end of the table. "I'll be sure to avoid it."

"Nah, I mean ridiculously *good*! Ah man, I'm kinda hoping they don't have any. It took me a week of extra PT to burn it off after my last trip out here. I think Mary even noticed. She is not attracted to Goodrich belly."

"Then why the hell did she marry you then, Porky Forkes?"

The men all chuckled, and Danny pointed a pistol finger at Jerry, his thumb hammer dropping as he took aim at his colleague's head. Gabby stood by the window, deep in thought, out of the banter loop. She was often referred to as The Method, because she was never out of character, and she *always* found the answers. She watched the traffic crawling along the streets far below, people as tiny as ants, scurrying from cars to doorways, buildings to cabs, oblivious to the threats and menaces that were being discussed within the walls of this very building.

Her process was trying to somehow put Alex out of the frame of events in Washington, but she was struggling. Her logic was being quite insistent. She ran through it again in her mind. Alex, Apex Labs, military, government, agents sent to watch him, the agents end up dead—murdered outside his apartment on the night before he begins a top secret project. The chances of coincidence were less than minuscule.

"God dammit," she said, and the laughter in the room stopped.

"Boss?" Jerry said, standing at the table as the other guys turned to look at her, silhouetted against the bright window. "Something up?"

Gabby turned to look at him as the door opened and three people walked in, a black suited agent followed by Marissa Cole, director of the New Religious and Extremist Cult investigation team. An older man whom Gabby didn't recognize filed in after Cole, and Gabby took her seat next to Jerry at the end of the table before making a round of introductions.

"Apologies for the wait, everyone," Cole said, taking a seat a few chairs down from Forkes. "There have been one or two developments since we last spoke. Agent Morgane, I'll need a few moments of your time alone before you leave today."

She turned as the older man handed her a black folio folder. She opened it and scanned a page before passing it down to Gabby.

"As of this morning, our man in custody, Lincoln Klick, is on suicide watch in Standon secure medical facility, here in New York. At 21:20 last night he put both of his arms through the bed frame of his cot, broke them, and then pulled out a bone fragment and tried to slash his jugular, hoping to bleed out in his cell."

Forkes winced and Jerry said, "Oh man," but Gabby didn't flinch. She had heard of, and seen, far worse. Things that would haunt her forever and yet had helped to forge her into the resolute, hardy, and somewhat thick-skinned agent she was today.

"What's his condition?" Gabby asked, flipping slowly through the report on Lincoln Klick, the self-styled leader of the House of the Serpent, a minor New Religious Cult that had sprung up in the northeast a few years before.

It had flown under the radar, posing no particular threat beside some unscrupulous money making scams and dubious recruiting techniques, until last summer when an ex-cult member accused Klick of the rape and torture of two teenage girls. The accuser barely escaped one such ritual in the basement of her own house, while her parents watched. She stabbed her father in the eye with a candle before setting his robe alight and making her escape through the house. Klick's members had been seduced by his promise of everlasting power and dominion over mankind under the rule of his master, Lord of Serpents. The Agency had yet to determine whom, exactly, that was.

"Touch and go for the first few hours, and he's probably going to lose his left arm. He slipped into a coma after surgery. He's being assessed as we speak and we'll get updates as they come in. You wanted to talk to him, I know, but I'm afraid this may be a wasted trip for you in that regard."

Gabby looked her in the eye. There was definitely a page or two missing from the report, and Cole was holding more than one piece of information back. The question was; why was there interdepartmental secrecy in what basically amounted to a ritual rape and assault case, and what might Klick have told them about the cult that they felt shouldn't be shared? There was nothing in the current investigation that suggested the group was anything more than an isolated, pseudo-cult. Low level, fairly localized and posing no immediate threat beside possible links to some fringe organized crime syndicates concerning the cash scams and hard-edged recruiting, the group was relatively small time, unless…

"What about the house," she said, dropping the file on the table, letting Cole know that she was aware of it's unimportance. Hawkins, the fourth member of her team, flinched visibly. He was the youngest and most inexperienced on the team. She would have to talk with him later. "When my team left, they were sending in engineers to open the vault we found in the basement."

"Nothing too out of the ordinary," Cole said, holding Gabby's gaze. "Paper trails, member records and a fetish porn collection mostly. The kind of stuff that Klick obviously thought was way more important than it actually is. He's already demonstrated an overdeveloped sense of self-worth, a belief reinforced by his recent transition from self-proclaimed cult leadership into ritualistic rapist. We will continue to build a full psychiatric profile on him, but it's looking like he's really manifesting some deep-rooted control issues, embedded within a previously introverted personality capsule that's now dissolving, allowing this septic, poisonous trait to emerge. It's fairly clear that he's been suppressing his urges to control, torture and rape for some time, possibly his pre teen years, and it's my belief that he began to use his role as a black cult leader, solidifying his position of power, to justify, to himself, not just his followers, his behavior as a serial rapist. In his subconscious mind, masking that act as a necessary ritual, or satanic rite, seemed like the perfectly normal thing to do and was the catalyst that set this chain of events in motion. I'm sure that, as we dig deeper, we'll find that this was most likely the first time he's even attempted such a ritual. It didn't go according to plan, people realized very quickly that they were in over their heads, and the shit, as they say, hit the fan."

A period of silence followed that told everyone in the room that Gabby wasn't buying it; at least not all of it. The buzz-rattle of her phone on the table relieved the awkward tension. She reached for it, leveling her gaze at Cole until she broke to look at the display.

"Excuse me." She stood and stepped away from the table.

Cole nodded and asked the others around the table if anyone wanted coffee while Gabby walked to the far end of the spacious room and gazed out of the window.

"Yes, sir."

Sorano's voice crackled in her ear. He was on-scene in Washington. "Two things," he said. She could hear him breathing. He was walking fast, probably away from the commotion of the scene. "Alex Bishop was seen at 05:15 this morning, getting into his car. Before he did, he waved or gestured down the street in the direction of the agents' car. It's not surprising. He probably knew they were tailing him and that they had been sitting outside his place all night."

Gabby could hear the sound of Sorano's footsteps changing as he walked up stone steps. She guessed he was at the door to Alex's apartment building. "What is interesting is that one of the other tenants says she saw a man leave the building shortly after Alex left."

"Ok, that's interesting, I guess," Gabby said dryly.

"What's *interesting*, Agent Morgane, is that she says she saw him leave *his* apartment, and that he was wearing an FBI field jacket."

Gabby frowned, as she was sure Sorano expected her to. "And I'm assuming we had no field agents in the area this morning."

"Nothing that would give us cause to be there, no," Sorano said.

Gabby heard a door shut and the background noise disappeared. He was inside. "So, two suspects, dressed as FBI agents, leave Alex's apartment a few minutes after he leaves. Do we have a time of death on the agents and the two civilians?"

"Preliminaries show some time between 04:30 and 07:00. The civilians were killed directly after the agents. No discernible time gap in between. Bishop left and this Mrs. Galasky is adamant that Alex walked directly out of the building, got in his car and left. He pulled a U and headed south toward the parkway. He arrived at Apex labs at 05:45. He didn't return home. And McCarthy says he didn't turn anything up in the apartment."

Cole approached Gabby, respectfully clearing her throat from a few feet away to get her attention. Gabby turned. "I'll need to get back to you on that, sir. Thanks for the update." She hung up and turned to Cole.

"Despite what you may think, Agent Morgane, we are all on the same team, all play for the same coach and are all working toward the same goal. Though I don't need to, I want to reassure you that any information I have, you have, and I will continue to see that is the case moving forward. I'm sure that goes for you and your team also."

Gabby looked past her to the conference table. Everyone was chatting calmly. The atmosphere appeared relaxed, friendly even. Cole stepped closer, lowering her voice.

"Like you, I am sometimes not privy to every morsel of information that comes out of either a scene or an interrogation room. Sometimes, I am left out of the loop with no explanation and, for all I am aware, no good reason. But that is how it is here, and in your office too, I'm sure."

Gabby hid her mild surprise at Cole's change in stance. She wasn't known to be the sympathetic type and was often referred to as the Ice Mother of the New York field office.

"We all have our strings to pull, favors to ask and aces to hold," Gabby said. "All I need from you on this case is just one simple thing; transparency.

If you can't give me that, then there is no reason for me to be here, no reason for me to share with you what I have, no reason to offer what experience and expertise I may posses, and no reason for our respective administrators to shuffle ultimately useless case updates, meeting schedules and office privileges back and forth, setting up meetings, just like this one, that lead to nothing but a gut full of frustration and a waste of time and taxpayer money."

Cole settled, raising an eyebrow. "I'm sorry you feel that way, Agent Morgane. Naturally I want both of our offices to work together, on this case and those moving forward. I can tell you that you know everything I know. Anything else and…"

"Then we are done here," Gabby interrupted, walking past Cole and nodding at Fawkes, who rose, immediately followed by Jerry and Hawkins. The four agents walked swiftly to the door. Gabby paused, turning to Cole, all pretenses dropped. "If I have everything you have, then you may want to send over pages four and five of the Serpents file. Whoever pulled them did a piss poor job of trimming the page numbers out."

She turned to leave and then turned back once more. "And serial rapists with an inferiority complex don't shatter both of their arms and then dismember themselves in a suicide attempt."

Gabby resisted the urge to call Sorano from the car on the way back to JFK. Sure, calls would be made, words would be spoken, and maybe some shackles loosened, but ultimately, only things that Cole wanted to share would be shared, and if she handed over anything, it would mean giving up the pretense of having nothing. There was something very off about Director Cole, and Gabby knew that the notion would sit in a corner of her subconscious, festering and being bothersome until she figured out what it was. Her mind switched gears to the new case in Washington. She would let Cole sit on the Serpents case. She could call when she needed them, as she most assuredly would.

"Let's get home, Jerry," She said, gazing out over the city as they crossed the East River on the Manhattan Bridge. The sun was setting over the city behind them. She hated flying at night.

Chapter Seven

LONDON, England. At precisely a quarter past eleven in the morning, the shade was pulled down over the office window and a curse silently aimed at an unusually sunny and mild November day. The offices of the Raven Group had resided in the old Blakenstock financial building at the end of Oxford Street for more than one hundred and seventy years. Most of the other big money firms had taken up new space in the Canary Wharf sector, but this was a very old firm, with very deep roots. It would not be moving for the sake of a better view of the Thames any time soon.

Today, James Devlin should, by any normal account, be in celebratory mood. But, for a man about to be elevated to full partner by his father, Thomas Devlin, in the centuries old firm of high level corporate banking and law, James's mood was far darker. With most of the annoying sunlight held at bay by the simple turn of a wrist, and the office now filled with a far more comforting twilight gloom, he sat in the large antique chair behind his enormous vintage bankers' desk and waited for his father. News of the promotion had already spread to many of his colleagues; a cascade of text messages and emails alerting him to their sycophantic electronic congratulations.

They all sickened him. Almost everyone in the company sickened him. If they weren't sneering down their pointy little snouts at him and whispering their stupid, juvenile jibes when they thought he was out of earshot, they were fawning over him for attention and approval. The last girl he'd screwed over the aquarium in the old man's office had just wanted a signature on some stupid form. He smiled as he recalled her expression when he had told her to lick him clean afterwards. They would do almost anything for a taste of power. It was pathetic.

There were three; no two people for whom he held both respect and trust, and both were out of the country, managing some project in the Middle East. The other, his father, managed his emotions more through fear and intimidation than through the building of trust and admiration. The prized aquarium and its inhabitants had seen its fair share of extra liquid food by way of retribution over the past two years. As long as there was a fresh supply of fresh, open minded secretaries and interns, he was happy to keep on donating.

A knock on a mahogany paneled door even *sounded* expensive, and his office door swung open an instant after three sharp taps. John Fisk, his father's senior advisor and CFO, entered.

"There will be a full showing of founders and senior partners in there today, James," he said, reaching straight for the antique cigar box on James's desk. He flipped open the lid with a fat finger and reached in, his gut spilling over the edge of the desk as he leaned forward. "You've been over this a hundred times, I know, but make sure you give the nod to old man Blakenstock *before* you even acknowledge your father or any of the other partners, clear?"

He clipped a meaty Cuban, the stub missing the silver ashtray and falling to the rug, and lit it with an old Zippo he pulled from his jacket pocket.

"I don't know why you pretend to like those things," James said, leaning back against the worn studded red leather. "You'll only take three drags, wave it around for a while for effect and stub it out in one of the plant pots that Mrs. Howell is always complaining about you destroying with your disgusting habit."

Fisk looked at him disapprovingly through a weak puff of cigar smoke.

"And it's a shameful waste of a two hundred pound cigar, *John*." James stood up and tugged on his shirt cuffs. "Let's go and make the old man proud, shall we?"

The old hallways were plush, carpeted affairs with lavish wood paneled walls and the smell of old furniture wax and money. Portraits of old men—there was a distinct absence of women in the ancestral hierarchy of the Firm—lined the hallways and adorned the walls of every office. This was an institution as arrogantly proud in its steeped tradition of wealth as it was successful at increasing it.

People came out of their offices as he approached, standing in the doorways to nod and offer their congratulations as he passed, heading for the old conference room, adjacent to his father's office. The double doors opened and he was ushered through to a room filled with navy blue and charcoal suits, white hair on nearly every head and picture perfect mustaches, trimmed daily for the price of a steak dinner. There was even a monocle or two. Fisk stepped beside him as the doors were closed and he was greeted with… silence.

It was a good thing that James wasn't smiling, even as he cast a glance over to the aquarium, because it would've begun to sag by now as two-dozen pairs of eyes glared at him impassively. The room resembled more of an old gentleman's club, with armchairs and couches and coffee tables adorned with cigar boxes and crystal decanters. There was not a conference table in sight. The silence stretched beyond the bounds of discomfort and James began to wonder if he was about to be fired instead of promoted.

A noise at the back of the room and James saw the tops of the doors swing open as someone entered the room. People started shuffling aside as a figure moved through the crowd and stepped forward. At six feet five inches and built like a Rugby Union professional, Thomas Devlin cast a very intimidating shadow. His hands were just enormous and when clenched, his fists resembled thirty-pound sledgehammers. James knew. He'd seen them up close.

"There are more than one or two skeptics in this room," he said, stopping a few feet from James.

Fisk stepped quickly away to take his place beside the elder Devlin. He still had the cigar, clenched between two puffy fingers. What an idiot.

"And I would be lying if I said that I don't have a few reservations of my own about what we are here to do today."

James snorted in his mind. He would never be above the put-downs, the lack of faith, the underestimating. His place would forever be in the corner. He would never be…

"But the days of not being able to trust you and your judgment are gone," Thomas said, "And I can tell you now, openly, before all who are here, that I welcome you into the fold, son, and I couldn't be more proud."

He stepped forward and bear-hugged his startled son before he could say a word, crushing his arms to his sides as applause began to ripple around the room, growing in intensity until it thundered in his ears and was joined by cheers and whistles from a dozen grinning faces. Moving away, Thomas gripped James by the shoulders and beamed down at him. James was speechless. He had expected a long, drawn out speech about the entire history of the Firm—probably since the Dark Ages—some stifling, overbearing nuggets of wisdom from the wizened old farts still commanding a seat on the board, and a sharp 'don't you dare fucking disappoint me, or else' comment from his impossible to please father and lord of the known universe. But that fantasy was in tatters now, blown away by the frankly absurd showing of affection and adoration at the newest addition to the board of partners.

"Everyone!" Thomas held up a huge hand, silencing the room within a couple of seconds. "There is, lest we forget, some formalities to attend to, before proceedings are deemed official. John, if you would assist Mr. Blakenstock."

Fisk scuttled over toward a couch on the far left side of the room; positioned in front of a fireplace that James could've fit his desk into. A small crowd of elderly suits moved aside, revealing a white haired old man, sitting, legs casually crossed, alone on the couch. He was looking down at an old pocket watch in his palm and as Fisk moved closer to speak, he snapped it shut and stood before he could open his mouth. James had only seen the man once before, when the heads of all the international branches had flown in for some big meeting. The only words his father had spoken to him that day had been, 'stay in your office'.

The old man walked forward. He exuded confidence, and there was a spring in his step that belied his outward years. He ignored everyone else in the room, and no one approached him. James found the obvious display of absolute power intoxicating. Stopping a few feet in front of him, he held out a hand. James looked at it for a moment before quickly reaching out to take it. The old man's hand was cool and smooth to the touch and his grip tightened immediately, just enough to show strength without crushing the bones in his hand.

"When you shake hands with someone you don't know..." he began to turn his hand slightly, rotating his wrist so that his hand was uppermost in the handshake, "always be sure to let the other person know who is in charge." He shook James's hand slowly and smiled thinly. "William Blakenstock," he said. "Nice to make your acquaintance, James. Your father holds you in the highest esteem. I trust you will not allow his opinion fall into disfavor."

"Thank you, sir. I'll do my best."

"Of course you will."

He withdrew his hand and turned to face the room. "The standard saying goes, with great power comes great responsibility. While this may be true elsewhere, we prefer to say, with great power..."

"*Comes great reward!*" The men in the room finished the sentence in unison and Blakenstock turned to face James once more.

"Play your part, James, and a great many spoils will be yours. A great many spoils."

"I'll work hard, sir. You have my word."

Blakenstock leaned in close, whispering in James's ear. "If you put in half as much effort as you do riding those young fillies over my aquarium, you'll do just fine."

He flashed a wolfish smile and then was gone, walking toward the doors at the back of the room as suits darted out of his way left and right, parting like the Red Sea before him. James was stunned. His face grew hot and he felt the dizzying nausea of the richly embarrassed. If he didn't get out of the room soon, he'd make a nice sticky mess all over the expensive carpet. His father approached, waving Fisk away with a dismissive flick of his hand. James struggled to compose himself.

"There will be a small private ceremony after lunch that you are required to attend. I'll send Fisk for you when it's time." He smiled, and then appeared to catch himself. There had been enough fatherly love for one day. "Mr. Blakenstock approves of you, but he will have his eye on you. Work hard, James. Do *not* let me down." He stepped back and nodded curtly. "Until later. You may go now."

James didn't hang around, turning and leaving the room, the doors opened and were closed behind him within seconds. It felt like the longest walk of his life back to his office, skirting more congratulations and handshakes as he fought the rising tide of anxious nausea. The most comforting sound he heard all morning was the soft *thump* of his office door closing at his back. He slid down the polished wood to sit on the floor, head in hands, as he relived the moment Blakenstock had called him out. Flashes of hitched up skirts, of grunts and moans, and all the while Blakenstock watching every thrust and slap.

"Oh my God. I can't get out." He looked up, took a deep breath. "I'm in. I'm bloody well all the way in."

The smile was slow in coming, but when it did, it was the most sinister he'd ever mustered. Two hours later, James was on a massage table in the spa, two floors down, directly under his office. He was fantasizing about a yacht party, somewhere in the south of France, and being surrounded by a horde of beautiful, panting women, all eager to do his bidding. Turning down the advances of a gorgeous, desperate woman was half the fun.

It had taken him less than ten minutes to accept the position he was in regarding Mr. Blakentsock. It was one of his strengths. He knew an untenable position when he was in one, and how to make the very best of it. It was one of the reasons he was such a gifted player in the markets and why he'd seen his own stock rise so rapidly. His father took all the credit, of course, but then he would do the same, he knew. The masseuse, a particularly firm-handed young girl from South America, was just starting to get somewhere with his tight hamstrings when there was a knock on the door. He heard Fisk's unmistakable, drawling tone in the hallway.

"Right away, Mr. Fisk," the girl said, and the door closed once more.

The lights came up slowly and he felt her hand on his back. "Mr. Devlin? I'm sorry, sir, but Mr. Fisk asked me to tell you that you're expected in your father's office right away. They are ready for you."

*　*　*

The same two doormen waited outside his father's office, one turning to open the door as he approached. The other watched him flatly, casting his eyes up and down as James paused at the door. He stepped inside and the door was closed silently behind him. His father's office was almost as big as the conference room and took up a good amount of floor space at a corner of the eleventh floor.

The fireplace behind his father's desk was dark and the mantel held several gilt framed pictures. He recognized his father in all but one of them, on various vacations, meeting famous people, receiving awards. There were none of James, though he didn't expect there would be. A small black and white photo, set in an old silver frame, caught his eye. A woman; pretty with flowing dark hair and a beaming smile in a short black dress. He guessed from the sixties or seventies. She was holding a baby, standing on a balcony overlooking the ocean, somewhere sunny. Could that be…?

"Go with Mr. Fisk, James. I'll be with you momentarily."

Fisk and his father were the only other people in the room. Fisk stepped forward and ushered James toward the far corner of the room. There was a pair of old leather armchairs beside a bookcase and a small table. When Fisk walked past the chairs and literally into the corner, toward the wall, James frowned, thinking that perhaps he should take a seat in one of the chairs. Fisk reached out to touch one of the wooden panels on the wall, and then mumbled something that James couldn't make out. A dull *click* from inside the wall was followed by a smooth rumbling sound as a door-sized section of the wall popped out and then slid slowly aside, revealing a doorway in the wall beyond. Fisk turned and nodded at James. "Follow me."

The passageway was narrow and smelled of old rugs. It was short, leading swiftly to another wooden door that Fisk opened with a push. The chamber beyond was dim, and James could see a few candles scattered around as he approached the doorway. He stepped through into a low, gloomy room. The angles were a bit odd and he realized that the room had five walls instead of four. It was dark, lit only by the candles, and there was a table against the far wall, and a large sheet covering something on the wall to his left. As he turned to the right, several figures stepped out of the shadows and moved toward him. He took a step back as he saw them, dressed from head to toe in black cloaks and all wearing white, featureless masks. He reached out for Fisk's arm as they moved closer.

"John...?"

Fisk grabbed his arm and produced a syringe. James could see the amber colored liquid in it and moved to pull his arm away, but in a heartbeat Fisk had the needle in James's neck and was pushing the plunger down hard. He cried out and several pairs of hands reached out for him. The room began to spin, the sounds grew muffled and distorted and things grew dark.

"Don't fight it, James."

Fisk's voice was the last thing he heard as he fell forward, tumbling into a numbing, senseless void of blackness.

Chapter Eight

Alex gathered up the data pad and made his way out of the lab toward the elevators, arm out, holding his ID for the nearest soldier to inspect.

"Very good, sir." The soldier pushed the call button and they waited for the elevator to arrive. The scientist and his trio of armed toy soldiers. None of them made eye contact with him, yet every trigger guard had an index finger for company, and the 'shoot first, ask questions later' stereotype so often associated with these kinds of soldiers was as thinly veiled as he'd ever seen. Still, he was tempted to offer the soldier who had pressed the elevator a tip as the doors opened and he stepped inside. He refrained.

"Come in, Alex," Drexler said as Alex pushed open the door to the conference room a few levels up.

The room was only a little larger than Drexler's office, and accommodated a large, twelve-chair, conference table with room to spare. The obligatory large screen TV adorned the far end wall, above a narrow table with all the refreshment goodies. Besides Drexler, the Colonel was present, along with an aide, a white coat he didn't recognize, and Charles, the man with the intense stare whom Alex had assumed was in charge of everything. He made his way to the first empty seat available and pulled out the plush leather chair.

"Before you sit, Alex," Charles said, from his seat at the head of the table, "Why don't you give us an overview of the project's… guts, so to speak. To get us all up to speed."

Alex nodded and pushed the chair back in, making his way to the far end of the table. He dropped the file on the polished mahogany and opened it, scanning a page or two before picking up a leaf and surveying the room. It took a moment for Alex to fiddle with the laptop on the podium as he logged in to the server. Finally, the screen burst to life with the Apex Labs Syndicate logo and Alex opened the first file.

"So, here we have a basic view of a DNA strand. It's the one we've all seen in textbooks and on your computer screen when you Google image search it. The specific gene we are interested in is called Monoamine Oxidase A, or

MAO-A, also commonly referred to as the 'Warrior Gene'. It's an enzyme responsible for the breakdown of neurotransmitters that we know to affect mood and behavior, such as dopamine and serotonin."

He clicked the remote and the slide changed to a close up of the DNA strand. "Our previous strategy has been to attempt to somehow 'activate' an MAO-A gene variant on a specific DNA strand, in order to influence a subject's behavior. Our challenges have been several-fold."

The screen began to slowly switch views, from technical diagrams of DNA structure and individual strands, to complex molecular diagrams and tables of data.

"Firstly, in order for this to be viable at all, we need to make it work in a living subject instead of theoretically, with random strands of God knows who."

Charles glanced at Drexler and he shifted uncomfortably in his seat, hoping that Alex wasn't about to embark on one of his über rants.

"Secondly, it needs to work spontaneously. We've had some limited success with this, as we saw in the rhesus monkey trial film, but it's fatally flawed and I believe that we need to rethink the entire structure."

Charles coughed slightly. "Do you have any theories as to where you might begin, now that you've decided to rip up the paper and start over, Dr. Bishop?"

Alex shrugged. "Anywhere would be better than where we are right now," he said, not caring if they appreciated his directness. He turned back to the screen. "And thirdly, how do we best transport the necessary gene switch into the subject? Our options are; either a dormant switch, embedded into the DNA strand and activated with discretion by some other, external or internal means, or the simpler approach of an immediate switch, where the subject would, perhaps, self-administer and the switch would be activated almost instantaneously."

"We have soldiers self-administering medication, sedatives, pain killers and what have you all the time on the battlefield, doctor. I don't think it would be a problem having our men giving themselves a shot in the arm."

"Well that would really help me out a lot. Thank you, Colonel. I'll add that to my notes."

"Alex," Drexler gave him a cautionary look and Alex took a breath.

"My apologies, Colonel. It's hard to keep my manners when I know I have two weeks to change the course of human history."

The Colonel nodded very slightly and Alex glanced at the other white coat in the room, diligently taking notes and stroking his grey goatee beard. His forefinger and middle finger were stained yellow from the chain smoking habit he knew must be causing him some ridiculous discomfort right now.

"We appreciate the pressure you're under, Dr. Bishop," Charles said, "As for today, we don't need to know the dirty details of the science. We would just like to hear your thoughts on your general approach to making this work, and if it's feasible within the next sixteen days."

Alex pondered for a moment. Drexler knew that he was running the entire process through his mind, accounting for what variables he already knew, and formulating his chances of success. He held his breath, knowing that Alex could just as well just say it couldn't be done than could.

"An additional three days for tail end testing would increase the chances of success by thirty-nine percent," Alex said finally.

The white coat dropped his pen and the Colonel snorted, sitting back in his chair. "Thirty-nine percent, my ass," he said, under his breath.

"Well then," Drexler interjected before Alex could get himself deeper into the Colonel's bad books. "Alex, tell us how you intend to proceed, if you would."

Alex had to pull his gaze from the Colonel and turned back to the laptop, scrolling through more files and clicking on one, changing the view on the screen to a new diagram; a 3D model of a DNA strand with one missing branch.

"In very basic terms, I will look for a way to synthesize a dynamic variant of the MAO-A enzyme in such a way that, despite its fairly limited influence on actual aggression and conscious behavior, we will be able to make it communicate with the area of the brain that produces other substances that will help us, like adrenaline, for example. If we can make the Switch talk the brain into believing the subject's natural state is one of heightened aggression and lowered moral barriers, without compromising alertness and tactical decision-making, then we have killed several birds with one stone and, perversely, skirted around many of the obstacles we have faced connected directly to the whole DNA issue itself."

The Colonel looked like a heart attack was imminent. Charles was actually smiling. The white coat was trying to remember everything he'd just said.

"So you're saying that we don't actually need to approach this as a genetics problem at all," Charles said. "It's more about the brain than the DNA?"

"Well no, not exactly, but you have the right idea." He approached the end of the table. "See, you have been focused solely on the manipulation, in its prime form, of the DNA and its variants, of a living, fully functional subject. Dynamic genetic modification at the highest level. I think we have muddied the water by not taking into account how big an asset the brain itself could be here."

"We've tried using the brain for behavior control," The Colonel said. "It's an old story, from before the cold war, only worked half the time and drove a good few men bat shit crazy."

Alex nodded, "I'm not talking about Agent Orange, psychedelic compounds or suggestive mind control, Colonel. I'm talking the actual, real, chemical drivers that directly influence and push our behavior between opening the door for someone and slamming it in their face. Those deep, dark corners of the brain, controlled by our baser instincts that are built on the very foundation of our own DNA. The genetics—and MAO-A in particular—are still the key, still the deciding factor in whether or not this will work, but the brain is the conduit, the brain is the computer. The DNA is the code we need to use to reprogram that computer. That's the terrifying simplicity of it all."

Drexler was nodding, his brain churning. Alex could see all the cogs in the room turning. He had set something in motion, and it would either help or hinder what he was about to embark on over the next two weeks. The white coat was writing again, scribbling and then scratching out, scribbling again. Charles leaned over to Drexler, whispered something in his ear. Drexler shook his head, and then nodded. "That's in your hands, Charles," he said, drawing away and standing, hands flat on the table. "Alex, thank you. We appreciate your candor and your insight. You've given us a lot to think about. I'll be down to discuss our conclusions in one hour. That's all for now."

Alex walked back over to the laptop and reached for the USB drive. It was gone. He turned to see Charles's aide handing him the drive.

"Thank you, Dr. Bishop," he said, showing him the memory device. "I assume you have the original files. I'd like to keep hold of this, for reference."

"It's all uploaded to my secure server too," Alex said, "I'm sure Dr. Drexler can give you access, if you don't have it already."

Charles smiled and stood, turning for the door. His aide and the white coat followed him from the room. Alex noticed an armed soldier in the doorway. He turned to escort the three men down the hallway.

"Son," the Colonel said, leaning forward on his elbows. "I'm not the kindest, and I'm sure as hell not the funniest, but I'm a straight shooter and I don't lie, unless it's under orders. I know who you are. Dr. Drexler holds you in the highest regard. I know that social interaction can sometimes be stressful for you, difficult even, but a man with your brains needs to grasp the importance of sometimes keeping your mouth in park instead of risking spitting in someone's eye who might not be so tolerant as to not kick you square in the balls. Do you take my meaning?"

Alex felt his respect level for the Colonel go up a notch and nodded. "I'll try to do that, Colonel."

"Very good, son. Now do me a favor and give us the room. I need to bend the good doctor's ear a few."

Alex left the file open on the table and left the room. The door hissed closed behind him and he heard a metallic *thunk* as the magnetic lock slotted into place. The privacy glass frosted a milky green and he turned away just as the soldier approached him. "Elevator to the Hub, sir?"

"Thank you."

For the ninety seconds it took to reach his lab, he wondered what he had done, and what he was going to do, and how many lives might be spared, or spent, by his actions.

* * *

Jerry pulled the SUV to the side of the street, a few yards before the fluttering cordon of yellow Police tape. With the rest of the team back at the DC field office, Gabby had wanted to get to the crime scene as soon as possible. Her inner anxiety was curiously higher than it should've been, and she put it down to the fruitless visit to the New York office and her barbed encounter with Director Cole.

"Agent Morgane?" A young agent, complete with tan trench coat and standard issue aviators, ducked under the cordon and skipped over. "Special Agent Patrick. Agent McCarthy asked me to show you over. Follow me."

When an agent took such delight in chaperoning colleagues from their car to his boss, you knew he'd been on his feet for just a few weeks, probably less. McCarthy would suck all of that youthful experience out in no time at all. They followed Patrick through a handful of civilians, under the cordon and around a pair of DC police cruisers. Gabby saw McCarthy immediately. He was chewing on the stub of a cold cigar, looking like a flatfoot of old, his fedora tilted back slightly and his pale, stubble-covered face screwed up against the cold November air.

"Morgane," he said, as they approached, ignoring Jerry. "One sec."

They waited while McCarthy tore a page from his pocket notebook and handed it to the officer standing next to him, who nodded and strode away.

"Pepperoni," McCarthy said. "Gianno's has the best deep dish in the city. And don't let that shit heel Keller tell you different. He wouldn't know a good pie if one landed on his face and forced itself down his greasy neck."

"I'll try to remember that," Gabby said dryly. "So, what have you got? Sorano said you'd get us up to speed."

"Well, what do you know?"

"Not what you know," Gabby replied, and McCarthy snorted, playing along. "Well no one knows what I know, Morgane. But, in the spirit of cooperation and wanting to get this pissant case zipped up before bedtime, I'll fill you in."

He walked over to the silver town car, doors open and the white tarps of the forensics team surrounding it on all sides. The bodies were gone, shipped to the morgue, and a man in a dust suit, mask and goggles was moving about the inside of the car, dusting hard surfaces and placing tiny items into plastic Ziploc bags.

"Bodies were discovered by two local residents. They're back with DCPD in the command vehicle." He pointed to a large truck, parked near to the cordon at the other end of the scene. "The woman is pretty shook up but the guy really couldn't give shit."

He stepped closer to the car, gesturing with his ballpoint. Gabby noticed the chewed blue cap, still attached to the pen. "No forced entry, no bullet holes, no GS residue, no fingerprints. It's as clean as you could expect anywhere outside of science fiction."

He looked through his notebook and sniffed, hard, wiping his nose with a sleeve of his coat. He wiped the same side every time. "I had forensics run blacklight tactile and dust tests on Bishop's doors, windows, surfaces and appliances. They're in the command truck now. Should have the results out nice and warm for you by tomorrow. If you'd like to take a seat I'll call your number when your order's ready. Nothing came up on-scene, so don't go gettin' all excited on me."

"Any noise?" Jerry asked, stepping to the car door. "Door opening, closing, a scream or cry for help?"

"Nothing. You could say it's like someone just parked the car here with the two bodies already in it. No one heard or saw a thing. We canvassed the entire street and the only nugget we got was from a neighbor of your friend, Morgane."

He turned to face her, pushing his trench open and stuffing his hands into his pants pockets. "And she said that she saw a suspicious-looking man exiting Dr. Bishop's apartment a couple of minutes after he left for work. Got anything on that?"

Mrs. Galaksy opened the door a crack and Gabby lifted up her ID and badge. "FBI, ma'am. I was wondering if you had another few minutes to…"

"I know who you are, agent lady. You're the doctor's friend. He likes you." She opened the door and nodded her inside. "Though I don't know what he sees in you. In my day you could trust the police. The local beat cop knew everyone in the neighborhood and there was no trouble that couldn't be straightened out with just a billy club and some harsh words."

Gabby smiled. "My dad used to say the same thing. I grew up with stories of local cops stopping by the neighborhood to play stick ball with the kids after their shift. It's a shame that they've had to move on with the world, isn't it?"

The old lady just nodded, and then drew back inside. Gabby walked into the living room. There were at least a dozen cats, all sitting silently on various pieces of furniture, the windowsills, beneath the coffee table. They eyed her suspiciously. Mrs. Galasky scooped a calico from one of the two armchairs and sat down on the other, petting the cat, which looked far from pleased. "But now, it's special agent this and special agent that, guns-a-blazin' and secret spies doing God-knows-what up and down the streets. Makes me wanna move back to Wisconsin with my sister. She doesn't have murders outside her door and she bakes the police captain a pie every Sunday. I don't have the fight in me to go out to stand up against who knows what anymore."

Gabby took a seat and tried to look patient. The cats continued to stare. It was a little unnerving.

"You know," Galasky said, "I've never seen the kitties act this way around someone they don't know before. Do you have a cat? You have a way with them."

"No, I'm afraid I don't. I travel too much to keep one. It wouldn't be very kind."

Mrs. Galasky nodded. "Uh huh. I guess. Now, what can I do for you, agent lady?"

"The man you witnessed leaving Doctor Bishop's apartment this morning. You stated that he was wearing a jacket, with the letters FBI on the back. Is that correct?"

"That's what I saw. That's what I said."

"Was he talking? Maybe on a cell phone, or to someone else? Did you hear anything unusual?"

"Nope. Didn't say a word, and it was just him. I saw him. He just came from the apartment, put his jacket on and walked by, down the stairs and out the door. Then I saw him in the street."

Gabby frowned. "Ok, let's back up a moment. You said he put the jacket on *after* you saw him leave Dr. Bishop's apartment? Then, when you moved to the window, where did he go when you saw him in the street?"

"I had a good view. That nice handyman, Rob Jones, put a brand new view glass in my door just last week. The old one was all scratched and foggy. Couldn't see a thing. No, he walked along the hall and I saw him put on this black or dark blue jacket—I couldn't tell exactly the color—you know, the windbreaker kind that the coaches wear, that kind of thing. It said FBI on the back in big yellow letters. I'm old, Miss, but I ain't blind yet."

Gabby chuckled, "No, I can tell that you're a long way from that ma'am."

"So then I looked out of the window. I had to move Whiner because he likes to sit right there and sometimes the drapes get all up under him."

She pointed to a fat black cat, sitting on the top of the old piano against the far wall. "And there he was, just walking down the steps. That's when he had a phone. He said something but of course I couldn't hear from way up here."

"And then what? Did he get into a car, or just walk away?"

Mrs. Galasky paused, hesitant, and Gabby knew that she'd seen more than she'd told the police earlier. She looked around the room. Small ornaments adorned almost every surface, yet everything was spotless and well organized, all in its place. Beside the piano was a trashcan—the woven wicker kind you get from Bed, Bath & Beyond—and near the top were shards of what looked like broken crystal or glass. Gabby rose and walked over, trying to look as if she was casually inspecting the tiny crystal figurines on one end of the piano.

"These are wonderful," she said, pointing to a trio of miniature ballerinas, each only a couple of inches high, meticulously hand-crafted down to their tiny crystal shoes. "The dancers of the New York Ballet Company?"

Mrs. Galasky shifted in her seat. The cat on her lap shifted with her, squirming momentarily at a fleeting window of freedom. "London. I've had that set for, oh let's see, sixty-five years."

"It's such a shame that it's not a complete set," Gabby said, reaching out to touch one of the tiny figures.

"Please, don't touch that," Mrs. Galasky said. "It's… it's a very precious memento."

Gabby looked down into the trashcan. The broken figures of at least three ballet dancer figurines were scattered amongst the trash. She didn't think for a second that they had gotten broken by accident during a daily dusting.

"They're beautiful," she said, stepping back from the piano. "I don't want to keep you, Mrs. Galasky." She turned for the door and reached into her jacket pocket, pulling out a card. "If you can think of anything else, please don't hesitate to give me a call."

Mrs. Galasky took the card and read the name. Gabby could see her mouthing the words.

"He does important work, you know," she said, still looking at the card.

Gabby paused. "Who does? Dr. Bishop?"

"Yes, he does important work, so he has the police and you agent people looking out for him. He left early this morning but I could hear him cleaning before. He does that a lot and sometimes it makes Samson a bit edgy. I was going to open the door to offer him some tea but I know he doesn't like to be interrupted and he seemed in a hurry. Poor man. He works a lot and doesn't really have anyone, besides you, of course. Not that I've seen."

"And the other… agent," Gabby said, "Are you sure he came out of Dr. Bishop's apartment? Right after he left? I know you have a fairly good view of the hallway, but Dr. Bishop's door is a few apartments down, and you mentioned that you didn't open the door."

Mrs. Galasky looked up and Gabby thought she saw something in her eyes, something sharp, meaningful. The older lady looked away, suddenly thoughtful, as if she'd forgotten herself for a moment. "Well, he did come from that end of the hall, and really just a few moments after Dr. Bishop went by."

"But did you *see* him leave Dr. Bishop's apartment?"

Mrs. Galasky looked down. "No, I suppose I didn't."

Gabby stepped forward and placed her hand on Mrs. Galasky's shoulder. The older lady calmed immediately, and she looked up, her eyes widening for a moment as she put her fingertips to her open mouth in a look of shock, before she relaxed and sat back down in the armchair. Gabby followed her down, patting her shoulder and smiling reassuringly. "That's ok, Ma'am. It was early. It was very nice of you to want to give Alex, I mean, Dr. Bishop, something for his drive. I'm sure he would've appreciated it."

Mrs. Galasky nodded and resumed petting the now almost sleeping cat on her lap.

"I'll see myself out," Gabby said, standing to turn for the door.

She took a step and noticed the mark on the wooden floor, between the edge of the rug and the baseboard. As she walked by, she got a clear view of what looked like the smudged shape of a boot tread, half on the floor, leading on to the rug. She walked on and headed for the apartment door, glancing over her shoulder to see Mrs. Galasky lifting a hand to wave gently. Gabby smiled back and left the apartment, standing in the hallway for a moment. Someone had paid Mrs. Galasky a visit and she had hidden that fact from her. The questions were; why, and who was he?

Gabby let the lobby door swing slowly shut behind her and stepped down to the street. Jerry walked over and said something that Mrs. Galasky couldn't hear from her second story window as she looked down through netted drapes, following Gabby with a cool gaze as she and her partner walked back over toward the police cordon. After a moment, she stepped away and picked up a cell phone, hitting a speed dial key.

"Tell Michael it's happening. He's here."

Chapter Nine

Nighttime in the lab was usually Alex's favorite time to work. No one around to bother him or fill his ears with useless gossip or small talk, and the freedom of the hallways to roam on the few occasions his tired eyes demanded a break from the harsh light of the computer monitor. Even though he had the lab to himself, he was on one such jaunt, thermos in hand, heading to the break room and the coffee pot. He was trying to think of something pleasant to disconnect from his work but all he could think of was how irritated he was going to be when he found the coffee pot empty, or worse, half full of cold, day old coffee that no one had bothered to refresh. As he rounded the corner and entered the spacious break room, his comms unit beeped in his pocket. Stopping in the doorway, he grabbed the small device and looked at the screen.

02:45 – Break Time

"I needed the reminder *before* I forgot to be reminded," he grumbled, shoving the unit back in his pocket and entering the gloomy break room.

Besides the few low powered recessed lights set into the ceiling above the coffee bar, the only light in the room came from outside, where the harsh white light from the floodlit courtyard and front lawn spilled in through the windows, between the vertical blinds, casting ghostly white stripes and swathes of light across the room. Closing the microwave, Alex tested his freshly warmed coffee and grimaced as the hot liquid burned his tongue.

"Goddammit," he hissed, walking slowly to one of the tables and taking a seat, cupping the hot mug between his hands.

Pulling his note pad from his lab coat pocket, he reviewed his notes, laid out neatly across the paper and interspersed with doodled diagrams and side notes. He had made some good progress over the past few nights, managing to isolate a half dozen promising codes to take into his next test phase. He was hopeful of having a solid Phase 2 to take to Drexler by the end of the week. One of the codes in particular was getting more of his attention than the others, and he suspected that it was one of Drexler's juvenile flies in his ointment. He had nicknamed the code *Keymaster*, though he was fairly certain it would end up being deleted from the file after he confronted Drexler about it. He didn't necessarily think that he was being tested like before, though he wouldn't put it past his boss to want to keep him on his toes, even on a project of this importance.

"One code at a time, Alex, old chap," he whispered, taking a sip from his still piping hot coffee.

He watched the pair of duty soldiers talking outside, over by the main entrance. He could see their rifles, slung over their shoulders, and he wondered absently if either of them had used them before. The sky was inky black and heavy grey clouds were rolling in from the west, carrying the promise of sleet and snow. He felt suddenly very cozy in the warmth of the break room and felt a pang of sympathy for the guards walking the grounds outside throughout the night.

He turned back to his notes, underlining and circling key numbers and phrases, turning formulas over in his head and rubbing some life back into his overtired eyes. At first he didn't notice the light outside changing color, but when it finally caught his eye he sat up, looking at his hands, now bathed in a soft pink hue from somewhere outside the window. Standing, he leaned toward the glass, pushing the blinds apart with his hands and peering through the window. The entire tree line that ran alongside the river was ablaze. Flames roared and pulsated skyward along a two hundred yard stretch of river bank, disappearing from view behind the far side of the main building. Thick black smoke roiled into the night sky and uniformed soldiers sprinted from their posts, some talking frantically into radios as others merely stood watching, powerless to help.

"What the hell?"

The window immediately fogged and Alex wiped the condensation from the glass and then watched as a fire truck with an Apex logo pulled into the courtyard. It was one stationed at the lab complex, out close to the main gate. He could see the flashing red and blue lights of more trucks beyond the perimeter fence as they headed toward the trees, the huge trucks dwarfed by the immense wall of flames. Then the sky began to change, the orange glow from the fire seeming to spread up through the clouds, low and foreboding, until the entire sky appeared a combination of fiery orange and red hues, like the most spectacular sunset he could imagine.

Another fire truck appeared in the courtyard and began to douse the main building with water as showers of glowing embers began to float and waft across the asphalt.

"*All personnel, report to your evacuation stations immediately. This is not a drill. I repeat, this is not a drill.*"

The programmed announcement went out complex-wide. Alex could hear the lag from the loudspeakers outside as the same message echoed across the property. He snatched up his coffee and strode from the room, moving fast down the corridor toward the Hub. When he reached the atrium he looked up. At the top of the open space, five stories above, the glass atrium roof gave him a clear look at the maelstrom of swirling orange clouds above. The sky seemed to be spinning, swirling in an almost pre-tornado formation; a dark pit at its center.

The soldiers in the Hub were gone, probably mustered to emergency posts elsewhere in the complex. His lab was as he left it, his laptop open, the word of the day screensaver scrolling '*Prophetic*' across the darkened screen.

Alex spun around at a loud noise from outside. *A scream?* He ran back along the hallway toward the Hub and main entrance, stopping just short of the atrium. Everything was fiery red and orange. Every room, office and lab appeared to be on fire. As he stepped into the atrium, terrified and yet unable to run back to the safety of his lab, he looked up. A monstrous swirling cloud rotated directly above the building like the gaping maw of an immense, fiery tornado.

"What the hell?" He flinched as the main door smashed inward with a deafening *crash!* and a figure stumbled inside, leaning on the doorframe as a blast of furnace-like air took Alex's breath away. He squinted into the heat flowing through the door as the man gargled something incoherent, struggling to speak. Alex didn't move closer. He couldn't, as much as he wanted to help. The man was on fire.

A loud *crack!* from above and Alex looked up to see spiderweb cracks appear in the glass roof. There was more fire amongst the clouds, swirling faster than ever, enormous flames shooting downward and bursting against the failing glass. Alex turned and ran for the door just as the burning man collapsed to the floor and the roof gave way, sending huge shards of deadly glass raining down on the Hub lobby. He hurdled the body of the man in the doorway and was hit by a crushing wave of heat and wind that threatened to force him back inside.

Cowering against the building, Alex looked out over the main courtyard toward the water. Everything he could see was on fire, from the trees along the river, the fire trucks—some with their lights still flashing kaleidoscope-like through melting plastic—the perfectly landscaped grass inside the perimeter fence, to the very asphalt itself, melting and shifting into oily black pools of burning tar. The people that were left standing wandered from vehicle to vehicle, wall to wall, desperately searching for cover in the hellish landscape.

The first he saw taken was a few yards to his right; a firefighter, golden yellow jacket half aflame, was screaming when the sound was abruptly cut short as something swooped down and snatched him from his feet, swirling and careening back into the burning sky on jet black wings, its prize gripped within huge talons. Then he saw more of them, swooping down out of the clouds to terrorize and snatch their fleeing victims as they scrambled for safety anywhere they could find it. A female soldier ran from the main doors toward Alex as he pressed himself against the wall beside the Hub doors. She made it to within twenty feet of him, her eyes wide with stark terror, when one of the black things flashed by, snatching her away in a mist of blood that splashed across Alex's glasses.

Alex felt the skin on the backs of his hands and face begin to tighten. His eyes were sore from the heat and began to water and swell, blurring his vision as something began to emerge from a slowly forming fire spout, twisting its way slowly toward him across the asphalt. It grew brighter and wider as it moved closer, and Alex could make out a dark shadow at its center, the silhouette of something immense. Then, as it began to step toward him from the fiery twister, Alex felt a hand grab his shoulder and he turned to see Gabby, crouching beside him, shielding her face from the heat with a raised forearm.

"Alex!" she screamed above the chaos. "Let's go! Come on!"

She pulled at him, trying to get him to stand, and Alex looked out once more, watching as the huge figure emerged from the fire, an image of a man, tall, huge, muscular. He could make out a mass of thick, slicked hair and vague, shadowy features, but he could see the eyes clearly enough. Red and glowing like a demonic apparition from some Friday night horror movie, they glared at him as it stepped closer, reaching out a burning arm, thick and rippling with muscle, flames licking up and around the flesh, and stretching out taloned fingers toward him.

"Alex, come on!"

He began to move finally, dragged back toward the doors as Gabby pulled and yanked on his lab coat. The creature was looming over him, reaching for him with outstretched hands, flames flicking between thick, gnarled fingers.

"*Alex!*"

He jumped awake with a startled cry, almost falling off of his lab chair, and stood, backing away from the workbench until he hit the wall, eyes darting around the empty room and gasping for breath.

"Holy… holy *shit!*"

It took several ragged seconds for him to get his breathing back under control, sitting back down on one of the work chairs and mopping his brow with a sleeve of his lab coat.

"Everything ok in here, sir?"

Alex looked up to see one of the lobby soldiers standing in the doorway, his partner behind him holding a rifle at the ready. The blatant display of heightened, on-edge security did little to ease his distress.

"Uh, yeah, fine. I'm fine. Should really just get some sleep. I'm a little jumpy."

The soldier stared at him suspiciously for a moment before scanning the lab. He made a point of staying outside. "Very well, sir," he said, backing out into the hallway. "Please let us know if you need help with anything. Maybe try to get some rest."

Alex nodded and the soldiers left. He watched them through the glass walls all the way back to the atrium, which had been a crumbling firestorm of hell just a moment ago. He glanced at the large digital clock on the far wall; its red LED numbers glowing brightly against the black display. 02:59.

"Actually, maybe I *should* get some sleep, dammit."

He rubbed his temples and looked through to the extended section of the lab at the cot against the far wall. At that moment it looked like the most inviting metal-framed, skinny camping mattress he had ever laid eyes on and he walked over to his computer on the workbench to pick up his comms unit. An alarm needed to be set. He had deadlines to meet. As he turned toward the cot, something caught his eye on the screen and he paused, turning to look at the large monitor.

The screen displayed an exploded view of a DNA strand—a 3D rendered model that Alex used to more easily visualize his work in progress—and tables of data connected to the three DNA codes he was currently working with. He leaned in closer. One of the codes was blinking, alternating red and grey.

"Oh come on," he mumbled. "Now what?"

He sat at the bench and began to navigate the file, running diagnostic checks in an attempt to isolate a fault in the data, the notion of sleep fading like a distant echo. He could find no errors and sat back finally, staring at the code, still flashing on the screen.

"What are you up to, Drexler?" he whispered. "It's a little later to be upping your game."

He reached for the mouse and moved the cursor toward the security settings, designed to prevent accidental manipulation of the actual code, stored in the archive at the back of his lab. As he clicked, warning boxes flashed up.

Caution! Access to physical code file. Are you sure?

He clicked 'Yes' and continued, clicking through several more warning pop-ups until he reached a final screen.

WARNING! Disabling this protocol will release all protective measures from this code. Unprotected codes may be damaged or permanently deleted. Proceed with caution. Continue?

Alex did not pause. The decision, and all of its consequences, had already been considered, weighed and justified in his mind. There was no point in hesitating. If the code was corrupt it could not be used. If it could not be used, it was useless in any case, and it was therefore irrelevant whether that code was left intact or not. He clicked the 'Yes' button and waited, looking at the rendered DNA code, a very accurate visual interpretation of the actual code—stored somewhere in the immense library that was his precious project resource—slowly rotating on the screen. For a moment, nothing happened.

Alex watched the display, the flashing code still visible in a small dialog window in the top corner of the screen, blinking a warning that all was not well with this particular code. Still nothing changed. He sat forward, about to reset the system, when something moved. At first he didn't catch it, a twitch so fast that he barely registered the movement. He waited, eyes fixed on the slowly rotating image. A flicker on one of the ladder rungs, followed by another, further up the strand. Alex clicked the visual diagnostic panel, checking for render anomalies in the computer's graphics card. It came up clean.

"Aw, come on now," he said, exasperated. "Stop playing hard to get. But, ok, if it's not the computer, and it's not me going crazy…"

He pushed the cursor to the *Delete Code* button. "… then it's trash time for you, my friend."

Click.

The button didn't respond, the code file was not deleted and the render continued to rotate slowly on the screen.

"Awesome," he said, sitting back in his chair. "You broke my computer."

He reached for the phone. "What are the chances that someone in I.T. is working this late?"

There was no answer on the directory line for the Tech Department, as Alex had suspected. As gifted a geneticist and all-round brainiac that he was, he fell short as a computer technician, or as a computer anything, really.

"Elmer's home in bed, sleeping," he said, dropping the phone into the trashcan. "Which is what I should be doing right now."

Alex rubbed his eyes and clicked on the delete button once more. Again there was no response and he tossed the mouse to the workbench, slumping in his chair and resting his chin on his palm.

"Ok," he said suddenly, standing up and reaching around the back of the computer tower to grab the power cord. "They told me never to do this."

He leaned on the tower and pulled the cord out. The computer whined down to silence, switching off with a final *click*. Standing back, he stared at the screen - and the still rotating image of the DNA strand.

"Wait a minute," he said, leaning around the back of the monitor. He followed the power cord to the back of the tower, which was definitely unplugged. Standing again, he pushed the *off* switch on the front of the monitor. Nothing. The screen remained powered on, the image still glowing on the display.

"Ok, I'm not *that* dumb," he said.

Reaching for the mouse, he swirled it around on the mouse mat and saw the cursor mimicking the motion on the screen. The computer tower was dark and silent and Alex snorted, smiling at the apparently still operating computer in front of him. Then, without warning, flames burst out of the sides of the monitor. Alex leapt back, hitting the chair and sitting down, his momentum carrying him backwards in the rolling chair until it hit the far wall. The flames rippled and danced around the monitor, framing the screen in a greenish-yellow fiery halo.

"Oh, you've got to be kidding me," Alex said, holding onto the chair armrests, the mouse resting on his lap.

The flames continued to bloom and flicker around the edges of the slim monitor. Nothing was melting, smoking or even actually *burning,* and yet Alex could feel the heat emanating from the flames, feel the fire as it rippled and licked at the plastic and glass. As he watched, a sense of calm settled over him. It eased his anxiety as if the flames were a soothing, hypnotic dance of warmth and light that began to appear more welcoming with each passing second.

Standing slowly, he walked to the workbench and reached out a hand toward the flames. He could still see the image of the DNA strand on the screen, untouched by the fire that covered the edges of the glass. His hand passed into the fire, the flames licking at the cuff of his lab coat sleeve until the fabric began to blacken and smoke. His skin remained untouched and Alex watched in calm fascination as the flames began to spread over his hand and wrist, and then up his arm, charring the white sleeve to a black smear.

Alex watched the code file on the screen, blinking steadily between red and gray. Before he realized it, he was moving the mouse with his burning hand, clicking on the file and sending it to a removable flash drive plugged into the front of the computer tower. A dialog box popped up.

Move original source file to drive: AB-01? Confirm Y or N.

Alex clicked 'Yes'.

WARNING: This action will permanently erase all data in file ALC-1701-NX *in all main server and archive utilities. Continue? Y or N.*

Without hesitation, Alex again clicked on 'Yes'. The sole file was moved to the flash drive, leaving no trace of its existence on the main system.

Alex reached for the flash drive, his fingers still engulfed in ghostly greenish yellow flames. He touched the small device and was jolted as his world was suddenly plunged into a hellish maelstrom of howling screams and sheer, infinite blackness. The lab disappeared in an instant, replaced by a black void all-encompassing except for the glow around his still burning arm, casting a futile greenish light in the endless dark. His feet hung beneath him as if he were suspended, floating weightless in the void. A sound reached up from below, like a low undercurrent beneath the banshee screams that were all around him. It was faint at first and Alex couldn't decide from which direction it was coming. A low rumble, like the menacing growl of some huge feral beast, Alex felt as though he was being stalked by something dark, powerful and infinitely evil.

"Who... isss... thisssss....?"

The voice, if you could call it that, resembled a multitude of hurtful, distressed sounds crushed and forced into syllables and words. It drained Alex of every last ounce of courage and curiosity, replacing them with a soul piercing fear he thought was impossible to experience. He could feel the blood draining from his face, his heart rate doubled and beads of terror-induced sweat formed on his clammy skin. His body was floating in the darkness, powerless, defenseless, and the only light besides the glow from his burning arm was a faint red and orange glow from somewhere far below, like the smoldering heat from some vast volcanic landscape.

"You dare.... to hold... iiiit? You daaaaare... to keep that which will beeeee reveeeealed?"

The voice was louder, clearer, and the howling seemed to die down in its presence. It surrounded Alex, overpowering him with a paralyzing fear.

"There isssss... nowhere to hiiiiide. Heeee isssss coming with the wraaaaath of daaaark angelssss. You will kneeeeel and perissshhh. All will kneeeel and perissshhh..."

Shadows began to swirl and roil beneath his dangling feet. As he watched, he could make out the rolling, swirling mass of slick black tentacles, reaching up for him through the inky darkness. He began to thrash and struggle helplessly, like an astronaut stranded in space and running out of air. A grasping tentacle flicked out and wrapped itself whip-like around an ankle, pulling him down toward the writhing mass below. Alex cried out, unable to resist as another, larger tentacle, gripped his other leg, wrapping itself around up to his thigh.

As he was drawn inexorably downward to the giant, squirming thing below his feet, another light appeared, this time above him. A bright, distant light that appeared like a faraway star, growing steadily brighter, expanding down toward him. His burning hand reached upward, the flame flickering toward the light, just out of reach. The grip on his leg tightened savagely, cutting into his flesh and drawing blood. He screamed in pain and stretched desperately upwards, straining every muscle and sinew as he glimpsed a chance at freedom. The light fell around him, enveloping him and banishing the fear, exiled back into the shadows. The voice roared in rage as one of the tentacles released its grip and fell away. He sensed his body being drawn upwards and the voice roared again. The other tentacle disintegrated, freeing him at last, and he ascended faster, floating up and away from the terror below.

"You… will… die," the voice roared. *"You will… all diiiiie!"*

Without warning, the light suddenly snapped off and Alex found himself back in the lab, suspended five feet in the air above the polished tile floor. As the realization hit home, he fell, crashing unceremoniously to the floor. Sweating and breathless, he struggled to get up, trying to make sense of what had just happened. As his logical brain tried to form a reasonable explanation—exhaustion, dehydration, malnutrition—a realization began to take hold, and it quickly became as undeniable as it was overpowering. Looking down at his hands, he saw the blackened sleeve of his lab coat, the skin on his arm and hand untouched. His other hand was clenched into a tight fist, his knuckles white and his fingers stiff and aching.

He stared at it for a moment before slowly—painfully—opening his hand to reveal the small flash device. In that moment, sitting there with a charred sleeve and a head full of nightmares, he knew everything. He knew what had just happened, he knew what he had to do, and, most importantly of all, he knew what he held in his hand. A single code, similar to millions just like it, and yet strikingly unique. And in that moment Alex knew that he was holding the DNA code of the Antichrist.

Chapter Ten

Gabby Morgane sat at her desk in the Washington field office, Jerry leaning on his elbows on the desktop beside her. The computer screen was on and although a few other agents were still at work in the building, the office was quiet at this late hour.

She looked up over the open plan office. One of the last two agents in the room was turning his desk lamp off and leaving for the night. The other, a much younger man, was sitting hunched over his desk, poring over an open case file about a small time auto theft ring causing some havoc in Brookmont. He was occupied with the file and a cold cup of coffee he turned absentmindedly on the desk. Gabby held her eyes on him, concentrating, and then began to rub her thumb and forefinger together, making slow circles, the skin barely touching. Jerry looked up, glancing between Gabby and the agent.

After a few moments, the young agent yawned. He stifled it with a closed fist and then rubbed his temples before leaning back in his chair and stretching his arms above his head. Another yawn followed and he tossed his pen onto the desk and closed the file before getting up to leave, reaching back to snatch up the coffee cup. Gabby's gaze did not leave him until he had disappeared from view through the double doors that led to the lobby. Relaxing, she scanned the room. They were alone.

"I still do not believe that you had anything to do with that," Jerry said, flicking a rubber band at Gabby's ear with well-practiced accuracy. Gabby chuckled, swatting at the incoming missile long after it had struck its target.

"It's all in the mind, Jerry," she said. "It's all in the mind."

"I've seen you do that yahoo, voodoo Jedi mind trick a dozen times and I'll say the same thing I always say. You have a talent for reading people and spotting an opportunity, and an uncanny knack for doing that at just the right time." He stood up, grabbing his coffee mug. "You'd make one helluva profiler."

Gabby watched him walk over to the coffee maker by the door and pour himself a cup. He dumped a fistful of sugar into the steaming black liquid before returning to the desk. "A fat lot of good you're going to be in about five minutes when those jitters hit you," she said, reaching into her bag to retrieve a case file.

"Well, I'm overcompensating for being a bitter old man," Jerry retorted, slurping the coffee and finishing with an exaggerated 'aaaahh' sound of mock satisfaction.

"Well, you got one part right," Gabby said, opening the file. "You're definitely old."

Jerry shrugged and went back to slurping his coffee. "So what are we working on tonight, boss?"

Gabby spread out a few pages of the file and handed him the cover sheet. There was a photo at the top right.

"Alexander Bishop," he said, nodding. "Socially awkward mega scientist and best buddy of one of our very own bright stars of the Agency. It says here that he has an Agency Warrant rating of five, and that's because..." he read further down the page, "he happens to work for one of the government's top military funded secret laboratories and has an IQ rating of 'Einstein who?', placing him firmly in the realm of 'possible threat to national security on the part of him being a little socially rebellious and a God-damned super genius."

He lowered the paper to the desktop. "Ok, I'm not biting. So what if he's smart and doesn't play well with others? Have you seen how most of the jerks in this building interact with each other, let alone with the general public? Bunch of ego-driven assholes with brains and weapons training. And nice pants. We have nice pants, too."

Gabby didn't miss a beat. She picked out another page of the file and put it on the desk between them. Jerry cocked his head slightly to look at it. "Two agents on babysitting duty get exed out right in front of their subject's apartment." She pointed further down a list of bullet points. "A witness claims to see one of *our* agents leaving his apartment building right after he leaves for work, though Chief Sorano confirmed this evening that no such agent was either dispatched or reported to be present in the general area, let alone on orders to follow or question him."

She paused and Jerry glanced up at her. "Is that it?" he said. "Is it those two flimsy facts that have gotten your panties in such a bunch?"

She said nothing for a moment and he could tell that her mind was working hard to put things together that may just not fit at all.

"I don't know, Jerry," she said finally. "The agents. It starts there. I can't believe this is just a simple car jack style drug hit. I don't care what McCarthy says in his report about dirty cops and drug gang turf wars. Those two agents were killed where they sat, and they didn't see it coming. I've never seen a cleaner kill, let alone two right next to one another." She looked at Jerry. "And neither have you."

Jerry nodded, acknowledging that the thread started there.

"Have you read McCarthy's report?" he asked, putting the coffee aside and leaning in, speaking softly. "The Chief is sold on the drug hit thing. McCarthy made a pretty strong case and it's not hard to make a connection between a recently raided safe house two streets from the murder scene and some drug clan spotting a loaded Fed car and getting paranoid."

Gabby just could not shake the idea of a link between the two agents' deaths and what Alex was doing at the lab. Ever since the day Alex had told her they had come to head hunt him away from MIT, she had hid her concern behind a warm, supportive smile. She was happy for her friend, but secret government laboratories were literally the stuff of dark themed conspiracies. Throw in the military and it was hardly worth thinking about.

"So maybe the Chief took the report as gold. I don't know, Jerry, something just isn't sitting right with me on this one."

Jerry nudged the coffee cup away and jabbed a finger at Alex's photo. "Are you sure you're not just looking for something that isn't there, boss?" He pushed away from the desk, his chair rolling silently backwards. "Maybe Alex just works at a big, government owned, lab. Maybe they sent a couple of their guys to babysit before he goes dark on this mega project thing, and maybe they parked in the wrong spot at the wrong time, two streets away from the safe house of a known cartel. The guys they have working for them now aren't your average, gang-banger type enforcer. They're mercenaries, ex-military, cops, Marines, you name it. They employ pros these days and it shows in the quality of their work." He leaned back, hands clasped behind his head. "I think Alex was exactly where he was meant to be; at home. The rest just follows a fairly decent thread of logic."

Gabby nodded, but inside she was shaking her head. "Well, the case is open until I file my report," she said. "And for the most part I'm sure it'll line up nicely right next to McCarthy's."

"Uh oh," Jerry said, dropping his feet to the floor. "I hear an enormous, mucho overtime and drastic cut down in valuable social life 'but' coming."

"But there's nothing stopping us sniffing around a few of those loose ends before that report lands on the Chief's desk."

Jerry's expression was blank, but Gabby knew he was in. He worked at keeping up a façade of aloofness, but she knew him too well to be fooled by it. He was loyal, not just to the agency, but to her, too. He'd go where she went, and not just because she ordered him to.

"Besides," she went on, "I'm saving you from a tortuous night of getting your ass handed to you by the nerd pool of interns at Call of Duty. But you can call it a social life if you want."

Jerry stood, snatching up the keys to the Tahoe. "So, where to first, boss?"

Gabby smiled, scooping up the file pages and jamming the folder back into her bag. "Apex. Let's see what they have to say about two of their own being murdered in cold blood right outside the apartment of the man they were supposed to be protecting."

*   *   *

The approach road to Apex Labs always seemed freshly resurfaced, with crisply painted road markings and bright roadside lighting. So bright, in fact, that it was hard not to feel like they were under numerous spotlights and keen scrutiny as Gabby and Jerry pulled up to the first gate at the main entrance in their sleet-rinsed Tahoe. The large, spot lit sign to the side of the gate showed the Department of Defense seal alongside the more prominent Apex labs logo.

"Good evening," the uniformed soldier said, stepping out of the guard hut and approaching the driver's window. "The complex is currently closed to visitors. If you have pressing business, there is a number you can call to get in touch with one of the administrators. The line opens at 6:00 am."

Jerry turned to look at Gabby, who was already leaning over from the passenger seat, holding out her identification. "FBI, here on an official business. We're here to see Doctor Henry Drexler. We'll wait while you make a call."

The soldier was clearly taken aback, and paused for a moment before stepping away. "Wait here."

He disappeared back inside the guard hut, sliding the door closed behind him. It looked warm in there, and Jerry rolled up the window before cranking up the heat a little.

"Who do you think he's calling?" he asked, watching the soldier talking on the phone through the fogged glass.

"Hopefully someone who will tell him to let us through," she said. "I for one won't be sitting out here all night, waiting for six o'clock to roll around so we can chat with an administrator."

The soldier hung up the phone and walked out. "May I see your identification, please," he said. Gabby suddenly noticed the other guard in the side mirror, standing silently behind the truck, armed with an assault rifle. His finger was on the trigger guard.

"One moment, please," the soldier said, taking both of their ID cards and stepping back inside the guard hut. He spent another minute on the phone, after looking at a computer monitor, and then returned to Jerry's window. He handed over the IDs and nodded. "If you would just pull up on the right inside the first gate, someone will be out to escort you in."

He stepped back and saluted crisply before ducking back inside and pressing a button on his small control console. A droning sound accompanied the sliding open of the tall, steel gate, topped with spools of glistening razor wire. Jerry glanced at the guard who waved him through once the gate was fully open. He drove through the gate, pulling over in front of a second, identical gate, thirty yards in.

"Like fish in a barrel," he said, turning to look back at the brightly lit entrance as the first gate slid slowly closed behind them. Gabby remained silent, watching the road ahead through the steel gray bars in front. After a few minutes a pair of headlights appeared, driving up the road toward them. As it drew up to the gate, Gabby turned at the sudden appearance of a flashlight at her window. A second light shone through Jerry's side and suddenly the SUV was surrounded by half a dozen uniformed soldiers.

A sharp tapping on Jerry's window was followed by the door being opened and a soldier shining his flashlight into Jerry's face.

"Please step out of the vehicle, sir. Security check."

Jerry looked over at Gabby, who nodded before climbing out of her door. They stood together as the soldiers inspected the underside of the

Tahoe with wheeled mirrors before opening all the doors and climbing over the seats.

"Jesus Christ," Jerry hissed. "I just had it detailed."

"Excuse me!"

They both turned at the sound of a voice, calling to the the m from the other side of the inner gate.

"Agent Morgane? Over here please."

Gabby glanced at Jerry and walked over to the gate. Two more armed soldiers stood close by. On the other side, an older man in a parka stood by the front of a town car. He peered at them through the bars of the gate as they approached.

"My name is Bennett," the man said. "Professor Drexler is our project lead. He is off site but asked me to take you in. He will be in within the hour."

The gate started to slide open and the man stepped back slightly. He kept his hands in his pockets. "Your vehicle will have to remain here, I'm afraid," he said, turning back toward the car. "I'll give you a ride to the main building, where you can wait for professor Drexler. If you'll come this way."

The ride to the main building took barely three minutes, yet the scale of the lab complex was hard to take in. It stretched from the eastern boundary fence almost a mile down to the bank of the Potomac, the main, central building surrounded by a myriad of smaller structures, all on their own signposted streets, so that it resembled a small town or military base. There were several checkpoints along the route to the main building, an impressive concrete and glass structure with a cylindrical atrium in the center that rose above the uppermost floor. The car moved away from the final security gate and onto the driveway up to the main doors. Bennett pulled up beside a pair of soldiers, talking casually by the curb. Gabby glanced at Jerry. Neither guard was wearing a jacket. They were both standing at the roadside, weapons slung over their shoulders, wearing nothing more on their torsos than a tightly-fitted olive drab t-shirt.

"That's right," Bennett said quietly, apparently to himself, snapping off his seat belt and opening the driver's door to get out.

The nearest soldier opened the back door. The wind whipped into the car and Gabby felt the ice-cold breeze sting her face.

"Sir, ma'am," the soldier said. "If you'd follow me, I'll show you inside."

Gabby and Jerry followed the soldier through the main entrance doors and into the Hub lobby. Bennett followed and presented his ID to the desk guard before turning away toward a frosted glass door in the back wall.

"This way," he said, swiping a key card and pushing through the door.

"Maybe they're Alaskan born," Jerry whispered, eyeing the soldiers outside as they turned to follow Bennett through the door. "This is probably like spring to them."

They walked along a short corridor and into what looked like a small conference room, with a central table, chairs and a TV monitor on the wall.

"There's coffee over there, fairly fresh I think," Bennett said, standing at the head of the table. "And some light snacks in the refrigerator under the counter. If you'd like anything else, just let me know.

"How were those two soldiers not freezing their butts off?" Jerry asked, taking a seat at the far end of the table. "It's minus ten out there."

Bennett smiled, glancing at the door as it slowly swung shut. "We are not simply an advanced genetics laboratory, Agent Walker," he said. Gabby made a mental note of Bennett's well hidden nervousness, and obvious careful choice of words.

"The two soldiers you saw outside are testing a new lightweight thermal garment for use as a base layer in extreme temperatures. It is the lightest, thinnest thermal material in the world and will keep them functioning in this climate for up to forty minutes. We are working to improve that, obviously."

"So you work with military equipment, too?" Gabby asked, taking her seat beside Jerry. "Research and development?"

"Some, yes. As part of our Advanced Research for Combat program, we pride ourselves in developing some of the leading technologies that will help keep our soldiers alive on the battlefield, our police safer on the streets and our government agents, such as yourselves, safer and more prepared, wherever the job takes you."

He didn't make a move to leave, and Gabby realized that he was the ice breaker, there to answer the light, non-threatening questions and generally to make them feel welcome and accommodated. An open arms policy of deflective answers intended to ease suspicion and lay a foundation of trust.

"We are attached to several branches of the United States Department of Defense and not only develop ways to keep our soldiers safe on the genetics game board, but also to find ways to enhance his chances of survival of critical injury through new applications of battlefield medicines and trauma kits. We already have several high level testing kits out in the field with a number of Air Force para rescue units in the middle east."

Gabby nodded. "Do you know professor Drexler well?"

"Of course," Bennett replied smartly, "He is our leading genetics scientist and one of the most respected teaching professors at Apex."

"And Alex Bishop? I've heard good things about him too."

Bennett's stiff smile wavered for a moment. "I... I'm not that familiar with our entire staff. Dr. Bishop may be one of the names I am simply unfamiliar with, I'm afraid. I couldn't say that I know anything about him, but perhaps professor Drexler can help you there."

A tone sounded on the wall-mounted phone by the door.

"Excuse me for one moment," Bennett said, stepping over and lifting the handset. He spoke in a hushed voice for a moment before replacing the handset. "Professor Drexler just arrived and will be here momentarily."

Gabby and Jerry both smiled and Bennett nodded before stepping out of the room, leaving them in silence.

"So what do you think of our little welcoming committee?" Jerry said after a moment.

Gabby was staring at the door, lost in thought, and Jerry nudged her chair with his foot. "What?" She said, looking over as Jerry shook his head.

"Our friend, Bennett," he said. "What do you think?"

Gabby turned back to the door, glancing at the clock on the wall. It read 2:49 am. "This Drexler guy better have a few really good answers for us at this time of night," she said, ignoring Jerry's question.

"Well he got out of bed to come in, so..."

"And I don't know how I feel about Mr. Bennett," she said then, "But I do know that those two guys outside are not acting like they're on the beach in Miami because of some super t-shirt. There was no blood vessel dilation, no 'rosy cheeks', their hands were normal color and there was not the slightest indication of tremors. It was literally as if they were operating in room temperature and not in sub zero temperatures. No way is that down to a fancy new base layer."

She swept her gaze around the room. As she looked at the oversized television screen, she squinted slightly. In the uppermost edge, above the screen, there was a tiny opening, about a quarter of a inch in diameter. A camera. Gabby had no doubt that it was probably used for conference calls and the like, but, at that moment, she was equally convinced that it was switched on and recording everything in the room. "And don't think for a second that Mr. Bennett didn't hear the Alaskan-born comment you made in the lobby." She turned to look at Jerry over her shoulder. "Mid-sixties, hearing aid in both ears, but he doesn't need them. When we pulled up to the doors, he said, 'That's right' because the two soldiers were talking and one confirmed that we're to be watched at all times, and if we slip our leash we are to be shot on sight."

Jerry's face dropped.

"I heard them when I cracked the window as we pulled up," she said before turning back to look at the door just as it opened and Drexler walked in.

"Good morning, Agent Morgane, Agent Walker," he said, stepping forward confidently and offering his hand. "Henry Drexler. I trust that Dr. Bennett accommodated you while you waited."

As Gabby shook his hand, Drexler smiled warmly. She had a good feeling about the man, and yet she knew, in that instant, that all was not right at Apex Laboratories.

"My apologies for all the security nonsense," Drexler went on, taking a seat in the chair at the head of the table. "Your vehicle will be brought down for you once it's passed security."

Gabby fished a small field notebook from her jacket pocket and placed it on the table. "Your security is nothing but impressive," she said, nudging the notebook straight. "I'm surprised, given its intensity, that we weren't asked to check our weapons."

Drexler smiled, leaning forward on the table and lacing his fingers. "It's not our policy to relieve government agents of their firearms when on official business. We could hardly justify that when we have sixty-eight fully armed military security personnel on complex."

"And besides those, what other security personnel do you have on staff at Apex Laboratories?" She reached for the notebook and flipped it open, readying her pen.

Drexler looked at both of them and then glanced down at the notebook. Gabby watched him carefully. "This isn't a social visit, then," he said. "Shame, I was about to order Gino's."

Jerry chuckled while Gabby made a mental note of Drexler's stiff grin and forced humor. He appeared cordial and relaxed, but Gabby could sense his discomfort as he squirmed invisibly in the chair. He was stalling, obviously dying to get out of there. He cast a subtle glance at his watch.

"Are we keeping you, Doctor?" Gabby asked. "I understand you were on your way in when we arrived. I hope we didn't interrupt something important that we're keeping you from."

Drexler laughed. "Well, it's a very busy place and, yes, I have something important to get to, but you have me in a spare moment. I'll excuse myself shortly, but please, what can I do for you?"

"Your security personnel," Gabby said. "What government and civilian assets do you maintain at Apex Labs, besides the uniformed military presence we've already seen?"

Drexler was nodding. He looked down, squinting at the table's polished mahogany surface. "Let's see. I don't have exact figures for you off the top of my head, but I'd hazard a guess at around twenty-five or so."

Gabby scratched a note in her notebook. Jerry cleared his throat.

"As you know," Gabby went on, "you recently dispatched two agents as security cover for one of your geneticists, a Dr. Alex Bishop. In the early hours of the following morning their bodies were discovered in their car by a local couple. Both had been killed where they sat. The couple that had most likely discovered the bodies were found half a block away, also murdered. Their bodies were stuffed into a dumpster. When were you first made aware that two of your agents had been killed while on protective detail, watching one of your leading scientists?"

Drexler stared. It was either a very convincing act, or he was genuinely shocked and was hearing the news for the first time. Gabby was having a hard time deciding which. He shifted in his seat.

"About twenty seconds ago," he said quietly.

A long silence followed in which Drexler stared at the table top. Gabby sat watching him, waiting for him to speak again, not willing to make any potential false front easier to maintain.

"I wasn't made aware that anyone had been hurt."

Gabby sat, observing the older man. After a few seconds, Jerry cleared his throat again. Before he could say something awkward, Gabby straightened. "We will need to speak to whoever is responsible for your internal security.

You're strongly affiliated with the Department of Defense, so would it be safe to assume that you have a military or government liaison who oversees your protection details?"

Drexler had a distant look in his eyes and Jerry was about to prompt him when he spoke suddenly, as if nudged out of a daydream. "In my time here, Agent Morgane, I have known of only two occasions where a security detail was attached to one of our employees, and one of those was for myself when I took a briefing to the Pentagon, three years ago."

Gabby scrawled something in her notebook, then looked up. "Then any records should be easy to find."

Chapter Eleven

Alex gripped the flash drive in a fist clenched so tight, that he began to draw blood as his fingernails dug into the flesh of his palm. His legs gave way and he slid down the wall, ending up sitting on the cool tiled floor. Staring at his now dark and lifeless monitor, he finally let out a breath, which lead to a wheeze, and then a chest-rattling cough. He fell to one side, clutching the drive in one hand and covering his mouth with a sleeve.

Just as he thought his lungs were about to make an appearance on the floor, the coughing fit eased and he began to pant for breath, leaning back against the wall. As he dropped his arm away, he noticed a dark stain on the white sleeve where he had covered his mouth. Looking closer, he frowned, confused. At first glance, it really looked like, well, oil, as if he'd used his sleeve to mop up a spill. It was black, spotted and slick. As he leaned in and took a breath, it smelled acrid, burnt and... dead.

"What the hell?"

It took some effort, but he pushed himself up and climbed gingerly to his feet, using one hand to steady himself against the wall. Shrugging off the lab coat, he draped it over the back of a chair, being careful not to touch the oily black stain. He stood still for a moment, then slowly relaxed his fingers, loosening his grip on the small device, hissing at the pain in his stiff joints. The thing looked small and insignificant in the palm of his hand, spotted with his blood and clammy with sweat.

"What in God's name am I supposed to do with you?" he said, holding the device up between his thumb and forefinger. He let out a sigh, feeling exhausted suddenly, and looked forlornly over at the metal-framed bed. The last thing he needed was another week of lab work and crappy cot sleep.

"Alex? What's going on? Are you ok?"

Alex quickly slipped the flash drive into his shirt pocket and turned toward the door. Audrey was standing there, holding the glass door open, a look of abject shock and concern on her face. He shook his head. "Audrey? What... what are you doing here?"

She pushed inside, walking over to him and taking him by the shoulders. Her hair was different; darker, fuller, like she was going out on a date. She looked striking.

"What the hell happened to you?" she asked, guiding him to his feet and helping him to sit in a chair. "I messaged you but you went offline. I thought you might have gone to get some sleep but then I saw you on the floor when I came down to the Hub to get coffee."

She crouched down in front of him and put his hands on top of his thighs, placing hers gently over them before looking around the lab. "What happened, Alex? It looks like a tornado ripped through here. Are you ok?"

Alex nodded. He didn't feel comfortable with Audrey holding his hands. He withdrew them, smiling weakly before folding his arms in front of his chest. He could feel the flash drive pressed against his chest in his pocket.

"It... it's nothing," he said, finally. Audrey looked at him intensely, waiting for him to go on. "I was working on some sec files and it was, you know, error after error." He rubbed his temples in mock weariness. "My frustration just got the better of me, that's all." He nodded toward the monitor, shifted at an awkward angle on the bench. "I'll have to explain this to Drexler, have IT come down to make sure I haven't broken anything too badly."

Audrey was scanning the lab, nodding absentmindedly, her hands still resting on his thighs. "Uh huh, well... I just saw you in here on the floor, you know. You looked like you weren't doing so good."

Alex watched as Audrey's eyes moved around the lab. There was something very methodical about the way she was looking around, as if she was searching for something. Alex could feel his chest tightening again. Another coughing fit was building. He cleared his throat and looked over to the chair with his lab coat draped over the back. He could see some spattering of the black substance on the floor beside it where he had been laying, coughing into his sleeve. The moment he saw the droplets of oil, the thought struck him like a sledgehammer. Turning his head, he looked across the lab toward the glass door and wall.

Beyond, slightly to the right of the doorway, he could see the Hub atrium, above the work bench and computer monitors. He turned back, drawing a mental line between the lab coat chair and the atrium elevator. The view was completely blocked, hidden from sight by the desk and computers.

"Did you manage to save everything?" Audrey asked suddenly, turning back to look up at him. "

Alex paused, his heart beginning to race. He could feel the beats growing stronger behind his forearms, crossed tightly against his chest.

"Everything I needed," he said after a moment. "Nothing lost that I can't rework, I'm sure." He forced a smile, convinced it just added to his nervous appearance. "Gotta give those IT guys something to do, right?"

Audrey looked at him, regarding him with her bright, searching eyes. She nodded, smiling back, and then stood suddenly, walking over to the small sink at the far end of the desk. She returned with a damp cloth, searching the floor as she walked, and leaned forward, dabbing gently at his face.

"Well that's true," she said, brushing the cool cloth against his cheek. "I think you should try to get some sleep. I can take care of your files for you. You look like you could really use the rest."

Alex glanced over her shoulder toward the atrium. The pair of soldiers that were usually stationed at the guard podium were nowhere to be seen.

"Uh, it's ok, really. There was nothing much to save besides some updates to what I was working on yesterday. It was a slow day today. Didn't get much done. Hey, how come you're here this late? Drexler got you working on something super secret?"

Audrey lifted his chin with her fingers, wiping his mouth like a mother wiping food from her child's lips. "Better to be safe than sorry," she said, ignoring the joke. "You don't want to leave this stuff laying around."

She straightened slightly, inspecting her work. "Did you put it on a drive? I hope you didn't rely on the servers, especially if you've had some kind of crash. Better to have everything on an external."

She looked around the lab again and, as she straightened, Alex noticed the bulge beneath her lab coat at her hip. His heart quickened further. Audrey was carrying a gun. She looked down at him and they gazed at one another for a moment.

"I know," she said, wrapping the washcloth around her hand and toying with the loose end. "I couldn't see you from the atrium."

Alex sat, frozen to his chair, unable to speak. He needed to move. He needed to get out and find help. Audrey was after what he had in his pocket, he was convinced of it, and, in that moment, he knew she would kill him for it if she had to.

"Why do you want my work?" Alex asked, shifting in his seat and hoping Audrey wouldn't notice the small device in his shirt pocket. "You're not even working on the project, and even if you were, we would be working on it together, so what are you doing?" He pushed the naive angle, trying to make her believe he had no idea what she really wanted. "Why are you even here at this hour? I thought Drexler had moved everyone off site to Carillon Field?"

Audrey smiled a little. "Where's the data, Alex?" Play time was over.

"I didn't save anything. I told you." He glanced quickly at the desk and the small stack of memory drives next to the keyboard. "Nothing was worth archiving today."

Audrey turned, following his gaze, and Alex seized the moment to jump out of the chair, intending to push her aside and make a run for the door. The chair slid backwards noisily and Audrey's head snapped back as Alex was throwing his arms out toward her. She parried them easily, swinging the washcloth-wrapped fist into Alex's face, knocking him sideways. He managed two more staggering, stiff-legged steps before his momentum took him crashing into the two file cabinets next to the door. She was upon him instantly, looking up to check the atrium before dragging Alex's dazed form back toward the desk. One of the guards had reappeared at the podium but didn't react to the commotion in the lab, thanks to the Hyperplex walls and door.

"Where is it?" Audrey said, kneeling on Alex's chest, one hand on his throat, leaning on his windpipe. "I saw you save it, Alex. Just give it to me and I'm out. Don't make me ask you again."

She leaned harder and Alex gagged, pushing against her arm and the knee on his chest. He could feel the memory device in his pocket, just beside her knee. It was only a matter of seconds before she decided to search him, and then he would lose the code, and most definitely his life. He had to get out of the lab and alert the soldiers in the atrium. There was an alarm button on the back wall, above the cot, but it may as well have been on another floor. He felt as though he was being crushed and was certain his ribcage would give way any second.

Choking and gasping for breath, he looked over toward his desk, pointing with a bloodied finger, cut in the fall a moment earlier.

"The desk?" Audrey said, looking over, before returning her gaze down at Alex. "It's on one of the drives on the desk?"

Alex nodded as much as he could and felt the pressure on his throat lessen slightly. Audrey shifted her weight, reaching inside her lab coat and drawing out a sub compact handgun. She rested the muzzle on his chest and pushed herself up, stepping away. "Get up."

Alex didn't move at first. He was scrambling in his mind for anything he could use to distract or appease Audrey and get out of the room. Even if he got to the door, he'd need a few seconds for the air seal to release and to get the door open long enough to shout for help.

"Alex," Audrey said, calmly. "You are not paralyzed with fear and you did not just lose the ability to comprehend the English language. Do not play dumb fuck with me. Do as I say and give me what I need and you get out of this alive. Now get the fuck up."

Alex rolled to his side, feigning a wince and clutching his chest to check the flash drive. Climbing slowly to his feet, he stepped forward when she motioned at him with the gun, standing just inside the extended part of the lab, out of view from the atrium. In the few steps he took towards her, he noticed everything around him, searching for any small item that might be of use in getting him out of the lab. Cables snaked all over the floor around the desk, pulled from conduits and cable ties. He stepped over them carefully and stood before her, the gun leveled at his chest.

"Ok, now show me which drive. I could take them all, but I don't want to have to check them all and find out it isn't here."

"The computers are down," he said, gesturing to the nearest lifeless monitor. "I need to plug it in to show you the data. I don't know which drive it's on."

She looked at him. After a moment, she nodded. "Fine, get your laptop. It's in your bag under the cot. I saw you put it there when you came in."

She had been watching him the whole time. That's how she knew he had saved the data on one of the flash drives and when to come down after all hell broke loose, or whatever had happened earlier. But she hadn't seen him put the drive in his pocket. She had already been on her way down to him by then. He knew that he couldn't let the code fall into Audrey's hands. He just knew it. It was his to protect. His responsibility. His to expose.

"Move it," she hissed, nodding with her head toward the back of the room.

Alex walked slowly toward the cot. He could see his messenger bag on the floor beneath the small bed, half covered by the grey blanket that hung over the side of the thin mattress. He dragged it out and set it on the bed, sitting down beside it.

"Bring it out here," Audrey said, staying close to the desk, and the flash drives.

"It's almost dead," Alex said, reaching into the bag and sliding out the small laptop. "I don't think the outlets over there are working. All the computers and the printer are dead, but the coffee maker in here is on, so I'll plug it in right there."

He opened the laptop and spun it around to show her the black screen while he tapped random keys in an effort to show that it wasn't booting up.

"Get it going, Alex," Audrey said, still pointing the gun at him. "Get the cable and plug it in."

"Can you bring the drives over?" Alex said, looking down at the laptop screen. He was stalling and it was obvious that she wouldn't fall for it. She grabbed the half dozen flash drives and walked over toward the cot. Tossing them onto the bed, she stepped back again, glancing out through the lab at the empty corridor and dark, deserted labs beyond. The screen flashed white and the hard drive started spinning up.

"Ok, it looks like there's some juice left in it," Alex said. "A couple of percent. Should be enough to..."

"Just plug the God damned thing in!" she blurted, taking a step closer. The gun waved ominously in front of her. "Quit fucking around! Don't think I won't put one in your leg to light that fire under your ass. Now do it!"

Alex put both hands up. "Ok, ok. I'll just get the cable out of my bag. I'll do it. I'm doing it."

He slid one hand slowly toward the messenger bag, it's flap laying open on the bed. He could see the grey cable, neatly coiled inside. As his fingers brushed the lip of the bag, Audrey stepped forward, raising the gun.

"Wait!" she yelled, the muzzle barely a foot from Alex's temple. "I'll get it. Sit right there and don't move. Not a fucking muscle."

Alex froze, then raised his hands again, straightening. "Ok, you got it. It's ok. It's right there, just inside the bag. See it?"

Audrey reached for the bag with her left hand, the gun in the other, still pointing at Alex's face. She pulled the coil of cable from the bag and examined it before handing it to him. "Plug the small one in."

Alex grabbed the small power connector at the end of the cable and slotted it into the laptop's power socket. Audrey held the wall plug in her hand and stepped to the side, toward the small counter that held the coffee maker and microwave. Both outlets in the wall were occupied. As she stepped closer, the cable unspooling as she went, she glanced at the wall, then back at Alex, still sitting, hands raised, on the cot.

"Just pull either one out," he said. "I can go without coffee or a burrito until tomorrow."

Audrey snorted and stepped up to the counter. She took another look at Alex and pulled one of the plugs from the outlet, then tried to plug the laptop plug in. Alex watched the plug dance around the outlet as she watched him, not willing to take her eyes from him for one second. She fumbled, trying to find the holes with her fingers before missing with the plug again. She began to grow frustrated. Alex watched as she almost got it, then dropped the plug to the counter top. She turned her head to grab it and in that instant, Alex shot his hand into the messenger bag.

Two seconds later, Audrey had the plug in her hand and turned back to Alex. He raised the taser pistol and squeezed the trigger. It was far easier than he had imagined. The trigger depressed with a satisfying *clack* and a high-velocity dart fired, trailing it's super conductive wire, striking Audrey in the cheek. She stood bolt upright, a distorted grimace on her face, and then fell, dropping the gun to the floor and collapsing in a spasming heap at the end of the bed, head jerking slightly as a flood of electricity coursed through her body.

Alex stood, dropping the laptop to the tiles, and ran for the door. He almost crashed into the wall and frantically hit the small activation panel to open it. Nothing happened. He hit it again, waiting for the familiar click of the magnetic lock as it released. Again, nothing. She had locked the door. He frantically looked for his key card, patting pockets and spinning in circles, simultaneously scanning the floor in case he'd dropped it.

"Where the fuck...!"

Then he remembered. His lab coat. The key card was clipped to the breast pocket. He scrambled over an upturned chair, tripped on the trash can and almost collapsed onto the chair that held the lab coat. Looking up, he could see Audrey leaning up on one elbow, shaking her head. He wished he'd kept hold of the taser.

Yanking the coat from the chair, he fumbled with it, turning it over in his hands until he finally grabbed the card, tearing it from it's clip. As he ran for the door he heard Audrey mumble something and glanced over his shoulder. She was climbing unsteadily to her feet. He could see the gun on the floor, just under the bed. She would have it in seconds. Slamming into the door, he pressed the card key against the panel and almost cried out when the lock clicked back and the seal hissed, releasing the door. He pulled it open and lurched into the hallway. Behind him, Audrey wasn't going for the gun. She slid her hand along the wall and pressed her palm against the alarm button.

"Hey!" Alex yelled, almost hitting the opposite wall. "Heyyyyy!" He looked toward the guard's podium, waving his hands frantically, as if signaling a passing plane from a life raft. The podium was empty.

WAAAAH! WAAAAH WAAAAH! WAAAAH!

The alarm sounded with a deafening wail, accompanied by spinning red emergency lights, high on the walls. He'd never noticed them there before. Turning back to the lab, he saw Audrey pick up the gun. She turned to face him, raised the weapon, and fired. The round struck the door at chest level. He barely heard the gun shot, but the round hit the glass with such a loud *crack!* that it made his ears ring. He almost dropped to the floor, hands instinctively covering his face. The door had stopped the round. She fired again and this time Alex ran, down the hallway, away from the atrium.

He knew the corridor led deeper into the lab complex, but he hadn't exactly explored the place, so he ran on a hunch, and then another, turning left and right, pushing through doors and running by empty office after empty office until he came to a door that offered the tiniest glimmer of hope.

EMERGENCY EXIT

He pushed the bar and slammed into the wall into what looked like a service corridor. He was standing at the top of a short flight of steps, leading down to a long, narrow passageway, lit by emergency lights and cocooned with masses of pipes and cabling on the ceiling and walls. The door was swinging slowly shut and he turned to look back along the hallway he'd come from. Audrey came running around the corner, gun raised. He went to move when he heard the gunshot. At first he thought the door had swung back open and hit him in the shoulder, like a hammer fist, knocking him back into the wall. When the second shot rang out and the round struck the wall just inches from his face, he knew he'd been hit. He turned, kicking the door shut, and reached out to grab a steel folding chair that was leaning against the wall. White hot pain in his arm and chest made him cry out, clutching his arm with his free hand.

Audrey was closing in, sprinting toward the door, gun raised. He grabbed the chair clumsily with his other hand, half lifting, half dragging it away from the wall. Propping it against the door, he jammed it under the handle just as Audrey crashed into it on the other side. Stepping back, he reached up and grabbed his injured arm again, cradling it against his heaving chest. The pain was subsiding, but he knew it would start to hurt like hell in just a minute, especially if he tried to use it again. Another shot rang out and a hole appeared in the door, followed by another. Alex turned and took the stairs two at a time, running down the corridor, toward the unknown.

Chapter Twelve

It took twenty seconds to apply the compressed foam explosive around the edge of the door, prime and detonate it, blowing the Dawn Gate out of the wall in a cloud of dust, splintered wood and chunks of sandstone. Checking corners and shadows, a trio of Western tourist-looking men expertly slipped inside, leading with their compact assault rifles as the team lead, Kessler, pale and muscle-bound, brought up the rear, checking the area before ducking inside the ragged entryway, his shirt sweat-plastered to his hulking body. Dust hung like a mist in the early evening air as curious onlookers began to gather at each end of the causeway.

Moving swiftly through the narrow passages, the team made their way deeper into the belly of the fortress. Kessler checked a handheld GPS unit, guiding the men forward in the semi-darkness. They met no resistance in the first three minutes; something they had hoped for in order to make a rapid penetration toward the inner chambers. As they moved toward the end of one of the wider hallways, Kessler stopped as the point man disappeared suddenly, yanked around the corner by unseen hands.

The three remaining men moved in unison, taking up a defensive posture, aiming at the corner, eyes unblinking, sweat rolling down their temples. After a few moments, something was thrown out into the passage. It landed with a wet *thud* on the flagstones and rolled a few times, coming to rest a few feet away from Kessler, his kneeling form coiled and ready to spring into action. He didn't take his eyes away from the corner for a few seconds, and then glanced down at the severed head of Sebastian, his point man. His eyes were squeezed tightly shut and his head rested perfectly straight on the floor, giving the impression he was buried up to his neck in sandstone.

Kessler made a small hissing sound and made some sharp hand gestures before gripping the barrel of his rifle and staring down the sights at the end of the passage once more. The two other men began to move as one, slipping silently away from the walls and inching forward as one pulled a flash grenade from his belt and pulled the pin while his partner covered him from a wider angle. He tossed it at the far wall and watched it ricochet around the corner. All three men covered their ears and closed their eyes. Still, the concussion from the explosion was fierce. Kessler felt the pressure on his face and chest as the grenade went off, the bright white pressing against his eyelids. Immediately, the three men were back on their weapons, targeting the end of the passageway. They moved forward, rounding the corner in a crouch, prepared to fire. The thin veil of smoke had almost cleared and they saw the body of their colleague, lying sprawled against the wall, a crimson stump atop his shoulders and a small pool of blood on the floor.

"Twos on corners," Kessler said. "I have six. Lothar is in position covering their exit route. Let's move."

*　*　*

From a vantage point behind a small dune ridge about ninety yards from the fortress wall, Lothar Venk could see the Land Rover on the stone ramp and the trio of Mamluks guarding it. One was under the hood, tugging on hoses and checking fluid levels. The bam! as he slammed the hood down came to Lothar's ears a moment later. He was thankful for the hour. It would've been a nightmare to be given the go at noon, when the sun was at its highest. Still, the air was hot and oppressive and he ducked down behind the ridge to wipe the sweat from his brow with his shirtsleeve.

"Kessler is breaching," One of the other three men said, pressing on a fitted earpiece with a fingertip. "Ten seconds."

Lothar nodded and the four men sat silently, waiting. A moment later, a deep *Boom* echoed in the air from the far side of the fortress. Lothar checked his watch. "Six minutes," he said, and the men began checking their weapons, pulling magazines to check rounds and tapping them on their kneepads before reinserting them into their rifles, looking down the sights and making small adjustments as they waited to be given the go to move. A second explosion sounded, this time more muffled, and the men continued to calmly ready themselves, working through a routine that had taken many missions to embed. The screech of a vulture above them made Lothar look up. There were a dozen of the birds, circling lazily a hundred feet above their heads.

"You won't be feasting on us today," Lothar said, flipping the safety off on his HK. He put the binoculars to his eyes and inched up to the ridge, peering through strands of tall grass at the group by the Land Rover. "Alpha, slide left fifty yards. I want a better angle on the rear of that truck."

One of the men moved away, making his way along the base of the dune in a crouching run before hitting the sand and crawling up the ridge to set up his rifle through the grass.

"Bravo; red sash, standing by the truck hood. That's your primary."

The man nestling between two bushes a hundred yards beyond the other side of the ramp settled on his stomach and removed the covers on his telescopic sights before nudging his way forward slightly and settling his aim. Anyone further than twenty feet away would've seen just another patch of desert instead of the well-camouflaged sniper amidst the rocks, half-covered in hot sand and beige netting. Of the four men on the team, Nikolai was the designated long-range target man. He wasn't the best in the world, but when the best in the world was currently measured in grouping rounds within a target the size of an apple at over a mile and a half away, there were only two or three men alive who could compete.

Nikolai drew his experience from the urban battlegrounds of Kosovo and Chechnya and was a great white among goldfish in the one hundred to five hundred yard range. He adjusted the grip on his Dragunov, relaxed, and waited. The Mamluk didn't know it yet, but in a matter of seconds he would be the first to drop, in what they planned to be a short and straightforward engagement.

"Delta, hold on target until it's moving. I want to make sure there's someone in it if we need to hit it."

The last man in the group signaled quietly from a few feet away, his gloved hand resting on the anti armor rocket launcher at his side. Lothar had all of the angles covered and all of the pieces were in play. Now they just waited for their target to appear. He swung the binoculars over to the Land Rover once more and almost immediately saw the bobbing heads of two men appear from behind the stone ramp. An older man stepped up first, followed by one much younger, whom glanced nervously all around and wrung his hands in front of him as he walked.

"*There you are*," Lothar whispered. "Stand by for target one go."

Target one go was their signal for all men to open fire the moment the first target was dropped; in this case, the red-sashed Mamluk standing by the Land Rover's driver's door that currently occupied Nikolai's sniper scope.

"Bravo, target change," Lothar said suddenly, eyes glued to the binoculars. "Rear of the truck, old male, brown robe. Confirm"

Nikolai adjusted aim quickly and settled again. "Confirmed. Ready to shoot."

Lothar pressed his throat mic.

"*Los.*"

He didn't hear the *click* of the silenced weapon as Nikolai squeezed the trigger a half second later. He saw the old man stumble forward into the boy, a fountain of bloody matter spraying over the youngster's face and tunic. As Nikolai was readjusting, the Mamluks reacted with surprising speed and coordination, immediately using the Land Rover for cover and turning to the desert to face the unseen threat. It didn't matter. He held the advantage.

The truck door opened and the driver jumped out as the man by the door was hit by Nikolai's second round. Lothar saw him disappear behind the truck as he fell. The man in the truck was fast. He took the boy down and they disappeared from view behind the ramp. The Mamluks were beginning to zone in on their general positions and his men reacted accordingly, backing down the ridge to move to a different position as they began to take fire.

Nikolai had the side of the ramp in his sight. Swathed in shadow, it offered his targets minimal cover behind a shallow ridge. He had forced them to the ground with a near miss that had struck the ramp wall close to the big man's head and now neither he nor the boy could be seen. He held the scope on the ridge, knowing that they would have to move soon as his teammates moved in.

Karesh's radio crackled as his support radioed in. He spoke quickly, keeping his eyes firmly fixed on the ridge in front of them. Then he looked up. Directly ahead, about sixty yards away, a trio of vultures circled in the sky. They were soon joined by a fourth and Karesh keyed the radio, barking an instruction. It was acknowledged and he dropped it into the sand, reaching inside his robe to pull out a Sig Sauer pistol. Aaron was frozen with fear, face pressed into the sand. Karesh patted him on the back gently. "Remain still," he said, his deep voice a resonating calm amidst the noise above them. "Keep your head down."

The radio buzzed once and a voice confirmed his order. He smiled, looking up at the birds and nodding. "We do not need eyes on the ground when we have them in the sky," he whispered, and then heard a dull *thunk, thunk, thunk* from behind him, high up on the fortress wall.

Lothar watched through the binoculars as another Mamluk fell, dropped by a shot from the well-concealed Bravo. He hadn't needed to fire a single shot and it looked more and more like his rifle magazine would remain full with only two more Mamluks to take out. The last remaining man on the ramp was tucked in tight behind the front of the Land Rover, out of his and Nikolai's field of fire. He would take some coaxing to bring down. The other—the one who had taken down the boy—would be a different story, and Lothar felt a twinge of urgency to get to their position.

"Delta, switch positions with me. I want cover for the truck. Move."

The man with the rocket launcher moved closer, hefting the heavy weapon in an awkward crouching scramble, his assault rifle strapped to his back. If someone got into the Land Rover, he would have a high explosive round put through the door as it backed down the ramp, if Nikolai didn't take out the driver first. The boy was the priority, though his handler had been clear that a catch-alive policy was not necessarily definitive. He just could not make it out of here to Damascus, one way or the other. A series of rapid *thud*s and *zip*s, made Lothar duck behind the ridge as the Mamluk on the ramp found his position and opened fire. It didn't matter. Delta would be covering him with the heavy machine gun in moments and then they would be free to advance on the ramp. Lothar drew back down the ridge and made his way slowly away from the fortress wall, out and away so he could cover the lower part of the ramp and assist Delta in covering the truck.

Nikolai could see fleeting glimpses of the Mamluk at the front of the truck, a shoulder here, a bobbing head there. He kept the scope on the area beside the ramp where he had seen the man and boy fall, and knew that it was only a matter of time before they either made a run for it or were forced from their position. He waited. Then he heard something unfamiliar. Three thumps, in rapid succession, two to his left, a few yards away, and another directly to his right. It was no animal, and no one had approached his position on foot. He risked a slight turn of his head and looked across the sand across his right shoulder. An M20 high fragmentation grenade sat perfectly nestled in front of a rock, three feet away.

"Oh, shi…"

The explosion disintegrated the rock and vaporized Nikolai, shortly followed by two more explosions that leveled an area thirty yards in diameter. The vultures would be disappointed.

Lothar dived to the ground, saw the plume of dirt and sand, and felt the concussion wave wash over his position a moment later. Glancing up at the fortress wall above the ramp, he caught a brief glimpse of a lone figure, silhouetted against the stark blue sky. "They have a grenade launcher," he said into his throat mic. "Watch the battlement. Alpha, move around to Bravo's position. We need cover on the far side of the ramp. Move, move."

He turned toward Delta's position and signaled his man there with his hand. The soldier nodded and began to arm the launcher before laying the machine gun on the top of the ridge. In the space of a few seconds three well-placed grenades had silenced their entire arsenal. Delta flattened himself against the top of the dune and took aim with his weapon, a powerful, large caliber HK assault weapon with a scope and forward bipod. He found the front of the truck and immediately began firing in a steady, three-shot rhythm, striking the front fender of the truck and stone around the front tire. He purposely avoided disabling the vehicle. There was still a chance they would make a run for it, and when they did, he would end things with the Scarab launcher. The Mamluk crouching at the front of the Land Rover stayed well hidden, keeping his head down. Lothar scoped the scene with his binoculars and made a mental note to punch their information handler in the face. Although he had far from underestimated the experience and intelligence of the Mamluk, he was realizing that they were far more 21st century than he had been told, no, *assured.* He would conduct his own reconnaissance and intel-gathering next time, and Michaelson could go fuck himself.

A second after the explosions showered them with sand and small rocks; Karesh hauled Aaron to his feet and dragged him backwards to the ramp wall. The door in the fortress wall opened and a trio of Mamluks emerged, weapons raised. They saw him and one rushed over as the other two moved past them along the side of the ramp, sweeping the area in unison. Gunfire started up again, from the other side of the ramp, and Karesh could hear rounds hitting the Land Rover and the ground around it. Suppressing fire. He turned to the two forward men as the other began checking Aaron for wounds and cleaning the blood from his face.

"Ray! They will move around to this side. They want the angle. Watch straight ahead, there." He pointed straight out along the length of the ramp and then slightly to the right, in the direction of the explosion. "And there. Expect three more contacts minimum."

The nearest Mamluk nodded, tapped his teammate on the shoulder and they began to creep forward together. Karesh turned back to Aaron.

"How are you, boy?" The other Mamluk was finishing wiping the gore from his face and neck. "Are you hurt? Did you get hit?"

"He's unhurt," the Mamluk medic said. "Just a little shock. He'll be fine. Maybe a bit sluggish, but you can move him."

"Your accent," Aaron said, staring at Karesh, a look of confusion on his red-stained face. "You're English?"

Karesh smiled briefly and nodded as a trio of rounds whizzed by overhead. "Born in the sands and raised in Cambridge. English mother and Burmese father."

Aaron went to speak when a blast of gunfire cut him off. Ray and his partner were laying down fire out toward a small ridge some way out over the dunes.

"Later," Karesh said. "We need to get you out of here. But we can't move for the truck until this is over. They'll hit it if we do."

The medic finished his work and picked up his rifle. "I'll have Tuya get some grenades out on the south ridge. There's one guy, maybe two, and one at least with a launcher for the Rover. One or the other is keeping the truck pinned."

"What about inside?" Karesh asked, as a ricochet pinged and whined overhead. "How many and where are they? We won't be able to hold this position if they make it out through the Dusk Gate."

"Only three. We took one out in the outer corridors, but we got lucky. They're good and they are moving. We're forcing them through to the Sanctum. We can trap them there, but Tuya has the only grenade launcher. We can't use that in the passages."

"Where's the other launcher?" Karesh asked. He still had a hand on Aaron's shoulder. The gunfire continued, both out amongst the dunes and across the ramp.

The medic nodded up toward the Land Rover.

"Wonderful," Karesh said. "Remind me to kiss Tuya when I see him."

Karesh nodded and the medic smiled before disappearing back into the fortress. They had their own battle to fight inside but Karesh wouldn't be able to get Aaron out of harm's way unless they could squash the threat on the outside. He needed Tuya's grenades and uncanny aim for that. He was the youngest Guardian in the fortress, and yet was, by far, the most incredible shot with the 40 mm grenade launcher that Karesh had ever seen, even through all of his years as a Royal Marine where he had seen combat in Afghanistan, Iraq, Syria and Kuwait, along with some other, less media-covered places. He slid down the wall, pulling Aaron down with him. "It's almost over," he said, and Aaron buried his face in his folded arms.

Lothar heard Alpha come under fire from somewhere near the end of the ramp. He couldn't make out any targets but could hear the distinct, disjointed overlapping fire from two weapons. He couldn't disengage from the Land Rover, but he now needed to regain control of the ramp. His target was there and now had fire support.

"Delta, can you put a Scarab round into the wall above the truck without destroying it?"

* * *

Kessler peeked around a corner, down the sight of his rifle, and surveyed the smoke-filled passageway. Two bodies lay close to the far end, in front of the only door, killed by the grenade he had tossed down there a moment earlier.

"Clear," he said, and Mita moved around him and across to the opposite wall. They moved down the hallway slowly, scanning for any movement, focused on the heavy black door at the end. They had lost Jonas to a crossbow bolt shortly after the inner breach, but they were close now and they knew very well just how lightly manned the fortress was. They were finally close to the perimeter of the inner fortress and yet Kessler couldn't shake the vague feeling that they had gotten this far on more than just luck and training. He put his ear to the wood, low down by the stone floor, minimizing himself as a target for anyone on the other side with a weapon and an itchy trigger finger. He stood, nodding at Mita who retrieved the foam explosive from a belt pouch. Kessler drew a concussion grenade and pulled the pin as Mita applied the sticky pink goo around the doorframe. Stepping to the sides of the door, both men turned away and Mita hit the detonator key. The familiar loud *crack*, followed by the crashing of the door as it fell forward to the hallway floor, boomed through the narrow passageway. The room beyond was gloomy and Kessler tossed in the concussion grenade the moment the door hit the ground. A split second after it detonated, he swung his rifle around the doorframe, flicking on the barrel-mounted flashlight. The room was twenty feet across and devoid of any furniture. Ornate stone carvings made for unique ceiling skylights and there was a metal grating set in the floor. It was empty.

"Clear," he said after a moment, and stepped through.

Mita followed and the two men moved swiftly toward one of the two doors set into the far wall. They had moved ten feet when a loud scraping noise filled the room and they both spun around to see a heavy metal grated barrier sliding down over the open doorway, trapping them inside.

"E-X! Now!" Kessler barked, and Mita rushed to the nearest door, pulling out the explosives can as he ran. He was already applying it to the doorframe when the first of three grenades dropped into the room through the skylight.

Tuya was creeping south along battlement when the radio call came through. The intruders inside the fortress had almost reached the Sanctum. Beyond that, they could breach the inner ring and then attack Karesh from anywhere on the fortress walls. He could hear the gunfire ringing out below, yet knew that his priority was to make it to the roof above the Sanctum where his brothers were waiting for him and his grenades. A moment's pause and he turned back, running down a narrow stairwell and sprinting deeper into the outer perimeter section. He had two halls to run, perhaps fifty yards, before he would emerge onto the small rooftop that looked down upon the ancient dungeon, commonly used for imprisonment and torture by the Romans in their day. Now though, it was a bare room used only for reflection and meditation, the blood long since washed from the floor and walls.

He rounded the last corner, skipped down the last five steps and saw his two brothers, one crouching by the skylight openings and the other climbing out of the trapdoor from the room below.

"Where *were* you?" The smaller of the two asked, standing and striding over as Tuya came to a breathless halt.

"They are firing on Karesh at the Dusk Gate. I need to get back." He reached into his tunic and drew out a belt with a trio of grenades attached to it. "Don't forget to close the steel trap!"

He turned and sprinted away as the skinny Mamluk shook his head after him. It took him less than twenty-five seconds to return to the top battlement, directly above the Dusk Gate. He could hear sporadic gunfire from both sides of the ramp below. Without pausing, he stoop-ran north along the walkway and then stopped, crouching by the wall and listening to the noises of the closest weapon, firing fairly steady three-round bursts at the truck on the ramp from somewhere, forty feet below. He took a deep breath, calmed himself and closed his eyes, holding the semi automatic forty-millimeter grenade launcher in front of him like a mortar tube.

Thunk, thunk, thunk!

As soon as the explosives were away, he sprinted south, past where the ramp was, and then stopped again, listening to a trio of automatic weapons exchanging fire in the sands below.

Boom, boom, boom! The fire pinning Ranah on the ramp stopped. Now there was only the fire from below his position, but he had to isolate it. He wouldn't be able to fire on instinct this time. Karesh was down there with the boy, and it sounded like two of his brothers had made it outside to help and were firing on a ridge about fifty yards to the east. He settled, moving and adjusting the launcher as he listened to the cracks and echoes of the machine guns. *Clack, clack, clack!* The sound came from slightly farther south. Tuya closed his eyes, turned slightly and waited. His brothers were splitting up, firing from two distinct positions near the base of the ramp. The desert replied again with the rapid *clack, clack, clack!* of a larger caliber support machine gun. Tuya gripped the barrel.

Thunk, thunk, thunk!

Delta glanced left as Lothar signaled him. He backed away from his machine gun and reached for the Scarab, hoisting it onto a shoulder before edging forward on his knees to the top of the ridge. Lothar took over the task of keeping the Mamluk pinned near the front of the Land Rover. He managed to knick the man on his left arm and saw him jerk away, tucking himself tighter against the front of the vehicle. He heard a faint popping sound from somewhere above and stopped firing to look up at the top of the wall. The top of a figure's head ducked down out of sight immediately and he knew what came next.

"Daniel…"

As Delta peeked over the top of the dune, he saw the Mamluk, cowering at the front of the truck, pinned by Lothar's expertly placed cover fire. He flicked off the trigger safety and moved the crosshairs up to the wall, around fifteen feet above the Mamluk's head. Any closer and if the explosion didn't take out the Land Rover, the falling debris would. He settled on a spot and was preparing to fire when he felt the small impacts of three objects close by. He risked a glance down and behind him. A few feet away on the sand lay two grenades. He could see the lettering stenciled on the side. High explosive.

"Oh, Good shooting…"

Boom!

Karesh heard the explosions and climbed to his feet the moment the echoes died away.

"Stay down, Aaron," he said, and made his way toward the end of the ramp, glancing back over his shoulder at the top of the fortress wall. Tuya was up there somewhere, casting his grenades into the sand with frightening effect. He knew their job was not done, though, and the intruders in the fortress could breach the Dusk Gate at any moment, should they get past their men inside. The two young Mamluks were kneeling in the sand, firing sporadic volleys into the brush and rocks ahead. Karesh whistled and motioned for them to pull back. Rounds whistled overhead as their quarry returned fire, an obvious attempt to mask his movements as he edged farther south to gain a better field of fire over the ramp and Land Rover. The pair returned fire as they drew back, and the shooter shot back a short burst that left pockmarks in the fortress wall, high above their heads.

Thunk, thunk, thunk.

"Down!" Karesh barked, and the pair dropped to the sand, Tuya's grenades sailing overhead.

When the echoes of the last explosion had died away, carried across the sands like an angry breeze, the pair stood and trotted over to him. The three of them stood in the shade of the ramp, looking down at a still prone Aaron, his face literally in the sand and his tunic spattered with Salomon's drying blood.

"We wait for two minutes," Karesh said.

He immediately tensed as the muffled sound of explosions rumbled toward them from inside the fortress walls. Ray drew away to the side, aiming his weapon at the door in the wall, prepared to cut down whoever stepped through it. When, a few minutes later, it did open, the skinny Mamluk from the Sanctum roof stepped out into the sunshine. "They are gone," he said, smiling at Ray as he lowered his rifle.

Karesh pulled Aaron slowly to his feet and dusted him down. He looked like a startled rabbit, scared out of his wits, but otherwise unharmed.

"Ok," Karesh said, clapping him on the shoulder. "*Now* we can get you out of here."

From his vantage point under a thick bush a hundred yards away, Lothar watched the Mamluks survey the Land Rover, checking it for damage before the boy and his minder climbed in. The others were moving out across the sand, looking for the bodies and weapons of his fallen comrades. The sun was drawing low toward the western horizon and he knew he would have the cover of darkness to make his withdrawal. For now, he would lie still and wait, and watch them haul the remains of his friends away to burn them, in the open, as a show of their victory. His grip tightened around the body of the binoculars and he smashed them down onto a rock, spilling glass shards to the sand.

"Mother*fuckers*," he hissed, drawing his rifle close. He would kill Michaelson when he saw him. Slowly.

Chapter Thirteen

Agent Director Marissa Cole walked with the purpose of someone very comfortable in her position of authority. Flanked by two agents, she stopped at the secured medical wing door and waited for the guard to process her through as he checked her image on the security monitor against his database of cleared personnel. After a moment the door hissed open and the trio breezed through. With clean, modern composite walls and lit by cleverly recessed ambient lighting, the facility looked more like the interior of a science fiction starship than a government medical building. They passed through several sectors, each with its own security control, and walked by several open labs with rows of white coat workers hunched over stainless steel workbenches.

At the end of a short corridor, the words *Sector Seven* appeared, stenciled along the wall in glossy, oversized lettering. Inside, the cold white linoleum floors were replaced with oil black marble tile and expensive looking art hung on the walls in the classic 'my kid could paint that' style.

"Wait here," Cole said, and the two agents pulled up to stand either side of a door marked S7-03.

Cole opened the door without knocking and stepped inside. Two armed agents stood close to the door, surveying a room that held a futuristic-looking bed, a comfortable-looking armchair and a flat screen television, mounted high on the wall.

"Ma'am," the nearest agent said, holding out a file as Cole stepped beside him.

"Any change?"

"Not since last night. First thing this morning he asked for his lawyer again, but nothing since then. The doc reports that his injuries are stable, though he'll lose some motor function in his left hand due to nerve damage from the surgery to fix the radius fracture. He's under light sedation for pain but he's lucid."

Lincoln Klick was lying silently in the bed, staring at the frosted glass window that hid a bland view of the medical facility's central atrium and garden, brightly lit on one side with the cold light of early morning. He turned his head at the sound of Cole's voice, his eyes widening as they met hers. He began to shake his head slowly and groaned, his expression sliding into one of tired hopelessness.

"Do you need anything else from us, ma'am?"

Cole shook her head, "No, this won't take long. I know Mr. Klick needs his rest."

"Very well. We'll be right outside if you need anything."

He nodded to his partner and both men left the room to join the others in the hallway outside. Cole stepped to the end of the bed and looked down at the almost despondent-looking Klick, his heavily bandaged arms held to the bed with thick restraints.

"It seems that you left one or two things out of your statement, Lincoln," Cole said, opening the file and pretending to read a random page. "Like this part. Wow, gang rape of two 15-year-old sisters a dozen times over the course of fourteen days in October, at your..." she snorted. "*Palace of pleasure* in DC."

She leafed through a few more pages, not lifting her eyes and shaking her head. She could see Klick squirming, pulling feebly against the restraints. "Or the fact that you aren't picky when it comes to the gender or age of your so-called 'becoming' guests. How many were there, Lincoln? How many defenseless minors did you violate in that basement before we pulled you out of there? Should we bring in Mr. Grey again to ask some more?"

Klick was shaking his head, his face a clammy mask of sweat. Cole looked up, peering at him over the edge of the file. A bloom of pleasure pressed against her temples as she saw the fear in his eyes.

"You've been a very bad boy, Lincoln. Sometimes bad boys like you need a little...encouragement when it comes to answering the difficult questions. It wasn't so bad once we got going, was it? I know Mr. Grey can be a little... focused on his work, but you did just fine after a while. Is that it? Would you like to see Mr. Grey again? It's just questions and answers, Lincoln. Questions and answers."

Klick was shaking his head, his eyes flicking between Cole and the door.

"Or is it something else?" Cole dropped the file to the bed and leaned forward, her hands gripping the footboard. "Something else you're not telling me, maybe?" She leaned in some more. "During our conversation yesterday, you mentioned a name and it's gotten me stumped. Who is The Rook?"

Klick visibly shuddered at the sound of the name. He stopped shaking his head and stared at Cole. When he spoke, however, the fear was not evident at all in his voice. The words came forth with the conviction and confidence of a well-educated man, comfortable in his own skin.

"You don't need Grey to make me tell you that I know who he is. You know I do, but I can't tell you much more than that," Klick said after a moment. "It doesn't matter where you keep me, or how many bomb proof doors there are between me and the outside, I'm as good as dead. And I don't mean just dead, I mean dead in the worst way you could *never* imagine. You think that Grey is evil and sadistic and, what did you say? Focused? You've no idea who these people are. No idea who they, *we*, take our orders from, who we *serve*. And I hope you never know, Agent Cole. In a world filled to overflowing with foul, evil, disgusting atrocities, all conjured and perpetrated by man, by *us*, it all pales into a cozy insignificance next to what is coming and what is going to happen to all of you.

"So go ahead, call your inquisitor, pull some more strips of flesh off me, break some more bones, drown me again. It won't make any difference. I know who you are, Agent Marissa Cole, and yes, I am afraid. I'm more scared today than I've ever been in my life, but not of you or your pathetic instruments of torture. You need to get to the top of my food chain because that's what you think your job is, and I'm just a rung on that ladder. You want that next promotion, you want that recognition, you want the adoration of your peers. Yeah, you want it all."

He laughed then, pushing his head back into the damp pillow. "It's funny, you know?"

Cole cocked her head to one side slightly. "What's funny, Lincoln?"

Klick smiled thinly, still casting his eyes toward the door as if expecting a sudden visitor. "If you knew the things I can't tell you, and had the opportunity, I think you'd jump on board. Ha ha, yeah, you'd fit right in. It's your kind of business model for sure."

Cole straightened. "No one is going to help you, Lincoln. No one from some big, shadowy cult organization is going to come and save you. As far as the world knows, you're just a small time cult weirdo that flashed a couple of girls who ran away and called the cops. To everyone out there who even gave a passing shit, you're a nobody, a rich boy with an insecurity complex and a short-circuited moral processor who likes to dress up in a fancy cloak and pretend he worships the Devil. The District Attorney hasn't even asked about you, and we dragged you out of that house on the fucking six o'clock news. I can take you wherever I choose and do whatever I want with you, and make no mistake, I'll do whatever it takes to dig out the sick rapist, drug dealing bastards you report to, even if I have to raid every God damned house with even the slightest semblance of a pentagram within five hundred yards of it."

Klick's expression dropped slightly and Cole smiled inwardly as she caught the gesture. Picking up the file, she turned for the door.

"He knows who you are," Klick said. "He knows where you're holding me, and he knows everything I don't know. He'll come for me, and after that, he'll probably come for you too, and everyone you've ever talked to about me."

Cole stopped, eyes fixed on the door. Some of Klick's words resonated inside her mind, even if she couldn't quite work out why. She remained impassive and cool, turning slowly to stare at Klick's twitching face, half turned on his pillow, his words a biting echo that hung in the air between them.

"And there's nothing you or your jumped up secret agent men can do about it."

Cole was pulling the door closed when Dr. Ferris approached. He strode toward her along the hallway, a chart tucked under one arm. Making a point not to acknowledge the director, he moved directly to the door and reached to open it, his hand pausing in mid air when Cole left her hand on the handle. He looked into her face, their noses inches apart. "Anything I need to clean up today, Ms Cole?"

She snorted, looking Ferris up and down. She despised the man and his holier than thou attitude. "He's all nicely tucked up in bed, just as you left him, Doctor." Ferris moved for the door handle, but again Cole didn't move. "I'm having him transferred. The order will be in your box by fourteen hundred. I'll expect him fit and ready to be moved by fourteen ten."

"You're not the only agent who wants to talk with my patient," Ferris said coolly. "And, seeing how he is of such high interest to the Bureau, I'm sure you will have the transfer approved through the proper channels. Chief Sorano would appreciate being kept fully apprised of Mister Klick's progress." He nodded toward the door handle. "Do you mind?"

With a final sneer, Cole wheeled away and strutted off down the hallway, her two agents in tow.

Cole was walking fast, clenched fists at her sides. She'd had run-ins with Ferris before, and he'd reported her twice, both times for excessive force during interrogation of a suspect. He hadn't tried to hide it, she'd given him that, but that had only cemented his place at the top of her shit list. And once you were on it, you didn't get off. Adding to that was another thorn in her side. One that she was going to have to think very carefully about removing.

"Get Sorano on a conference line in G-2. I want to know everything about Agent Wonder Woman Morgane and what the hell he thought was great about the idea of sending her and her lap dogs up here to stink up my investigation."

The last security door thudded closed behind them and the security guard watched them appear to grow smaller as they headed down the hallway that connected the medical facility with the administration building. When they had pushed out through the last set of double doors, he picked up the phone.

"They're out. Yes, sir. She's headed back now. No, sir, everything went as planned. The subject is still secure. Yes, sir. He'll be in transit tomorrow. The usual route."

*   *   *

The conference room was spacious and well furnished with the plush leather swivel chairs that Cole had become accustomed to using since she had insisted on having the ridiculous, and ancient, 'Cold war cots' replaced, as she used to refer to the old grey metal chairs and furnishings that had adorned the conference and meeting rooms throughout the New York building. The office budget hadn't even taken a hit, thanks to her special relationship with the director of internal financing, or rather the special dirt she had on him. It wasn't really anyone's place to judge his personal cross-dressing preferences, or voice opinion on his choice of weekend fetish bars. No, much better to keep those photos somewhere safe, far away from prying, manipulative eyes—all except hers, of course.

Cole tapped a button on the conference remote speaker at the center of the long table and sat down.

"Go secure, authorization Cole, Gamma two seven echo."

"*Authorized, Director Cole. Line secure,*" a female voice said from the loudspeaker.

"Chief Sorano, good morning."

"Agent Cole, what can I do for you?" Sorano's voice was relayed with perfect clarity from recessed loudspeakers placed throughout the sound and RF-proofed room.

"Agent Gabby Morgane," Cole said dryly. "She and her team paid me a visit yesterday, I assumed to follow up with the investigation into the sect house in DC. Lincoln Klick and his associates."

"Yes, she returned yesterday with good words to say about it. What's on your mind, Agent Cole?"

"Is she still attached to the case in DC? I was working on the assumption that once she had effected Klick's arrest and he had been transported to my facility I would have full autonomy on the pursuing investigation. While I respect Agent Morgane's experience and dedication, I have the utmost faith in my team's ability to work both ends of the case. I wondered where you stood on that."

There was a moment's silence. "Though I have Agent Morgane on another case, she is available to you should you need further assistance at this end. Besides that, the case is yours, Agent Cole."

Cole smiled. Knowing that she had Morgane on call but kept at a good arm's length and out of her hair was exactly what she had hoped for.

"Thank you, Chief. I'll be sure to keep you appraised should anything become relevant this end. Please pass my thanks to Agent Morgane."

"I'll be sure to do that, Agent Cole." There was a pause, and Cole reached forward to cancel the call.

"There's one more thing," Sorano continued, Cole's hand frozen mid air above the call cancel button. "I would be very disappointed if I were to learn that you had manipulated the case, Agent Morgane's visit, and subsequent availability, to further your own professional ends. I make no assumptions, but inter-office cooperation is still a sticking point in some parts of the agency and I know that communication between the DC and New York offices can sometimes be… patchy. Any information you purposely hold back that's pertinent to either case will be deemed a breach of agency code of conduct and you will be disciplined accordingly. Do I make myself clear, Agent Cole?"

Cole glared at the microphone, her hand now a tightly clenched fist. "Of course, Chief. You have the full support of my team and myself. Please don't hesitate to contact me with any concerns you may have."

"Very good."

Click.

Cole sat back and slammed the arm of the chair. There was probably nothing to it, but she could only assume that either Morgane had said something to Sorano, or the Chief was playing favorites. Everyone was well aware of Gabby Morgane, the super agent, and poster girl for the FBI. Cole had only met the woman once, and already Morgane was proving to be a major pain in her ass. Her comms unit chimed and she touched the small Bluetooth device behind her ear.

"Cole. Yes, have them bring it in."

A moment later the door opened and one of her personal agents walked in. He handed her a file. "This is the name Mr. Grey got out of Klick. Seems straight forward, but it was unusually sticky trying to dig around on this guy."

Cole nodded, "Thank you, Matt."

The agent turned and walked to the door. When he had left the room, she opened the file and began to read the first page. At the top was a cleanly printed photograph of a young man, perhaps in his mid twenties. Slicked back dark hair and a spark of arrogance in dark brown eyes, he looked like a lawyer or a stockbroker with no concept of the value of money, or emotions, or relationships. She pictured him driving a million dollar Italian sports car and still only dropping the valet a couple of dollars. As she read further down the page, she smiled a little. Being proven right was only one of the small things in life she had grown accustomed to. Now, though, it was almost expected. It was one of the things that kept her in a job. One of the things.

"Wealthy father, wealthy grandfather, born into old money." She started to read aloud. "Hmm, wait. *Old* money. Blakenstock investments. Went to the London School of Economics and barely passed, entered the firm at 22, division manager by 24, owns a four-million dollar apartment in Chelsea. No ties, no steady girlfriend, no record."

Cole snorted, flicking through a couple more pages before returning her gaze to the picture on page one. "You really haven't been anywhere, have you? Born into a life of money and power and had your hand held all your life by dear daddy. Now where are you going? Let's just wait and see."

On instinct, she reached for the phone, punching an extension and holding the handset to her ear, staring at the file. "I want extra security on a subject over on the high level medical floor, Downtown. That's right. Klick, Lincoln. J. He's under the care of Doctor Ferris, but is scheduled for transfer tomorrow. No one gets in to see him. I mean no one. Even if Doctor Ferris attempts to get into that room, I want to know about it first. Yes, authorized."

She hung up, putting her finger on the paper, and tapping the man's picture. The name beneath the photo read; *James Devlin*.

Chapter Fourteen

Gabby and Jerry followed Drexler out of the conference room, on their way to the office of the Director of Security. Drexler walked fast, like a man in a real hurry to get somewhere, and Gabby juggled the notion that he was hiding something with the idea that he was just a very busy, hyperactive scientist nerd who wanted to get back to his chemistry set.

"David Akers came to us from the White House," Drexler said proudly. "He served four years as Director of the Secret Service and was personally responsible for the safety of the President." He turned to look at them while he walked, almost immediately bumping into a fire extinguisher on the wall. "He came very highly recommended and is very thorough," he said, rubbing his arm and moving on.

Gabby didn't think that Drexler was usually a nervous, clumsy man, but he was definitely on edge about something. She had the subtle feeling that, whatever it was that had Drexler so twitchy had something to do with Alex, and anything to do with her friend was something that she wouldn't let go.

"Ah, it looks like Director Akers is not in his office," Drexler said as they stopped in front of an office door at the end of a plush hallway. The lights were off, along with every other office, and it was clear that there would be no summoning Akers for an interview at three o'clock in the morning.

"Well that's fine," Gabby said, reaching into her jacket and drawing out a business card. "Thank you for your efforts, Dr. Drexler. If you could please make sure Mr. Akers gets this and gives me a call when he comes in to the office later today, I'd appreciate it so we can get our investigation wrapped up and out of your hair."

Drexler looked visibly relieved at the prospect of the two agents leaving. His return to the demeanor of the cool, intelligent super scientist was instantaneous and impressive. He nodded slowly and stepped forward. "And thank *you*, Agent Morgane, for being so diligent in your duties and wanting to come all the way out here to get to the bottom of something that has deeply affected us all, here at Apex." He held out his hand and Gabby shook it. His grip was firm and clammy. He turned to shake Jerry's hand. "Agent Walker, a pleasure. Thanks again."

Drexler stepped back and clapped his hands together. "Right, perfect timing, as I have to get back. I'll have someone take you to your car. It's been brought down for you. Thank you again for being so understanding of our security procedures. I know they can be a pain. It's the same for every one of us."

Gabby nodded. "Thank you, Doctor. You need to keep all of those crazy experiments of yours safely under wraps. Especially the super thermal compression t-shirts you've got going on out there."

Drexler's expression wavered slightly. He caught it and laughed, but Gabby had already seen through it, and he knew it. "Well, someone's got to keep our boys warm without dressing them up like Eskimos, right?"

The three of them chuckled together as Drexler guided them back along the corridor to a guard station, where a giant uniformed soldier stood, ready to check IDs.

"Sergeant, please see to it that Agents Morgane and Walker here get back to the vehicle dock so they can wait for their car to be brought around." The soldier nodded, stepping between them. "This way, please."

Gabby shook Drexler's hand in thanks once more before she and Jerry turned to follow the solider down the hallway. Drexler watched them go. As soon as they had disappeared around a corner, he darted away, running down the hall to the nearest elevator, repeatedly pushing the button as if in some vain hope of summoning the car any faster. When he finally exited on his floor, he sprinted to his office, fumbling with his key card before barging in and heading straight for the TV monitor control on his desk. He locked the office door while the system booted, waiting for the security camera image to appear. The image was of the inside of Alex's lab, from a vantage point somewhere above the door. It looked like the scene of a burglary. Equipment and furniture was strewn around the room, cables snaked across the floor and the computers were dark, still and dead.

"What the hell is this?"

Suddenly, the alarm went off, sounding like a cross between some wounded banshee and a diving submarine. It droned outside in the hallway and Drexler jumped at the sound, before reaching for the phone. It rang before he could pick it up.

"Drexler. What the hell is... what do you mean 'someone hit the main alarm in the Hub'? Who? Dr. Bishop? He's the only one in there. Well you're the ones down there! What do you see, God dammit? Bullet holes? What the hell is going on down there, Johnson? Where is Dr. Bishop?" Drexler glared at the monitor. The two soldiers were looking around the room, one of them holding a phone to his ear.

"Find Dr. Bishop," he said. "He needs to be ok, do you understand? I'm coming down."

He hung up the phone and watched as the soldiers spoke before one hurried from the room. Sergeant Johnson stood amidst the disarray, poking around and waiting for the doctor. Drexler picked up the phone again and dialed, punching the keys with angry frustration.

"Something has happened in Dr. Bishop's lab. Yes, we're locking down now. I don't know, missing. I'm on my way down there. Guards report gunshots, but no blood and no sign of Dr. Bishop. Well, I can't rule that out. Akers will be on his way in. No, nothing unusual. Well, we had a visit from a couple of FBI, wanting to talk about two of our men who were killed. Why wasn't I notified of that? I just sent the kid home to get some sleep, for Christ's sake." Drexler sighed, running his fingers hard through his hair. "Yes, I'll do that. They'll be gone as soon as I can get them out of the gate. They were leaving when the alarm sounded anyway. I'll call you when I know more."

He hung up the phone and stood for a moment, staring at the top of his desk, eyes unblinking. There were scenarios to be expected with this project, and he had been notified about the FBI agents' visit *after* he had been called to be told that there was some unusual activity in Alex's lab. Bennett hadn't lied when he had told them he was on his way in. But it wasn't the breakthrough he was expecting to walk in on. Not at all. Now, instead of a slice of good news and perhaps a huge step toward their goal, he had a vandalized laboratory, a mysterious gunman and his lead geneticist—and key to the project's success—missing and possibly shot.

"Shit, Alex," he said, turning for the door. "Where the hell are you?"

*   *   *

Alex clutched his arm as he ran. The pain in his shoulder was dizzying and he dare not look at the wound. He could feel the hot, sticky blood oozing beneath his fingers and shirt sleeve as he tried to keep a tight hold over the wound. Every few steps he glanced over his shoulder. He was alone, for now. No sign of Audrey, or any other crazy person with a gun. He came to several intersections and stopped to check around corners carefully before dashing forward along the narrow passageway. His vision suddenly swam alarmingly and he barreled into a stack of crates against the wall, falling to the floor and crying out as his shoulder hit concrete. Laying on his side, he pushed with with his feet and inched his way around the crates, squeezing himself against the wall, out of sight.

His breath came in ragged, wheezing gasps, and the bullet wound was bleeding a lot. He couldn't lift the arm at all and clutched it a little tighter. The red alarm lights continued to spin, with one on the wall directly above him, and he could hear the muffled groan of the alarm sirens. As he sat catching his breath, he patted his shirt pocket and pulled out the flash drive, holding it between bloodied fingers.

"You," he gasped, in between breaths and staring at the small device. "What the hell have you gotten me into? You've already nearly gotten me..."

Clang!

A loud noise from somewhere back along the passageway made Alex freeze. He slipped the drive back into his pocket and drew his feet close, away from the edge of the crate. Someone was coming down the hallway. Peeking through a gap in the stacked crates, Alex looked back down the corridor. At first, all he could see was grey walls, wall lights, piping and one red emergency light. There was silence for a moment, until another sound of movement echoed down the passageway and he saw a shadow on the wall. He held his breath as someone approached, their rhythmic, scuffing footsteps accompanied by a faint, high-pitched whine. Alex immediately got an image of an electric powered scooter.

The footsteps drew nearer, and finally, Alex saw the shape of a small palette cart appear, pushed by a young man in overalls and an Apex Labs ball cap. He guided the palette cart, loaded with plastic box-like containers, to the intersection and stopped. Alex watched as he looked left and right, then seemingly right at him through the stack of crates, then pulled a cigarette from behind his ear and lit it, flicking the zippo closed with practiced ease before tossing it into the air and catching it in his breast pocket. He took a few hard drags before turning left and walking away down the corridor.

Alex held his breath until the sounds of lazy footsteps and electric motor died away, then let out a long, shaky sigh, bowing his head to his knees. His shoulder was bleeding down his arm and had pooled a little next to his hip, staining his pants. The pain was suddenly very intense, and he shook his head, trying to clear his vision and regain his composure.

"It's just a little shock," he said to himself, daring to take a look at the bloody wound. He couldn't see much through the torn sleeve and clotting, sticky blood, and quickly clamped his hand back over it, wincing at the sharp jolt of pain. He shook his head once more and grunted, slowly climbing to his feet and trying to keep from toppling over again. He started off down the corridor, away from the intersection. He knew he was headed east, out toward the delivery docks and service yard. Now he just needed a door to get him out there, so he could, in all reality, get shot or freeze to death before he got through the tree line and out to the perimeter fence. Ten steps later and the red flashing lights went out and the alarm stopped its groaning dirge. Maybe everyone was going back to business as usual. He laughed, in spite of the pain, then cursed as a lightning bolt shot down his arm.

"Fucking psycho assassin Audrey," he said. "I knew there was a reason I didn't date her."

*   *   *

Gabby and Jerry followed the soldier along a wide hallway, with one glass wall looking out over a dimly lit grassy area. She guessed they were at the back of the main building, making their way to some lesser attractive part of the facility. There were no more pictures adorning the walls and all the doors they passed through were plain, cold, and sterile. Even the perfectly clear windows seemed to add to the unfriendliness of the place.

"You may still have time for a round or two of Call of Duty when you get home," Gabby said. "Just don't use fatigue as an excuse when the kiddies kick your ass."

Jerry snorted. "Nope, it's a school night. All of my worthy adversaries are tucked up in bed, sucking on their thumbs and cuddling their teddybears."

The soldier glanced over his shoulder, a smirk on his face, then walked on, pushing through another set of double doors. As they hissed closed behind them, the alarm sounded, echoing along the hallway and stopping the trio in their tracks. The soldier turned toward them, immediately reaching for his radio mic.

"Juno one-one, command. Alarm sounding. Can you confirm a drill? Over." A tiny, metallic sounding voice responded and the soldier nodded. "Roger that. Heading in. Juno one-one out."

He stepped forward, towering over the two agents. "The facility has a lockdown alert. You're supposed to come back with me until we get the all-clear. Please follow me. Keep your firearms holstered and stay close. He strode off and the two agents took off after him, struggling to keep up.

They had only gone a few yards when the soldier put his hand up to his ear before slowing to a stop right in front of a pair of doors. "Juno one-one, copy. Go ahead."

The voice was speaking rapidly in his ear and he turned to glance at Gabby. His hand was on his weapon, finger resting dead straight on the trigger guard.

"What do you think is going on?" Jerry whispered, looking around, hand instinctively resting on his hip next to his holster. The closer his hand was to his weapon, the better he felt.

"It's probably a drill. I hope it's a drill. I'd like to get out of here before sun up."

The soldier—Gostalk, it said on his name badge—nodded, turning toward them. "Roger that. Copy all." He dropped his hand away from his ear and stepped forward. "Change of plan, ma'am, sir. We're conducting a lockdown drill. I'm ordered to show you the way to the service dock. Your vehicle is waiting for you. If you would just sit tight there until one of the line patrols swings by to lead you out, it shouldn't take too long."

Gabby shrugged. "Lead the way, soldier."

Gostalk nodded and started off at a pace, back toward the service dock. Gabby and Jerry both had to jog to keep up.

"Is this a regular thing?" Gabby asked, running just off Gostalk's shoulder. "The alarm?"

He didn't turn this time. "Uh, yes ma'am. They do it every once in a while. Mostly during or right after a shift change. They like to try and catch us napping."

They continued along the desolate hallway as it gently curved along the entire back wall of the main building. The soldier's pace was constant. He didn't waver in a single step and, after what seemed like a solid few minutes of running, finally slowed. He stopped in front of a pair of blue doors with windows set in the top halves. "Ok, straight through these, then another hallway to the last set of red doors. They'll be labeled D2 - Service and will take you out to the dock. You're vehicle is right there."

Gabby peered through the window. The hallway was bathed in intermittent red flashing light from an emergency alarm beacon on the ceiling. "Ok, thank you, soldier. We'll be fine from here."

Gostalk nodded, turned and took off, running back along the hallway and disappearing around the bend. Gabby turned to Jerry. "Age before beauty."

Jerry shoved the door open, slipping through and purposely letting it swing closed in Gabby's face. "Assholes before Angels," he said as she shook her head in mock disgust before kicking the door open and pushing through. As it closed with a *thunk* behind them, the light stopped flashing and the alarm went silent, leaving a vacuum of footstep-marred silence in the hallway.

"Ok then," Jerry said, not missing a step. "Just a drill. I guess they got their man, or put out the fire, or whatever it was they had to do."

"Well I hope Gostalk didn't miss too much of the party babysitting us."

"Are you kidding? Did you see that guy? Two hundred and thirty pounds of corn-fed all-American athlete, right there, boss. He probably made it back, sorted everything out and turned the alarm off himself."

The red doors appeared in front of them and Gabby could make out a floodlit area beyond. As they stepped outside, they were caught off guard by the chill in the air.

"Where's my new super tech thermal t shirt when I need it," Jerry said, pulling his collar up and shoving his hands into his pockets.

"You're too cold-hearted to feel the cold," Gabby said, gesturing to their Tahoe, parked by a large metal roller door some fifty yards away at the end of a row of Humvees. "Let's get in and turn the heat up, shall we?"

They set off, taking a short flight of stairs down to a large loading dock area. A long, raised platform stretched away to their left, while the building on their right towered above them like some huge warehouse. There were no guards and no employees outside.

"I hope the keys are in the damned thing," Jerry said, walking around the truck and reaching for the driver's door handle. "If it's locked, I'm going to throw a hissy fit. Just a heads up. Like, on the ground, full kicking and screaming. The whole show."

Gabby stepped up to the passenger door and watched Jerry through the window. He pulled on the handle and the door swung open. As he moved to step up to climb inside, the building exit door burst open, crashing into the wall beside the roller door. Jerry was half in the truck and jumped, freezing as the figure of a man burst out of the building and fell to the ground beside the Tahoe. Gabby saw the door burst open and then lost sight of whoever came through it on the other side of the truck. She ran around, reaching Jerry as he was rounding the open truck door, hand gripping his sidearm.

The man was laying on the ground, face-down on the frigid asphalt. Gabby saw the bloody wound first.

"Blood," she said, scanning the area and drawing her weapon as she moved slowly forward. Jerry moved beside her, turning a full circle as he checked the dock area for movement. The man was barely moving and Gabby knelt beside him, reaching out to carefully touch his neck, feeling for a pulse.

"Oh my God," she said as Jerry knelt opposite her.

"What is it?"

Gabby gently turned the man over. He barely moaned when she touched his arm. Laying flat on his back, Jerry's face fell too. "Oh shit."

Gabby leaned in close as Alex looked up, staring blankly at the sky, pale and deliriously weak from his injury. His lips were moving but only a weak, croaking sound came from his throat.

Chapter Fifteen

The room swam in and out of a slurring, smothering darkness, punctuated by fuzzy flashes of yellow light and the echoing, garbled sounds of muffled voices and murmurs. James Devlin came around sitting in an ornate high-backed chair. A pair of firm hands rested on his shoulders, holding him back against the plush fabric. As the sounds became more distinct and the shadows beat a slithering retreat, he began to tentatively survey his surroundings. The room was small, low ceilinged and smelled of dust and incense. The floor and walls looked like grey flagstones, giving the distinct impression of a medieval dungeon, and the kind of room any story's hero would not want to wake up in.

"And so, he is with us," a voice said, somewhere to his right. "Carefully now, David. Give him a moment."

The hands on his shoulders loosened their grip slightly and he let his head roll back, resting it on the back of the chair.

"Where…where am I?" he said, his voice barely more than a cracked, ragged whisper. As his eyes struggled to focus, he made out the forms of several figures standing around the room. At least a dozen. Every one of them wore a blood red full-length robe, their features hidden within the shadows of a deep hood. They shuffled closer when he spoke.

"You are standing at the threshold of a magnificent journey, James." That voice again. It sounded very familiar, yet James couldn't quite place it. "A journey that you were literally born to take. A quest that will change the course of human history and restore a rightful balance that was torn from us millennia ago."

James shook his head, clearing the last dregs of whatever drug had been used to knock him cold. One of the robed figures moved forward, stepping out from the gathered throng.

"This is your time, James. A great time. Every breath, every beat of your heart, has led you to this moment. You have been bred from the finest stock.

Your bloodline is the purest on the planet, and your ancestors nothing short of legends of their time."

The figure reached up and drew back the hood, revealing a head of white hair atop a very recognizable face.

"Mr. Blakenstock?" James almost buckled beneath another wave of dizziness and confusion. The room swam and nausea rose like an acidic tide in his throat. He choked it down, not wanting to suffer the indignity of vomiting before a crowd.

"That's right, James. You have nothing to fear. I know this is a terrifying and confusing ordeal, but you will come to see this as a true turning point in your life. It will finally have more meaning than the paltry search for wealth and power. You will know true purpose, true sacrifice and the ultimate reward."

James's wits were returning to him. The room did indeed resemble a dungeon. There were lit sconces on the walls, giving the room a dim, oppressive feel. He couldn't make out much more through the wall of red robes before him.

"Where is my father?" he asked, looking around at the hooded figures. "Where am I?"

Blakenstock regarded him closely for a moment and then took a step back and nodded at whoever was holding him in the chair. The hands released him and he slumped forward slightly, still weakened and unsteady. A robed figure stepped from behind the chair and moved in front of him to stand beside Blakenstock. Whoever it was stood almost a full foot taller than the older man and made for an imposing figure. He knew it was his father before he reached up to reveal his face. As the hood fell across his broad shoulders, James felt a sudden stab of betrayal and helplessness, knowing that his only real ally, however stern and harsh, was standing before him, alongside this carnival of identical freaks.

"James," he began, his tone deep and soothing. "This is a lot to take in, and I…"

"You drugged me!" James blurted suddenly, spittle flying from his lips and staining Blakenstock's sleeve. He knew the old man noticed it and he felt a momentary spark of glee at the thought of his disgust as he stood there, resisting the urge to wipe it off.

"Yes," his father said coolly, "and I would do it again. Look at yourself."

His father nodded, glancing down and James looked at his arms. He, too, was wearing a robe, similar to the others except that his was pure black. He pushed a sleeve up and saw the first tattoo, snaking down from his upper arm with tendrils and scales and an odd circular marking, onto his forearm. The black ink was fresh and his skin still raised and welted from the tattoo artist's needle. He quickly checked the other arm and saw a similar tattoo there, too.

"How…? What…?"

His father leaned in close, the firmness in his voice increasing slightly.

"James, a big factor of why you are here, why you were chosen, is how you react and adapt to all of this. I cannot tell you any more, and you know that I do not play games, but you *need* to take stock, evaluate, and trust your instincts. Acting like a spoiled brat will do you no good whatsoever. Do you understand me?"

He straightened, standing beside a stern-looking Blakenstock, and glared down at him. The look in his eyes was one of fretful anticipation and readiness to make a hard decision. James had seen it many times before and knew he was at a crossroads, where his next decision, his next few words, would shape the rest of his life. He nodded, more to himself than to his waiting father, and drew a calming breath. Looking around, he took inventory of the things around him, justifying and clarifying, ordering his thoughts and letting his logic take over. He knew most of the people in the room. That much was certain, even if he couldn't see their faces. He had awoken in the middle of some kind of ritual—the robes and burning torches gave that away—and he was its subject. Ok, so he had no idea what they wanted of him, but if they were going to do anything twisted and satanic to him, they wouldn't be trying to fluff his ego and talk him around, would they?

His father had never acted this patiently. He stood silently while James gathered his thoughts, allowing him to get his head around what was happening. His arms were beginning to sting from the tattoos. And so were his back, legs and the top of his chest. He shoved the thought away, not wanting to think about what other ink now adorned his body. There was no getting out of the room, that was clear. He looked at his father, his mind at least calmer for now, yet far from at ease.

"I want to know what happens next," he said, and his father looked at Blakenstock, his expression slipping into one of relief and resignation.

"There it is," Blakenstock said. "It's time to meet your destiny."

Without another word, the crowd of robed figures began to withdraw, melting away into the corners of the room and out through two doors in the far wall. They filed out silently, each disappearing through the dark openings until only Blakenstock and his father remained, standing in front of him. Then Blakenstock nodded and stepped back, replacing his hood over his head before turning and following the others out of the room.

His father reached up, drawing his own hood over his thick hair, and smiled. "Do not search for your answers, son. Just speak your mind and answer openly and honestly. It's all he will appreciate, and he knows you far better than you can imagine."

He stepped back slowly, hesitantly. James could see that he wanted to say more, but he turned suddenly and walked away. Then the doors closed, leaving him alone in the gloomy room. He sat still, looking around a room that was furnished only with a single red rug on the gray stone floor, four burning scones on the walls and the chair in which he sat. As he shuffled forward to sit on the edge of the seat, bracing his arms to help him stand, a door opened and a woman stepped in.

"Mister Devlin," the lady said, with a slight bow. "If you would please follow me. He will see you now."

She was dressed in a smart business suit and immediately clashed with the archaic surroundings of the stone-lined room. James hesitated as a wave of dizziness caught him off guard.

"Take your time," the woman said. Her dark skin and black hair were almost hard to make out in the shadows at the far end of the room. She waited, standing with her hands at her sides, and as he began to push himself gingerly to his feet, James couldn't help but picture her in her underwear, bent over the aquarium in Blakenstock's office.

By the time he had walked over to her, his head was finally clearing and he was steadier on his feet. "Where are we going?" he asked, knowing that she wouldn't answer him.

"This way, please," she replied, leading the way through the door and out into a hallway, its walls lined with flagstones, just like the room. They walked a short distance to a large red leather paneled door, set back into the wall. Two red candles lit the entrance, their holders wax covered skulls, with mouths agape.

The door opened by itself and the woman led the way inside. James walked through, emerging into a large wood-paneled office with a fire raging in the large hearth to the left, framed by black marble with ornate gold inlays. A large desk sat by the old windows on the wall away to the right, the view of city rooftops and grey clouds warped by the antique glass. In front of the desk were two studded red leather high back chairs, separated by a simple wooden coffee table. A man was standing by the fireplace, staring down into the flames, a glass of amber liquid in one hand, a walking cane in the other. His navy blue suit was immaculately tailored and his thick wavy hair was onyx black, slicked back and lustrous, ending in neat, tousled waves just above the collar of his jacket. He didn't turn when James entered and only moved when the woman had retreated back through the door, shifting his weight and taking a measured sip from the glass.

"There are only five Algiers crystal tumblers in the world," he said, his voice low and husky and immediately seductive. "Commissioned and hand made by unknown Florentine craftsmen, four hundred years ago, from the finest cut crystal. They put even the exquisite works of Calleija to shame."

He raised the glass, examining the fire through the swirling liquid. "They say that to own one makes you a part of an elite group of human beings. To own all five…" he turned to look at James. "Makes you a God among Kings."

As their gazes locked, James was taken aback by his eyes. They appeared the darkest black and yet seemed almost to glow in the firelight. James felt the man's gaze penetrate him, searching him, probing inside his body and soul. It was the most unnerving ten seconds of his life and he could neither move nor speak the entire time, frozen to the spot until the man looked away again, returning his gaze to the fire.

"Tell me a secret," he said after a moment.

James paused and then said, "When I was in my last year of college, I cheated on a final exam. A few of us got a copy of the paper before the test."

The man smirked, keeping his eyes trained on the flickering flames. "Ah, come now, James. I was hoping for something a little more... *liberating.*"

James didn't move, and didn't know what to say. "I really don't..."

"How's Miss Jennings doing these days?" He turned then and walked slowly forward. Not slowly because he wanted to emphasize the weight of his question, he just walked easily, slowly, without the need to move faster. It was very unsettling. The name. It sounded familiar, yet James couldn't quite place it. "Five foot three, classy brunette, hazel eyes, legs up to her eyeballs and a body constructed specifically for the sticky kind of sin."

He stopped a few feet away, tapping the cane on the expensive rug. James' stomach fell. The man smiled. "There it is," he said. "There it is. Oh she was a filly all right. And she sure enough remembered your name quite loudly in old man Blakenstock's office, did she not? Just yesterday morning, as I recall."

James felt the blood draining from his face, leaving his skin drawn and pale, the skin around his cheekbones tightening. Images of hidden office cameras and dim control rooms filled with monitored images of his sexual escapades in every nook and cranny around the building filled his mind. He was going to throw up all over the expensive rug.

"Conquests, James," he said, stepping close, barely a foot away. "A man's life is defined by his conquests. Do you really think that you are just conquering these poor girls' womanhood?" He stepped back, holding James' gaze. "Why don't we take a seat over there," he said, making no gesture to show James to any particular chair. James turned away and walked over to one of the red chairs by the desk at the far end of the room. He glanced back at the man, still standing by the door, then rounded one of the chairs and sat slowly, the leather creaking a well worn welcome as he settled. Sitting in a red leather chair, clad in only a black robe and fresh tattoos, James felt, he suspected, just as he was supposed to feel; vulnerable and exposed. He leaned forward and peered around the side of the wingback. The man was gone.

"You can tell a lot about a man by how he acts when he feels vulnerable."

James gasped, startled by the sound of the man's voice as he turned to see him sitting in the chair opposite him. The man shifted slightly in his seat, resting the tumbler on the armrest.

"When King Richard the First returned to England from battling Salah al-Din for Jerusalem in the third crusade, his ship was wrecked in a storm on the shores of Venice. Leopold, of Austria, captured the King, intending to hold him to ransom. He was, instead, sold to the Emperor of Germany and a ransom was demanded from the people of England for his safe return. The amount was so large that the people of an entire country had to be taxed into poverty just to raise the money, about $12 million in modern currency."

He held up the glass, turning it in his hand. "The value of just one of these," he said. "And it's only one of five, designed simply to hold liquor to satisfy thirsty men."

James didn't know what to say. He sat rooted to the chair, afraid to utter a single syllable. The man drained the liquid and then suddenly tossed the glass over his shoulder across the room. James turned, mouth open, and watched the glass sail through the air and crash into the fire. At least a twenty yard throw. The equivalent of making the half time free throw from the half way line in basketball. James turned back to the man, eyes wide in silent shock.

"It's ok," he said, settling back and laying his cane across his lap. "I have another four."

"Who are you?" James asked, finally.

The man smiled, and James thought he caught a glimpse of a pair of canines a little more pointed than usual. "Who do you think I am?" he replied, rolling the cane up and down his thigh. The handle was a silver wolf's head with ruby red eyes. His expression was playful, cocky. "We're on a game show. You have, say, one guess to win a million. What do you say?"

"The most important man in the building," James said without hesitating.

The man laughed, his head rocking back and his wide grin exposing those pointed canines. There was a great feeling of honesty in that laugh. There was no pretense, no false, strained joviality. It was a genuine, rib-squeezing, from-the-gut laugh and James felt that he had just heard the first real, genuine laugh of his entire life.

"Well, there is something that I have not had to confirm in a while," he said. "My name is Roland Black, and yes, I am the most important man in the building. And only six people, besides yourself, have ever laid eyes on me here." The man leaned forward slightly. "So you want to know why you're here."

James nodded.

"You want to know whether to turn left, or right, or run home to momma."

He regarded James for a moment. Was he waiting for an answer? A reaction?

"Every man reaches a number of crossroads in his life, James," he continued. "He has the choice, should he turn this way, or that way, or carry on going the way he's headed. And like the branches of a great tree, the farther out you get, these crossroads become fewer and farther between. I can tell you that you have reached a few in your lifetime and every decision you have made has led you here, to this moment, to the biggest crossroad of your entire life."

He sat back again, regarding James with those onyx black eyes, and sighed, as if in defeat. "Would you choose differently if you already knew your full potential? Not a rhetorical inkling of what you may one day be capable of, or the warm and fuzzy feeling you get after a really good motivational pep talk, but a real, tangible knowledge of what you already *are* capable of, and how it could be best used to serve your interests."

James thought for a moment, imagining the things he could do if he could pretty much predict the outcome. Knowing exactly what he could do would mean he could just operate beyond the limits of his confidence. He was smiling before he knew it.

"Of course you would," Black said. "Anyone in their right mind would. It's a numbers game, James, and I'm going to show you just how much potential you have, and how it's going to help us rule the world."

James snorted a laugh before he could help himself, then covered his smirk with a robe covered hand. Black was smiling too.

"It's ok, James. I would laugh too, were I in your position. It's the cowards and the lepers who cry, shamed by their fear and weakness. But look at you, embracing the unknown, operating in a realm of possibilities and improbabilities that would send most sheep scurrying back to the herd, content with a life of self-sustaining purgatory, safety nets everywhere."

"Well this isn't what I had in mind for the day's events when I got out of bed this morning," James said, after a moment of uncomfortable silence where Black just looked at him, regarding him with a sort of calm assurance, as if waiting to hear the answer to a question he hadn't asked yet. "To be honest, I'm just going along for the ride because I've no idea what the hell is happening around here, and, if you'll excuse me, I'm scared shitless, so I'll more or less do just about anything you say."

Black simply nodded slightly. "And you very well should be scared shitless, James. Not to throw any added pressure your way, but you are the first and only person in *history* to be in this position. You are one of a kind, James. You are unique, special, rare, priceless. Care to add anything? This is good stuff for an epitaph."

James didn't move. He sat silently, becoming more scared by the second, regardless of whether he was supposed to be or not.

"Oh, come now, James. Nothing is going to happen to you. I know what you're thinking, and no, you are not a pawn in some international drug cartel, nor are you being roped into some perverted sex trafficking ring, though that one is an insanely profitable enterprise should one decide to go down that route. No, you are what you think you are; your father's son and a valuable part of the Raven Group's future." He stood and rounded the chair, leaning against the back on his elbows. "Now, of course I know you're not an idiot. You've had enough time to gather your thoughts. You're sitting in a black robe, in a strange office, and you've been through something that, while you recall fully, have absolutely no idea how to rationalize or explain. The chanting, the red robes in that room. That was just the very end of it. Very melodramatic, of course, but I allow Blakenstock to follow his theatrical whims. Keeps things... authentic."

James glanced down at the robe, catching a glimpse of part of the tattoo on his right arm.

"Do you know what The Overwatch is?"

James thought for a moment. The term seemed very familiar to him, yet he couldn't place what it was attached to.

"You've more than likely heard of it here and there, from movies to video game titles and cool kid social media handles."

He stepped around the desk, laying the cane on the worn leather desktop and reaching down to open a drawer. He pulled out a small glass vial, filled with what looked like water and held it up. "This," he said, gently shaking the small bottle. "Is power. This is one of the world's best kept secrets, the things that myths and legends are made of."

"Water?" James said, instantly regretting the weakness in his voice.

Black tilted his head slightly. "Of course it's water, but it's where it's from that makes it... special."

Walking around to the front of the desk, he looked at the vial before slipping it into his jacket pocket. "But we will get to that later. The Overwatch has been written about, in pseudo-religious texts mostly, although most of the definitive works on the subject have been lost through time, forgotten about and discarded as some sort of mythical enigma. And it's very old. Older, for example, than Christianity."

He let that sink in, though he knew full well that James was more concerned with the ink on his skin than the big picture being painted for him.

"They are something you will get to learn about first-hand." Black leaned in, his lips a few inches from James' ear. "But for now, I can tell that you're eager to hear about your new... markings."

James pushed one sleeve up slightly. The skin was slightly raised and red, still tender from the needlework. He dare not look at the rest of him. The skin all over his body was sore, burning and itching beneath the robe.

"Come with me," Black said, suddenly turning and walking away, back toward the far end of the room and the still burning fire. James followed, picking up the robe slightly when it caught on his bare feet as he walked. Black walked over to the wall to the left of the fireplace and pressed something imperceptible in the paneling. A door-sized slab pushed out from the wall, then swung outward, revealing a full sized mirror set back into the wall. It's frame was uniquely ornate; a mixture of brass and bronze and reddish gold, and the glass carried a few stains in the corners, showing its age.

"This," Black said, leaning his cane on the wall beside the frame. "Is an Infinity Mirror. Every man should have a mirror like this. One should be admired by others as you are by yourself. Your self appreciation will be reflected back onto you by those you meet. Come, stand here and see what you what you've become."

James walked hesitantly to stand in front of the old mirror and Black guided him by his shoulders until he saw his full reflection in the glass. At first the image appeared dim and unclear, but after a moment the reflection seemed to brighten and sharpen into crisp focus, drawing out his features and every facet of his persona.

"Ah, yes," Black whispered, stepping to the side slightly. "It sees you, welcomes you. This will be the moment you identify with your true self, your true purpose, James."

Black stepped behind him and reached around his shoulders, grasping the robe and suddenly tearing it effortlessly away, letting the shredded pieces fall to the floor. James flinched, then stood frozen, eyes wide, taking in the image of his naked form in the mirror. The tattoos adorned a good deal of his body and appeared crisp and fresh, inky black, surrounded by a hue of red, irritated skin. At first he thought it was an intricate, abstract dragon or serpent, but as he looked more closely, he saw the shapes and symbols that made up the swathes and patterns of ink. It started at his chest, spreading out over his shoulders and down, wrapping around both arms to half way down his forearms, where it ended in wavy, pointed tendrils.

A line of archaic symbols was placed over the top of his shoulders, the same symbols appearing on the sides of his calves. More of the strange letters were interspersed throughout the piece, woven amongst a multitude of complex, interlaced lines, tendrils and shapes. It was so shocking to James that he had to think it was beautiful or else he would have screamed in horror. Perversely, all he could think about at that moment was, how the hell was he supposed to get laid with this crap all over him?

"Would that that be your sole dilemma," Black said, glaring into the mirror over James' shoulder. "But no, it's going to be the very least of your concerns, James. The very least."

Black stepped away and James swooned a little as a dark shadow seemed to fill the space behind him, casting the room around him into darkness. When he turned, the room was still there and Black was standing a few feet away, hands clasped in front of him. In the mirror, he stood alone as dark shadows swirled at his back and nudged at his ankles like a billowing wall of inky smoke.

After a moment, his head cleared and a strange sensation started to move over his body, like a cool breeze blown over warm skin, fresh out of a hot bath. Still the darkness swirled behind him and yet he felt a sure sense of confidence growing within him. He stood a little straighter, noticing that he was sucking in and tightening his stomach as he always did, trying to emphasize his mediocre abs. But they were tightening on their own. They were literally tightening, the skin seeming to shrink against muscles that were becoming more defined by the second.

Other body parts were changing too. His shoulders grew more defined as his arms swelled in size and his chest expanded. He heard small popping noises as his back spread slightly and his legs grew before his eyes. He was too enamored by what he saw to complain, let alone be as terrified as he should have been. His vanity was caressing his swelling ego with its intoxicating touch and he marveled at the almost perfect physique he now saw standing before him. Even his skin tone had darkened slightly, softening from borderline pale to a light, even tan.

"Holy mother of..."

"Not the kind of mother you would want to go home to," Black interrupted, stepping forward, half concealed within the swirling folds of smoke that filled the image behind James in the mirror's reflection.

"This is who you could be, James. This is what you've desired for yourself, the tool you've yearned to forge yourself into to get what you want, *do* what you want. Do you feel how empowered you've become, how unstoppable, how perfect?"

James was nodding, enchanted by his own image, the tattoos suddenly seeming so perfect.

Black was smiling thinly. "Come," he said. "Let me tell you about my son, and how you are going to help me save him."

Chapter Sixteen

Damascus was an old city. Widely regarded as the oldest continually occupied city in the world, it was sprawling, vast and a visual mix of ancient roadside history and slapdash modern catch-up. The term 'old' was now more of a physical description of its general state of overall appearance than a label of being the ancient and historic cradle of civilization it was used to.

Karesh drove the Land Rover west toward the city at a measured, even pace. Aaron had nursed his shock in numbed silence for the first hour, before turning to his keeper and speaking for the first time. He thought his voice sounded small and weak.

"Were those men there to kill me, or Professor Salomon?" he said suddenly, squinting in the bright desert sunlight.

"Neither," Karesh said, keeping his eyes on the road. Ever watchful, he considered even the occasional stray camel on the highway a possible threat. "They wanted to take you alive. They no doubt hit the professor as a target of opportunity."

Aaron sat silently, considering that. He had left the fortress with Karesh as the other men had begun to gather bodies, and body parts, left behind after the battle. He had never been exposed to bloodshed before and had thought long and hard about how it had affected him. Coming to the same conclusion over and over, he decided that it hadn't shocked him nearly as much as he had thought it would. It was horrific, yes, seeing men, friends, killed before your eyes, yet there was an undercurrent flowing through his life that he didn't comprehend. An undercurrent that seemed to carry him through the darker moments, the more dangerous times, just like the battle at the fortress. It was as Salomon had told him. he was supposed to be destined for something else, something bigger. And, he supposed, if he was destined for something else, the stars in heaven would keep him safe until he could fulfill it.

"So I am protected, then," he said after a moment.

This time Karesh did look over at him. Aaron was sitting in the passenger seat, looking just a little taller than he had when he had fist laid eyes on him. He sat straight, swaying with the movements of the car on the uneven highway, eyes fixed firmly forward towards the horizon. "That's quite a leap," he said with a smile. "I would grant that, during that engagement, you were surrounded by the armor of God, and you are not even fully protected yet, as you will be after the awakening. I have fought in many places and seen similar things. But with you, it is very striking. It was not only my eyes that saw the hand of God upon you." His smile faded. "And you will need it, my friend, for what is to come. You will need every ounce of divine protection there is."

They drove on in silence; Aaron lost in thought and fantasy while Karesh checked the GPS as they bore down on the eastern outskirts of the city, sprawling across the horizon before them.

"I know that I'm meant to meet someone here who'll show me what I'm supposed to do," Aaron said, keeping his eyes on the road. "After the fighting, after I saw the professor fall, the words he had said to me became very clear, as if they had changed color in my mind and I could finally read and understand what they meant." He turned to look at Karesh. "I am to be his champion. Somewhere far from here, far from my home. I know what I have to do, I just don't know how."

Karesh felt for the young man sitting beside him. He was to be thrown into battle against a vastly powerful and ancient adversary, and, at this point in time, he had nothing to his name but his wits. At twenty-four, Aaron had become a man long ago, ritualized into manhood through a secret initiation ceremony, after years of meditative combat training that he remained unaware he had even undertaken. Only in the deepest ranks of *The Overwatch* were these things permitted, and many had been tested over the centuries, only to fail through lack of focus, vision, and faith.

Aaron was different. He had taken the *mind walks*, as if born to them, training his body in an out-of-mind state, his consciousness left behind so that his senses were sharpened and honed to an almost supernatural level. His home secure, and his identity safely guarded, Aaron had walked among his peers as the one who would fight for humanity in the face of the greatest evil ever to walk the earth, and he had no idea.

Only at the final moment had they discovered his true identity, trying to snatch him so they could take him into the shadows to torture and kill him, spilling his blood and dismembering his body in the old ways, the slow, agonizing, unclean ways.

Unbeknownst to him, Aaron's destiny was already mapped out for him, and it was a path of urgent discovery and the most perilous danger one could imagine. Karesh could imagine a lot, and yet he knew that whatever enemy Aaron had yet to face would far eclipse even his most dangerous opponents. And now, with barely the faintest notion of awareness of what he was to become, Aaron sat calmly, hand resting on the old book he had taken from the professor, blissfully unaware that he would soon be a very different man than he was now.

"We have not too far to go now," Karesh said. "We need to stop for gas and water, a few miles up ahead, then around to the south of the city to Artoz."

Aaron kept looking straight ahead. "Artoz, isn't there fighting there?"

Karesh nodded, "There have been some conflicts there in the past, but now…we should be fine. We will be going directly to see the Teacher. When we arrive, make sure the book is well covered." He reached behind him into the back seat. "Here," he said, pulling out a handful of hard-bound books from the back. "Mix it in with these. Perhaps better to keep it in plain sight than try to hide it in here."

Aaron wrapped the pile of books with a scarf, tying a knot at the top so that it resembled an old school book bundle. Karesh smiled. It's what he would've done. Aaron tossed the bundle onto the back seat. The gas station appeared ahead, a ways back from the road, and Karesh checked his mirrors. There had been only one vehicle behind them for the last thirty miles, and that had been an old flat bed truck with a stack of bathtubs on the back. It had dropped farther behind them until it had been lost in the shimmering heat haze that danced along the horizon. Karesh kept the Land Rover steady, pulling off the highway and immediately onto a heavily potholed, rough dirt road. They kicked up a cloud of red dust and sand as they drove, leaving blissfully smooth asphalt behind.

The gas station was barely a run down shack with one rust pitted pump standing under the shade of a hand made lean-to. Karesh pulled alongside it, barely squeezing under the tarp, rolling and flapping lazily in the hot breeze. A small bell sounded as the tires ran over an air line and almost immediately an old man appeared from inside the shack, hobbling over with a gap tooth grimace. His left leg was gone, replaced by a worn, ill fitting prosthetic that poked out from badly torn and frayed pants. The flesh colored plastic shin was chipped and cracked with age.

"Cash only," he said, stepping up beside the pump. "No machine. Only cash."

Karesh nodded, pointing to the pump handle and then back to himself. "May I?" he said, reaching for the pump. "So you may rest, or perhaps get the boy some water."

The old man didn't release the pump at first. His dry, sand-crusted hand rested on the rusting metal as he squinted up at Karesh, who cleared him by at least a foot. "Only grade two diesel," he said, drawing his hand away and scratching his scraggly grey beard. "Maybe no good for your truck. Is gas, no?"

"No, diesel is fine. Please, some water for the boy." Karesh nodded toward the passenger door as the old man grabbed a bucket of water from behind the pump, walked around to the driver's door and dunked an old rag into the dirty liquid, ignoring Karesh's request. He started to wash the buildup of sand and dust from the windshield, the brown water dripping and pooling around his feet. Karesh shook his head as he began refueling, watching the ancient number dials on the pump roll as it clunked and wheezed the fuel into the tank.

"You are going into the city?" the old man said, his Arabic smooth and laden with the tone of wisdom. Karesh regarded him as he continued his window washing, soaking the front of his tunic as he worked. "My nephew makes very good Shawerma. You would like it, I'm sure. Go and see him, he will welcome you. The Falafel is perhaps not so good, but he is young and he still learns."

Karesh watched the old man through the truck windows, keeping one eye on the pump dials. These old ones had no automatic cutoff and he didn't need fuel spilling all over him and the truck in eighty-five degree heat. The old man picked up the bucket and walked awkwardly around to the passenger side, squashing the soaked rag against the windshield and making rough, rigid straight line strokes of streaky water over the thick glass. "And the coffee," he continued, "The best in all of Damascus. I swear it. I will go there just for the coffee. And then come right back, because there is no one to watch the pump, and if there is no one to watch the pump, well, the gas doesn't sell itself."

More rag dunking. "Ah, but the coffee." He straightened, smiling. "So good. Almost worth it. Almost, but not quite." He went back to washing. Karesh was smiling, despite himself. The old man couldn't reach all the way to the center of the windshield, so there remained a stripe of dry, crusty glass.

"The Shawerma though," he went on again. "Well yes, I would go for the Shawerma. It's just so..." He stopped, his arm frozen outstretched, pressing the soaked rag against the windshield. Karesh saw him pause, then noticed the fuel begin to overspill and cut off the pump, cursing silently at the small amount of gasoline running down the side of the truck and dripping onto the sand. He quickly replaced the pump and moved alongside the truck to stand next to the old man. He was standing so still that Karesh thought for a moment he was having some kind of seizure on his feet and was about to collapse. He reached out to touch the man's shoulder.

"Harun!" The old man said, raising his hand, dirty water streaming down his arm and up his sleeve. "He is here! He is here!" He stepped back, bumping into Karesh and stumbling over the bucket, spilling the water into the dirt. Karesh caught him as he fell, helping the old man to his feet.

"What do you know of that name, old man?" Karesh asked, propping the man against the hood of the Land Rover. He was breathless and obviously in shock, still staring at the windshield, directly at Aaron.

"Harun," he said again, trying to calm his breathing. He shook his head, making some small gestures with his hand before kissing his fingers and looking up at Karesh, obviously trying hard to keep his eyes from the passenger seat's occupant. "The Bringer of Light. He is here, now, with you. Do not tell me this isn't so, for I see it with my own eyes, here, right before me. This is a sign, a great and holy sign. You must go, if he is here then so is the other. You are needed far from here. Go!"

He turned suddenly, wheeling away on his prosthetic leg before disappearing inside the shack. The door slammed shut and Karesh could hear the man praying over the gusty breeze and flapping of the tarp. He left more than enough cash for the gas under a rock beside the pump before climbing in and starting the truck.

"Who was that?" Aaron asked. "It sounded like he knew my name."

"He doesn't know your name," Karesh replied, gunning the engine and pulling away from the station. "He knows what your name means, and what you are here to do."

Chapter Seventeen

Drexler stepped out of the elevator into the Hub atrium, met by a half dozen armed soldiers. One stepped forward to intercept him, holding out a hand.

"Screw my ID!" Drexler yelled, pushing past and striding across the atrium floor toward the corridor and Alex's lab.

There were already two of Akers' men inside. Both wore crisp blue suits and resembled the FBI agents who were, hopefully, leaving the complex right about now. The farther away they were from this mess, the less he had to worry about. At least for the time being. One of the men stepped forward.

"Dr. Drexler, we are still in the process of securing the lab, but what I can tell you is that, judging by what evidence we have here, and here—he pointed to the two bullet holes in the door—Dr. Bishop was not wounded when he fled the scene. What I can tell you is that a data file *was* downloaded to a removable drive and deleted from the main system. I'm having tech dig deeper to see what they can find about what data was stolen exactly."

"Stolen?" Drexler said, snapped out of his stupor as he surveyed the wrecked laboratory. "What do you mean, 'stolen'? No one is saying anything was taken yet, agent..."

"Fisher, sir."

"Agent Fisher, right. Well, until we have definitive proof that Dr. Bishop, or anyone else for that matter, has taken anything, or indeed even acted in a way that violates project security or Apex codes of conduct, he will be treated as a missing person and possibly wounded, is that clear?"

The agent nodded, unfazed. "Yes, sir. We are searching the complex right now, starting with the main building, and all checkpoints are on high alert. Nothing is getting in or out."

"Ok, very good. Do you have the surveillance feed? Walk me through what happened here."

The agent lifted his data pad and pulled up the same camera image of the lab that Drexler had been watching in his office. The agent scrubbed the video to the point where Alex was sitting in a chair with a figure in a lab coat standing in front of him. Whoever it was knew there was a camera above them and stood so that it was impossible to see a face.

"We thought you might be able to help us identify this person, sir. We've looked through the whole segment and at no point does she give us a clear enough look to make a positive ID."

Drexler watched as the woman—he had to assume that it even was a woman—and Alex talked. He saw Alex try to stand and push her aside, wincing as he was struck in the face and wrestled to the floor. The image showed the woman's back and Alex's legs for the next minute or so, until the woman got up.

"Wait," Drexler said, pointing at the screen. "Back up, just a second. Is that...is that a gun?"

The agent clicked back a few seconds and then paused just as the woman moved her arm close to her side. The frozen image showed what looked like a gun in her hand.

"I can't say for sure, but it looks like one from where I'm standing," the agent said.

"Oh, Alex," Drexler said, as the agent continued the video. He watched in silence as both Alex and the woman disappeared out of shot, probably into the lab extension. A few minutes later, Alex could be seen rushing around and then out of the lab, apparently none the worse for wear. Another minute passed and the woman walked quickly across the lab, following Alex from the room.

The agent paused the video. "That's about it, sir," he said. "We have Dr. Bishop in the lab, working, before the incident, but there is some missing video where the feed went down at 02:59."

The alarm droned outside in the hallway. Drexler was momentarily distracted by it. "What do you mean, the feed went down? It stopped recording?"

"No, sir, it didn't stop recording. It just recorded a blank screen for about four minutes. When it came back online..."

Drexler just stared at the agent.

"Well, sir, when the feed came back on, the room was pretty much as you see it now, and Dr. Bishop was on the floor, over there." He pointed to where Alex had been laying, coughing up an oil slick.

Drexler shook his head. "So you're telling me that what *actually* happened wasn't even recorded on camera?" He balled his fists and slammed them down on the nearest worktop. "Will someone tell me what the *hell* just happened in here?" He took a few steps forward, then turned back to the agent. "And turn that damned thing off!"

*   *   *

"Help me get him up," Gabby said, holding Alex's head off the ground and quickly looking at the wound in his shoulder. "He's going to need blood if we can't get this stopped."

Jerry opened the back door of the Tahoe, then rushed back to help Gabby lift Alex to hit feet, maneuvering him to the door and into the truck, laying him along the back seat. "There's a field med kit in the back," he said. A moment later, the tailgate opened with a hiss of hydraulics and Jerry started moving plastic ballistic cases around until he found the bright orange med case.

"Put it right there," Gabby said, pointing to the center console between the two front seats. "We stop the bleeding, clean and wrap, and then get the hell out of here."

"Not sure if you noticed all the checkpoints we went through getting in here, boss. I'm thinking it'll be a little harder getting *out*."

They worked fast, Gabby pressing on the wound while Jerry tore open packets of gauze and pulled out sterilizer fluid. The bullet hole was in the side of Alex's shoulder, toward the back. Gabby couldn't see an exit wound. "It's either in his delt, or it went deeper somewhere," she said. There's no way we'll be able to pull it out here, either way. Get the quick clot on him and let's pressure wrap it for now. The sooner we're off this complex, the sooner we can get him looked at."

Jerry's hands worked with practiced, methodical speed. As soon as he placed an item on Alex's abdomen, Gabby scooped it up and applied it, discarding blood and fluid-soaked gauze and working fast to get a clean dressing on the wound.

"Ok, I think that's good," Gabby said, folding a fleece jacket and putting it under Alex's head before reaching for a blanket. As she drew it up over his body, her hands brushed his chest. She felt something, small and hard, and drew the blanket back, feeling over his shirt until she found the pocket. She drew out the flash drive and held it up.

"A data drive?" Jerry asked, leaning in the door and squinting at the small device.

"Looks like it," Gabby said, standing back from the door and looking down at her friend. "And who knows what's on it."

"This is getting real weird, real fast," Jerry said, stepping back and closing the door. He walked around the car and stood beside Gabby, bending to pick up a piece of gauze from the ground. "I'm not even going to try and guess what kind of protocol we should be following here, but I'm going with 'let's get him out of here first and I'll ask a boat load of annoying questions later'. However we play it, we can't just drive out of here with him taking a nap on the back seat, tinted windows or not."

Moving the cases around in the back was easy. Putting Alex's unconscious form back there, then stacking what cases they could in front of him before sliding the cargo cover into place, was not.

"If he moves, stretches, wakes up, whatever, it's over," Jerry said, standing back and looking at, what appeared to be, a normal, innocent, totally filled cargo space in the back of the Tahoe. He nodded. "I think we did pretty good. I mean, look at it..."

"Well let's hope they don't," Gabby said, pulling her coat around her. "Come on, the longer we wait, the longer our odds get. And it's freez..."

They were both suddenly caught in the bright glare of a pair of headlights as a car swept into the service yard. It drove right up to them, lights blinding like searchlights. Gabby shielded her eyes as someone got out of the car and walked toward them.

"Agents Morgane and Walker?" A soldier appeared, stepping forward in front of the car. Gabby nodded. "Guilty." Jerry almost laughed.

"I'm here to escort you back to the main gate," the soldier said. He suddenly stepped between them, to the open back of the Tahoe. "Picking something up?" he said, touching one of the black tactical cases.

"No, those are just field equipment cases," Gabby said. "Camera equipment, crime scene accessories. That kind of thing. You can open one up if you want."

The soldier put his hands on one of the upper most cases, then paused, appearing to look further into the back of the truck. Gabby and Jerry looked at one another as the soldier pushed one of the cases aside and reached between them.

"Well it looks..." he said, pulling his arm out, "you're holding out on me."

He turned around, raising his hand. He was holding a Snickers bar. Jerry immediately patted his jacket pockets.

"I'm guessing that is about to be confiscated," Gabby said, smiling.

The soldier reached up and pressed the button on the tailgate then stepped away as it swung down, slowly closing with a satisfying *thunk*. "Well yes ma'am. This is grade A contraband and I'm afraid I need to take it in as evidence."

Gabby held her hands up. "Well, you have our full cooperation, soldier," she said, clapping Jerry on the shoulder. "Isn't that right, partner?" Jerry looked a little disheartened. "Yes, that's right. Full... cooperation."

The soldier walked back to the car. "Well ok. Now this investigation is wrapped up, I'll lead the way back to the main gate. You have a lovely morning now."

The bitter cold had covered the windows with a layer of frost and it took a minute of running the heat at full blast to fully clear it. They followed the car to the first checkpoint and were just waved through. The same went for the second and third checkpoints. As they drew up toward the main gate, the area brightly floodlit, Jerry began tapping his fingers on the steering wheel.

"Don't do that," Gabby said. "You look like a guy who has an unconscious man in the trunk that he's trying to smuggle off a high security government installation."

"You're not helping."

The lead car pulled through the first gate as it slid open, stopping by the guard hut. The gate rattled closed behind them and another soldier appeared, stepping in front of the Tahoe, walking around to the driver's side. Jerry rolled the window down.

"Good morning sir," the soldier said dryly. "Just waiting for clearance. You should be on your way shortly." He tapped the windowsill and moved away, walking back around the front of the truck and over to the car. Gabby and Jerry sat silently as he talked to the car's driver and then straightened as the car pulled a u-turn, heading back through the gate and out of the bright pool of light, disappearing from view into the darkness. The front gate remained agonizingly closed.

THUMP!

Jerry jumped visibly at the heavy sound from the back of the truck. "Shit," he whispered. The guard looked over at them and slowly walked over.

"Come *on!*" Jerry whispered as the soldier approached. A murmur from the back and Jerry coughed, covering the sound.

"Everything ok, sir?" he asked, looking a little more intently into the Tahoe's interior, craning his neck so he could see between the seats into the back.

"Yeah, sorry," Jerry said. "My foot is still numb from standing around outside, waiting for our ride." He stamped a hard *thud* on the floor. "Trying to get some life back into it."

The soldier nodded, standing back slightly. "I need you to open the back, please, sir."

Jerry looked over at Gabby. She nodded slightly and Jerry turned back, smiling at the soldier. "Sure thing," he said, reaching down and pushing the tailgate release button.

"Good to go!" A voice yelled from the guard hut. They looked over as another soldier ran out, trotting over to the truck. The tailgate swung open slowly behind them. "Word came from Dr. Drexler himself," the young soldier said. "These guys are already searched and cleared. Priority clearance. They're good to go."

He turned and ran back, presumably to get out of the cold, and disappeared back inside the guard hut. Jerry went to open the door but the other soldier stopped him, holding the door closed with gloved hands. "It's ok, sir," he said. "I'll get that for you. You sit tight."

He walked to the back of the truck. Jerry could see him in the rearview, looking into the back. One more sound and they were toast. The seconds dragged. The soldier looked. Jerry held his breath.

"These cases," the soldier said, stepping back to Jerry's window. "You should secure them. Don't want them rolling around back there."

Thud.

Jerry went pale. He looked into the rearview, expecting the soldier to order him out of the car. The tailgate had closed.

"You drive carefully now," the soldier said, stepping back and waving at the guard hut.

"Thank you," Gabby said, as Jerry just sat there, staring at the soldier, barely managing a weak smile and a nod. "Have a good morning."

Chapter Eighteen

The business departure lounge at Heathrow International Airport in London, was, to all intents and purposes, a barrel full of fish, eager and waiting to be caught by the smooth, stealthy predator among them. A few feet away, a young priest sat, waiting for one of the two waitresses to bring him his Earl Grey. James noticed the way his gaze lingered on the waitress's skirt, a little longer than it should, and he smiled, offering a mental nod toward the man in turmoil.

"What takes you to the US?" James asked, as his own drink arrived. Coffee, black and unsullied by dairy or sweeteners.

The priest looked up from his book. "Convention," he replied, as James nodded a hello. James didn't prod and the priest raised the book, revealing the cover.

"The survival of Christianity in the technological age," James read aloud. "They have conventions for that?"

The priest smiled, unsure of whether he had suffered an insult or not. "It's actually the tenth anniversary this year. They moved it to the big convention center, next to the airport. I would think that it's quite a big deal."

"I'm sure it is," James replied. "All of those bible bashers under one roof. How many do you suppose will be there?"

The priest didn't flinch at the slight barb. "I am told upwards of two thousand. We are traveling from all over the world. Even Rome will have representatives there this year. It's a pressing issue."

James looked away, pondering. "That's one hell of an opportunity to make a difference."

The priest brightened. "Exactly! That's what we are all there for, to make sure that, as Christians, and those who drive the message around the world, starting with the people who need to hear about it on our very own doorsteps, we are able to utilize technology for good, instead of crumbling under the pressure of cyber-vilification and conspiracy theories that might, if left unchecked, weaken the faith of those less fortunate to be able to read the one true message."

James was nodding, eyes widening in mock awe. "Wow, Father, that is truly impressive. What a very well founded, thought out and articulated presentation. Are you going to speak?" The priest went to answer, but James continued, "Though, let me ask you a question." He shifted forward onto the edge of his seat. "Doesn't it seem odd to you that, with the power of the Almighty behind you, a religious fan base and foundation based on standards set two-thousand years ago, and your worldwide, unshakable faith, you need the help of the internet to stop, how did you put it...the vilification of Christianity?" A couple of pairs of eyes were turned their way, sensing the beginnings of a juicy debate.

"It's a simple way of saying that there is no need to pay heed to everything you read on the internet these days that diminish the power of our faith and make false claims of being able to disprove the existence of God."

"There are more ways to disprove the existence of God than to prove that he is real," James said. "Have you seen him?"

The priest smiled. He knew he was cornered now. There was no way to go except forward. "I see God every day, in the acts of kindness of real people, and every..."

"No," James said sternly. "Have you *seen* Him? Don't read more into the question. It's really very simple. Has He appeared to you? Has He appeared to anyone you know, have met or have heard of? Has He made his presence known to you in a real sense, not through the feelings of closeness with your maker you experience through your prayers and wishes and outdated, meaningless gestures." He waved his hand loosely in the air in the form of a crucifix. "But where is He when you really need him? When *you*, as a race, really need Him?"

A handful of other passengers had stopped what they were doing to spectate. James felt their eyes on him. He reveled in it, bursting to life inside as people hung on his every word. The priest stayed calm, but James could see the 'uh oh' in his eyes. He went for the jugular. "How about the Devil? You have absolute belief in God, ergo, you believe in the Devil, too. One cannot exist without the other, am I right?"

"Of course, we all know the story of..."

"And so, you are looking for strategies to counter the threat that modern social media and its burgeoning subculture poses to the very belief structure of Christianity itself, and all because of a few ardent atheist bloggers and their keyboard warrior followers who are making life more than difficult for all of your potential recruits, especially those who, God forbid, have internet access." James stood up and stepped close to the priest, who sat back in his chair. "I don't think that the Devil could've played a better hand, do you?"

"Ladies and gentlemen, we are now boarding executive class passengers, rows one through five. Please make your way to the boarding area. That's executive passengers, rows one through five. Thank you."

Suddenly, a man appeared at James' shoulder. Tall, solid and with an almost unnaturally chiseled jaw, he was bodyguard personified. "It's time to go, sir," he said, looking around the lounge, scanning faces, bags and exits.

James held the priest's gaze for a moment more before breaking into a wide grin and holding out his hand. The priest reached out and took it, and then winced as if he had suffered an electric shock. He quickly withdrew his hand and James smiled, holding up open palms. "I'm sorry, Father, my manners are shocking. Enjoy your conference. I hope the venue is as full as you hope it will be."

The priest watched James as he strode off, followed closely by his bodyguard. When he had disappeared down the boarding tunnel, the priest let out an audible sigh and collapsed back into the chair, sweating and pale, absently rubbing the palm of his hand.

"Are you all right, Father?" the business man to his left asked, reaching for a glass of water on the mahogany coffee table. The priest took a sip, hand shaking. "Yes, yes, thank you. I'm fine. Just... just a little taken aback. He... he was certainly very passionate there, wasn't he?"

The business man smiled, patting the priest on the back sympathetically and looking over toward the boarding tunnel. "Yeah, he put you through the ringer all right. Overstepped the mark, if you ask me."

The lady standing behind them nodded, frowning her displeasure. "Damned well rude, if you ask me."

In the forward section on the upper deck of the aircraft, James settled into the plush leather seats and eyed the stunning flight attendant as she moved from seat to seat, checking safety belts and fluffing pillows. He had bought every seat in the executive section, and his bodyguard, Matt, settled on the back corner seat on the far side of the cabin. James looked over at him, adjusting his seat, refusing an extra pillow and pulling out a copy of Recoil magazine from his bag. He noticed the picture of the half naked girl in camo paint and a torn tank top on the front cover and wondered absently if that kind of role playing might be worth exploring. He doubted he could get past the combat boots.

The plane was filling up behind and below them. He could feel the masses shuffling down the narrow aisles to their cramped seats, crammed in like the cattle they were. In a few hours he would be in New York and one step closer to his prize. He was under no illusions that this would be easier than Mr. Black had warned. Since his awakening before the Infinity Mirror, he had felt a steadily growing sense of knowledge and absolute confidence in himself and his abilities. Even though, at first, it had been something more than difficult to comprehend, let alone accept, Roland had shown him his true purpose. A purpose that would see him, and the Raven Group, as the newly established elitist power on the planet.

He felt excitement then, and struggled to keep from giggling out loud. He was still James Devlin, son of Thomas Devlin, the infamous financier, but he was now so much more. More than he could have hoped he would be and much more than his father, left behind now to run the stocks and money management systems he had been doing so well for his whole professional life.

He snorted, giddy at his meteoric rise to the top of the tree. Even old man Blakenstock himself could not order him around. And Mr. Black. *The* Mr. Black; first and only of his kind, and the one true heir to this cesspool that humanity had made of the world. James would make him proud and wanted nothing more than to find Alex Bishop, retrieve the Code and return home, jubilant in his victory. He glanced over at Matt again, nose deep in the magazine, and wondered how long it would take for the novelty of his presence to wear off.

Their contact would be waiting at JFK to take them to the Akron hotel in lower Manhattan, a high end, exclusive building owned by The Raven Group. Mr. Black would be very happy if he could wrap this up and be back in London before the end of the week. As he reclined the seat, he smiled, and began to imagine the ways he would screw the flight attendant in the private bathroom after takeoff.

"First play, then work," he said to himself, a wolfish grin playing on his lips.

Chapter Nineteen

Karesh pulled the Land Rover into a wide dirt road, lined on either side by lush palm groves. The sun was low in the west, accentuating the natural red of the dirt and sand, kicked up into a quarter-mile long dust cloud behind them on the road from Damascus, a low, hulking mirage to the northeast. The tree-lined road led them straight to a solitary farmstead, a group of low stone buildings set back from the road amidst the palms. As they approached, Karesh spotted the guards; first at the stone arch, marking the entrance to the grounds, then at various points along the half-mile driveway, half-hidden but visible enough to act as a subtle deterrent to any would-be visitor.

Pulling into the courtyard of the main building, a small entourage appeared, walking over to greet them as they came to a stop behind another Land Rover, identical to their own, just a lot cleaner.

"Stay here," Karesh instructed, and then climbed out, walking around the truck to meet the greeting party. Aaron could see no weapons, save for the ceremonial daggers that each man had tucked into his sash. Their white smocks gleamed brightly, even in the approaching twilight, and Aaron thought that they must have an impossible task keeping everything so clean out here, surrounded by red dust and sand as far as the eye could see. Karesh was talking and Aaron noticed that he kept his arms at his sides as the men watched him intently. Every expression was blank and they seemed to be regarding him with a sort of suspicious curiosity.

None of them looked toward the truck, until another man appeared, older, from the open doors of the main building. He emerged from the shadows of the arched doorway and ambled slowly toward them, his movements that of relaxed ease, unhurried and exuding a calm that soon washed over the men as he drew close. He stepped through the group and extended a hand toward Karesh, who took it, stepping forward as both men exchanged kisses to the cheek, nodding and mouthing their respects.

All eyes turned toward the Land Rover and Aaron felt suddenly as if he was being inspected, like a sideshow curiosity, or exotic pet. The old man moved slowly past Karesh, walking up to the passenger door and opening it slowly. His expression broke into a warm smile and he bowed slightly. "For many generations we have been expecting you," he said. His voice was low, rasping and dried out by a lifetime of living in the desert. The deep creases on his face and hands painted a portrait of a man who had lived and worked outside, baked and beaten by the sun. The laughter lines, Aaron noticed, were the deepest.

"Please," he said, stepping back and gesturing for Aaron to get out. "Welcome home."

*   *   *

As the waning desert sun broke through the lined drapes in shades of golden yellow and warm orange, Aaron awoke to the sound of running water. Sitting slowly and swinging his legs over the edge of the simple bed, he stood and walked to the nearest window, pushing aside the drape and peering outside. The inner courtyard was a lush oasis of palms, foliage and exotic flowers, surrounding a sparkling pool of water that was fed by a rocky waterfall, set against the far wall of the courtyard.

"The purest sense of life and serenity," a voice said from behind him, and he turned to see the old man, standing in the doorway, a folded white robe in his arms. He bowed slightly and stepped into the room. "It is an oasis, not just of water and life, but of free spirit and light."

Aaron let the drape fall back over the window, leaving a single, golden shaft of dust-filled light stabbing the floor between them. He nodded awkwardly as the old man approached, holding out the robe. "Thank you, uh..."

"Abdul-Rahim Bayhas," the old man said, bowing again. "But Rahim will more than suffice."

"Servant of the merciful," Aaron said, taking the robe. "And a lion of the desert."

Rahim smiled. "This old lion is perhaps a little wiser today than he is courageous. Some call me The Teacher." He moved to the small table beside the window and poured a glass of water from the clay jug, lifting the glass and examining the liquid in the shaft of sunlight. "I hope you are well rested. When you are dressed, please join us in the garden. Sahim will be outside. He will show you the way."

"What is in the garden?" Aaron asked, as Rahim walked toward the door.

"The reason why you are here," he said, turning with a slight nod before disappearing into the hallway. A stocky man in a red robe leaned in and pulled the door closed after him.

A few minutes later, Aaron was walking along a wide, shaded hallway. He could feel the cool tiled floor through the bottom of his sandals. The air carried the scent of jasmine, freshly cut grass and lavender. The gentle burbling of running water echoed around the walls and arches. As the hallway opened out to the courtyard, Aaron paused and took a moment. The garden was even more breathtaking from out here and he looked down at his toes, touching the edge of the lush grass that ran the entire length of the courtyard, thick and soft and vibrant green. A wall of palm trees enclosed the garden, open to the cloudless evening sky, and a multitude of exotic flowers and plants—many the likes of which he had never seen—were blooming amongst the trees and shrubs. To the far right, the waterfall fed a large rock pool. As Aaron looked, he noticed that it wasn't a water feature, constructed by people for decoration and effect, but a natural rock formation that tapped into a water source somewhere beneath his feet, deep underground.

"This is why this place was built," Rahim said, stepping up beside him. He placed his hand on Aaron's shoulder and gestured to the garden with the other. "When the very first builders here finished this part of the main house, they saw that the palm trees were starting to grow, placed just so, as you see them now. They planted nothing. Not a single plant or blade of grass. This is just, well, as it was then. While the house was built around the waterfall, the garden appeared by itself, forcing the builders to extend the courtyard and push out the south side of the structure."

Aaron was mesmerized. It appeared to be the perfect oasis, manicured and pristine, at the center of a house that seemed to exude peace and calm. He felt at home here, at peace. "When did you find this place? How did you find it?" he asked.

"Do you see the walls, here? The pillars over there?" Rahim pointed to a nearby wall and then across to the other side of the courtyard. The upper level was a row of open Roman arches, their edges worn and softened by sand and time.

"Yes," Aaron replied.

"They were built in the time of Tiberius, Emperor of Rome. You can see that they cannot at all be mistaken for anything other than Roman in design." He stepped onto the grass and Aaron followed him to the center of the courtyard garden so that they were surrounded by lush plants and sandstone walls, directing shafts of dying sunlight through their high arched windows.

"It is written that Tiberius spent year after year in Campania, a hundred or so miles south of Rome, but..." Rahim waved his finger. "...he spent only the first two years in Campania. The reason he was away for so long, and was thought to have disappeared entirely, was because he was much, much farther away."

He turned and walked beside the rock wall that led under the upper level. Aaron followed as Rahim walked toward the back wall. He led Aaron to a narrow recess, covered with a long drape of linen that wafted slowly in the breeze of his approach. He pulled it aside and stood back so Aaron could see. In the recess, carved neatly into the rock of the wall and decorated with fine carved edging and tile work, was a small pillar, perhaps four feet high. Sitting on top was the chipped and worn white marble bust of a man, obviously Roman.

"Is this...?" Aaron said, pointing clumsily at the bust.

"Tiberius, yes," Rahim nodded. "By the time our people came to call this place their permanent home, Tiberius was gone—back to Campania—but not before he passed on ownership to what is now the extended family of the people you see all around you. Some say he was later poisoned, as seemed to be the way of the Romans and their politicians. What he left us was a legacy of peace, of wisdom, and of the divinely spiritual."

Rahim dropped the drape and guided Aaron back out into the garden. The shadows were deep now, as the sun dropped below the horizon to the west. Walking past the waterfall, they sat by the glistening pool. Aaron dipped his fingertips into the water. It was crystal clear. "And so, Tiberius found this place, this oasis in the middle of the desert."

Rahim nodded. "He did, but he found it only because his former governor, Piso, had plundered every village and caravan from the deep desert to the shores of the Mediterranean. One such caravan was encamped here, on this very spot. It was the famous general, Germanicus, who clashed with Piso, and attempted to have him recalled to Rome, which ultimately led to his poisoning at the hands of the governor, later that same year.

"And so, Piso, seeking Tiberius's favor, wrote to him describing a wondrous discovery, a hidden gem, deep within the Syrian desert. It was this secret, this place, that drew Tiberius out of Rome on his so-called vacations. In the years that followed, this place was built and defended and tended by the ancestors of the men and women you see here today. These ancestors were the beginnings of The Overwatch, and they have been protecting this place, and its prophecy, for nearly two-thousand years."

"Prophecy? What prophecy?"

Rahim looked at Aaron, placing a hand gently onto the younger man's arm. "That, my young warrior, is where you come in."

Aaron frowned and shook his head slightly, confused. "Warrior? Me? But there's... how can it be me?" He looked at Rahim, steadily holding Aaron's wide-eyed gaze. "There is a mistake," Aaron said. "I've been a cleric since I was a boy. A messenger. Nothing more."

"Every man has his place in this world, Aaron, except that your place is very different than anyone else's." He paused, resting a hand on Aaron's shoulder. "Come, you will understand everything after the awakening."

Aaron looked up at the old man. He was afraid. Rahim nodded, he could see the fear and uncertainty in his eyes clearly enough. Still, he knew how well prepared the young man was, even though he didn't yet know it himself. He knew Aaron was ready. His training was complete, undertaken as part of a daily 'meditation' routine that was intended, outwardly, to reinforce an overall sense of peace and focus as Aaron was secretly groomed from birth to fulfill a prophecy written nearly two millennia ago.

Rahim led Aaron across the grass and through an archway to a wide, gloomy passageway that led into the belly of the main building. Long sheets of linen drifted and billowed in the warm evening breeze and Aaron could taste honey in the air. The old terra-cotta tiles were warm beneath his feet and, as he passed into the deep shadow from the garden, his robe held the warmth of the evening air against his back. Even with the events of the past few days, and the information he was trying to process, he felt calm, like the cool, relaxed calm of an experienced fighter about to engage in battle. He had always considered that his greatest gift was being able to remain focused and relaxed in the face of great pressure and stress, but had considered it nothing more than a fortunate personality trait. Now, though, he was wondering if it was more than that, and was thankful for it.

They approached a wide, heavy wooden door—so big that a car could pass easily through it—set into the wall at the end of the passageway. Aaron looked back, the opening to the garden appearing as a subtle pastel portrait at the end of a long, wide tunnel. He could see the linen sheets moving wistfully across the entryway, offering glimpses of grass, plants and rocks beyond. Rahim touched his shoulder and he turned back to the door. After a moment, the sound of bolts being drawn thudded through the thick wood and echoed down the hallway. The doors swung open slowly, pushed by two robed men, heads down, straining against the heavy wood. The hinges were as thick as Aaron's forearm and he wondered what was so precious that it needed to be kept behind such fortifications.

"When you enter," Rahim said, guiding Aaron slowly toward the doorway, "Say nothing. Reserve any questions until we are together again in the garden." He paused, stepping forward to stand in front of Aaron. "Do not fear. There is nothing behind these doors except good people who have dedicated their whole lives to doing good things for good people. Your confusion is a fog, Aaron, and it will soon be lifted. Trust me when I say that everyone who has been standing beside you has been leading you to this moment, to your destiny, and it is a truly wonderful thing."

Aaron nodded slowly and took a deep breath, still painfully uncertain, and obviously afraid. "Will Karesh be here?" he asked.

Rahim smiled. "He will be waiting for you. He has high hopes for you. As we all do. Now come, it is time for you to fulfill your birthright."

They walked through the opening and the two men pushed the doors closed, their heads bowed, eyes on the floor the entire time. As the doors thudded shut, Aaron looked behind him. The men slid the heavy bolts across the doors and a wave of panic washed over him. He took another breath, feeling Rahim's hand squeeze his shoulder. Linen sheets hung from the ceiling, forming a moving wall of partitions that were pulled aside as they walked toward the center of the large room. Aaron could sense the number of people in the room with them, even though he could only make out the vague shapes of unmoving figures, standing aside, obscured by the sheets and backlit by the golden glow of low burning torches that lined the room in wide, bowl-like copper sconces.

More sheets were pulled away before them until, finally, the center of the room opened up and they stepped down into a circular area, ringed with burning torches and stone benches, a low stone platform at the center. The entire room, and indeed the whole building, was constructed in the old roman ways, using blocks of granite, marble and sandstone, some transported from vast distances, others carved from local quarries and all aging in the most comforting and magnificent way. The room felt warm, inviting and cozy; the soft orange-red tones of the stone walls and floors only intensified by the numerous flames that were burning in the beaten copper and stone sconces all around. The shadows were extensive, yet inviting, and Aaron felt a clear sense of peace and safety amongst the room's occupants, of which there were perhaps two dozen, all identically robed and standing quietly with an almost tangible sense of anticipation.

Seated in an arc around the central 'circle', like a sort of informal court, were seven older men, all clad in soft white robes, immaculately kept, but worn with the age of years of daily use. They all wore deep red sashes around their waists, except for one, the oldest of the men, sitting at the top of the arc. His sash was as his robe; white, and worn with years of use and washing. As Aaron approached, guided forward gently by Rahim, the elder stood. Aaron noticed that there was a hole in the ceiling, directly above the center of the circular area. He couldn't see to where it led from where he stood, but it disappeared up into the ceiling, shrouded in deep shadow, like the mirrored image of a deep garden well.

The elder stepped forward, moving past the other men, still seated and watching Aaron intently. "Welcome to my house," he said, his voice deep and welcoming, dried by the desert air. "And I welcome you, Abdul-Rahim Bayhas, faithful servant and lifelong friend." He bowed slightly and Aaron turned to see Rahim return the gesture as he stepped to the side and took a seat on a small stone stool, just outside the stone tiled circle. The elder stood in front of Aaron and looked him square in the eyes, a custom Aaron was very familiar with. It gave the older man a chance to gauge the young man standing before him, measure him and look him over, without doing him the discourtesy of physically inspecting him in front of the entire room.

Finally, he reached up and clasped his hands on Aaron's shoulders. "Since I can remember, my father, and grandfather, have told me the story of the one who would come to us, the one who would do battle with the forces of darkness in a time of great turmoil, the one who will bring light back to the world from which it had faded, the one who would cast the beast's offspring back into the abyss and give the world of man a new chance at an existence free of evil."

He gripped Aaron's shoulders and grinned briefly, flashing rows of perfect teeth in a brilliant smile. "And here, finally, you are. You have no idea how very pivotal this time is, Aaron. Not just for us, or for you, but for all of mankind." He stepped back and dropped his arms to his sides. "I know this is a lot to you, but I also know that you understand the gravity of what is happening, even if you don't know how you understand it. Come, sit here with me. Soon you will know everything there is to know, your secrets unlocked and your mind and heart set free. Soon, you will feel only strength and knowledge and the solemn, singular confidence you will need to face the journey ahead of you." He bowed slightly. "I am Merek, the guardian of the bloodline of light. It is my honor to meet you, Aaron."

* * *

Aaron was shown to one end of the low stone platform in the center of the circle—what looked like a low stone bed. He sat, straight and proper, on the thin mattress, draped with a simple woven blanket. When he was seated, Merek took his seat opposite him. It was only then, when everyone was settled and the room was silent, that the six other men in the circle stood and bowed, deep and long, before sitting quietly once more.

A moment later, two women appeared, moving between the linen sheets as they made their way toward the center of the room, carrying a large, flat wooden box between them and clad in flowing white linen gowns that brushed and swept the floor around their feet as they walked. When they entered the circle, everyone stood. Aaron moved to do likewise, but Merek waved him to stay seated. The two women placed the box on the bed behind him. He wanted so badly to turn and look at what they were doing, but instead stayed still, staring straight ahead as Merek and the others looked at him. Merek stood suddenly and stepped forward, gesturing for Aaron to stand.

He turned and looked down as the two women lifted what looked like a soft white shawl from the box and placed it carefully on the bed, unfolding it and laying it open with great care, its frayed edges hanging over the side of the platform, almost touching the floor. When they were satisfied with how perfectly it was placed, they closed the box and carried it away, disappearing in the forest of slowly wafting linen sheets. Merek stood beside Aaron and they looked down at the white fabric in silence. There was a sense of awe in the room and Aaron was about to ask what it was, when Merek spoke.

"For over two thousand years, this has been in our keeping, to be safeguarded, protected and kept until the time came to honor its true purpose. That time has finally come, and now, as you have arrived, just as it has been written, the time has come for your awakening." Aaron was trembling, more with anticipation than through fear, and Merek placed a warm hand on his back. "My son, do not be afraid. When this is over, you will see everything, know everything and rejoice in the knowledge that we have unlocked in you. This is your destiny, and while a great burden rests upon your shoulders, so does a great power kneel at your side. You will never be alone, and every moment of doubt and fear will be dispelled by His guiding hand as He stands by you, shoulder to shoulder on this, the most important quest any man has dared to undertake."

He turned Aaron and guided him to sit once more. The other six men in the circle stood and stepped up to the sides of the stone bed, three on each side. As Merek pushed Aaron back gently, half a dozen pairs of hands reached out and held him, easing him back until he was almost touching the mattress. He saw, then, that the hole in the ceiling went up through every level above to the open air, giving him a narrow, tunnel-vision view of the sky above, dark purple and with a spattering of twinkling stars. Then, as hands slipped behind his legs and one hand cradled his head, he was lifted effortlessly, suspended perfectly horizontally above the bed. He stared at the darkening sky through his own personal telescope in the ceiling above him. Merek walked around to stand above his head and placed his hands on either cheek. His palms were warm and comforting, and Aaron found himself relaxed, despite his precarious position.

"In the time of man, we mould you," Merek said, his tone smooth and somber. "In the time of angels we guide you, in the time of peril we turn to you, in the time of victory we honor you."

The six men repeated his words, their timing perfect, as if they had been rehearsing this moment their whole lives. The pressure on Aaron's face increased, and he felt the room swim for a moment, tilting as if he was dizzy from spinning, feeling as though he would roll and fall to the floor at any moment.

"From the light, you were born to us, and into darkness you lead, a champion among men, willing to give all so that all evil can be banished."

The room continued to spin and Aaron felt a rising panic as his vision became ringed with a mist of darkness, beginning like a shadow on the edge of his senses, and growing steadily deeper as he tried to breathe and turn his head. Merek held him tightly as he continued, rubbing his temples with his thumbs. "The Hidden One awakens, breathe your spirit into his soul. The Hidden One awakens, cover him with your shield of light. The Hidden One *awakens.*"

Aaron felt himself begin to fall, slowly at first, and then faster and faster until he could hear the air rushing past his ears in an incessant roar. He wanted to scream, to cry out for them to stop, to let go, but he couldn't feel their hands on him anymore. He was just falling, rushing toward a warm, deep abyss, and just as he felt convinced he was about to hit the bottom and smash his body on some unseen rocks, he suddenly felt softness beneath him and the warm, inviting feeling of being enveloped in something other worldly and infinitely comforting.

Merek looked down at Aaron's limp form and checked his eyes. They were rolled up into his head, his breathing steady, and his heartbeat strong and measured. "He is there now," he said, and the other men stepped away softly, returning to take their seats on the stone benches. The soft white blanket had been wrapped around his body, cocooning him, and he looked like a swaddled infant, calm and peaceful in an oversized crib.

Turning toward Rahim, Merek held out a hand. "Old friend, the Grail." Rahim lifted a simple wooden cup, filled with water, and held it out to Merek with both hands. Standing over Aaron's head, he dipped his fingers into the cool liquid and anointed Aaron's forehead with the sign of the cross as everyone in the room simultaneously made the sign of the crucifix in the air before them. Merek stepped back, looking up at the ceiling and opening his arms wide. "He is here," he said, his tone stronger, more confident. "Your right hand is among us, safe at last, as you wished. And now we send him out, out into the darkness, into the chaos for which we have spent his life preparing. He is your spear, your guiding hand, your voice and your faith. Watch over him, as we have done from afar. Keep him as you intend, on the path of righteousness, as he takes up the Holy sword against your sworn enemy, in the war to end all wars."

He looked down and reached out, holding the cup over Aaron's upturned face. "Fill him now with your divine strength and protect him as he takes up arms against those most foul. Protect this, your champion, your warrior, your child of light!"

He tilted the cup and the liquid poured out, streaming down toward Aaron's face. As the stream fell to within an inch of his skin, it suddenly exploded, ignited into an ethereal flame, like a liquid fire, sparking and crackling, bright and harsh in the dimly lit room. Everyone gasped, leaning back from the fiery spectacle. The fire spread quickly over the entirety of Aaron's prone form, touching nothing but the air an inch from his body, enveloping him in a flaming sarcophagus of crackling fire.

Merek stepped back, almost dropping the cup to the stone floor before handing it back to Rahim, who took it as if holding the most precious thing on earth. Merek clasped his hands tightly together, as if in urgent prayer, and leaned forward, a few feet from the head of the bed. He gritted his teeth against the fierce heat of the fire, turning now from a bright white yellow to a greener hue and finally to blue, casting a cool ghostly light over every face in the room. The ends of Merek's hair began to curl and burn as he stood there, unmoving in the heat. He cried out then and the flames intensified, glowing hotter, the roar of the flames growing even louder.

He reached out a shaking, clenched fist toward the fire, grimacing with sheer effort. As his fist hovered over Aaron's throat, he opened his hand. The silver crucifix fell from his palm and turned to a shiny, molten stream that passed through the layer of flame and onto Aaron's exposed chest, just above the blanket that covered the rest of his torso. A blinding white light formed there, growing brighter and larger until no one could help but shield their eyes as the light filled the room. Suddenly, a flash of blinding blue white light exploded upwards in a stream of liquid fire, up through the opening in the ceiling and out, up into the night sky.

On a hillside, four miles to the west, two shepherd boys sat stunned, their eyes turned toward the thin, arrow straight, shaft of light, reaching for the heavens in the middle of the deep desert. One stood, raising his hand and pointing toward the inky black sky, his friend too dumbfounded to climb to his feet. They were not alone. The next day, the social media tongues would be wagging around the world over the phenomenon that would come to be known as the 'Finger of God'.

In the room, the roar of the flames intensified once more to a tremendous crescendo and people began to back away, some kneeling, their arms covering their heads as if waiting for the ceiling to cave in upon them. Merek drew back, unable to bear the heat and brilliance of the flaming shroud that covered Aaron's body. As he turned away, the roaring sound grew still louder, filling every nuance of space in the room before, finally, exploding in an immense thunderclap, and sending a shockwave outwards, knocking the men from their seats. The flash of light abruptly disappeared and the room was filled with a sudden and complete silence.

After a moment, Merek sat up on the floor, dropping the arm that was shielding his face, and turned toward the bed. Aaron was sitting up, facing away from him, a steady mist of steam flowing from his skin and the white shawl still wrapped around him. Merek could see his shoulders slowly rising and falling as he breathed, slow and deep and steady. As Merek climbed slowly to his feet, the other elders in the circle were still on the floor, seated throughout their stone bench seats. They cast wide-eyed glances amongst one another, but none of them made a move to get up. Merek walked slowly around the bed to stand in front of Aaron, sitting straight and still, hands resting on his lap as the white shawl hugged his shoulders.

"Aaron," he said quietly. The steam was still lifting from his exposed skin and head, like an athlete who had just come inside from a bitter cold run. "Aaron, can you hear me?"

Aaron lifted his chin and looked up at the older man, his expression calm and unreadable. He seemed to regard the old man for a moment, tilting his head slightly as he stared, almost curious with his gaze. He went to stand and Merek reached out a hand, helping the young man slowly to his feet. Immediately, the other elders rose to their feet, a few of them moving forward, reaching out their hands as the shawl threatened to slip from Aaron's shoulders. He held onto it, though, and they hesitated, keeping their distance as Aaron stood straight, stretching with a deep sigh.

"Hello, Merek," he said after a moment. "Yes, I can hear you."

"Do you remember what happened?" Merek asked, frowning as Aaron stood slowly, gathering his bearings. Although the Guardians were well prepared for the ceremony, every pair of eyes in the room was wide in silent awe at what they had just witnessed. To live a life guided by a code, determined by a prophecy more than two-thousand years old is one thing.

To actually see that prophecy come to pass with your own eyes, is another thing altogether.

"I remember the water," Aaron said. "And I could see only the stars." He lifted his head again, looking up at the opening in the ceiling. "Then..." he drifted off, closing his eyes and swaying slightly. Merek moved closer, anticipating the need to help if Aaron should fall. He opened his eyes, still staring up at the night sky above. "Then I saw my past, my childhood, and every moment since, and I heard every word ever spoken to me about my place, my purpose." He dropped his head, looking at Merek, his eyes full of knowledge and cool wisdom. "I see the path ahead of me, and I see know what I must face."

Merek nodded, "You will need to rest, and bathe." He stepped forward, reaching for the shawl where it crossed over Aaron's chest. "And this..." he pulled the shawl apart and revealed Aaron's chest. "Will need to be cleaned and covered until it heals." Aaron didn't look down. A metallic ring of silver was embedded in the skin of his upper chest. Perhaps an inch and a half in diameter the symbol of the Guardians was formed inside; a crude crucifix with a slanted bar half way up the central post. The skin around the edges was raw and crisped, as if the ingot had been branded into the flesh.

Aaron seemed untroubled by it and Merek nodded. "And this, we should return it now to its resting place. It has been kept for this very moment and is sadly too fragile to be handled too much." He touched the shawl and Aaron nodded, releasing his light grip on the old garment, allowing two of the other elders to step forward and gently lift it away, placing it carefully on the bed once more.

"Until today, this is something I never knew existed," Aaron said quietly, looking down at the almost threadbare fabric on the bed.

"The last shoulders this warmed were those of Jesus Christ himself," Merek replied. "Kept in secret, for but one use, and handed down through generations of Guardians until the time came for the prophecy to be realized. And now it has passed its divine grace on to you. You will need its protection, and you will need the protection and guidance of every Guardian on earth, for that is the purpose of The Overwatch, Aaron, to serve you and your quest, because should you fall, humanity falls with you."

Aaron turned to look at him as one of the elders placed another light blanket around his shoulders before bowing and backing away. "It sounds so simple, doesn't it?"

"Well, it really is," Merek replied, guiding Aaron past the bed and up the two steps, out of the circle. "If we were to sit here and dissect the whole thing—what lies ahead of us—we could pick at many, many details and get no further than a simple discussion."

They paused as a man walked toward them, holding a package, wrapped in cloth. He stopped in front of Merek, bowed, and handed him the package before withdrawing silently.

"You remember this?" Merek asked, unwrapping the object to reveal a large, hard back book. "This is what brought you here, what set you on the first steps of your journey." He held it out toward Aaron and he reached out, taking it in both hands.

"I took it with me to the fortress at Palmyra," Aaron said. "That was my task. My counsel in Aleppo made this very important to me." He looked up. "I'm sure you know this."

"Indeed," Merek nodded, "We are all connected, as you well know." He reached out and tapped the book gently. "This is the key to the final part of your journey here."

Aaron held it up, examining it, but didn't open it. "A token of importance to keep me focused? Something to add urgency to my step? I thought it was something important, and Professor Salomon..." he drifted off, recalling how the old professor had been shot right in front of him. His old robe, stained with his blood, was gone now, and he suddenly wondered where it was and how he could see it again.

"I am sorry about the professor," Merek said. "He was a father to us all, and his passing is a huge loss." He reached for the book, sliding it from Aaron's hands and opening the front cover. "But this is no token, no mere object of incentive." He held it up, showing Aaron two pages, crammed full of hand-inked writing, the swirling, cursive lines covering the pages from edge to edge. "It is the journal of the Guardians. It chronicles our time from the days of Tiberius, when alliances were struck, the buildings you see around you were first built and the secret of the spring were recorded."

Aaron cocked his head, and Merek smiled. "Come, I'll show you."

* * *

The garden was lit with burning torches, hanging from ornate metal sconces on the walls. Guards were posted on the upper levels, some with long rifles and others with binoculars, standing in the archways and looking out into the darkness, scanning the rows of palm trees and the darker depths of the desert beyond. Merek led Aaron back to the waterfall, gurgling cheerily into the rock pool and disappearing into a number of natural channels as the water ran back down into the rock below.

"We know that Tiberius learned something from Piso that he felt needed to be kept secret at all costs. We think that he recalled Piso to stand trial in Rome simply to remove him from the equation so he could pursue this new interest alone. It's also true that he came to form the Overwatch, and to help shape our purpose. Tiberius determined that he would aid us with a neutral governorship of the desert provinces, withdrawing some of the fringe garrisons and effectively giving us breathing room to exist here under the secret protection of Rome, without the senate or the new governor ever being aware of it."

Aaron nodded. "So what made him do all of that? What made him change his life, commit political murder, abandon his position of Emperor of Rome? Why did he do all that?"

Merek reached down and scooped a handful of water from the pool, letting it drain through his fingers. "Because this changed him. This water, blessed by God, gave him new life, and new purpose." He tilted his hand and the water dripped from his palm. Aaron watched the new ripples mix with the undulating surface of the pool. "And when he died, he was one hundred and fifty-nine years old." Aaron rose to his feet silently, his eyes wide as he absorbed the incredible words. Merek smiled, shaking his head, unable to hold back his laughter.

"The fountain of youth?" Aaron asked, his voice cutting through the relative silence in the garden. "Is that what you are saying? That this is the fountain of youth? Right here, in the middle of the desert?"

"It's not what we would call it," Merek chuckled. "To us it is the most special place and the source of something divine that we have been charged with protecting for two millennia. We cannot help the properties that the water holds, any more than you can help the prophecy that brought you to this place and will soon send you out to earn a great victory. This place, and its properties will ultimately play very small a part in what is to come, and yet it is the foundation of what brought us all together, what created the faith we all share."

"Faith? In God?"

"Faith in you."

Aaron smiled, nodding his concession. He believed every word that Merek had told him. There was no need for anything but the truth. Within the folds of the inner layers of the Overwatch was where he had been raised. Nothing that had ever been told to him was untrue, and what he had been told about the journey that lay ahead of him now frightened him to the core.

"It's time for you to rest," Merek said, guiding him away from the waterfall, the old book clutched under one arm. "You have a long trip ahead and you need to be prepared."

"I can't stay," Aaron said as they walked back toward his room. "I'm leaving tonight. The enemy is already ahead of us."

Chapter Twenty

Marcus pulled the car up to the front of the old red brick building. The thirty feet of white painted curb was reserved for special guests only and Marcus planted the big car squarely in the center of the space. He got out, grimacing slightly at the frigid temperature, and opened the back door for Mrs. Galasky. A doorman approached, tipping his hat in greeting and gestured for her to walk on, toward the polished brass revolving door. Marcus stepped beside her and she took his arm.

"You go on ahead, Marcus," she said. "This will take a little while and I'm sure he will arrange for someone to take me home after we are done."

Marcus smiled, "Sorry to refuse an order, ma'am, but I'm responsible for your safety. I'll be fine right here. I have a good book and a thermos full of hot tea."

She looked up at him and smiled, shaking her head. "I swear, you're as stubborn as your father. He would tell me the same thing, I'm sure, from under the hood of some old jalopy. He is very sweet, as stubborn as a mule. You're just better looking."

Marcus laughed and paused as they reached the door, letting her hand slip away from his arm. When she had disappeared inside, stepping into a private elevator just off the lobby, Marcus went back to the car and settled in. Drawing a worn paperback from the glove box, he poured a steaming cup of tea and turned a page, thanking his lucky stars for car seat warmers.

The building was not very old, but had been under the same ownership since it was built, in nineteen twenty-nine. It rose thirty-one stories into the night sky and housed one of the largest top floor suites in the city. The elevator doors opened to an expansive, blue marble-floored room, softly lit with large off-white shaded lights, hanging low from the darkened ceiling. The high windows that made up the entire far wall offered an unobstructed view of the city, stretching away like a sea of pinprick lights in the darkness. A slender man in a grey suit stepped forward, the coiled wire of his earpiece giving him away as inner sanctum security. "Leonore," he said, extending a hand in greeting. "Very good to see you again. It's been some time."

Mrs. Galasky took his hand, smiling as he bowed, touching the back of her fingers to his lips.

"Far too long, Eric," she replied. "Thirty years by my count. You look no different, as usual. How are things? Keeping busy, I trust."

"But not too busy," Eric replied with a wry smile, turning to lead the way toward a group of couches and armchairs by the windows. The set up was open, and yet immediately warm and inviting, with worn suede furniture, dark wood accent pieces and the most eclectic group of lamps and table ornaments, as if they had each been collected from a different part of the world, representing a completely different culture.

"Please, make yourself comfortable," Eric said, standing beside one of two arm chairs, facing one another and separated by a beautiful, heavy raw wood coffee table. "Michael will be with you in a moment." He bowed and turned, walking away across the highly polished floor. Leonore noticed that his feet did not make a sound and she watched him walk away, disappearing around a corner in the far side of the room. She knew he could feel her watching him as he went, they all could.

It had been over seventy years since Leonore had first met the ethereal being with whom she was about to have her first full conversation in over a decade. Raised on the hard graft streets of North London, Leonore Galasky was not one for nerves, but she felt them now, strumming in her chest as she waited. Her father, a butcher by trade, had worked all hours to keep a roof over their home, a modest house beside the train yards. She had felt truly at home and safe in that house. And she had her fair share of fond memories, not least the time that their next-door neighbor, Mrs. Dawson, set fire to her kitchen and ran into the street where she had yanked off her burning apron, along with her entire dress. She had been Pantyhose Patty ever since.

Leonore reached forward and picked up a small crystal figurine of a dancing girl and held it gently as she turned it slowly, the memories of her mother cascading through her mind like a bursting floodgate. Her mother was her hero. Born into a wealthy family, she became a famous ballerina by the time she was sixteen. Her family had called it fateful that she took an extra practice session one night and snuck outside the dance studio for a sly cigarette, where she bumped into, literally, the local butcher, delivering cuts of meat to the restaurant next door. The man who would go on to be her husband, and Leonore's stern, hard-working father, was despised by her in-laws. Such was their snobbishness, that they not only struck her from the family will and refused to see her at all, but they disowned her legally in name, taking a petition to a city magistrates to have her name removed from the family line.

And she hadn't cared. Not one iota, because she had found the man of her dreams, in a cobbled alleyway, carrying a side of beef on his shoulder and lighting up her world with his smile. It had been hard, but they had everything they ever needed, and things were good. They were good for a long time. Long enough to make the good memories seem like a fair price to pay for the losses they had endured. Losses that had etched a lifetime of pain and heartbreak into her father's face in a single, fateful night in war-torn England.

On December 29th, 1940, the German bombers came, as they always did, and laid down a rainstorm of fire that cut a swathe of destruction across the center of the capital in a night that became known as the second great fire of London. It was the most devastating single night of bombing of the entire war.

Earlier that day, her mother and brothers had left for the zoo. George had been whining about going for weeks, and when he had been joined by his older brother, she had finally relented.

Her last memory of her mother and brothers was as they walked through the small white garden gate, all waving, before George had pulled his ears and stuck out his tongue and they had all disappeared along the street. She would never forget her father's words as they went back inside, a cold drizzle starting to fall. 'I don't believe anything should be kept in a cage. I'm with you, Leo.'

"A human's past is a wonderfully terrifying thing," a voice from behind her said. The tone was low and smooth, the words spoken with the unhurried ease of someone who had been speaking for a very long time and had little else to do. "Without direction, and all caution thrown to the mercy of life's wind, every single lifetime should be cherished and regarded as nothing less than a priceless thread in the story of all humanity."

Leonore turned in her seat to see Michael walking towards her. His ash grey suit and white shirt was still his preferred attire. She looked down. "And I suppose that even an old lady who had lived such a life wouldn't be able to convince you to wear shoes every once in a while."

Michael smiled, his chiseled face softening as he approached, leaning down to place a gentle kiss on Leonore's cheek. His wavy brown hair fell and tickled her face and she wrinkled her nose, chuckling as he drew away to take a seat in the armchair opposite.

"I see Eric looks wonderful, as always," she said, placing the figurine back on the coffee table. "How long have you been playing 'son of his father' for now? Three, four generations?"

"It is a consequence of who we are that drives us to certain, imaginative, extremes," Michael said. "But you didn't come here to see me about Eric's eternal youthfulness and how we weave it into everyday life." He sat forward, elbows on knees, his face brightening like an expectant teenager. "I've actually been waiting a long, long time for this conversation to take place," he said. "And, knowing that just two days ago you made the decision to visit me, and seeing you here now, carrying news that my ears cannot wait to hear, is exhilarating."

Leonore smiled patiently. "I'd almost forgotten how you find it hard to talk in straight lines. It really has been a long time."

"July first, nineteen ninety-eight," Michael said brightly, like a small child answering a question right in class. "You wore a blue dress and your glasses were different."

"Not as fancy as these."

"Not as strong."

Michael sat back. Leonore could see him squirming slightly, looking for the most comfortable spot. "The Nemesis is traveling," he said, his tone back to mature and smooth again. "He will arrive in New York in thirty-five minutes. The plane is on time."

Leonore pondered for a moment, half knowing that Michael knew exactly what she had driven all this way to talk with him about. "I'm going to put the life of someone close to me at great risk. He may appear ordinary to you, and to most people, but he is about to enter a chapter of his life that will not only put it in grave danger, but will also help determine the future of humanity." Michael said nothing, but sat listening politely. Leonore went on, "When I first met Marcus, he was in Danny McCane's auto shop, head under the hood of an old Camaro that Danny was convinced would never run again. He let the kid take a run at it—thought he could use the practice—even though he already showed an uncanny knack with cars and most things mechanical. Danny had found him one day, sleeping under a tarp in the back of a truck he was fixing up. He was just a child, orphaned and alone, on the streets. Now, I've told you about Danny before. You know how he is. He could've taken him to child services, dropped him off at a police station, or worse."

"I should tell you that Marcus's time of worrying after Danny is almost over. All of us have our paths to walk, Leonore, including me, and Danny is needed elsewhere, though he has still one more important task to undertake, in the name of his adopted son."

Leonore felt her heart sink, and hoped that it didn't show too much. There really was no hiding your feelings from a creature like Michael, but she took pride in keeping a lid on it, for her own sake, and disliked the idea of anyone seeing past her longstanding and well-manicured façade. She went on, "Despite my best efforts, I grew close to Marcus. Over time it became clearer to me, as it did a long time ago to you, that he is meant for something else, something...bigger."

"For the first time where there are actual stakes," Michael added. "And yes, I have seen Marcus, how he cares for you. He will need every ounce of his skills if Aaron is to make it into the city alive, although something tells me he is going to make it look very easy."

Leonore sat silently, simply looking at Michael, knowing that he probably knew whether or not Marcus would be successful, or if he would die trying. Being able to see a man's destiny is one thing, daring to look is another.

"I cannot tell you what the immediate future holds for Marcus," he continued, "Any more than I can tell you yours. We covered this a long time ago, shortly after we first met. I know you remember. You haven't raised the subject since. That kind of discipline, knowing what you know, is impressive."

"I didn't come here to be pacified or misdirected. You've known me long enough to be able to see when I'm fighting, and when it's best not to poke. That damned juvenile streak of yours. I swear, Michael."

He held up his hand. "All right, Leonore, all right. Let's continue another way. Shall we?" He stood, holding out his hand. Leonore took it and he helped her out of the seat, turning to guide her toward the windows. The balcony outside ran the entire length of the building and was furnished with sets of simple chairs, a small table here and there and a spattering of gas heaters. They stepped outside, into the crisp night air, and then seemed to step into a bubble of warmth as Michael lead her to the low wall, where he leaned, looking down toward the street, thirty-one stories below.

"It is one of my failings that I sometimes do not take seriously some of the very important things entrusted to me by my human companions," Michael said after a minute, scanning the skyline and breathing in the sharp winter air. "I've been to war, Leonore. The war from which all wars were born. I've seen the most terrible things done unto others, that mankind's most evil could not begin to imagine. I was solemn, my heart as heavy with blood as my hands were soaked in it, and yet I knew, because my cause was righteous—and it was a conflict between the dark and the light—the blood that had been spilled, the blood of angel and demon alike, would not be in vain. Mankind would reap the lessons sown by the deaths of the divine."

He turned to look at Leonore, a heaviness in his eyes that she had not seen before. "And now we are here, in this moment, a moment that has been written of since before the Son of the Almighty walked this earth an unknown and free man. And this could be the fall of man. Imagine the incredulity of it all, Leonore. Imagine how many gave their lives, how many divine souls were lost to the cause of good over evil. And now, everything, *everything*, rests in the hands of a few humans, the very pivotal of which has *no idea* what is coming, and what to do when it does."

Leonore touched his arm as he stared out over the city. "You're afraid," she said quietly. "It's all right to be afraid, Michael, even you. Fear is not an emotion reserved for lower mortals, especially the fear of losing everything, like *all* of mankind. You have every right to be fearful. And no one feels it because only a precious few of us have any idea what is coming. You are carrying the fears of the world on your shoulders. Everything is finely balanced and the stakes are as high as they could possibly be. Fear is what keeps us grounded, aware, alert. We need it, however much we despise it. Humans have become accustomed to handling and using their fears, even if it sometimes means not standing up to it. Just its presence is enough to galvanize most of us into action. But you..." she squeezed his arm and he looked down at her hand, white and frail-looking. "You can do nothing but dwell, and wait on the sidelines, and hope we come through."

Michael smiled softly. "It isn't fear, Leonore. Fear is something that holds no sway over me, nor any of my kind. It isn't fear that you see when you look at me." He turned to look at her. "It's doubt." He straightened, patting Leonore's hand gently as she held his sleeve. "There is nothing after this if you lose," he said quietly. "Nothing but sorrow and darkness and wretched agony, forever. There is no coming back, no rising up, no fighting back. If he succeeds and rises to power, the earth will be his torture chamber, and mankind his victims. He will bleed every last one of you for all eternity, and he'll laugh while he does it."

*   *   *

The arrivals gate at JFK was unusually quiet. The last plane in from London was only half full, and James made his way quickly through the various security checkpoints and immigration formalities. He stood back from the baggage carousel, away from the light throng of passengers as they began to arrive, gathering around the baggage claim in a silent, shifting mass. Matt hovered like a hawk, eyes scanning the stream of bags as they began to slide down the chute and onto the moving platform. James tapped away at the screen of his phone, an email to Mr. Black, letting him know, as instructed, that he had arrived without incident. The customary 'swoosh' let him know his email was on its way and he pocketed his phone, scanning the crowd, momentarily distracted by a trio of flight attendants as they made their way through baggage claim.

The crowd started to disperse as bags were picked up and wheeled away toward the exit. Matt turned to look at him and shrugged. It would be typical that only his bags were delayed, lost or on another plane to Alaska by now.

"I'll give it ten more minutes and then I'll go and find someone," Matt said, turning back to the carousel, his stance unchanged and his eyes darting, surveying their surroundings. If there was one thing that James liked about Matt it was that he was disciplined enough to be on the job when he was supposed to be, instead of just some meathead ex-military grunt who wanted a fat paycheck for looking the part and doing little else.

A few minutes later, after everyone else had left, the first of their bags appeared, sliding down the metal chute and dumping onto the carousel. The others followed a minute later and James sighed, watching as Matt made short work of hauling their bags onto a cart and turning for the ramp that led to the exit. They emerged into the waiting area, where people waited eagerly for relatives and friends to appear. James saw a small group of Catholic priests, gathered next to the newsstand, and wondered if they were waiting for the one he had spoken to in London. He paused as Matt pushed the cart over to a large man in a black suit, holding up a sign with James' name on it. He watched the steady stream of passengers beelining for their friends, and then the priest appeared around the corner, a small rolling bag and an old messenger his only luggage, the book he had been reading was nowhere to be seen. The priest looked pale and weary, as if he was coming down with the flu, and James watched as his compatriots hurried to help him with his bags, looks of concern on all of their faces.

"Enjoy your stay, Father," he whispered, and then turned away, the large man nodding a greeting to him as he guided them out through the door to a waiting limousine. Three cars back, parked curb-side behind an Alamo rental car shuttle, sat the charcoal grey town car of a pair of FBI agents. They pulled out, slipping expertly into the flow of traffic, keeping a safe distance behind the stretch Lincoln among the sea of headlights.

Chapter Twenty-One

"Keep pressure on it," Gabby said, as Jerry held onto Alex on the back seat of the SUV. They were parked amongst some trees, out of sight of the road, barely two miles from the Apex Labs. Jerry had fought the urge to floor it and just get as far away as possible, as fast as they could, instead of sticking to the speed limi't for the benefit of any eyes that may be on them as they skirted the perimeter of the Ark complex.

"He's out," Jerry said, leaning forward to put his ear over Alex's open mouth. "Breathing's ok, pulse is weak but steady."

They worked with the emergency medical field kit to patch up the bullet hole in Alex's shoulder, but they both knew that he would need a doctor, and soon. He had lost a good amount of blood—was still losing it—and the bullet was still in there.

"We have to get him to a hospital," Jerry said, pressing a pad of gauze onto Alex's shoulder. "You can't help it any more than I can, boss, but he needs proper medical attention, regardless of what happens after."

Gabby worked silently, preparing a fluids IV, her mind working furiously amidst an overload of information. "He's not going to bleed out, Jerry, not if you keep that thing on there anyway. We'll get him some help, but first we need to stabilize him and get away from here. I don't trust Drexler, I don't trust whoever the hell this security director, Akers, is, and I sure as hell don't trust any of the suits above them, either here or in the offices downtown." She wrapped a rubber tourniquet around Alex's arm, holding the IV needle tube between her teeth. "Whatever happened to Alex in there is part of a much bigger picture, and I'm going to find out what it is." She paused, holding her breath as she positioned the needle over Alex's skin, nudging it into a vein and sliding it in.

"Corporate espionage?" Jerry said, holding Alex down while Gabby worked. "I know it's extreme, but Apex has some of the most secret and enviable programs in the world. It's no secret that Alex is a top geneticist and that the military projects flooding into that place account for billions of dollars of defense spending. Who the hell knows what they had him working on? It could be the Chinese, the Russians, the…"

"It wasn't the fucking Chinese, Jerry. This is something else, something closer to home, and it all started with those two murdered Apex agents. That was either a message that we aren't getting, or someone didn't want eyes on Alex that morning." She taped the IV down and wrapped it with bandage, straightening as much as she could in the back of the SUV. "And that Mrs. Galasky," she continued. "There was something very off about her."

"Like what?"

"I don't know. Everything. We are going back there at some point. I need answers about that morning, and she has some." She got out, standing just outside the door. "And I think she knows that I know."

Jerry looked down at the gauze. It was soaking through again. "I'm going to need to plug this with something real soon, boss, or we'll have more to worry about than some crazy upholstery cleaning."

The rear wheels spun on the damp asphalt as they got back on a road glistening with a sheen of frigid water and patches of deadly black ice. Gabby sat in the back, Alex's head on her lap, checking the IV bag and keeping his body secure as every innocuous bump and dip seemed about to rock Alex awake and jerk the life-giving needle from his arm.

"Remember," she said, looking ahead through the windshield. "Take the 190 up. We'll need to go around. We need to avoid Rockville and Bethesda."

"I got it, I got it," Jerry said, obviously uncomfortable with his superior's plan of action. "It'll turn a thirty-minute drive into an hour. You sure this guy is ok?"

"I'm sure. He knew Alex's father. Mine too. He'll know what to do."

"Yeah, but does he know what he's doing? Wait, he's not a vet or some kind of animal psychologist, is he? That kinda shit always happens in the movies. Why doesn't anyone know a doctor? They always know a vet, or a chiropractor, but never a doctor."

"He was a combat medic. Best corpsman in the Latrang Valley. Now slow down, the last thing we need is a highway patrol uniform coming on shift with an itchy trigger finger on his radar gun."

The drive out to Brookeville took less time than they thought. At almost 5:30 am, the sun was still tucked beneath the eastern horizon, but the work day was beginning for a lot of people, and the morning commute was showing signs of starting to build.

"How's he doing back there?" Jerry asked, as he watched mirrors and fought the urge to weave through the moderate traffic on the 97, picking up a morning rush out of Olney to the south.

"The same," Gabby said, brushing a strand of damp hair from Alex's forehead. "I'm guessing we're about fifteen minutes out. I know this is suburban, but once we're clear of Olney, it'll be fields and trees and easy to miss the turn."

"You just tell me where to go, boss, and I'll get us there."

Gabby looked out of the sleet-spattered window. A fine mist was being kicked up by the cars on the road, turning headlights into foggy halos all around. "Thanks, Jerry," she said after a minute, still staring out through the armored glass. "Unless you're planning on turning me in and seeing me go down for treason, I really appreciate you sticking your neck out for me."

Jerry looked at her in the rearview. "Boss, I've worked for one or two real douchebags in my time, and every single one of them I would've called in by now. But, and I'm not looking for a promotion here, I've just never worked for anyone like you before. You've always been upfront, fair, by the book and still a helluva lot of fun, so I think I can honestly say that your secret's safe with me."

Gabby smiled, nodding toward his reflection in the mirror. "Well, it's going to be a long day. I'm going to have you head back to the office and cover for me while I take care of this. I don't want you any deeper than where you are now."

"Which is up to my neck, in case you hadn't noticed."

"I still need you back there. I'll come in as soon as I know Alex is stable. All we've done is go out to Apex to ask a few questions. We didn't get anywhere with that, and that part's the truth, so we'll go with that. If anyone gets nosey down the line I'll figure something out, but besides the alert on the base, nothing happened, and they couldn't wait to see the back of us, so I doubt we'll be hearing anything from them any time soon."

"Ok," Jerry said, nodding. "There's something I really need to do when I get back."

"What's that?"

"Take a nap."

Gabby wasn't kidding. The entrance to the small road was tightly shrouded on both sides by thick, bushy trees and shrubs. There was no sign, nor mailbox, and the road surface was gravel and dirt, although, if you looked closely, you could tell the entrance was maintained. The gravel was raked and even, but not too much. For all intents and purposes, it looked like a small dirt road leading into the fields. Nothing more.

"Nice and slow, Jerry," Gabby said from the back seat, one arm still protectively covering Alex's torso. "He'll know we're here by now. Trust me, you don't want to spook him."

"You make him sound like Rambo or something," Jerry said, guiding the Tahoe along the narrow track in the darkness. The landscape opened up around them and they left the road, and the noise of passing cars, behind them. The hedgerows seemed to crowd the Tahoe on both sides as they wound their way toward a set of low buildings, a quarter mile ahead on the right.

"Pull around to the front of the garages. He has security lights. They should come on."

"There's a light on. Someone's up," Jerry said, pulling into an open area in front of a large, single story house, with a detached three car garage and what looked like a barn and a grain silo behind it. The gravel crunched beneath the tires and Jerry eased to a stop facing the garage, looking right toward the house. The solitary light cast a yellow white rectangle on the driveway. The only light for what seemed like miles. Suddenly, the Tahoe was bathed in bright white light from high intensity halogen lamps above the garage doors. As Jerry shielded his eyes, he sat back, turning his head toward the driver's window, and stared straight into the barrel of a Mossberg 12 gauge, an inch from the glass.

"Hands on the steering wheel, son," a gravely voice said from outside. "Nice and slow. And let's get everyone out of the back, shall we?"

Gabby opened the door, stepping out slowly with both hands raised. "I know it's been a while, but do you have any cinnamon sticks?"

The shotgun swung toward the back door, paused, and then slowly lowered as the sound of a deep chuckle broke the early morning silence. "You're too sweet for cinnamon sticks."

Gabby lowered her hands and stepped forward, her face breaking into a wide grin. "Hello, Gant. I hope we didn't get you up."

The man stepped forward, pressing a button on a small remote control unit in his hand, dimming the lights to a normal level. Tall—well over six feet—and lean, his face was chiseled with age and a lifetime of maintaining a strong physical presence. He screamed ex-military, with close cropped steel grey hair and the posture of a man used to standing tall.

"Lady, if you'd had to get me up at this hour, I'd feel obliged to pull my .45 and end it all right now." He stepped forward, leaned the shotgun against the truck and bear hugged Gabby, almost lifting her from her feet. After a moment, he released her and stepped back, holding her by the shoulders. "Good to see you, Gabby. What brings you out here at this time of the afternoon?"

Gabby turned back toward the rear door, nodding toward the back seat. "I brought someone else you know. He needs your help." Gant peered inside. "Oh, Lord," he said. "Alex? What the hell happened, Gabby? What have you brought me?"

Gabby slumped against the side of the SUV, exhausted."Gant, right now I just need you to make sure Alex is ok. After that, I'll tell you most of everything I know. Can you do that?"

Gant leaned inside the door, reaching out to touch Alex's face and neck. He took his pulse, closing his eyes as he counted, then straightened, putting his hands on his hips.

"Nice work with the IV, Gabby. Wound looks clean, but it's still leaking some. We'd better get him inside." He picked up the shotgun and walked around the front of the Tahoe. "I have a wheelchair in the guest room. And tell Slick to get out of the damned car already. He's making me nervous."

Gant and Jerry manhandled Alex's limp body onto the table in the kitchen. Gabby followed, carrying the orange med kit from the Tahoe. Gant left the room, reappearing a minute later, pushing what looked like a steel tool chest and IV stand. "Hook that up on here, Slick," Gant said, and Jerry obliged, attaching the IV bag to the hook, maneuvering it to the head of the table. Gant spun the tool chest around and pulled open the top drawer, revealing a tray full of medical instruments, neatly spaced out on white linen.

"Wow," Jerry said, holding onto the sides of Alex's head. "I don't want to know what your favorite hobby is."

Gant didn't miss a beat, handing Gabby a pair of medical scissors. "Cut his shirt off, Gabby. Slick, grab a blanket from that closet over there, and then a bowl of clean hot water. I need to re-open this thing."

Alex was laying in trash. The pile of garbage rose up around him, leaving him only with a ragged view of the alley rooftops and inky black sky above. He could see the thin, ruffled clouds scudding by, and debris flew across his field of vision, whipped around by a gusty wind, icy and unforgiving. As he tried to sit up, he immediately fell back, white hot pain stabbing at his side. He drew his hand away and looked at his palm. It was slick with black blood. Grimacing, he squirmed up to a sitting position and looked around.

The alley was long and dark, littered with overflowing dumpsters and random piles of garbage. The wind howled down the alley, moving a dumpster on creaking wheels until it hit the wall, taking a chunk of brickwork with it. It took immense effort, but when he finally managed to stand, one arm braced and shaking against the wall, the pain in his abdomen subsided a little. Looking down, he saw a ragged, bloody hole in his shirt that revealed a large gash in the flesh on his right side.

Gusts of wind, at first cold and then blisteringly hot, blasted down the alley. There was no fire and no snow, yet the temperature fluctuated as wildly as the wind, now picking up again and hurling more trash against him as he stumbled forward. He could see the moon, oversized and orange hued, as if reflecting some immense fire somewhere below.

Alex grimaced at the constant, throbbing beat in his side as he stumbled to the end of the alley. It opened onto a deserted street, littered with shadowy, silent cars, their ashen hulks abandoned with doors open to cold, empty interiors. The road stretched away to darkness in both directions, and he winced as the wind gusted red hot again, prickling his exposed skin. Ducking into a nearby police cruiser, he pulled the door closed to shut out the noise and the heat. Slumping back in the seat, he closed his eyes, fighting a rising tide of despair and waited for the wind to die down again.

Alex snapped awake after what seemed like a few seconds, grimacing in pain and staring through the dirty windshield at the snow now falling in near horizontal slashes of white and grey in the driving wind. He sat back, eyes fixed and solemn on the empty street.

At first, it looked like just a shadow, a smudge that shifted among the misty, billowing snow and the shadows between cars and buildings. There it was again, darker this time, more defined. It was a figure, walking through the blizzard, directly toward him. With a shove, he opened the door and climbed awkwardly out into the storm. The snow-laced wind howled around him and he stumbled to the front of the car, leaning heavily on the hood and hugging his chest against the cold.

He could see the figure more clearly now. It walked toward him down the center of the street, slow and steady amidst the swirling snow. His skin was ice cold, numbed by the stinging snow and sleet, and he slipped to one knee, eyes fixed on the approaching figure. It was wearing some kind of immense cloak that appeared to flap and billow around it as if with a life of its own. A deep hood kept the stranger's face hidden in darkness.

As he struggled to hold his head up, he looked down at the snow-covered ground and the pool of blood growing there, fed by the constant drops from the gash in his side. He felt himself heave a cry of anguish, the sound snatched from his lips by the wind. Still the stranger drew closer. He slipped further down, his hand sliding through the snow on the hood of the car until his hip hit the ground and he grunted, sitting up against the grille between the headlights.

The stranger stepped close to him and Alex looked up at the looming countenance of this strange figure, cast against a backdrop of tumbling grey and black sky and driving snow. Still, the stranger's face was hidden within the deep shadow of the large hood, and Alex found a vague comfort in the presence of another human being. The stranger stood over him, watching him freeze and bleed into the snow.

"Who are you?" Alex croaked, his words barely audible above the gusting wind. His wound throbbed with the effort of speaking. The figure stood there, silent and unmoving as a statue. He waited for an answer and then bowed his head when one didn't come as he slid toward an end he realized was now very close.

"Dabit deus his quoque finem." The voice cut through the raging wind, and stirred something deep within Alex. A familiarity that creased his brow and lifted his head, hair plastered in icy tendrils to his forehead. He stared up at the figure as it raised one hand toward him, the voice coming from within the shadows of the hood.

"God will bring an end to this," the stranger said, one hand extended, reaching out toward him, as if to help him to his feet.

Alex began to struggle, to lift his hand toward the stranger's outstretched fingers, but barely had the strength to hold his head up. "I can't…" he croaked, his side throbbing, blood spilling onto the snow.

"If you find the strength," the stranger said, the voice seeming to envelop and surround him. "God will bring an end to this."

Alex looked at the hand. It was barely two feet from him, but may as well have been two miles. He could feel the strength draining from him with every drop of blood, that fell to the frozen ground. His head dropped again and he looked at his own hand, laying loosely by his side, resting in the blood-stained snow, thin, and weak, the skin a blue-tinged hue.

"Who...? I can't..." he whispered breathlessly. "Just leave me. I can't..."

"Find the strength, Alex. Find the strength so you can bring an end to this."

Alex faltered, and yet his heart stirred, a distant nerve touched. He knew then. He knew everything. It was all inside him.

"Find the strength, Alex" The voice sounded as calm as when it had first spoken, and yet there was a deeper strength there now, urging him to act, driving him to move.

He grunted, shifting his weight slightly, his hand still pressed against his wound. The stranger's hand hovered above him, tantalizingly close. Raising his arm, he roared in agony as the pain speared him below his ribs, the blood gushing from the tear in his flesh, spilling onto the snow in a gush of red. As his fingers stretched outward, the stranger remained still, unmoving, unwilling to move forward even an inch. Alex screamed again, the air leaving his lungs in a roar that seemed more than amplified to his frozen ears. There was more than pain in the sound now.

And then their hands joined, the stranger's fingers wrapping firmly around his cold and trembling hand, and he felt the strength, the seemingly infinite power as he was pulled forward away from the car and up off the frozen ground.

And as he rose upward, he saw now that the cloak was not a cloak, blown and billowed by the wind. They were wings; ash grey, immense and majestic, flexing and beating steadily in the storm. And then the stranger reached up, grasping the hood and pulling it back to reveal strands of golden hair atop a perfectly smooth, ivory complexion. Alex cried out then, tears suddenly welling in his eyes, and streaming down his cheeks to freeze in icy crystal drops on his frigid skin. It was Gabby.

"Aaah!" Alex jumped awake with a yelp, arching his back on the table and almost knocking the suture needle from Gant's hand.

"For Christ's sake, hold him down, Slick! Unless you want to take over the internal stitching, and something tells me your needlepoint ain't so good!"

"Alex!" Gabby was leaning over him, a bright light behind her head, skewing his vision to a bright, blurry smear of face, eyes and light. Alex tried to focus on her eyes amidst the noise and chaos and searing pain. He screamed again, flailing with his one free arm as Jerry finally managed to pin the other at his side.

"Damn it, man!" Gant yelled, trying to keep Alex from bucking off the table. Alex's wound was only partially sutured.

Jerry finally got ahold of Alex's other arm, and between Gabby and Gant, they managed to hold him down until he had stopped thrashing, his eyes rolling back up into his head as he passed out, finally falling limp again.

Alex awoke with a start, a cry echoing in the small room as his vision filled with a slowly turning ceiling fan on a reclaimed wood paneled ceiling. Within seconds, the door opened and Gabby appeared, moving quickly to his bedside, followed by an older, stern-looking man with a military haircut and expression to match. He stood by the door, hovering.

"Alex. You're awake. Thank God." She leaned over him, immediately pressing her hand to his forehead. "Ok, just relax, you need to rest, so lay back for me, ok?"

He eased himself back into a mound of soft pillows and heard himself take a long breath, looking at Gabby's face, her expression a mixture of happiness and concern.

"Where am I?" he asked after a moment, gingerly looking around what appeared to be a bedroom in some kind of ranch house. "I remember..." he trailed off, his face scrunching into a frown.

"It's ok," Gabby said, touching his arm. "You don't need to think about any of that right now, Alex. The important thing is that you're here, and you're safe. We'll get to everything that happened when you're ready."

"I was working," he continued, turning to look out of the window at a scene of green fields and distant tree lines. A trio of birds flew across the grey sky. He remembered the geese. The geese that flew over the lunch room toward the river. The lunch room. "The lab. I was working at the lab."

"Alex, it's ok. We have time. Just try to relax, ok?"

Gant stepped up beside her, holding out a glass of water. "He'll need this," he said, stepping back as Gabby nodded, taking the glass. "I'll be right outside. Holler if you need anything."

"Thank you, Gant," Gabby said, turning back to Alex as Gant stepped out and closed the door. "Alex, you need to listen to me now, ok? Alex, look at me."

Alex turned his head away from the window and looked Gabby in the eye. "Who are you?" he asked suddenly, his expression vague and searching. "Why did you believe in me?" Gabby watched as Alex's hand moved to his abdomen, pressing gently on the sheet that covered his torso, as if pushing at some area of mild discomfort. She was about to answer when Alex continued, "In the snow, by the alley, why did you believe in me?"

Gabby frowned, stroking his arm. "You mean at the lab? You ran outside. Jerry and I were there. You were hurt."

"It went through my ribs," Alex said, frowning down at his body, drawing his other arm away from Gabby's hand as he tried gingerly to pull the sheet aside, his IV tube snagging momentarily on the bed frame.

"Alex, wait." Gabby reached forward, freeing the tube before he pulled it out. "You really need to rest. Alex, please. We can talk about everything when you're feeling stronger."

Alex's head fell back onto the pillow again, his hands falling still in his lap. His eyelids fluttered and then closed as he muttered something beneath his breath that Gabby couldn't make out. She pulled the sheet over his arms, and then felt his forehead again before unfolding the blanket at the end of the bed, drawing it up to his chest. She stood, looking down at her friend for a moment and then turned to walk out of the room.

"I saw your wings," Alex whispered, and Gabby froze, hand reaching for the doorknob. She turned, a deep frown creasing her features, and looked at Alex. He was staring at her, but his expression was one of calm reassurance, all signs of doubt gone from his features.

"What did you say?" Gabby asked, still reaching for the door. Alex closed his eyes and turned his head away slightly, falling back into an easy sleep. Outside, the green fields were turning white beneath a lead sky and steadily falling snow.

Chapter Twenty-Two

"He didn't look feverish to me, but you got a closer look at him," Gant said, reaching out and refilling Gabby's mug with steaming black coffee. "He's been through a lot. I've seen plenty of men—trained men, who were used to being in harm's way—have similar reactions to shock and trauma. I'm kinda surprised that he's not climbing the walls and jabbering like a monkey, after what he's been through. He'll come around pretty quickly, I bet. Then you'll get some sense out of him."

Gabby took a sip of coffee, staring at the swirling liquid. She was exhausted. No sleep in twenty-four hours, and every one of those hours a stress-fueled roller coaster ride of tension and anxiety. She was a walking ad for Zquil and Xanax, and Jerry would have been too if he hadn't been tired enough to fall asleep on one of Gant's not-too-comfortable reading chairs, by the window in the living room.

"I need get in to the office," she said, pushing the mug away on the table and getting up, swaying slightly as she stood.

"And I need a lemonade enema," Gant replied, standing and holding her arm to steady her. "But neither of those things are gonna happen anytime soon."

Gabby smiled, in spite of herself, and slowly sat again, leaning forward and putting her face into her hands. "Then I at least need to call in," she said. "And Jerry should be going. I need to brief him before he leaves."

Gant walked over to the sleeping Jerry and kicked him gently in one out-stretched leg. "C'mon, Slick," he said, as Jerry stirred, blinking at the bright grey light from the snowy sky outside. "That truck ain't gonna drive itself to work."

"And if he asks for a report, just start to write one. You can go all the way to when we left the complex. I'll call Sorano and ask him to have you bring me the case file. I'll pull a sick day. Grab the files—the ones in the file drawer in my desk—and come back out here. That'll give you the majority of the day to poke around *quietly* and see what's come out of Apex, if anything."

Jerry sat in the Tahoe, leaning out of the open driver's side window. He reached to turn the heat up. The snow was beginning to come down now, but with rush hour almost over, he should have an easy drive into the field office, perhaps an hour away. He yawned. "Got it, boss. You want bagels or donuts? Estelle always brings a box up from Bennie's first thing."

Gabby shook her head, Gant's parka wrapped around her shoulders. "If the Chief asks why I'm not there, just tell him I'm following up a lead."

"I thought you were gonna pull a sick day?"

"He'll believe it more if I call in sick then get some work done anyway. He loves my work ethic. Stay in touch, and don't forget the files. Leave in time to make it back out here before dark. The weather's closing in and it'll be bad for the next couple of days. I don't want to have to come dig you out of some drift somewhere."

"That doesn't give me much time for any poking around, but I'll keep my ears open," he said, nodding at Gant, standing impassively behind Gabby, the Mossberg tucked under one arm. "Call my cell so I can show the incoming before you call the office. You're sick, but following up a lead. Got it."

"I already called your cell. I even left a sickly-sounding voicemail."

"Of course you did." Jerry patted his jacket pocket, then paused, looking down. "I don't know what the hell happened at the lab, boss, but you'd better find out what's going on soon, because if this thing blows open and you don't have things straight from the get-go, the Chief is gonna skewer you alive, not to mention all the unmentionables at Apex, and the higher-ups at the DOD."

Gabby nodded. She knew she was dragging Jerry into this with his eyes closed, and with a wounded government fugitive tucked away inside the house, that they had helped to escape, there were plenty of loose ends to clean up before the dust could settle, and she wasn't sure anything would settle for a good while.

"Ok," she said, tapping the side mirror. "Get there and back in one piece."

The tires crumped and cracked over the fresh snow and Gabby watched the tail lights glide away, finally disappearing in the mist of falling snow. Gant stepped beside her. She could sense him scanning the road and hedgerows. Once a Marine, always a Marine.

"We'd better get inside," he said, his breath a cloud of billowing steam in the frigid morning air. "You need some rest too." They turned together, walking back toward the house. There were a few level inches of fresh snow, thick and wet, but growing more powdery by the hour.

"Before you do that, though," Gant continued, "I'd like to know if you've gone and bought hell with you when you came up here. Now, you know me, Gabby, I'm not one to preach or whine, but I am one to be prepared." They stepped inside, shaking off their coats and stamping snow on the thick door mat.

"Honestly, Gant, I can't tell you right now. Not because I know but can't tell you, but because I just don't know. Everything I told you about what happened last night is all there is. I don't know who will be coming for Alex, or when, but they'll come."

They walked through the kitchen and Gabby stepped down into the dining room, sitting back down at the table. Gant started a fresh pot of coffee.

"Go on into the living room," he said, nodding toward the far room at the back of the house. "More comfortable in there."

Gabby ended up in the same chair that Jerry had fallen asleep in earlier, the Native American patterned blanket across her lap.

"So we don't know if we're dealing with government security, military investigators, or some shadowy, secret corporate group that wants Alex, and whatever he has or knows, back." He walked over, ducking slightly beneath the wood beam that separated the kitchen from the bright living area, the large windows on the far wall giving an inspiring view of the surrounding countryside. Today, though, all he could see was fields of drifting snow and the misty haze of distant trees. The sky appeared almost the same shade of silver grey as the ground, the daylight uniform and bright, casting a cold, refreshing light throughout the room. He stepped down into the living area, hands in pockets, and walked to the window, looking out. "It says we'll have this for the next few days, but the worst will be today and tonight. I hope your friend has snow tires on that thing."

When Gabby didn't respond, he turned to look at her. She was sitting upright in the old armchair, fast asleep. Gant pulled a foot stool over and lifted her legs up, tucking the blanket around her. Taking one last look out at the snowy landscape, he went back to the kitchen, and fresh coffee.

*   *   *

David Akers walked into the security control room and turned, standing beside the open door. "Everyone out," he said. The four other people in the room stood, pushing their chairs out and dropping their headsets on their consoles. When the room had cleared, Akers closed the door and walked over to the front console, beneath a giant split-screen monitor on the far wall.

Snatching up the phone, he punched in an extension. "Akers, I'm in the monitor room. There's something you should see. Yes, sir."

Five minutes later, the door opened and Charles stepped in, closely followed by Drexler. Charles closed the door and punched in a key code, securing the room.

Akers nodded, gesturing toward the back row. "Take a seat, gentlemen."

Director of Security Akers was as lean, marathon runner-looking man, in his mid fifties. He defied his age in numerous ways, not least of which was regularly outboxing any member of the security team, including Jonas Halssen, the big Swede of Brownsville.

Even though he was raised in the halls of government security, his appearance and demeanor suggested a disciplined military man, probably of higher rank, retired into the lucrative world of private security contracts.

"I've sifted through the video feeds along the timeline after the attack on Doctor Bishop in Lab Three. We know he was shot in the process of barricading the door behind him when he took off down the main access corridor."

Akers worked the keyboard on the console and turned to the main monitor. "So, here we see Bishop shoring up the door after he's hit. He pauses, and then flinches again, before hitting the stairs. He's hurt pretty bad, he just doesn't know it yet." A moment later, a flash of white appeared on screen as a figure crashed through the door, sprinting down the stairs and out of shot.

Drexler edged forward on his seat, opening his mouth to speak, but Charles reached over and touched his arm, stopping the question in Drexler's throat before he could ask it. He sat back and Charles withdrew his hand as Akers moved the cursor on the monitor, switching to the other image of the service yard. The loading docks were clearly visible on the bottom left of the image, and a lone black SUV sat parked facing the wall on the right, the open expanse of the service yard stretching away behind it.

"Ok," Akers said. "This is where it gets interesting. We only have one camera in that service corridor. I've already put in the order for two more, but I'm fairly certain that he had to stop somewhere between the gunshot wound and this shot here." He pointed to the image of the service yard. "This is running almost parallel to the other feed. Watch the door on the bottom left of the screen."

The double door swung open and two figures emerged. They made their way across the yard toward the SUV.

"Those are the two FBI agents who came to talk to you, Mr. Akers," Drexler said.

"What do they want?" Akers asked, clearly suspicious, and, Drexler observed, a little worried.

"They want to talk about the two Apex security agents who were killed outside of Doctor Bishop's apartment, the night before he started work on Project Icarus."

Charles looked at Akers. "I thought we had that taken care of," he said dryly.

Akers looked thoughtful for a moment. "I was told the report had been filed and sanctioned. Case closed."

"Well it looks like your asset didn't close it enough."

Akers was already nodding. "I'll make a note to take care of it myself, sir."

"Make sure that you do."

Drexler squirmed in his seat, obviously uncomfortable with the sudden left turn the conversation had just taken. Akers turned back to the monitor. "My guesses here are that whoever was chasing Bishop was either delayed, thrown off his trail or decided to terminate the chase, which brings us to the most interesting segment of the feed. Keep your eye on the small emergency exit just to the left of the SUV."

They watched Alex as he stumbled out of the exit door, falling forward onto the ground. No one spoke as Gabby and Jerry rushed over to him, and then picked him up to put him in the back seat of the SUV. Akers didn't fast forward any of the service yard segment, and they watched while they patched Alex up in the back of the Tahoe before placing him into the trunk, carefully hiding him behind some boxes. Drexler was getting fidgety by the time the escort guard arrived, talking to the two agents before they followed him out of the yard.

"Oh my God," Drexler said finally, slamming his palm on the console. "Alex isn't here, in the building, or even on the complex, and he's certainly not crawling along some God damned escape tunnel and into the fucking woods!"

"No, he left with the help of two FBI agents," Akers said soberly. "And now he's on the run, with sensitive Apex project data and who knows what else." He leaned forward, glaring at Drexler as if the whole ordeal was his doing. "That's US government property, Doctor Drexler. Top *secret* government property. I would not be doing my job if I didn't suspect that this was a planned attack, orchestrated in order to steal sensitive Apex project materials. Now, orchestrated by whom, that's up for speculation at this point, but the fact is, Doctor Bishop downloaded project data to a portable drive before *erasing* that data from the mainframe. There is *no trace* of the data file. And from what I've seen of the video feed of the incident in his lab, it could easily be surmised that he was in the midst of stealing the data when he was interrupted by a corporate rival, looking to take the data for himself."

Drexler stood, his face angry red. "I still don't see any *evidence* to suggest that Doctor Bishop acted in anything besides self-defense during this whole thing. And now you're telling me that he's some kind of corporate spy who got into a fight with *another* corporate spy. This is not some shady underground shadow corporation, trading in government secrets and super weapons, and Alex Bishop is not James fucking Bond!"

He walked around the console to stand directly in front of the monitor, the frozen image of Gabby's Tahoe taillights just above his head. "For all we know he could be dead or dying right now, more than likely in a hospital somewhere, and he'll contact us as soon as he's able to." He folded his arms defiantly, leaning on the edge of the console.

"Is that your final assessment, Doctor?" Charles asked. Drexler ignored him, too incensed to reply. "Very well. David, where do we stand as of this morning?"

Akers tapped a few keys on the console keyboard. "Major Keene is awaiting your arrival in briefing room 3. Blackwing is geared up and ready to deploy."

"Deploy?" Drexler asked, stiffening. "Deploy where? For what?" He turned to Charles. "Who are you setting your wolves on now, Charles?"

Charles sat impassively, staring at the monitor. "Please, continue, David."

Akers glanced at Drexler, then looked down, reading from the screen. "My agency asset is working on intel I handed over this morning. He knows the subjects, so it shouldn't take too long to narrow down a list of possible destinations they might hole up." He looked up at Drexler. "Nothing at any hospitals within forty-five miles. My hunch is they're shacked up somewhere not too far away. A friend or relative maybe."

Charles nodded and then stood, turning for the door. "Very well. Thank you David. Keep me in the loop." He glanced at Drexler. "Doctor?"

Drexler pushed away from the console, heading for the door. In the hallway, Charles led him to the elevator and removed a card from his jacket. He inserted it into a slot beneath the number pad beside the door. A small panel slid open, revealing a single unmarked button. Charles pushed it before returning the card to his pocket.

"Do not ask any questions and please do not fidget. She hates peripheral movement and will likely not look at you directly. If she asks you a question, answer as directly as possible. She is the last person to want to go around the houses with you."

"Who is 'she'? Where are we going?"

"All you need to know, Doctor, is that she is the reason this place exists today, and the whole reason for our successes with the government and the military over the years."

Drexler took a deep breath. "Ok, so the most important person imaginable. That's all you had to say. The most important person imaginable."

Charles smiled in spite of himself. He liked Drexler, despite the man's sometimes unpredictable behavior.

The elevator door opened to a dimly lit, narrow hallway. The walls were wood paneled, as most of the other executive areas were, but the wood was much darker and there were no pictures or other decorations. The walls were plain and clean and the only source of light was a trio of recessed spotlights that cast pools of blue white light on the burgundy carpet. Charles stepped out and led the way down the hall toward a recessed doorway. There were no guards or soldiers. No one to check IDs. No security.

"There is no personal security outside of the Sanctum," Charles said, as if reading Drexler's mind. "But there are strict security measures so stay close to me."

Drexler swallowed and slowed his pace, falling slightly behind Charles as he approached the door. It opened before they could reach it and Drexler looked up at two glossy black panels set into the wall, just above the door frame. Charles walked in and Drexler hesitated for a moment before stepping through the door. It closed automatically behind him. Stepping beside Charles, a few feet inside the door, Drexler looked around as much as he could at the dimly lit, low-ceilinged room. It resembled a circular lounge, with a few low, wide arm chairs to one side, a large, dark wood desk with a bank of television monitors across from it, and a row of large, heavily tinted windows running around one half of the room's circumference.

"If you would like to sit, please do so," a voice said, from the direction of the desk. Charles immediately walked over to one of the armchairs and sat down. Drexler followed Charles's lead. There were no chairs in front of the desk, and behind it, Drexler saw, was a high-backed chair, its back facing out toward the room.

"Our window to retrieve the data is closing," the voice said.

"Yes," Charles said, his tone serious and flat. "It has become starkly apparent, as you surmised, that the staff we have available to us may not be as diligent, or skilled, as we require. We will need a different strategy put in place when the time comes to bring new people in. People who can share and understand our visions and be fully committed to them."

"The female FBI agent," the voice said from the shadows. "Gabby Morgane. She is the key to everything." Charles said nothing. He sat, listening. "If you go back to her family, back to her parents, her father, and then her father's friends, you will find Alex Bishop."

Charles was nodding then. Drexler wanted to ask why an FBI agent's family and friends could have anything to do with Alex's whereabouts.

"Doctor Drexler," the voice asked. "You have a question." Drexler realized that the voice, low and husky, was the voice of a woman. He had never heard it before and could place neither the accent nor the age of the speaker.

"What will happen to Doctor Bishop if he is brought back here?" Drexler said, his voice sounding weak and feeble in the silence of the room.

"What are you afraid of, Doctor?" Charles said from beside him. "That he'll be brought in handcuffed with a bag over his head and then tortured by bad men with guns? I think you said it yourself; we are not some shadowy corporation. We do not employ such tactics, or reasoning. We need to find

Doctor Bishop, and we need to find him as soon as possible. There are many questions, and, as it stands, he is the only one who has the answers."

"And this is where you come in, Doctor Drexler," the woman said, still hidden behind the tall back of her chair. "It's obvious, at this point, that Doctor Bishop is in possession of something valuable. Valuable enough that, as you surmised to mister Akers earlier, someone else would threaten his life at gunpoint, in his own lab, to get it."

Drexler looked at Charles, who just stared back, nodding very slightly.

"Yes, Doctor Drexler," she continued, "I see that your conclusions regarding the incident are the most logical—and the closest to my own—and we feel that you have the best chance of talking Doctor Bishop into turning himself back into us and helping to locate any data that is... missing."

Drexler sank back into the chair, weighed down by the knowledge that he was to be used as some kind of emotional leverage in order to get Alex to give himself up. At a huge disadvantage, he knew then that the people for whom he worked were far darker and more untouchable than he could ever have imagined. He was floating over the abyss, and there were dark monsters swimming beneath his feet.

"Well, naturally I want Alex's safe return as much as anyone," he said. "But my question stands. What is to happen to him if he returns?"

"Look, Doctor," Charles said, turning to face him. "There will be a thorough investigation. That is inevitable. Once we have explored all the facts and exposed the truth, we can set about getting things back on track and Alex back to work. You saw the surveillance video, you saw how Alex managed to escape his attacker, but you also saw him download, and then deleted all trace of, an encrypted data file from the secure mainframe, minutes *before* that intruder even showed up. That needs some frank explaining."

Movement to his right caught Drexler's eye and he turned his head. The chair behind the desk was turning around. Charles immediately stood up, so Drexler did likewise. They stood there, watching the chair make its slow turn, until it was facing the desk, and they could both see its occupant.

"It is not my liking to issue veiled and shallow threats, Doctor Drexler," the woman said, still a shadowy, moving figure in the gloom. "You were responsible for bringing Alex Bishop to the Apex family. You say you looked at his background, but it is clear to me that you did not look nearly hard enough."

Drexler could see the movement of a face and hands, but everything else was hard to bring into focus, and he had to refrain from overtly squinting to get a better look.

"I will make a proposal to you, Doctor Drexler," she continued, and Drexler saw the flash of a lighter, followed by the orange glow of the tip of a cigarette, pulsing brighter as she drew a breath. "You will do everything in your power to help us bring a peaceful and satisfactory end to this debacle, or you shall find it impossible to get a job as a cashier at a corner drug store." Another pull on the cigarette and a long, slow exhale of grey smoke, bitter and acrid, even from twenty feet away. "How does that sound?"

Chapter Twenty-Three

Four cups of 7-Eleven coffee, half a dozen breakfast claws and half way through The Martian Chronicles audiobook, Special Agents Kyle and Neeson played rock paper scissors to see whose turn it was to run for coffee number five. Across the street, the Akron Hotel rose like a polished black marble monument to all things opulent and rich. Since the limo had dropped James Devlin and his escort at the front entrance right around midnight, they had sat in their cruiser and watched precisely seventeen people come and go, none of whom were Devlin, or anyone who looked remotely like him.

"Ok, that guy looks familiar," Neeson said, staring at the Akron's front door through a pair of field glasses. "No, wait, it's the doorman." He dropped the binoculars to his lap and took a sip of long cold coffee. "Jesus, doesn't anyone stay at this damned place? How the hell do they stay in business?"

"It's a weekday," Kyle said, taking a bite of the last breakfast claw. "Better for us it's not a Saturday. Can you imagine how many people would be coming and going in and out of that place? You'd be losing count right about the same time as you'd be losing your Goddamned mind." A dollop of jelly dripped onto his tie. "Ah, shit. That's the second one this week. Hand me a napkin, will ya?"

Neeson reached for the bundle of napkins in the cup holder, easily within reach of Kyle's outstretched hand, and tossed one onto his partner's lap. Kyle was reaching for it when his cellphone rang. Neeson picked up his scarf, a bright red Calvin Klein birthday gift from his fourteen-year-old daughter. He was about to wrap it around his neck when he paused, distracted by the look on Kyle's face as he took the call, issuing the occasional grunt and 'uh huh', followed by a final 'Yes, Sir', before dropping the phone away from his ear.

"Everything ok?" Neeson asked, tucking the scarf into his standard issue trench.

Kyle snapped his cell phone shut. "We're out." He turned to look at his weary partner. "You know that crazy bitch from the New Religious Extreme Cult division, or whatever?"

Neeson turned his head. He was putting his gloves on—the paper loser to Kyle's scissors—about to run for that coffee. "Huh, yeah, I think everyone has heard of her. Why?"

"She's sending a relief unit. They're gonna want our surveillance drive."

"Ok, so what? That's SOP. They can have it."

Kyle leaned in close. "And they want our key codes and audio hub too."

Neeson blanched, stiffening in his seat. "What? We always erase those things as soon as we get back to the office. Why would they want to hear every belch, fart and stupid joke we made over the last twelve hours?"

Kyle shrugged, "Beats me. They'll be here in thirty. Better get that coffee in, Ollie."

Neeson snorted, muttering obscenities under his breath as he pushed the door open and stepped out into four inches of snow.

"And make sure it's not burnt!" Kyle yelled after Neeson slammed the car door shut, flipping his partner off with two gloved hands before disappearing in the sidewalk crowd.

Kyle didn't see the three men get out of the Mercedes SUV, parked farther along the street. He was rubbing bear claw jelly from his tie with a cheap napkin when they grabbed his partner and dragged him from the sidewalk, bundling him into the back seat and speeding away from the curb in a flurry of snow and ice. He was just about to lick the napkin again when a shadow passed by his window. Kyle stopped, turning his head as a gloved hand knocked on the glass. He reached inside his coat, wrapping his hand around the grip of his Sig Sauer 9mm, then lowered the driver's side window.

An older man stood beside the car. Kyle took a mental snapshot; nice suit, expensive-looking scarf, long trench coat, neatly trimmed greying hair, clean shaven, early to mid-fifties. He looked like he could be a banker, or attorney. The street was busy. Snow was still falling in sporadic flurries, and the traffic rumbled by, the sounds of their engines mixed with the *slushing* of the wet, grey snow and water as they moved by. Not even this kind of weather stopped New Yorkers from going about their daily business. The sidewalks were as packed as any weekday. His hand remained on his weapon.

"Excuse me, sir," the older man said. "I work in the Keller building, right over there, and I noticed you were here late last night. I usually see the mail van park here, but he was on the other side of the street this morning. You seem to be in his spot. I don't mean to be a busybody, but do you think you could find somewhere else to park? There are plenty of spaces along Miramar Avenue, just a block down that way. I know it's no fun to walk in these conditions, but I think you would be better suited to..."

"I'm sorry sir," Kyle interrupted. "I'm on official business."

The older man straightened a little, looking the car up and down. "Well, if you'll excuse me for saying so, it's very easy to say that, especially in this particular model of vehicle. It does *look* very official, but then, anyone can buy one of these, and I feel that it's my civic duty to ask you for some identification."

Kyle sighed. A do-gooder busybody was right. Still, at least someone was paying attention. He slid his hand away from the gun and reached inside his jacket pocket, pulling out his ID wallet. Looking down, he opened the wallet and then held it up, looking back up at the man, and straight into the muzzle of a suppressor.

Clack!

Kyle's body slumped forward and The Rook stepped calmly away from the car as a panel van drew alongside and a trio of men got out. Within a matter of seconds, Kyle's body had been shoved across into the passenger seat, a driver had started the car and both vehicles had driven off, leaving The Rook to cross the street after handing off his weapon to one of the men in the van. A black car was waiting on the opposite curb. Ninety seconds after Agent Neeson was bundled from the sidewalk, The Rook was settling into the back of his car, a sleek Mercedes S-Class. He pulled his cell phone from his pocket and dialed a number. "I'm afraid our cleaners couldn't make it today. Yes, two, that is correct. Please call if you would like to reschedule, thank you." He hung up and straightened his jacket. "All right, Mister Pennyman, let's pay a visit to the FBI."

Chapter Twenty-Four

Aaron felt full. At first he couldn't really put his finger on what kind of full he felt, but, after an hour sitting beside Karesh in the Land Rover as they traveled toward Damascus airport, he realized that he felt at ease with the sensation, and began to understand what he was feeling. He did not remember all of the awakening ceremony, and he did not remember *not* remembering everything he knew now, revealed to his subconscious during the ceremony in a way that, while he understood its origins, held nothing but mystery for him. He was a new Aaron, with a lifetime of experiences that he recalled now as if he had been aware of them his whole life, and yet his memory of the youthful, naive man that had carried his consciousness, and memories, was fading with each passing minute.

"We will have only two hours in Moscow," Karesh said, passing an old Toyota pick up loaded with goats on the otherwise deserted highway. "I suggest that we stay at the gate. No exploring this trip."

Aaron nodded. "I've never traveled outside of Syria."

Karesh glanced over at Aaron. His youthful, awe-ridden demeanor was now replaced by a sort of world wise calm and sense of ease way beyond his years. A look in the mirror showed only the diminishing image of the goat truck as the airport complex loomed up ahead. Within two hours they would be in the air, with stops in Moscow and London before a final leg that would take them to their final destination; Washington DC. He had been told who they were to meet, and yet knew enough of where they were going, and why, to know that getting safely into the city may well be much harder than they imagined.

Aaron had never seen fully armed soldiers, like the ones he was seeing as they walked through the airport. Their uniforms said that they were there for their protection, but their faces told a different story, and the hundreds of passengers mingling throughout the airport all carried an air of apprehension, anxiety and false guilt, heavy and cumbersome, like the oversized backpacks that many of them bore. He wondered if it would be the same at the other airports they would visit, or in the cities and towns, if armed men would be watching over their every move, looking at the clothes they wore or the color of their skin. He dismissed the notion as it began to snowball in his mind. They were here, it was their job, and he had nothing to fear, just the same as the vast majority of people, making their way through the run down terminal building.

"Who will be waiting for us in Washington?" Aaron asked, as they picked up their bags from the security checkpoint and made their way toward the departure gate. Karesh slung his duffel over a shoulder. He looked markedly different from the black-clad, sword-wielding desert warrior he had first seen at the fortress. Now in an olive utility shirt and loose cargo pants over dusty hiking boots. Both of them were dressed in entirely western clothing, chosen specifically to resemble a pair of travel weary journalists or photographers.

"There are many things that you know now, Aaron," Karesh said, reaching into his shirt pocket for a stick of gum. "And I'm sure that you know far more about many more things than I ever will. But you do not know many of the details of our journey, and who we may meet along the way, for your own protection." He handed a silver wrapped stick to Aaron, who happily accepted it. "Just as you have been prepared for many years of your life for this great quest, so too have I been prepared. It is my purpose in this life to ensure that you reach your destinations, talk to those with whom you need to talk and stay alive until the end, and I shall do so until either I am dead or we have completed our task."

Aaron raised his eyebrows as they approached the gate area. Karesh guided them toward a pair of empty seats against the far wall, giving him an ample field of view over the concourse and other passengers waiting to board. "Did you rehearse that? In the mirror?"

Karesh gave him a sharp jab in the ribs. "No, I did not. I am not just a wild haired fighter, desperate to lay down my life for some highly righteous cause. I believe, just as I know you do, that this will be the greatest battle ever fought, and that the prize for our enemy, should he triumph, will be the souls of all of humanity." He turned to face Aaron, lowering his voice, almost to a whisper. "All of these people, Aaron, every single human being that you see, and the billions that you don't, are facing damnation if we fail; if *you* fail. There is *no one* on this earth better prepared for this fight than you. I am here to protect you from the shallow threats, the men who will be sent to kill you, or worse, take you. Every black-hearted, sadistic soldier, assassin, mercenary and gun-for-hire that is pointed in your direction. These are the threats that I am here to face for you. The threats that you will face, the ones that I'm powerless to help you with, are far, far worse."

*   *   *

Gabby awoke with a start, kicking the blanket to the floor. She immediately covered her eyes against the bright, uniform light coming in through the windows that offered an uninterrupted view of the fields and trees to the north of the ranch. The sky was an unbroken, ash grey and the landscape resembled a picturesque winter scene from somewhere in Lapland, not rural Washington. The snow was so thick that it almost blended with the horizon, a distant misty haze through the heavy snow still falling all around.

"I'm not sure your friend will make it back by tonight," Gant said, stepping down from the kitchen, two cups of steaming coffee in his hands. "I've never seen those weather folks on the TV look so bemused. They're saying there's basically no reason for this storm, that it literally came out of nowhere. People are worried." He waited for her to shift and shimmy in the chair and then handed her a cup. "I looked in on Alex. No fever and sleeping like a baby. He's looking great, all things considered. He's a very lucky guy. Lucky that you got him here when you did."

"And the bullet?" Gabby took a sip of the hot drink, allowing her eyes to close, savoring the moment as Gant stood in front of her, looking out upon the snow-covered landscape.

"Got it all. Entered through the shoulder, punched down through into his chest. Took a neat little chunk of bone with it and landed up a hair away from his aorta. And I mean a hair. Like I said, he was lucky. Someone was really looking out for him."

Gabby nodded wistfully, cupping the mug of hot coffee in both hands as she breathed in the bitter steam. "Someone at that lab tried to kill him, Gant. He was running for his life, terrified and alone. His best shot of luck was that he ran into us when he did."

"Or fate."

Gabby looked over the rim of her mug. "If you believe in that sort of thing."

Gant snorted and turned to walk over to the bookcase against the far wall. "In the spring of seventy-two, we were sent out on a trap and catch mission. Intel shot us over some pretty good aerial photos of a VC forward operating base, just over the border, in Laos. Some bigwig Colonel or something, gearing up for a push on Da Nang, they said. There was nothing there, just heavy jungle, so what little assets we had were like needles in the proverbial haystack."

He reached up to move a few books aside, then drew down a polished wooden box, perhaps eighteen or so inches long and half as wide. He turned, carrying it over, and sat down in the chair opposite. "We didn't know if we would find anything. Hell, we didn't even know who we were looking for exactly." He held the box on his lap, running a finger along the top edge.

Gabby stared. She knew that Gant had served with Alex's father in Vietnam, but she had no idea how close they had been, if at all.

"It was a shit storm of a mission," Gant said, staring at the box on his lap again. "And I told everyone after that someone must've been looking out for us that day." He looked up. "Because, with every little thing, the more I go over it in my head, just the way it happened, there's no way we should've gotten out of there alive. No way, let alone with God damned medals and a presidential handshake."

His eyes drifted somewhere far away for a moment, before he spoke again. "You know, when they cleared the tunnel system, they found the mine that took half of your father's leg."

Gabby stared. "No, I didn't know that. Dad didn't talk about it. At least not to me, anyway."

"Only a quarter of the explosives had detonated," Gant said, his eyes still focused somewhere far away. "Divine intervention if I ever heard of it."

Gabby frowned. She had not heard that story, and yet the fact somehow didn't seem too far fetched to her, as if the luck they had been afforded was in a way deserved, paid for. They had earned their safe passage out of the war, and from the moment that was decided, by fate, or destiny, or whatever, there was no way they were not going to make it out.

"Why all the fuss over a tunnel network?" She asked. "The South was pretty well being suffocated by that time, and surely one Colonel couldn't have given them *that* much intel to have made too much of a difference." She paused. "You know I don't mean..."

"Yeah, I know. It's ok Gab. I get where you're coming from all right. Asked myself the same questions a hundred times. But it wasn't just the Brass that we found down there. There was something else. Something that we didn't expect to find." He trailed off and was silent for a moment before suddenly clapping his hands on the box and straightening in his chair. "But hey, they treated us like kings for a while, gave us a fat early retirement and pinned some silver on our chests. We even got to meet the President. Well, except Gary, but you know that. You know they..."

"They still have it," she said, nodding. "Yeah, I know."

Gant sighed, and scratched his head. "So anyway, we were young, ya know? However ballsy or war-wise for our ages we were, we were still young. Barely more than kids. And then, when I thought it had all really died down, when I thought it was behind us, they called us in and gave us these." He tapped the box and paused before reaching out, handing it to Gabby. She put her coffee down on the window sill and took the box into her hands. Gant seemed to sag a little, looking suddenly relieved, as if he'd just shed a great weight from his shoulders. Tag, you're it. "And I've kept it ever since."

He leaned forward, his eyes dark with a serious intent that put Gabby instantly on edge. "But the moment you showed up here with Alex, I knew that I didn't have to keep hold of it anymore."

Gabby looked at the polished surface of the finely crafted box. Her reflection stared back up at her.

"I really didn't get it at first. Neither did Warren," Gant said. "I remember how calm and serious the guy was. The suit who gave these to us. And if there's one thing more than anything else that we took away from that meeting, it was that these could never be lost, ever. Never fall into the wrong hands. That sorta thing. He made us promise to keep them and hand them down. Hell, it was that meeting that pretty much decided for us that we were supposed to have kids, ya know?" He chuckled and then went quiet for a moment. Gabby could see pain in his eyes, and wondered where that was coming from. She had never known whether or not he had ever had kids of his own, but the mask he wore in that moment was the mask of a father in pain. It was unmistakable.

"He said we would know when the time was right," Gant continued, coughing away the raw edge to his voice. "We just thought the whole thing was cool as hell, ya know? And kinda spooky. The things he told us..."

"What things? What is it?" Gabby asked, her fingers reaching over the edge of the lid.

"Open it and take a look for yourself."

Gabby opened the lid slowly and peered inside. After a moment of pause, and then numbing realization, her expression fell and her eyes opened wide in disbelief.

"Oh... my God." She looked up at Gant, his expression as knowing and relaxed as hers was animated. "Is this *real*? Do you have any idea what this is? Where *this* is from? Gant, this thing... is it *real*? Is it the one? The *real* one?"

Gant just nodded solemnly, and Gabby returned her awe-drenched gaze to the open box.

"What's going on?"

Gabby almost cried out, slamming the lid shut and nearly jumping out of her skin. Gant couldn't help but chuckle, turning to see Alex standing in the open doorway to the bedroom, rubbing his eyes and looking like he had just woken up the morning after the world's last ever party.

Gant got up and walked over. "You really shouldn't be out of bed, son. Come on, don't take another step. Let me come to you." He led Alex over to the old armchair he had been sitting in, next to the window, and motioned for him to sit down, laying the blanket over his torso and legs as he settled back into the old chair. Gabby looked down at the box for a moment, her fingers lingering on the lid, before putting it on the small table beside the chair.

"Okay, she said, smiling broadly and reaching out to pat Alex's knee. "How are you feeling?"

Chapter Twenty-Five

Jerry topped up his coffee and sauntered back toward his desk, eyes scanning the control room. The office had grown steadily busier since his arrival, but there had so far been nothing to indicate that anyone had heard a whisper from Apex Laboratories. In fact, the biggest news to hit the floor was the weather. He looked to the far end of the room and the Chief's glass-walled office. The room was dark, the Chief yet to appear, and Jerry wondered for a moment if maybe he had heard anything personally about what had happened at the complex in the small hours of the morning and was in some kind of high level meeting about it, watching security monitor footage of Gabby and him driving onto, and then away from, the lab complex. A jaw-clicking yawn suddenly struck him and he stopped, leaning against the nearest desk and almost losing his balance as his hand slid across a stack of paperwork. He caught himself and began to rake the papers together when he paused, staring down at one of the printouts. A single word caught his eye, barely peeking out from beneath another sheet.

"Oh, hello." Glancing up, he put the coffee cup on the adjacent desk and slid the single sheet out from the pile before hastily tidying the papers and moving back to take a seat at his desk.

The paper was a standard printout from the International Arrivals Watch List, transmitted to every security and immigration desk at every airport in the country. As part of the inter-departmental communications mandate, put in place by Chief Sorano, every division that placed a watch flag into the system, on any incoming international traveler, automatically synched that information with every other division, segmentedand prioritized by jurisdiction and interest level, and included any known associates or sources—such as confidential informants and court subpoenas. The name that had caught Jerry's eye was none other than Lincoln Klick. It sat directly below a photo of what looked to Jerry like an Armani model named James Devlin.

"Oh, thank you, Chief." He kissed the paper and jumped from his chair, grabbing his jacket and making for the door, just as Chief Sorano pushed through it.

"Ah, Walker, just the man I want to see. I hope you're just running to get more coffee."

Jerry cursed under his breath, pulling up right in front of the Chief. "Good morning, Chief," he said brightly. "I was about to head out to meet up with Agent Morgane. We're following up on one last lead from the murder, the Apex Labs security detail."

The Chief started off toward his office. "That can wait. In my office, please. And don't think too hard about heading out anywhere. It took me an hour just to drive four blocks on my way in."

Jerry followed Sorano to his office and stepped inside while the Chief settled, hanging his jacket and putting his briefcase on the floor beside his desk. He sat down and leaned forward on the desk.

"Take a seat, Agent Walker," he said, fingers interlaced on the desk in front of him. Jerry sat, having hastily folded the print out and shoved it into his jacket pocket. "I'm concerned," Sorano said, looking down, at nothing in particular.

"Chief?" Jerry said, a familiar seed of concern germinating in his gut.

"Agent Morgane," Sorano said, without looking up. "I'm concerned about her movements, and, honestly, I probably wouldn't have brought this up to you now, had she been here when I arrived this morning."

"Well, Chief, she's..."

"I know that you and your team were led a bit of a wild goose chase with New York and the whole Lincoln Klick, Serpent's Lair cult house thing, but there are times when you go it alone to tie up loose ends of a case, or pursue important leads, and there are times when you go back to the drawing board, sit at your desk and write your God damned report."

The Chief did look up then, meeting Jerry's gaze with practiced timing and penetrating glare, searching for even the slightest twitch or gesture of a lie.

"We spoke with McCarthy, sir," Jerry said, staying calm and being sure to hold the Chief's gaze, looking away only within the tempo of his dialog. "And although he filed his side of the report—which we have no issues with—there were one or two things we felt we should clarify, for ourselves, just for the sake of our own thoroughness, before submitting our reports, sir."

Sorano glared at Jerry, unmoving and obviously making the mental decision on whether to openly call bullshit or not. He leaned back with a sigh. "And I suppose that if I asked what those one or two things were, you would reel off a couple of indeterminate, vague points in the hope that I would, no doubt, not bother to follow up on."

"Oh, no, sir, we both are completely..."

"Shut up, Walker." Sorano leaned forward again. "As a sidekick, I'm sure Agent Morgane could do far worse than you, and as a cover up artist, you're doing her proud, but—and I hate to even have to remind you of this— you are a *Federal Agent*, whose primary responsibility is to me, your team and this department, which serves the government and tax payers of the United States of America. I will allow every agent under my command some latitude in the pursuit of valuable, authentic intel while on case, and even a little rule bending, within the bounds of the law, but I'll be damned if I will tolerate some loose cannon, Sherlock Holmes and Watson detective circus, while I try to put out fires you both feel obliged to light under the ass of a New York division director, who, this morning, filed an official complaint of professional harassment and badgering, personally naming both you and Agent Morgane!"

Jerry laughed before he could help himself. Director Cole. What a bitch.

"I'm assuming that you find humor only in the Goddamned magnitude of what landed on my desk this morning, and in the fact that Agent Morgane is nowhere to be seen to cover your ass, when I asked for her Apex report to be on my desk first thing this morning."

Jerry blanched. "Of course, sir. All I know is that Gabby, er, Agent Morgane, told me that she was following up one more lead and would get the report in today. I thought she might've got stuck in the snow somewhere, just like you almost did, sir."

"You said you were on the way to meet with her," Sorano said, nothing moving except his lips as he spoke. "And, I'm not even going to ask where. At this point I doubt you would tell me the truth if I did ask." He stood and walked to the window, a bright white square in the far wall. "Okay, get out of my sight, Walker."

"Yes, sir." Jerry stood, turning to leave.

"And Walker," Sorano said, still looking out of the window. "Whatever it is that you're up to, I hope to God that it doesn't blow back on this department, or there *will* be hell to pay. Do I make myself clear?"

Jerry stood, half way to the door. "Yes, sir. Completely clear, sir."

"Okay, get out of here. And make sure you grab some snow chains from the car pool. You're gonna need them, even for 5th Avenue in this stuff."

Jerry left the room and Sorano sighed, staring out over the white-blanketed city. A storm was coming, and he had a feeling it had nothing to do with the weather.

*   *   *

The flight was glass smooth, and Aaron sat, chin resting on his palm, staring out of the window at the sky beyond. Karesh was sitting beside him, re-reading a copy of a National Geographic magazine. There was a picture of Jesus being crucified on the front cover, with a title that read, 'Messiah, Warrior, Son of God? The Enigma of Christ.'

"I wonder what they would do if they knew," Aaron said.

"If they knew what?" Karesh replied, not lifting his eyes from the magazine's pages.

"If they knew what I know. If they knew what we are facing, what's real."

"You know more now than many have known throughout history," Karesh said, "But this is not your only weapon. You will need much more if you are to defeat the evil you must face. It makes no difference what people would do. They will make no difference. Only you can do that."

Aaron sighed, leaning closer. "Is it just us? Just the two of us? I mean, I know we are going to meet people that will help us somehow, but, when it comes to it, when we have to fight, who will fight with us?"

Karesh dropped the magazine to his lap. The business class cabin was half full and most of the other passengers were sleeping, or trying to. "If the whole world fought with us it would change very little. There is only one sword, and that is you." He pointed at Aaron's chest and it was as if Aaron felt the weight of it somehow, like the whole world was pointing at him now, watching and waiting to see what he will do.

"I remember things," Aaron said, quietly. "Things from my childhood. Things that I know to be true, because they are my memories. I lived them, but it is as though I am looking at my life through the eyes of a stranger, like it wasn't my life at all, but another life, being lived by someone else."

Karesh looked over. "I cannot even begin to try and comfort you, or justify any further the reasons behind why your life was kept a secret. You know, as well as I, that there really was just one choice, and that was to bring you to adulthood the way they have. You have been prepared in a way that can barely be imagined. Every day, *every single day,* you have be taught, trained, honed into a man filled with wisdom and peace but also sharpened to a razor sharp edge." He paused, nodding slightly. "This is a war that only you can win, Aaron. A war that only you are capable of winning." He returned his gaze to the magazine. "So, you see, it doesn't matter if the whole world fights alongside you or not."

"And what about you? You have training. You were a soldier. A good one. You can help me, can't you?"

"Of course, I will always do whatever I can to help you. I was a soldier once, different to the kind of soldier I am now. I hope that, when my time comes, it is with my sword in my hand and by your side as you cry victory to the heavens." He grinned infectiously, and Aaron couldn't help but return one in kind. "What is your biggest concern?" Karesh asked gently. There was a moment of turbulence and Aaron saw him grip the armrest just a little tighter.

"I fear that I have no place in this war. That I am not really who everyone thinks, and hopes, I am. I'm afraid that I'll fail, because I am not brave, and that I won't know what to do when the time comes to fight."

"Well," Karesh said, "That is plenty enough fears for one day, my friend. It will take some time for you to acclimate to the knowledge you have now, that your subconscious needs to absorb and recognize, before you begin to feel settled again. This is the most vulnerable time for you, and for all of us. That is why I changed our travel arrangements, to give us some more time, and to keep the wolves from our door just a little while longer."

Aaron nodded, biting at his fingernails as his thoughts wandered. Karesh sighed, settling back, allowing the young man to become at ease with his fears. They had a long way to go, having changed their flight from Moscow to New York to a new route that took them instead into Paris and, now, to Toronto. The upgraded class was a rare privilege, and yet an obvious choice as far as security was concerned. Karesh looked at his watch. Four hours until they landed. More than enough time for him to make a sweep of the main cabin and keep a watchful eye out for anyone with deception in their eyes.

"I'll be back in a moment," he said, patting Aaron's arm. "You really should try to get some sleep. You're going to feel it once we have to move around tomorrow." He got up from his seat and scanned the cabin. Of the other three passengers in business class, only one was awake, and elderly woman, reading a book and nursing a tall glass of champagne. She glanced up as he walked by, her eyes quickly returning to the paperback on her lap.

The main cabin was just as sparsely populated, with only around a third of the seats occupied. The window shades were all drawn down, making the cabin gloomy as people did their best to get some sleep on the eight-hour crossing. A few reading lights were dotted about the room, yet most illuminated only the tilted, distorted faces of slumber. Karesh walked slowly down the aisle, head turning slowly from side to side, scanning faces, looking for anything out of the ordinary. Anything at all.

One man, sitting in an aisle seat on the opposite side of the cabin, followed him with his eyes as he walked. Karesh took a mental note. Caucasian, mid-forties, overweight, clammy, thinning hair highlighted by a truly magnificent combover. He was highly suspicious, of anything and everything, and a very nervous flier. Karesh moved on, approaching the restrooms at the rear of the aircraft. A flight attendant stepped through a curtain, stopping in the aisle, her practiced smile bright and perfect. "Anything I can get you, sir?" she asked, as Karesh stepped beside her.

"Thank you, no. Just stretching my legs. A couple of laps should do the trick."

"Well, you let me know if I can get you anything at all, all right?"

She stepped away, disappearing behind the curtain again. He could hear her chatting with another attendant. Theirs were the only two voices back there. The soft glow of a laptop screen to his left caught his eye, the small computer's screensaver a swirling pattern of random colors, it's owner asleep, chin on palm, leaning on the narrow arm rest. Karesh turned and began to make his way slowly forward again. As he moved away along the aisle, the laptop man opened his eyes, lifting his head from his hand, watching as Karesh walked away. He took the metal framed spectacles from his head and wiped them absentmindedly on the hem of his shirt. Lothar did not take his eyes from Karesh until he was out of sight, stepping through the drawn curtains that led forward to the upper class cabins. He was the only one who knew the target and his minder were on this flight.

After tracking them to Damascus airport, he had managed to follow them to Paris via Moscow, only once almost losing them, during the terminal change at Charles de Gaul, not knowing which flight they were planning on taking. He had watched the soldier make the decision after a series of phone calls, guessing that he was changing their route on the fly. Lothar had considered calling in, but wanted this to go down his way, by his hand, and when he walked into Michaelson's office with the kid's head in a beer crate, he would smash his righteous fat face in with it.

* * *

"What the hell do you mean, 'They didn't arrive in London'? So where are they now? Do we even know if they're in England? Did they get there at all? What the fuck am I paying you people for!"

James stood at the end of the long conference table on the top floor suite of the Akron Hotel. It was the first setback in what he thought would be a smoothly executed operation to grab this Aaron kid, put him on a private plane back to London and hand him over to Mr. Black. That all hinged, however, on actually knowing where the kid was, and was going be. Matt stirred uneasily by the door.

The others in the room, five members of the Raven Group assigned by Roland to assist James with whatever needed to be done, were all older, wiser and far more experienced in such matters, than James was, and yet they looked up to him like some kind of worldly presence. A leader, *their* leader. Mr. Black had chosen him personally. He was the one, the champion of their cause. It was up to them to throw away their lives in order to help him, if it became necessary. Four men and one woman, all top level business executives, chairing the boards of five of New York's largest corporations, sat silently, weathering the barrage of James' wrath as he paced back and forth between the end of the table and the immense flat screen monitor on the wall.

"Our assets on the ground had solid information that the target and his aide would arrive in London from Moscow before catching a Delta flight into Washington. We were never led to believe that they would deviate from this plan."

James stopped, turning to plant his hands on the polished mahogany table. "Then why didn't we have someone in Syria, or Moscow, to make damned sure that they didn't deviate from their precious plan?" He leaned forward, eyes almost glowing with fury. "Because, ladies and gentlemen, you were complacent, that's why. *Complacent!*"

He stood and waked over to the window. One of the older men coughed, his thick white mustache twitching as he spoke. "Sir, we did have people on the ground in Syria. They were attached to the group we had move on the fortress in Palmyra with orders to follow them and report all movements. As our other source gave us good information about a flight to Moscow and then London—and we have a reliable contact in the Russian capital that confirmed that—we feel that we observed prudence, covered the targets from several angles and..."

"And still you lost them," James said, cutting the older man off. He turned and walked slowly back to the head of the table. "He is coming, and when he gets here, I want him. I want him in one perfect piece or his head in a God damned box on my desk. Either way, he is one man, with one person with him. It really shouldn't be that hard."

There was a knock at the door and Matt moved to open it, checking to see who was outside. Stepping aside, he pulled open one of the double doors. A young woman, dressed in a smart blue business suit, walked in, holding up a folder. "They are on an Air France flight, heading into Toronto. They land in two hours."

James froze, and then looked from face to face at the table. "That gives all of you two hours to get some people over there and redeem yourselves." A moment's silence followed before five chairs simultaneously pushed out from the table and the group filed quickly out of the room. The young girl who had come in with the folder, turned to follow them out. James looked up. "And where are you going?" he said, the girl pausing to look back. "You don't have to leave. Come and sit down. I want to hear how you managed to find him while those idiots, and all of their expensive resources, could barely find their way to this office."

The young girl flicked her long blonde hair over a shoulder and walked toward the end of the table as James pulled a chair out for her. As she went to sit down, Matt walked to the door and stepped outside, closing the doors behind him. He was due a coffee break. Half an hour should be more than enough.

The Boeing triple-seven landed at Pearson International precisely eleven minutes ahead of schedule. Aaron was awoken only by the touchdown, having fallen asleep almost on command when Karesh had left him to walk the cabin. He stretched, looking out of the window at an alien world of heavy gray skies and a blanketed white landscape. The sight filled him with a mixture of boyish excitement and a sort of subtle, creeping dread at the thought of being so far away from home and the surroundings he had grown up in. He suddenly missed the deep desert.

"When we clear immigration we will hire a car. Remember, we are visiting Canada, not the United States. Even though your passport says Egyptian, they will judge you on your looks, not your nationality, so act as yourself, as you always do."

"And how is that?" Aaron asked, pulling his backpack out from the overhead locker above his seat.

"Like a little boy with the wonder of the world in his eyes," Karesh replied, grinning as he clapped the young man on the back. "Come on, let's get through this and on the road. We still have some way to go, and people are counting on us."

They moved through customs and immigration far more quickly than Karesh had even hoped. They were first to the baggage carousel and Aaron stood watching the people file through the checkpoints. Everyone was different, looked different, dressed different, and yet they almost all wore the same expression of a sort of resigned exhaustion, mixed with relief. They were all happy to be home, they just didn't look it.

He wondered then; would he wear the same face when he finally returned home, to his friends, his family, his life? He watched them, one after the other, scoop up their passports with a nod or a thin smile as the officers waved the next in line forward. Another man stepped up to the counter. He didn't smile, but handed his passport over with a curt nod, nudging his spectacles up on the bridge of his nose. He didn't look as tired as everyone else. Aaron imagined him sleeping the whole flight, an enviable trait he didn't think he would ever share, despite his exhaustion-driven nap the last few hours of the flight.

The man stood waiting, tapping his fingers against his leg, the light reflecting off the face of his black sports watch, and the handmade woven bracelets jangling on his wrist. Red and orange woven bracelets, with three silver beads on one end. Aaron looked down, lifting his hand and pushing back his sleeve to reveal a red and orange woven bracelet. The three silver beads glinted under the fluorescent light. He watched the man carefully through the crowd. He looked like a pretty average tourist. Maybe someone returning home from Europe, except they hadn't come from Europe, and judging by the dust-stained desert boots and fresh tan lines, neither had he. Average build, messy light brown hair, he had a scar on his forearm, pale and straight, and another on his neck, just below his ear.

Aaron could feel his anxiety building, when, suddenly, a warm sense of calm fell over him, like a wave of sedative medication taking effect. He stepped closer to Karesh, nudging his arm to get his attention.

"I know," Karesh said, not taking his eyes from the carousel. The bags were beginning to slide down the chute and onto the rotating metal conveyor. "He's been following us since at least Moscow, though, by the look of him, he was with us in Damascus. I have a feeling exactly where."

"It takes one soldier to recognize another," Aaron said, touching the bracelet. He remembered the look on Professor Salomon's face in those last seconds before he was murdered. Fatherly, loving, full of wisdom. That was the memory he chose to keep as his memento from that day. Karesh reached forward, snatching two bags from the carousel. Turning, he smiled, handing one to Aaron. "Okay, let's find a car, shall we?" As they turned for the exit, his smile vanished. "We do not have to go far, but we have to move. He is good, so he will already have considered the same options we have. Out here, then to the right."

They exited the terminal and Karesh immediately stepped to the curb, arm raised. Within seconds, a blue and white cab appeared and the driver jumped out, hurrying around to help them with their bags. Aaron resisted the urge to look behind them, wondering if the stranger had his bags and was standing right behind them.

"Okay, get in," Karesh said, the driver trotting around to the driver's door. As both rear doors slammed shut, Karesh leaned forward. "Universal Car Hire, but please take us out to route 427, to the 401, exit Dixon."

The cab driver frowned for a moment and then shrugged. "As you say," he said. Aaron guessed Ukrainian, maybe Russian, then chuckled to himself, as if he'd know from three words and a lifetime of learning from books, computers and holy people in the middle of the desert. The cab lurched away from the curb and into a fast moving stream of traffic. They made their way quickly to the freeway, merging into post-lunch time traffic, about as quiet as it was likely to get. Aaron allowed himself a small sigh of relief, confident that they had managed to give their pursuer the slip. Glancing at Karesh, he realized that he didn't share his optimism.

Lothar grabbed his passport and walked toward the baggage claim, carousel two. He could see the targets moving toward the exit, having already picked up their bags. He could only hope that his was already on the conveyor. They were walking out as he stepped up to the moving line of luggage, squeezing between two large men wearing Maple Leafs hockey jerseys.

"Hey, watch it, pal."

Lothar raised a hand in apology, not needing a scene, however much he would enjoy the scuffle, and looked down the line of advancing bags. His khaki duffel was just dropping amongst the other bags and he waited, counting in his head, knowing that each passing second gave his quarry a better chance of gaining a lead on him and slipping away. The fourteen seconds it took for his hand to close around the duffel's handles seemed like an eternity. He snatched it from the carousel and walked down the line, in front of a few passengers, before cutting out of the crowd and heading to the exit.

The hockey fans were waiting for him to turn into them, but getting ugly in an airport was the last thing he, or his mission, needed. Closing in on the exit door, he could see the cars and cabs moving by outside. Now he would see if his forward planning was worth a damn.

Exiting into a thin crowd of passengers looking for a cab or a pick up, Lothar scanned up and down the line of vehicles. A Range Rover caught his eye, but it wasn't the one he was expecting.

"Major?" A German-accented voice said from beside him. He turned to find a tall, chiseled man with cropped sandy blonde hair and bright blue eyes, standing before him. "Hans Bruger, Sir. We have a situation change. We will need to take a cab. I'll brief you as we go."

He turned to the curb and hailed a cab, stepping in front of the nearest one. It screeched to a stop two feet from his knees. Lothar climbed into the back seat, joined by Hans a moment later, holding his cellphone to his ear.

"Right, okay, stay on the line." He leaned forward. "Head to Dixon Road, toward the 427," he said, the driver nodding and pulling sharply away and into traffic, drawing a few honks from drivers as he cut them off. Hans turned toward Lothar. "We saw them come out. They took a cab before you could get here, so Mikel is tailing them. He'll relay their movements to us so we can intercept."

Lothar nodded. It seemed he had been met with a good team. It was the single biggest advantage he could've hoped for.

"Good," he said. "They will either drive across the border, or head for an airstrip. Either way, they are going into the US. Either New York or Washington. I want them intercepted on the US side of the border. Make sure Mikel knows to keep a good distance. The bodyguard is good. If he makes Mikel, we will lose them. Make it clear."

Hans relayed the message. Lothar could hear the insistence in his voice. He knew Lothar, but only by reputation, and he had no intention of crossing the Major of the Red Guard.

The car rental office was busy, busier than on most days, and Lothar was grateful for the busy street as they left the cab and joined Mikel in the Range Rover, parked a hundred yards south of the office, across the street. Hans already had the powerful binoculars to his eyes, scanning the forecourt of the office, faces magnified to almost point blank range through the high powered lenses.

"They are inside," Hans said. "The front is glass, but it's too crowded for me to keep a visual. I can see the exit road though. Looks like only one way out, running beside the building and out onto this street. We'll see them when they drive out."

"I don't like it," Lothar said quietly. "He's a slippery one, the bodyguard. I'll be surprised if he didn't make us already."

"Well there's only one way out. Even if they know we are here, they have to leave sooner or later. They don't rent panel vans. They have no choice but to drive out of there, and we'll have them when they do."

Karesh stood at the front of the rental office, standing beside a pop-up ad and staring out of the windows at something down the street. He broke away suddenly and walked over, guiding Aaron through a busy lobby area with service counters on three walls and a snaking line of people waiting to be served in the center of the room.

"Are we going to drive all the way to Washington?" Aaron asked. "In a hire car?"

"We aren't hiring a car," Karesh replied, scanning the room slowly. "The one from the plane is still with us, I'm sure of it. We are going to need a way out of here." He paused, frowning at something across the room, and then appeared to relax, turning to Aaron. "Okay, this is what we are going to do. Just play along, and act excited, okay?" Aaron nodded, unsure of what was going on, and anxious about what was about to happen. Karesh walked away and Aaron followed him, until they broke into a trot, jogging toward a young man in a bright yellow polo shirt, swinging his bag onto his shoulder and waving a fist full of car rental forms at the counter clerk. They caught up with him just as he was about to walk out to the parking lot at the back of the building.

"Hello!" Karesh said brightly, Aaron almost skidding to a halt beside him. "I'm very sorry to bother you, but we really need your help."

The man, no more than twenty, Aaron guessed, stopped in his tracks, a look of uncertain surprise on his pale face. He looked from Karesh to Aaron and back again, taking a small step backwards. "Um, hi. What... what's going on?"

Karesh was acting tired and out of breath, as if he had just run a mile to get here. Aaron followed suit, panting and standing with his hands on his hips as Karesh spoke.

"We're contestants on a reality TV show, and we have to get somewhere without being caught by another team. We could win a million bucks if we can get there first!"

The man's face immediately brightened. "Oh my God! That's awesome! I love this! I was just talking to my girlfriend the other day about how cool it would be to get on a TV show like this! She absolutely *loves* The Amazing Race! Is this what that is? The Amazing Race? Where are the cameras? Are there more teams coming this way? Do you need to find a clue?"

Karesh grinned, and Aaron knew it was genuine. "It's a new show, even *better* than The Amazing Race. The cameras are very small, but they're everywhere. If we break the rules we're out, but the only thing we can't do is pay for help. We are being hunted, and if we are seen or caught, we get thrown into a sort of jail and we have to wait there. We could lose too much time to win, and we are in first place, and we're *so* close! The other team is outside. They're parked in a Range Rover down the street, waiting for us to drive out so they can catch us. Could you give us a ride? They won't be expecting that and we could get away. You would really be helping us to win! Can you do it?"

"Yes, please," Aaron chirped. "If you help it would be amazing."

Barely a half second pause and the young man thrust out his hand. "I'm Benjamin. Okay! Let's do it, yes! Okay, okay, you need to wait here so I can get the car close to the doors and you can jump in. I'll be right back!" He darted through the doors and the stopped, turning back. "Is anyone from the show going to contact me? Am I going to be on TV?"

"Oh, you will be on TV," Karesh said, still grinning. "Your girlfriend will have a famous boyfriend!"

Benjamin did a stiff, awkward fist pump, "Yes!" and then hurried out into the parking lot, head sweeping left to right as he searched for his rental.

"We could be here an hour before they even get a damn car," Hans said, staring at every car that drove out of the rental office, scanning the face of every driver.

"Be patient," Lothar said, his eyes on the road and his mind working through possible scenarios and options. "They've been inside for only ten minutes, but we could use another angle. Mikel, take a walk up there and go inside. Neither of them have seen you two. Take that backpack, and ditch the leather jacket. Call in whether you see them or not."

Mikel was a large man; over two hundred and forty pounds, though he had more of a Viking warrior's build than any kind of couch potato. The Range Rover rocked as he got out, and Lothar reached forward, adjusting the video camera mounted to the dash to make sure it was pointing at the car rental exit. He watched as Mikel made his way casually down the street, first toward a fast food restaurant, before jaywalking across the street and stepping up onto the sidewalk between the line of parked cars. Hans watched him through the binoculars as he crossed the exit road, casting a quick glance to his left, and then turned into the forecourt, disappearing through the sliding glass doors, guarded by a pair of floppy armed inflatable characters with yellow streamers for hair.

Karesh scanned the room through the glass from just outside the rear doors, while Aaron sat on a bench on the opposite side of the exit. A metallic *swoosh* noise accompanied the doors opening and closing as someone walked through them, which seemed to happen every few seconds. He remained by the doors, switching his gaze from parking lot to rental office floor. Suddenly, a bright red Chevrolet Impala pulled sharply up to the doors and Benjamin hopped out, beaming and full of jittery excitement. "Okay! Let's go! You're in a race, right? Let's go!"

Karesh turned once more as he picked up his bag, looking over the crowd of people in the main office, scanning faces, demeanors, body language. He turned away and stepped to the car, opening the back door. Aaron ducked inside and Karesh followed, closing the door as Mikel appeared through the crowd, walking toward the back doors, looking at every face and khaki shirt. Benjamin pulled away as the doors opened and Mikel walked out.

"Get down," Karesh said, and Aaron laid across the back seat as Karesh dropped his shoulder, squeezing in front of Aaron behind the front seats. "Okay, Benjamin," he said calmly. "You need to be calm and drive normally. We can't let these guys know we're in here and they'll spot you in a second if you drive like a maniac, okay?"

Benjamin nodded enthusiastically, then took a very exaggerated deep breath. "Okay, okay. I got it. Nice and easy. I'm cool, I'm cool. Let's give these guys the slip, and... Oh! Oh! I see them! A Range Rover! There it is! Oh my, they are really close!"

Karesh cringed. "Nice and easy, Benjamin! We don't want to get caught!" Another loud deep breath and Karesh felt the car lurch slightly as it rolled down the curb and onto the street, accelerating away, not too fast. He could hear Benjamin humming nervously in the driver's seat, directly in front of his face. "Let me know when we're clear of the street."

"Oh, I think we're good now," Benjamin said, and Karesh pushed himself slowly up, twisting to look out of the back window. They were speeding away from the car rental office, out of sight around a long curve in the road. He sat up, guiding Aaron up so they were sitting beside one another.

"How did I do?" Benjamin asked. "Did I do okay? I don't think they saw us. I think we made it! I got you out!"

Karesh kept his eyes on the road behind them, looking for any sign of the Range Rover he had noticed earlier when two men had pulled up in a cab before climbing into the SUV. The windows were too heavily tinted to see who was inside, but with their guest in tow since Moscow at least, it was a fair bet that he had been at the fortress in Damascus and had called ahead to a team here to try and coordinate an intercept.

"You did just great, Benjamin," he said, turning to look at the road ahead. "Now, let's get off this road. Pull into that rental place up ahead."

Benjamin nodded, grinning broadly. "Fake a stop at one car rental, slip away unnoticed and grab a car at a different rental place. Genius! Oh, I hope you guys win!"

Hans dropped the binoculars to his lap as his cell phone buzzed in the cup holder. "What have you got?" he said, lifting the glasses back up to his eyes with his free hand. "Are you sure? Did you check outside? Well you need to be sure, dammit!"

Lothar reached over to touch Hans' arm and the younger man paused, looking at him, phone in one hand and binoculars in the other. "It's okay," he said. "They're gone." He nodded then. A small gesture of respect for, what he was learning to be, a respectable adversary. "Call him back. We'll get on the road. There's no point in checking airstrips. They could call a chopper in to just about anywhere. The road is our only chance, and that chance will fade as soon as it gets dark, so we need to move."

A few minutes later, with Mikel back behind the wheel, they headed for the freeway, and then onwards toward the border at the Falls. Lothar knew their chances of finding them had just evaporated, but he was still anxious to get to New York. He had a report to deliver and an asshole to put in the hospital. "Let's go," he said. "Head for the crossing at the Falls. We can reroute as we go." Mikel pulled the Range Rover into traffic, punching keys on the GPS. "And hand me the monitor. I want to check the surveillance video before we get too far."

Hans passed a small, hand-held video monitor from the back seat. A long cable connected it to the back of the video camera, fixed to the dash by a self-adhesive mount. Lothar began reviewing the footage, rewinding in high speed to the beginning of the segment. Mikel was moving quickly through the traffic as he headed for Queen Elizabeth Way, the road that would take them all the way to the border. He played the video, a zoomed in image of the rental office exit. A consistent stream of cars appeared, pulling up to the curb before turning onto the street. Not a single face sparked recognition. Businessmen, couples, families, none of whom bore even a passing resemblance to the soldier and the boy. Just a constant stream of... wait. He paused the video and then jumped back two ten-second gaps, the image freezing on the front of a bright red sedan, approaching the exit. He went to push 'play' but almost dropped the monitor as Mikel swerved across two lanes.

"Sorry."

Lothar was stony faced but said nothing. He knew they had to move fast if they were to have even a slight chance of catching their quarry. He played the video. The red sedan pulled up to the exit. He could see the driver clearly. White, light brown colored hair, completely average-looking. It was no wonder he slipped by without a second glance. Then he pointed, directly at their position in the parked Range Rover. It was so obvious that he seemed to point directly into the camera, a huge goofy grin spread across his face. He appeared very animated for a few seconds, even bouncing behind the wheel, but then stopped abruptly, sitting up stiffly in his seat before driving the car steadily onto the street. Not too fast, and not too slow. Lothar smiled, saying to himself, *'Good move, my friend. Good move.'*

"They are in a red Chevrolet. A sedan. We need to catch them inside the US border. Timing will be critical because they will undoubtedly switch cars, assuming that they don't have someone waiting for them already."

Mikel gunned the engine and the SUV surged forward as Lothar checked the map on his phone. It showed two obvious crossings; one north, on the General Brock Parkway, and one farther south, close to Niagara Falls. What were they trying to do? Would they attempt deception, or had they played that card at the rental place and would now just make best speed to the border? He nodded, zooming in on the map. "They will cross north of the falls. Mikel, take the General Brock Parkway. They will cross there."

Chapter Twenty-Six

The secure medical wing at the FBI's New York field office comprised of a vault-like entrance to a short corridor, with two private rooms on each side. A small desk was positioned out front, in a small lobby area, and the entry way into that lobby was an open, steel-barred door with an armed guard, a coded entry pad, ID card key reader and three CCTV cameras, all remotely operated from a separate control room. Anyone attempting to get in to one of the secure rooms was either delusional or just plain stupid. The Rook was neither. He watched from the back seat of the Mercedes as unmarked FBI vans and medical ambulances pulled in and out of the auxiliary facility.

What looked like an ordinary, red brick corporate structure, built and then remodeled a few times over, was the only place in the city that held every suspect, criminal and person of interest that the FBI had in custody outside of Washington DC and San Francisco. The medical wing was located on the thirteenth floor. There was a long suspended pedestrian bridge that spanned the two main buildings, separated by the access road that lead to the processing areas, one level above the basement.

"Very well. Seven-seven-nine-one-four. Yes, that will be all." The Rook hung up the phone and slid it into his overcoat pocket. The driver glanced in the rear view. After making the mistake before, he had learned well enough not to ask questions or make suggestions. The Rook would move when he wanted to move, sit and wait when he felt that he needed to wait. He was never rushed and never missed a mark. After thirty minutes, the windshield wipers fighting the heavy flakes of snow, a dark blue ambulance appeared, moving up the slight incline of the access road toward the street. The Rook watched as it reached the crest by the curb and paused. The driver flashed his headlights before the ambulance pulled into the street, the thick snow cracking and shifting beneath the tires.

"Follow him, and stay close," The Rook said from the back seat, stoic and dry. The driver shifted into gear and pulled out behind the ambulance as it passed by. They tailed the vehicle for two blocks, until it turned into a narrow side street. The snow was piling up against the dumpsters and walls, and both vehicles drew to a quiet stop about forty yards down.

The Rook opened the door and stepped out, walking toward the back of the ambulance. The back door swung open and a uniformed officer climbed out, stepping aside as The Rook walked by, climbing up into the back of the truck without a word, and pulling the door closed behind him. The officer pulled a cigarette from a pack in his jacket pocket and lit up, walking to the side of the narrow street and shoving his hands deep into his coat pockets.

The inside of the ambulance was, like every other like it, lit with a sterile, cold luminescence that almost begged you to feel sick. The Rook closed the door and stepped forward, slightly hunched over the end of a yellow framed gurney. Lincoln Klick lay with both cast arms strapped to the guard rails. An IV hung from a hook in the roof. He appeared lightly sedated, his head lolling from one side to the other, yet he lifted his head, straining to see who was standing over him. The Rook stared, his face expressionless, and reached into his coat, drawing out a pair of syringes, one filled with a pale yellow liquid and the other empty.

Klick's eyes struggled to focus, and he shook his head, looking up and squinting in the harsh light. "Who... who is that?" he said, his voice tinged with the effects of medication. "Doctor Ferris? Where are we?"

The Rook reached down, lifting the sheet covering Klick's lower body, revealing his shins, knees and then his thighs. He squeezed and prodded Klick's thigh, searching for the artery.

"Hey, what's going on?" Klick said, his head beginning to clear as the realization that something was very wrong began to hit home. "Who are you? What is this?"

The Rook looked up briefly, his eyes meeting Klick's for the briefest of seconds, yet that was all it took for Klick's eyes to relay that image to his brain, which processed it, attached it to a memory and sent the spine tingling wave of realization to his adrenal gland, which instantly went into overdrive.

"Wait, oh no. Wait, just wait. Please, I didn't say anything. Not one thing, to anyone. I swear! *I swear!* You have to believe me! They even tortured me! And I didn't say.. wait.. what are you doing? What is that? What are you...? No, don't!"

The Rook took the cap off of the syringe with the yellow liquid and leaned in closer. With one swift *jab*, he slid it into Klick's inner thigh, pressing the plunger before withdrawing it, replacing the cap and stowing it calmly back inside his coat pocket.

"What was that?" Klick was terrified, his arms and legs thrashing at the heavy leather straps, his IV tube flailing and whipping in the air above him. "Help! HELLLLP!" He screamed as The Rook took the empty syringe, and then stood there, waiting, at the end of the gurney.

"What are you doing?" Klick said, red faced and petrified. "Why are you just standing there? What...why...I mean, *please!*"

The Rook simply stood, as if waiting for a bus or train, calm and patient, knowing that, in just a minute, his job would be done and another problem would be neatly solved. After another minute, he slowly withdrew the plunger on the syringe and moved to the side of the gurney.

"No, no...no...please, just...can you stop? Can you? I want to be good. I can be a great servant. I can! Please, can you just take me with you? I'll do anything you ask, just please let me live. Please, I beg you."

The Rook paused, looking down at Klick's wide and bloodshot eyes. The tiniest glimmer of hope appeared there, just for a second.

"I'm afraid it's too late for that."

"Oh my God, no, please!"

A stream of yellow urine flooded onto the sheet as Klick lost control, terror now the only guiding sense he was aware of. He was going to die. The only question in his mind was how much it was going to hurt. He jerked suddenly, his head slamming back into the mattress, and The Rook stared at him, gauging the sudden physical reaction, and then slid the needle into the IV junction, pushing the plunger and sending ten milliliters of air into Klick's bloodstream.

A few seconds later, Klick's eyes grew wide and his body stiffened. His expression collapsed and his head fell to the side, eyes staring up at The Rook, accusing and lifeless. The Rook put the syringe away and grasped the edge of the sheet between two fingertips, tossing it back over Klick's legs, covering the cooling flesh and pool of stinking piss.

Outside, the officer flicked the cigarette butt into the snow and climbed back into the ambulance without a word. The Rook brushed a few flakes of snow from his lapel, closed the car door and settled in his seat.

"Let's go," he said, after a moment. "Mr. Devlin will want his update."

The driver nodded, backing the Mercedes out into the street. The traffic had lightened up considerably as the day drew on, and the city was quiet, as if hunkering down, preparing for a storm. Across the city, in the sky, high above the airport, a bank of heavy clouds moved slowly in, darker than the even gray, snow-bearing clouds that hung low over the skyline. A darker, roiling maelstrom, the clouds turned in a slowly rotating vortex like the menacing eye of a sinister hurricane.

People hardy enough to brave the weather stopped to take pictures with their smart phones, pointing at the building phenomenon. A looming sense of foreboding accompanied the roiling clouds, and many mumbled gestures of faith and fear before disappearing inside, locking doors and pulling shades.

Father Peter adjusted his collar in the mirror, tugging it up to cover the creeping, bruise-like tendril that snaked up the side of his neck. The room was gloomy, yet he saw his reflection as if illuminated by some hidden spotlight in the ceiling. He turned his head from side to side, patted his neatly parted hair and straightened his spectacles.

"Let's get this show on the road," he said, smiling at himself and turning to pick up his coat and scarf from the bed. His reflection remained in the mirror, watching him as he slung his coat over his arm and walked by toward the door. As he reached for the handle, a strange thrumming noise began from somewhere behind him. He paused, turning to look at the window, still covered by the heavy drapes. Walking over, he pulled them aside. The noise instantly increased as he watched the glass being pounded by torrential rain, the large droplets smashing into the window with surprising force, turning the built up snow into a heavy, wet sludge that slid and slopped down the glass and onto the sill, before slipping over the side and down to the street below.

"Well, rain, snow or shine, it's only up the street."

He turned to leave, the drapes hanging open to the dull grey sky beyond. In the hallway, he was greeted by a small moving crowd of priests, all making their way down to the lobby. They all nodded a greeting, and he returned each one, until the last had moved by and he fell in behind, walking a line toward the elevator he would not take.

* * *

"What do you mean, they're gone? What the hell happened to them?" Marissa Cole was standing over her desk, glaring at the phone—on loudspeaker—sitting on her desk. The news just came through that the agents she had sent two of her own to relieve, were nowhere to be found.

"As I said, ma'am, we arrived on scene forty-five minutes after the call came down. They were not here. It's like they just drove off. I've tried raising them on their cells, as well as the secure-net. No luck so far. They could be driving in with some technical issues. We should give it some time. This weather is playing all kinds of havoc down here."

Cole bowed her head and took a deep, calming breath. "A little God damned snow doesn't suddenly relieve my agents of all sense of procedure and common sense, Lambert. Something doesn't sit right with this. Stay put. I'll have a second team sweep the area, see if anyone saw anything suspicious."

"Yes ma'am."

She disconnected the call and looked up. "And you were about to tell me that Klick isn't due here for another two hours, is that right?"

The agent standing in front of her desk knew he was in trouble. Director Marissa 'Hot' Cole lived up to her nickname almost to the letter, because when she was so inclined, it felt like you were being dragged over hot coals, such was her wrath, all-encompassing and, to be fair, totally indiscriminate.

"Er, yes, ma'am," he said, trying to stand up a little straighter, appear a little more relaxed. He was not relaxed. "We got the call a few minutes ago. They're about ready to transfer him. Just waiting for a signature from Doctor Ferris and he'll be in the wagon and on his way over here."

Cole could not hide her fury, and the agent blanched, even taking a small step back. "Ferris, that meddling piece of shit. I should go over there myself and break his arm while I make him sign the damned order. Messing with my shit, asshole." She looked up again. "And what about Devlin? Who the fuck is this guy, and why is he here? Why the hell do I care? And why in hell is he so damned hard to get a look at, huh? Tell me that. And where are those two agents? Agents who were supposed to be watching a fucking hotel door!"

"Well, um, I don't really..."

"Oh, get the fuck out."

The agent didn't need a second invitation and turned on his heels, disappearing out through the door a few seconds later. Cole punched in an extension on the phone. "Get a second team over to Lambert's twenty. The Akron Hotel, yes, and get me Mister Grey. I need him up here asap."

She sat down and opened James' file, sitting on the desk in front of her. She reread everything they had on him in two minutes flat, and that just served to fuel her already boiling frustration. Beyond what Klick had given them on day one, and what they had in their standard archive, they knew next to nothing about the young financier, and yet Klick had been terrified to give up his name, suffering through the agony of having both of his arms broken and one almost dissected before he blurted the name out, seconds before passing out and vomiting all over Grey's shoes. He hadn't said anything, but then, Mister Grey hardly ever said anything anyway.

She had brought him with her from her time as an NSA interrogator at the Charikar black site in Afghanistan. An Afghan by birth, he had shown an uncanny ability to extract information from even the hardiest subjects, his favorite technique being the slow breaking of bones, which he then pulled out fragments of to show the subject, before using them as nails, and hammering them into various sensitive areas of soft tissue and between fingers and toes, impaling them with their own bones.

He had become Mister Grey when literally no one could pronounce his name and he insisted on wearing an ash grey shirt every day. She had lost a subject after one particularly hard night of questioning, and when the spook from Langley had showed up, demanding her head for 'torturing a high value asset to death', they made it all go away by sending her home and reassigning her to the New Religious and Extremist Cult division in New York. A shitball assignment, with one enormous advantage; No one else was on the ladder, and it was a clear shot all the way to the top. All she had to do was break a few big cases. She had a Senator who liked to screw goats in his back yard on a full moon before slitting their throats and washing in their blood, and a high ranking police chief of a major city who had repeatedly been caught soliciting young teenage girls for 'fashion shoots' in his basement 'studio' that more resembled a dungeon from the Spanish Inquisition.

There were plenty of sick assholes who thought they were in league with the Devil, or the moon, or both, and would gain power by doing the most ridiculous, awful things. She was there to make sure that they didn't get away with it, and owed her a pocketful of huge favors to keep them out of prison and their dirty habits off of the internet. That was her key to the top, and the office of Chief of the FBI. From there, who knew, she might take a run at Governor.

A noise made her turn her chair toward the windows. The huge snowflakes that had been falling all morning had been replaced with a torrential rain that hammered noisily at the glass and obscured her view of the city.

"Terrific," She said, as her phone rang. Turning back to her desk, she reached forward and hit the speaker button. "Cole."

"Director Cole, this is Special Agent Miles, with the District Homicide Division, downstairs. We just caught one on a transfer from the secure medical facility Downtown. Your name is on the transfer article, so you get the call." Cole's stomach tightened. This could not possibly be good news. Not today.

"Go on, Agent Miles."

"Well, it would be better if you could see for yourself," the agent said. *"If you'd care to come down, I'm sure you'd find the time worthwhile. I'm..."*

Cole hung up, her chair rolling back into the wall as she stood and strode from the room. In the hallway, she snapped her fingers at Agent Benizek, gesturing for him to follow. He hurried to catch up as a handful of his colleagues made throat-cutting gestures from behind their desks. He flipped off the group with his hand behind his back as he reached the elevator door, pulling up beside Cole, arms folded and bristling with pent up anger.

The basement level was one of the most brightly lit and clinical-looking in the building. Both a detention and medical facility, it also served as a temporary morgue, for cases where the victim was either in Federal custody at the time of their death, or was of specific interest to one or more of the cases at hand.

Today there was only one body in the room, laid out on an autopsy table and half-covered with a pale blue medical sheet. Cole walked in to a crowd of four agents, surrounding the Homicide Division's medical officer, Agent Miles. She knew him by reputation only, and what she knew she didn't like, but then, she really didn't like anyone.

"Give me the room," she said, striding toward Miles. The other agents moved away without a word, reluctantly turning to leave.

"Good afternoon to you, too, Special Agent Cole," Miles said, placing a clipboard on the nearest stainless steel table.

"*Director* Cole," she corrected, walking past him to stand by the table at the far end of the room. She looked down at Klick's pale and lifeless body, his head resting on a stone block, adams apple jutting up from his crooked neck. "Who brought him in?"

Miles walked over, standing on the opposite side of the table, leaning on the metal surface. "The same two guys who signed for him over at the Downtown building," he said, reaching for the clipboard hanging from a small hook on the end of the table. "Noonan and Kessler. Nothing out of the ordinary. Been driving transfers for, let's see, Noonan eight years and Kessler two. And before you go getting yours in a bunch, this is the first time anything like this has happened on their watch."

Cole pulled the sheet back, exposing Klick's blue veined abdomen. "You're going to tell me that this was either the result of his self-injury, or that he had some kind of episode. You will look him over, maybe even cut him open, but you won't find anything. Nothing that can't be medically explained, anyway."

She seemed almost distracted, meditative, and Miles had to look up at her to make sure she was still present. "I will run some tests, of course," he said, replacing the clipboard. "But, in all honesty, judging by what I have in front of me, and the officers' accounts, it would appear that you lost a subject during transfer, most likely due to a clot, say, disturbed when he was moved. He's been supine and resting, and had a couple of nasty breaks, so it's not a huge leap to make that connection. Bouncing around in the back of an ambulance with a couple of rogue clots is a recipe for disaster."

Cole nodded vacantly, frowning at Klick's body but not really looking at it at all. Her mind was somewhere else, on someone else.

"Are you all right, Director?" Miles said.

"He had extra security," Cole replied thoughtfully. "No one saw him. No one got close to him. There's just no way anyone could have..." her voice trailed off and she shook her head, straightening and stepping back, regaining her demeanor. "Thank you, Doctor," she said, nodding toward Benizek as she made to leave. "Please keep me informed." She reached the door, Benizek holding it open for her, then paused, turning back toward the room. "And Doctor, if you find anything out of the ordinary, and I mean *anything*, you have my direct line. I suggest you use it."

Miles nodded and Cole walked out, Benizek shooting the doctor a cautionary look before turning to leave, letting the door swing shut behind him. Walking around the table, Benizek looked down at Klick's serene expression, the bright overhead light giving a brief impression of a sleeping man, rather than a dead one.

"Well, what did you do, Lincoln?" he said. "What did you do?"

Chapter Twenty-Seven

"But I'm going to New York! I'm from there!" Benjamin was more excited than ever, and almost tripped over himself getting out of the car at Pinkerman Car Rental, a small, private company, off the franchise car hire grid. Karesh pulled his bag out of the car and looked across the roof at Aaron, who offered only a shrug by way of support.

"I'm not sure that the rules allow us to hitch that kind of a ride," he said. "What if we get to our next pit stop and find out that we've been penalized, or worse, disqualified?"

Benjamin stepped forward, almost too close. Karesh could smell the scent of wintergreen breath mints. It made his left eye water. "But you said you just weren't allowed to pay for help. I don't want anything. I just want to help." He stepped back and spread his arms wide, raising his voice as if the whole world was watching. "I want to help, and do so gladly, and of my own free will, so you can't disqualify this team!"

He stepped forward again, dropping his voice to an exited whisper. "See? Let's get going! Who knows how long we have before someone picks up our trail?"

Aaron walked around the car, standing beside Karesh. "Less paper trail," he said, and then looked up at the sky. "And he has a point. We should probably get moving."

Karesh raised his eyebrows. "Oh, is that right? Well, if he has a point, and we aren't breaking any rules, I suppose there's no reason why we shouldn't."

Benjamin clapped his hands but Karesh stepped forward, his expression darkening. "But we also have a duty not to put anyone else in harm's way, and I don't know that we can avoid that by accepting your help, Benjamin, however much I'd like to."

Benjamin's shoulders sagged, defeated. Karesh stepped forward and clapped him on the shoulder. "You have more than helped us already, my friend, and the whole world will owe you a debt of gratitude for what you have done today."

Benjamin smiled and was about to speak when a man, wearing a bright green polo shirt, appeared from the small office and strode toward them, waving his hand.

"I'm sorry gentlemen," he said, stopping a few feet away. "I hope you weren't waiting for a return vehicle to rent. Our last available just called in. Stuck in bad weather, down in New York, would you believe it. They were supposed to be here this morning, but they went and got snowed in. Some crazy storm just blew up out of nowhere, so they're sayin'. So, anyway, I'm sorry guys, but I have to shut up shop for the day. You're welcome to rest up for the night and come by tomorrow, if that helps. First return is due at 10:00. Martha's Bed & Breakfast is just a mile or so down the road there. It's a nice little place, if you're interested. Let's hope that weather doesn't hit us up here, eh?"

He turned and walked back to the office, and Karesh looked at Benjamin, his face lighting up. "Looks like I get to come to your rescue again! Now we *have* to get on the road!"

Aaron shrugged again, unable to hold back the grin, and Karesh looked thoughtful for a moment, before opening the back door and tossing his bag inside. "Okay, Benjamin," he said. "One condition."

"Shoot," Benjamin said, unable to contain his enthusiasm.

"You will do everything I say, and go exactly where I tell you to go. And if at any time I tell you to get away and leave us, you will go. No hesitating. It could mean the difference between our success or the end of everything. Do you understand?"

Benjamin nodded. "Whatever you say! Let's get going! We've got a long way to go, and you've got a million bucks to win!"

The skies got progressively darker as they made their way to the border crossing, and by the time they moved through the immigration checkpoints over the river and made their way down the 190, past Niagara and skirting the city to the west, rain was beginning to spatter the windshield and the gloom of a storm front was pushing toward them from the south. Barely two miles behind them, inching forward in the crowd of cars as they funneled into the immigration station, Lothar sat impassively, staring out at the darkening sky and scanning every car in front of them.

"What makes you think that they are even in the same car?" Hans said from the back. "They could have gone just a mile up the road and got another car."

"We would have seen it," Lothar said, squinting at a red Toyota a few cars ahead, before dismissing it, rubbing his eyes with a yawn. "We were barely twenty minutes behind them. The only rental places on that road would've taken more than that time to get them into a car, and the two we passed were closed anyway. No, they are in the same car. They need to save time and are gambling on the fact that we didn't make them. It makes sense for them to get a good lead. Even if we were following on the same road, under different circumstances we could pass them on the freeway and never even know it. It's what I would do. Time is more important to them."

As they pulled closer to one of the kiosks, an immigration officer looked over, scanning the approaching vehicles before settling his gaze on their Range Rover. He moved to one of the other officers and leaned in, whispering something in his ear. The officer nodded and walked away, disappearing inside one of the kiosks. The new officer waved them forward and they pulled up to the automatic gate as Hans lowered the back window.

"Good afternoon," the officer said, stepping up close to Hans's window.

"Good afternoon, sir," Hans replied and held his passport close to the open window. Beneath it was a thick brown envelope. "A beautiful day."

The officer reached inside the window and took the envelope, sliding it quickly inside his jacket. Hans extended his hand and the officer took the passport, leaning down to peer inside the vehicle. Lothar stared at him coolly from the front seat.

After a moment, the officer handed the passport back and smiled. He didn't check the others. Stepping back, he waved them on their way. "Enjoy your visit, gentleman, and do drive safely."

"Americans," Hans said, as they pulled away from the checkpoint. "Arrogant and cheap." He sat back, resting his head on the headrest and folding his arms over the H&K submachine gun on his lap. "Works for me."

Benjamin was turning out to be a more effective driver than Karesh would've given him credit for. From the moment they pulled onto the freeway from the immigration station, he became focused, silent and more aggressive on the road, driving as though someone were in hot pursuit and out for blood. By the time they began to draw south of the city, the rain was turning to sleet, covering the roads with an icy sludge. The roads were still clear, though, the northern most cities far better equipped to deal with harsh weather than their own, more southerly, neighbors. They had driven for a couple of hours when Karesh decided they should stop for a few minutes to stretch their legs. Aaron had been watching him carefully since they had crossed the border.

"Who are we waiting for?" he asked, after Karesh told Benjamin to pull off the freeway and into a gas station, a brightly lit mini mart beside it. Benjamin parked the car and killed the engine, stretching in his seat. "Okay, kids, go grab your goodies. Don't go too far and no talking to strangers, okay?"

Karesh opened the door and stepped out into the freezing rain, Aaron following a moment later. He pulled his jacket up over his head, running to catch up as Karesh walked toward the brightly lit mart entrance.

"What makes you think we are waiting for anyone?" Karesh said, walking through the automatic doors and into the store. He paused, turning to look out through the rain toward the car in the lot. "We should get some gas while we are making good time, and we need food, water."

"You've looked at your watch over a dozen times since we crossed the border, and we drove half way across the Syrian desert with a back seat full of gas cans without stopping to stretch anything."

The clerk was a young man with a scowl and impressive sideburns. He was leaning on the counter and didn't look up when they walked in. The ball cap he wore said 'The Don't Stop. NY'. The place was deserted, and they walked down the center of the mart, along one of the narrow aisles, toward the glass refrigerator units along the back wall. Aaron had never seen such an array of different products, stacked neatly on shelves in brightly colored packaging. He thought it reminded him of a toy store. Karesh remained silent for a moment, opening one of the refrigerator doors and pulling out two liter-sized bottles of water.

"Well, he should be here any minute," he said, finally, opening another refrigerator, filled with yogurts and cheeses. "We were due here fifteen minutes ago. Not too bad, considering our revised travel plans." Aaron followed with a shopping basket, Karesh dropping items in as they went along.

"So, who are we meeting? Why are they coming all this way? We could have just flown into a different airport, closer to Washington, and then met him there, no?"

Karesh smiled. "One day, when it is not even your job, you will make plans, and you will understand timing, misdirection, tempo. For now, though, allow me to continue to make those plans, so that we may get to where we are going, whether the help we need comes to us way out here, or greets us at the door when we arrive at our destination."

"And what about the men who are following us? There was only one on the plane with us, I think, but there were more outside the airport. The one who came with us was at the fortress." Karesh stopped, turning to look at Aaron, a frown of concern crossing his face. The refrigerator door swung slowly closed beside him. The defense of the fortress had been planned for, but unfortunate, nonetheless, and Karesh felt for the boy, having lost what was to be his teacher and mentor, after only having known him for a few precious minutes.

"Yes, he was there," he said, solemnly. "He is very dangerous, determined and well trained, and he lost men in the fight. He will be more motivated to succeed now, because of that. I know I would be. It's a shame..."

Movement in the reflection of the glass door caught Karesh's eye. A figure stepped into the aisle behind them, the silhouette of the MP7 sub machine gun unmissable.

"*Get down!*" Karesh yelled, pushing Aaron aside to the end of the aisle and down to the tiled floor. A trio of bullets smacked into the refrigerator door as Karesh fell, rolling forward and coming to a stop beside Aaron. He looked along the back aisle to the far corner, and the door there. It said 'Staff Only' in poorly stenciled red paint, below a small wired glass window. The room beyond was brightly lit. Another three round burst exploded cans of soup above their heads, and Karesh bobbed his head quickly into the aisle. A big man in a leather jacket was stalking down the aisle. He carried an MP7 with a suppressor, and from the way he was wielding it and moving toward them, Karesh knew he was dealing with a man with training.

"We need to get through that door," Karesh whispered, nodding to the corner. Aaron turned his head, kneeling on the worn tiled floor, his body pressed tightly against the end of the shelf. The door was a few aisles over. It may as well have been a hundred. "There is more than one," Karesh said, reaching up to pick a dark green can of peas from the shelf. "One is for sure covering the back, so we may run into him if we make the door. If we get through, keep low and get to one side as soon as you can. Do you understand?"

Aaron nodded, pressing himself against the end of the aisle. He was scared, but felt strangely in control, his breathing calm and steady. "Yes, I understand. Down and to the side."

Karesh nodded. On the end of the next aisle, he spotted a rack of utensils. He squeezed Aaron's shoulder, leaning around him to look down the other aisle. It was clear. No one sneaking up along their flank, for now. "Stay here," he said. "I will be just a moment."

A second later, he tossed the can of peas into the aisle, and yelled, "Grenade!"

From farther down the aisle, Mikel heard the shout and turned to see the green cylinder hit the floor and roll toward him. He turned to dive along the aisle, crashing to the floor and sliding into a rack of breakfast claws. They were on sale. Two for a dollar.

Karesh rolled across the end of the aisle, reached up to snatch a metal potato peeler—the cheap kind with the open metal handle—and rolled back before Mikel had a chance to realize he had been duped. As Karesh rose to his knee, another man appeared at the end of the far aisle, in the corner of the store, blocking their way out. He saw the handgun coming up and the even, short-step walk of a trained soldier, aiming on the move.

"Back into the aisle!" Karesh said, leaning into Aaron and moving him around the corner into the open aisle he had checked a moment before. Two rounds struck the end of the aisle as they moved away, spraying them both with canned broth and shredded chicken. Aaron fell back into the aisle, his head almost hitting the floor as Karesh dived, almost landing on top of him.

"Give me the gun!" he said, loudly, knowing it would give their attackers pause, slowing their advance. He lowered his voice. "Two in here, with us," he said. "The third either covering the front or moving in through that room. We have to move quickly."

He knew that they were trying to force them away from the back aisle, and the prospect of an escape route through the staff door.

"Follow me to the intersection, just up there," he said. 'Stay close, and grab that jar of beets, on the shelf right there. Aaron turned and reached across the aisle, pulling a large glass jar of beets from the shelf, the dark red liquid swirling as he pulled it to his chest.

"Okay, trust me with this."

A few moments later, Karesh moved down the aisle, all too aware that the man with the handgun was moving along the back aisle toward them, squeezing them between himself and the large man with the MP7. But that left the intersection—a break in the aisles half way down in the center of the store—open, so long as the third man wasn't there, waiting to spring a trap. When he reached the intersection, he peered around the shelves, and then into the next aisle over. The large man was there, creeping away from him toward the back of the store, weapon raised.

He felt suddenly very vulnerable. If he had miscalculated, and the third shooter was coming in the front, instead of covering the back, he could expect a round in the side of his head any second. When it didn't come, he rose to his feet and crept toward the large man, his wide back stretching the leather of his very large jacket. The handgun man would be appearing at the end of Aaron's aisle any moment, so when he stepped close behind the big man's creeping form, he moved fast, keeping the hulking figure between him and the open end of the aisle, about ten feet away.

He swung his left hand up to the man's head, grabbing a handful of hair, and *yanked,* pulling it hard down and back. The man made a strange '*gaack!*' sound as Karesh plunged the peeler into his neck, just below his right ear, before drawing it out and kicking the back of his leg, dropping the man to his knees. Two more stabs to his neck and head and the man slumped forward to the floor, dark red blood spilling onto the faded tile. Tossing the peeler to the floor, Karesh reached down to recover the MP7 as a noise in front of him caught his attention. Instinctively he ducked, step/falling over Mikel's body, as shots were fired at him. A round grazed his torso and he twisted his body as he fell, hitting the ground on his side and trying to raise the gun to aim up the aisle.

Hans rounded the corner by the staff exit and saw the bodyguard, the target crouching behind him, at the end of Mikel's aisle. He raised his gun and fired two quick rounds through the stacks of produce, just as they dived for cover. He was uncertain if he had hit anyone. He guessed Mikel was inching toward the end of his aisle, and moved forward slowly, eyes focused on the corner the targets had disappeared around. Two aisles away, he heard the bodyguard ask for his gun and paused, considering his options, and cursing himself beneath his breath at having rounded the corner into the back aisle too quickly.

With Mikel moving toward the back of the store, the targets were in the next aisle over, between Mikel and him. They had the aisle clear behind them, to the front of the store, and as it stood there was nothing stopping them from running out the front door.

Hans moved forward again, heading toward the end of the aisle that they had dived into. He crouched at the end, gun raised, then peeked quickly around the corner and into the aisle. A body lay on the floor, face up, blood pooling around his head. It was the primary, the boy, Aaron.

"Fuck!" he hissed, moving into the aisle and carefully leaning over Aaron's still form, his eyes staring blankly up at the ceiling. He was about to reach down to feel for a pulse, when he heard a noise, definitely the sounds of a struggle, somewhere over in the next aisle. Moving quickly, he turned out of the aisle and peered around into the next one, just as Mikel's body hit the floor. He saw the spurt of blood spill out from his neck and the potato peeler skitter across the floor toward him as the bodyguard tossed it to the tile, crouching to pick up Mikel's MP7.

A surge of rage filled him, tingling his cheeks with a hot flash, and he swung his gun up, moving into the aisle. The bodyguard straightened, checking the weapon as he rose, and Hans's finger tightened on the trigger as his foot brushed the potato peeler, moving it barely an inch on the floor. Hans lost a half second in pause and then fired as the bodyguard moved aside, dropping to the floor and twisting to land on his back so that he could bring his weapon to bear.

But Hans was already on him, kicking the weapon from his hand and sending it clattering into the shelves. Stepping forward, he raised the pistol, sneering as he aimed down at Karesh's head, one booted foot pinning the fallen man's ankle painfully to the hard floor.

"You killed my fucking friend, you piece of shit!"

He tensed, and Karesh closed his eyes, praying that Aaron had taken the opportunity to slip away to safety, his final moments filled with regret at having failed to deliver him safely to Leonore, and, as rumor had it, Michael himself.

Shfft!

Karesh opened his eyes at the sound, and looked up as a hand appeared under the man's gun arm, pulling it away, and then snaked up, striking the man crisply in the throat with the peeler. Hans choked, reaching up to grab his damaged windpipe as Aaron stepped out from behind him—his chest and neck stained with red juice—and struck him with a blinding trio of hard blows to the kidneys, ribs and thigh, pulling him down hard and finishing him with a smashing knee strike into his face, which sent him to the floor in a twisted, bloodied heap.

The handgun clattered to the tile and Aaron stepped forward, calmly reaching down to pull Karesh to his feet. "It's time to go," he said, and Karesh reached up, allowing Aaron to pull him to his feet. He winced, feeling the graze in his side.

"The guns," he said, as Aaron started moving along the aisle. "We'll need them."

Aaron stooped to collect the two weapons and Karesh took the bloodied peeler from him, shaking his head at the simple weapon before stowing it in his back pocket. Aaron handed him the machine gun before moving toward the front door, standing open invitingly an aisle and a half ahead. They had just reached the intersection when Lothar appeared, blocking their path to the door, swinging his own assault rifle into the aisle and raising it, staring down the sights at them as he moved expertly forward.

"Drop them," he said, moving slowly, his finger poised on the trigger.

Aaron dropped the two weapons, kicking them aside. Karesh was able to stand, but he would be in poor condition if it came to a fight. He had seen how Aaron had taken care of the gunman, yet didn't rate his chances as highly against a seasoned killer like the man standing before them now.

"I should kill you and take the boy," Lothar said, glaring at Karesh. "My priority is him. Everything else is secondary, and expendable." He nodded toward Karesh. "That means you."

"What do you want with him?" Karesh asked, gently pushing Aaron aside, away from him.

"Don't play stupid with me," Lothar hissed. "I have a job to do, just as you do. My employers want you, Aaron, to come with me. I'd prefer that you come uninjured, but I'll do what I have to if it means I get you to where I'm going."

"How many did you lose at the fortress?" Karesh asked suddenly, and Lothar bristled, the question catching him off guard. "Were you the only one to make it out?"

"What do you know about how many of my men were lost? What do you know of them?"

"I know that we were far more prepared than you expected. I know that you lost a team trying to abduct an innocent young man who has pledged to do only good in his life. I know that you are a paid mercenary who, despite what your reputation suggests, has a conscience and is not simply a gun for hire, and to hell with the morals."

Lothar smiled, stopping just short of the intersection in the aisles. His aim did not waver, and his eyes remained fixed down the iron sights of the rifle. "There are pros and cons to being such a worthy adversary," he said. "And you are one. I'll give you that. But the higher the league, the tougher the opponent, and that's me. I'm the tougher opponent, Karesh Harrison, ex Royal Marine Commando, Victoria Cross recipient and pride of his troop. Leader of the assault on El Karjul, where your team rescued the German ambassador from a compound held by forty armed extremists. I know about your service record, your achievements, your history."

"And I know yours, Lothar," Karesh said, his hands held slightly away from his body, fingers spread. "Shame is a powerful motivator, and yet you have nothing to feel ashamed of to have made you fall so far."

"Shut *up!*" Lothar spat, stepping forward slightly, his entire body tensed, ready to shoot. Aaron patted Karesh on the butt and took a step away, distancing himself slightly. Karesh frowned, glancing down, and then at Aaron, who was a few feet to his right.

"Don't move!" Lothar said, keeping his aim level with Karesh's chest.

A blinding light suddenly appeared through the doorway, and the loud noise of a revving engine filled the store as a vehicle skidded to a halt, right at the curb, its headlights a pair of blinding white spotlights against the darkness of the parking lot beyond. The car horn sounded, blaring a deafening tone throughout the entire room.

Lothar flinched, not wanting to take his eyes from his quarry, but aware of the potential threat to his rear. Aaron dived to the right as Lothar hesitated, momentarily caught between three targets. In that instant, Karesh dropped to a crouch, his hand moving to his back pocket and finding the peeler there. He drew it, gunslinger style, and threw it underhand at Lothar. It struck the German in an instant, the crude blade sinking into the flesh between the knuckles of his trigger hand. Lothar yelped, instantly releasing his grip on the weapon, which fell noisily to the floor.

Aaron sprung from the intersection in the aisle, aiming a flying punch at Lothar's jaw as the mercenary stared at his injured hand, his other coming up to grip his wrist instinctively. Even through the pain he was still not unaware, and managed to slip Aaron's first punch, bobbing his head back and turning, so that Aaron simply sailed by, his clenched fist hitting nothing but air. But Karesh was far more measured in his attack, approaching from the front and staying low, flashing a hand out to grab Lothar's injured fist.

The German screeched as Karesh's grip tightened around the peeler's handle, twisting it into his flesh. As Lothar's eyes widened, Karesh swung his other hand, balled into a tight fist, from below his waist and upward, striking Lothar hard in the jaw, just on the side of his chin. Lothar dropped away, knocked out cold, and landed hard, his arm slapping the floor and knocking the peeler free, sending it skittering across the floor.

Karesh stood over Lothar's unconscious form, and then lifted his head, shielding his eyes from the bright light of the car in the doorway. Aaron moved cautiously to stand beside him. After a moment, the engine cut off and the lights dimmed, revealing the chrome grille of a Cadillac SUV. Aaron and Karesh looked at one another.

"I thought..." Aaron said, a look of confusion on his tired face.

"Benjamin," Karesh replied, his lips slowly curling up into a smile that Aaron mirrored.

"Who's Benjamin?" A voice said as the door opened and a man in a pristine black suit stepped out, walking around to the front of the SUV. Karesh and Aaron looked at one another again as the man walked over to the checkout, leaning over to look behind the counter. The clerk was laying on the floor, curled into a ball, his arms covering his head. He glanced up. He was terrified. "I didn't see anything! I'm not looking at you! I.. I won't say a word! Just... please.. don't kill me!"

The man leaned over and pulled the security system hard drive before hopping up to sit on the counter, smiling at the two men he was there to pick up.

"So," he said, "I'm sorry I missed the party. I hope you guys are ready for a road trip."

Karesh glanced down at Lothar, still unconscious, but he couldn't stay on the floor of the mini mart all night. He looked out into the parking lot, amazed that no one else had driven up. He turned to the man, still sitting on the counter. Aaron stood by, watching.

"A road trip sounds good," Karesh said. "But these days you don't know who you can get into a car with."

"Well you don't need to worry about me," the man said, hopping off the counter and stepping forward. "I'll be your archangel."

Karesh smiled and stepped forward, acknowledging the safe word, and held out a hand. "Good to meet you..."

"Marcus," the man said, taking Karesh's hand. "Marcus Novak. Likewise. Now, let's get this guy somewhere quiet so we can hit the road. The weather's pretty bad down through to the city. We'll hit the edge of it in a couple of hours."

Within ten minutes, they had bound a groggy Lothar and put him in the back seat of the Range Rover, parked off to the side of the parking lot behind a clump of bushes. Marcus tossed the keys into the undergrowth.

"There," Marcus said, "That should slow him down. Give him some time to reflect on his poor decision-making."

Aaron turned from putting the bags he had retrieved from a terrified Benjamin's car into the open back door of the SUV. "He's a good man. He's just forgotten, that's all."

Karesh looked off toward the gas station as Benjamin pulled onto the road, tires spinning on the wet asphalt, and sped away, taillights quickly disappearing down the dark highway.

A minute later, with all three men in the SUV, Marcus pulled onto the road and headed south once more. He glanced in the rearview mirror more than a few times, each time hoping that Aaron wouldn't notice, taking stock of the man who, according to what he was led to believe, was going to save the world.

Chapter Twenty-Eight

"We may have them," David Akers said, as Charles and Drexler walked into the control room. "We got a solid hit on a number of traffic cams that show them heading north on the 197, around twenty minutes after they left the main gate. I had Morgane's life history pretty much dissected at the atomic level—you can thank our inner circle friend at the FBI for that—and got an interesting hit on her father's timeline."

He tapped a few keys and the grainy, black and white image of the Tahoe driving along a freeway was shunted aside, replaced with another, equally grainy, image of an American soldier, standing in front of a row of Huey helicopters, holding an M16 rifle.

"This is Gary Morgane, Agent Morgane's natural father. He served three tours as a combat medic in Vietnam—all voluntary—from 1967 to 1972. Saved more Marines than the atom bomb. Honorably discharged in '77. Later married, had the one daughter, Gabby. And then he just disappeared, completely dropped off the grid. Left his wife and daughter behind. No one has heard from or seen him since. He even pulled a no-show at his own Congressional medal of Honor ceremony. It's been in keeping ever since. And get this; according to a record from his original CO, he begged to get into Bishop's unit, and I mean *begged*. He went way up, pulled strings, asked for favors, just so he could get a posting at Da Nang at the same time Bishop was there."

Charles was in deep thought, glaring at the monitor. He was under enormous pressure from the upper powers to retrieve whatever data Alex had taken. He prided himself on knowing *everything* that went on at Apex Labs, including every byte of data that circulated within the mainframe and also in and out of the every system. He had an uncanny ability to remember numbers, figures, codes and combinations, no matter how complex, and so, as his conscious had almost merged with the system's main data archives, he felt a very real sense of loss for the gap in the data flow that was now present in the mainframe.

"So how does her missing father help us find where *she* is right now?" Drexler asked.

Akers tapped more keys, and another image popped up, sliding next to the one of Gary Morgane. "This is how," he said, jabbing a finger at the screen. "Billy Gant, Marine corpsman, served through the exact same tours as Warren Bishop, and, after he put in so much effort to get the transfers, Gary Morgane."

"So," Charles said, smoothly, his inner cogs spinning. "These two men here," he pointed at the images of Gant and Morgane, "Served with Bishop, through several tours, out of the same base, and both of them were medics?"

"Not just medics," Akers said, not seeing Charles's train of thought. "Specialist medics. These guys were elite. Closest thing I could compare them to today would be Air Force PJs or SEAL combat medics. Pretty rare back then to have two such skilled and experienced guys in the same battalion, let alone the same fire team. One might call that a blatant misappropriation of valuable resources."

"Sounds like this Bishop guy wasn't running short of a few band aids," Drexler said, taking a seat beside Charles.

"Or," Charles said, quietly, "Someone worked very hard to make sure he got home in one piece."

After a moment's awkward silence, Drexler coughed. "So, what happens now, today, with this information?"

Akers brought up a satellite view of what looked like a rural area, the lush green fields dissected by roads and tree lines. There were buildings dotted randomly around the image, what looked like ranches or farms, and Drexler whistled. "Wow, that's amazing. Some secret CIA spy satellite?"

Akers looked over. "Google Earth," he said.

Charles was unmoved. "What are we looking at? Where is this exactly?"

Akers zoomed out and clicked a few icons, bringing up the map label overlay. "This is literally a mile north of the outskirts of Brookeville," he said. Moving the cursor on the screen, he pointed to various landmarks. "This is the 97, north of Olney." He zoomed back in, the image centering over what looked like a ranch, with a long driveway leading up to a main courtyard and house. There were a few smaller buildings, what appeared to be a grain silo, and a large red barn. "This is Gant's property. He's owned it since 1982. Bought it outright. It's well isolated, with nothing nearby, save for a golf course to the east and the Hawlings River Regional Park to the north. Lots of open land, with only one access road, here." He pointed to the driveway. "With so much open area to work with, we should be able to get a team in there, no problem. No disturbance, minimal fuss, nice and clean."

Charles stood. "Where are we on local law enforcement out there? That's still a main road. The slightest glance at a convoy of blacked out assault vehicles and it'll be all over social media before they turn into the gate."

"We'll go in with the lightweight fleet," Akers said. "No tactical gear. We'll keep everything else teched-up. Drones will relay visual and audio data ahead of the strike team. That's assuming we can get anything up in this weather."

Charles looked at his watch. "Too late to go in tonight. Bishop is still going to need to recuperate, regardless of how skilled Mister Gant is with a scalpel and his band aids. Have the team ready to move out in two hours, and find them somewhere to sit up for the night. Somewhere they can move out from without raising eyebrows. Give me a pro-rep within the hour. I'll pass the update along. Thank you, Director Akers." He turned to leave, Drexler falling in behind, his face a storm of uncertainty.

Out in the hallway, Drexler shook his head as they walked toward the elevator. "Are... are you sure this is the best course of action?" he said, his hands stuffed into his lab coat pockets to prevent him from waving them around, which he did a lot when he was anxious. "Sending in an armed assault team? Can't we just drive up, let them know we know where they are and try to talk to them? Perhaps Doctor Bishop will just come in of his own accord." The elevator door slid quietly open and they stepped inside.

"Put yourself in Doctor Bishop's shoes, Doctor," Charles said calmly. "He works on a top secret project, seconded from his home, unable to leave, and surrounded by armed guards at every corner. Just when you think you have a breakthrough, you are attacked in your own lab—at gunpoint—and are shot trying to escape, with, potentially, the most valuable genetic data in history. Tell me, Doctor, would *you* walk back to our corporate smiles and open arms?"

Drexler always put the human component first. Charles, though, watching the older scientist squirm and struggle under the weight of unfolding events, was far more pragmatic when it came to interactions with people and relationships in general. It didn't matter one way or the other whether that relationship was personal or professional. It was cleaner that way, easier to manage. He saw Drexler's conundrum very clearly, though, and, in some detached way, felt some empathy for the man. It was natural that he felt some kind of paternal bond with the young geneticist. He had invested a lot of time and energy in, what he had turned out to be, the brightest prospect in genetics in the country.

Charles had watched as Drexler had mentored, encouraged and wrapped in cotton wool, protecting Alex from the spiky, slippery world of high-stakes, government contracted projects and programs that had crushed and broken down many before him. And yet he had blossomed. No matter how Drexler—the country's foremost scientist in his field—had tried to trip up his young prodigy, increasingly testing his abilities and knowledge, Alex had continued to astound him. And in the end, Drexler had been right. Alex had known he was being tested, that his errors were really Drexler's wrenches, tossed into his working machine in an attempt to stump him. He had known all along. Charles snorted at the thought, and Drexler was distracted from his emotional turmoil, turning to face him as the elevator doors opened on the uppermost floor.

"What's so funny?" Drexler asked, as they headed along the solitary corridor towards the Sanctum.

"I'll ask you to wait out here, please, Doctor," Charles said, as the door opened and he disappeared inside. Drexler looked around for a chair that wasn't there and began pacing slowly back and forth in front of the door, which he would do monotonously until Charles reappeared.

"You found Bishop," she said, as Charles approached the desk, as usual shrouded in shadow, the dim outline of the high back chair visible in the gloom as he moved closer. "He's hurt. It was hard for him, for a while, but he's strong enough to be moved now." Charles saw the chair swing around toward him. "I trust you will have what we need back before the council gathering tomorrow."

"That is looking very likely, Madam Founder," Charles said, standing a few feet away from the desk. She didn't like people standing too close, looking at her, and Charles was one of a very few whom she allowed this. "We have a team preparing to move out tonight. They will lay up overnight somewhere close to the target and move in first thing."

She shifted in her seat and Charles saw a sliver of red-tinged hair in stark contrast to the pallor of her cheek. "I always favored more subtle, direct, methods," she said quietly, her hands resting on the desk in front of her. "But Black Wing has proven, as you advised, to be very effective thus far. It's the times we live in, I suppose." She coughed slightly, and Charles tensed, ready to move forward, but she raised her hand, anticipating his move. "It's all right," she said, her voice suddenly dry, and rasping. "Just a cough, Charles."

"Yes, Madam Founder," he said, stepping back slightly. She appreciated that he made a show of keeping his distance. His reverence and flawless loyalty was precious to her.

"How time flies," she said, pulling a long, slender cigarette from a silver box and lighting it, the yellow glow from the lighter momentarily illuminating her face. Charles looked away, but caught a snapshot image that stayed in his mind. A pale face, smooth like alabaster, and those stark, green eyes in sunken sockets, framed by blood red hair.

"It seems like only yesterday when you began your adventure with me, back in the cold country," she continued. "Things were very different then, over there." She took a long drag, the hiss and crackle of the burning tobacco the only sound in the room. "And you," she said, blowing a long stream of ash grey smoke into the air. "Were it not for the prospect of the firing squad, you would never have taken the risks you did, would you, Charles?"

Charles shifted uneasily on his feet, squirming. She smiled, but he didn't see it. He stood, silently taking the weight of her words, as he always had.

"You worked so very hard," she said, after another long draw on the cigarette. "So very hard, to betray me."

Charles bowed his head, his hands clasped tightly behind his back, and squeezed his eyes shut. "I... am... sorry, Madam Founder. I..."

"It's all right, Charles," she said gently. "I have these moments of recollection, and these words come. I know it hurts, but we all need to remember where we come from, don't we? What drives us forward. And besides," she stubbed the cigarette out into a thin glass ashtray. "You are mine now. You have been since my resurrection. I haven't forgotten how you tried to make amends, Charles. I won't forget."

Charles straightened. "For the rest of my life, Madam Founder," he said, his voice strong and clear in the quiet, sound proofed room.

"And today," she said, "You may call me what you used to call me, before. Before you stopped being that to me. Just for today."

Charles nodded slowly. "Yes, Mother."

*   *   *

James sat on a plush leather couch, in the living room of the penthouse suite of the Akron Hotel. A large split screen TV showed four separate news feeds, all apparently reporting on what was fast becoming known as a bit of a phenomenon. The snow that had plagued New York and Washington for the past couple of days was rapidly turning into a heavy, sodden slush that was blocking roads and flooding large areas of the cities.

He swirled the whiskey in the expensive crystal tumbler, the large fire in the hearth refracting through the amber liquid. He was alone, save for the newscasters on the TV screens, and sat perfectly still, staring forward over the rim of the glass, slowing his breathing. The rain lashed at the balcony windows, a muffled hammering like the thundering of a thousand frantic fists on the tinted glass. In the distance, the first rumble of thunder announced the coming climax to the storm.

James closed his eyes, holding the tumbler between his fingertips, and continued to swirl the liquor. A ragged fork of lightning split the darkness, and the thunder duly rolled a moment later, a cacophonous, crackling rumble overhead. James frowned in deep concentration. The lightning crackled again, closer this time, and the thunderclap rattled the glass in the doors.

Across the city, above the airport, a dark, swirling mass of cloud was becoming more defined, hanging menacingly low, just beneath the charcoal storm clouds that now blanketed the city, dropping water in sheets of torrential rain as the streets began to empty.

It had been hours since the sun had disappeared to the west, hidden by clouds and snow, and the night seemed somehow darker than usual. The security officers stationed outside the convention center gazed skywards from beneath the cover of the main entrance porch, their faces clouded with worry as one pointed up at the slowly turning vortex above. It was moving closer, edging across the sky like an immense, other-worldly craft, and when it became clear that it was not going to stop until it was directly above them, the two officers decided enough was enough.

James was humming now, the sound low and monotonous, like a vibrating machine inside his chest. The whiskey was swirling, but slower now, as if it were thicker, taking effort to move within the glass. James's frown deepened and beads of sweat appeared on his forehead as he worked and stretched his newfound powers.

The swirling vortex was directly over the convention center now, spewing rain and debris and hurling bolts of lightning at the ground. The airport was shut down, all flights in and out of the New York area canceled for the night. The weather channels were at a loss as to where the violent system had originated, all issuing the same, clichéd safety one-liners in an attempt to keep people off the streets. James gripped the tumbler tighter, forcing the liquid around and around in the glass. Outside, the storm growled.

*   *   *

It was as if someone had turned the heat up in the back of the auditorium, and yet Father Peter Howell could not stop shivering. His foot, sticking out slightly into the aisle, was tapping and shaking as if he had just downed a few cups of espresso. He drew more than a few curious glances, and would have garnered more attention if he was anywhere but on the very back row, the exit doors invitingly close behind him. The first speaker was drawing applause as he finished up his presentation; a strategy for utilizing mobile apps as prayer recorders. He found the idea childish and contrived, and sat, arms folded, smirking at the man on the stage as he walked away like some kind of celebrity, waving to the crowd.

Peter found himself to be suddenly irritated with the whole show. Everyone had their ideas about how technology was helping and hindering the spread of various religious ideals. He didn't think a show and tell of homemade science projects was the answer, and suddenly laughed out loud, just as the applause had died away. He saw an ocean of faces turn to look in his direction and couldn't help but snigger at all the frowning, serious faces. Someone touched his arm and he turned to look at a young priest—younger than he was—in the chair beside his, a look of genuine concern on his face.

"Father?" he said, his hand still resting on Peter's arm. "Are you all right? You don't look well, feverish in fact. Can I get you anything? A cup of iced tea perhaps?" His accent was distinctly English, and Peter thought about asking him where he was from, but dismissed the idea, realizing that he simply didn't care. He closed his eyes and took a deep breath, and focused on not telling the young man where he could stick his tea. *What the hell is wrong with me?* he thought, dismayed at his attitude. Opening his eyes, he forced a smile. "No, but thank you, Father. You're right, I'm not myself at all. I'll give it a few more minutes and if I don't feel any better, I'll step out and get some fresh air. How long until the intermission?"

The young priest looked at his watch. "About thirty minutes more. Perhaps you would be best going to get some air before the break, to avoid the crowds."

Peter nodded. "Thank you, Father. A good idea. I'll do that, in just a minute."

The young priest nodded, smiling, and then turned back to face the stage, where they were putting up large posters of artwork and concepts in preparation for the next speaker. Peter looked down at the program. *Professor Dominic Benoit - How Wi-Fi is the Devil and why we must defeat it to destroy his message.*

"Oh, Jesus *Christ!*" Peter hissed beneath his breath. He sat back in despair, rocking his head back and closing his eyes, just as a large drop of water landed square on his forehead with a loud *smack!* He opened his eyes, staring up at the auditorium ceiling. Directly above him, he could see a darkening of the ceiling panel, like a damp area that warped and buckled the paint. Another drop landed on his head, in exactly the same spot as the first. Then the ceiling above him groaned. A long, low, wailing moan that seemed to reverberate throughout the entire building. Peter looked around. Everyone was busy talking, writing notes and waiting patiently for the next presentation. The young priest to his left was chatting away to his colleague.

"Excuse me, Father," Peter interrupted, tapping the young man on the arm.

"Yes, Father, can I help you?"

Peter looked up. "Did you hear that? From up there? Do you see water leaking from the roof?"

The young priest looked up, frowning at the ceiling for a minute before shaking his head. "Hear what? I don't see anything. What did you hear, Father?"

Peter thought about trying to explain, but thought better of it. "Nothing," he said with a smile. "It's probably just the storm. It sounds like we have thunder now, as well as this dreadful rain."

The priest looked confused for a moment, but nodded, smiling back. "Thunder? Well, you have far better hearing than I, Father," he said, as the lights in the room suddenly dimmed and flickered before brightening again. The young priest laughed. "Well there you have it, Father," he said. "Do you know something we don't know?"

Peter smiled as the priest turned back to his friends. The roof groaned again, and as Peter looked up, two more drops landed on his face. He stood, looking around, but could see no other leaks, or anyone who looked like they were hearing what he was hearing. Indeed, they were all focused on each other, or the commotion on the stage as the speaker tested the microphone and said his hellos. Peter wasn't paying attention, until an image appeared on the large video screen behind the speaker. Peter paled where he stood as he stared at the image. The building, the roiling clouds, the giant fist smashing the building to the ground, spilling rivers of blood out through every crack and crevice. The building in which they all now sat.

Peter turned, knocking the chair over as he ran for the door, bursting into the lobby and sprinting past a small group of startled volunteers toward the main doors and torrential rain beyond. The sky lit up with a blinding flash of lightning as he pushed at the glass doors, the thunderclap almost instant on its heels. His chest thudded with the sound, and his ears rang as the people in the lobby cowered and covered their ears.

"Get out!" Peter screamed, turning back to face them. The door was stuck, and no matter how much he pushed and shoved, it would not move. He screamed again as more lightning struck, seemingly right above their heads, and the thunderclap took his breath away. "We need to get out! Get them all out!" He could hear the building creaking and shifting around him, and suddenly felt a hand grasp his shoulder. He turned, crying out in fear, to stare into the face of a young woman, wearing a burgundy convention center vest and metal name badge. Serena, it read.

"Sir, can I help you? It's okay, it's just a storm. You're much safer in here. Why don't you come with me and we'll get you something hot to drink?"

Peter was beside himself with fear, still leaning hard against the door that refused to open. "Can't you hear it? Can't you *feel* it? It's going to fall, all of it! We have to get out!"

Another man quickly approached, holding his hand up as he aimed for calm. "Sir? Sir, please try to calm yourself, you're scaring some quite nervous people back there. Now, what seems to be the problem? Can I get you to come back away from the door? The storm's pretty bad out there."

"No!" Peter cried, pushing harder against the door. "We all need to get out, now!" He shoved as hard as he could, and suddenly the door gave way, spitting him out onto the rain spattered porch.

James opened his eyes, his shirt damp with sweat and his brow finally relaxing. The whiskey was swirling rapidly in the glass and he turned his head to watch it, a sense of power filling him as his lips curled up into a wolfish smile. Power. He was bursting with power, and he liked it, he reveled in it, learning more with each breath and stretching his senses as his thoughts turned toward his favorite priest.

"Walk away, Father," he said, watching the liquid change color in the glass, shifting from a warm amber to a dark, blood red. "Walk away and watch the power of the one true God."

As Peter turned to look back, the door swung shut as the man put his hand out to stop it. As he watched, the man tried to push the door open again, but couldn't. He was trapped inside. He walked to the next door, pushing and shoving with his hip, unable to open it. He could see them talking and pointing at the exits, more and more staff trying different doors as he edged back on the wet concrete, finally climbing to his feet and backing out from under the porch roof into the rain.

"I'm sorry," he said, as an enormous lightning bolt struck the top of the building, sending sparks flying to the ground like an immense firework display. The thunderclap rocked the cars in the parking lot and deafened him momentarily, and yet he didn't flinch, instead just backing away across the parking lot toward the road, saturated and heavy with guilt. Overhead, the vortex was roaring like an inverted tornado, a dark, bottomless funnel stretching up into endless darkness. He continued backing away, the rain lashing at his face and body, until he crossed the road and came to a stop at the airport perimeter fence. He stood, frozen, taking in the horrific scene before and around him. The rain, the howling wind, the sinister vortex that sat squarely above the convention center. He closed his eyes and pictured the painting from his nightmare. The building, the storm, the clouds, the lightning.

"Oh, dear God," he moaned, sliding down the fence to sit in the freezing mud, his fingers gripping the chain links behind him. "Please, no. Please."

A loud *crack!* filled the air, echoing across the parking lot from the convention center. A sort of rushing, hissing noise followed, and a window exploded above the main doors. He thought he heard a faint scream from inside the building, but all other noise was suddenly wiped out by the loudest thunderclap he had ever heard. A thick, blinding bolt of lightning pulsed down from the center of the swirling storm cloud, momentarily blinding him, as the pressure wave hit him like a tidal wave, crushing the air from his lungs and snuffing the scream before it could leave his throat.

The noise of twisting metal and cracking, crumbling walls came to him as the sound of thunder rolled away, and he opened his eyes to see the front of the entire convention center building buckle and sag, followed by the right wall, as it began to implode, unable to take the weight of a roof saturated with tons of water and thick snow. He sobbed as he saw the people running to the doors, crushing against the glass, screaming for their lives and unable to find a way out as the building came down around them. Sparks flew and dust clouds erupted into the air as the immense roof finally gave way, falling in and down, onto the heads of everyone inside. Peter cried out in anguish as he witnessed the faces, twisted in terror, disappear beneath tons of metal, rubble and glass, before the building was lost in a thick cloud of acrid dust, spewing out in all directions and covering him with a fine layer of grey dirt.

When the noise had subsided, and the building had settled into a massive pile of destruction and death, Peter noticed that the rain had stopped, the wind had died down and the storm had suddenly blown itself out. He looked up to the sky, glimpsing patches of twinkling stars among the rapidly clearing clouds. He wasn't sure how long he sat there, soaked to his skin and freezing to the bone, but it wasn't long enough. He felt he should sit there forever; cold, wet and in freezing agony, asking for the forgiveness of every soul he had abandoned in that place. There were no more screams, no more cries for help, and yet he could hear them in his mind as clearly as if they were still real, and barely yards away.

The sirens seemed so far away, even when the first fire truck pulled up on the street, blocking his view of the ruined building. And still he sat, barely noticing the firefighters as they scrambled from their trucks, all of their efforts and training in vain. He didn't react when one of them spotted him, sitting back against the fence in the dark, and came over to him, calling for help. He didn't respond when they asked him things, wrapped a blanket around him and shone a light in his eyes. He didn't hear anything. He didn't feel a thing, except the deaths of three thousand innocent souls weighing heavy on his heart.

Chapter Twenty-Nine

Leonore sat, quietly fidgeting at the long table, a glass of wine before her. She was vaguely concerned about her cats. Mister Arnesen was a nice man, but he was the most forgetful person she had ever met, and she couldn't keep fleeting imagery of her starving felines at bay. He was still there, moving from conversation to conversation and walking quietly between the main room and and the glass-walled conference room, positioned like a giant glass display case on the far side of the open room. It had been some time since she had heard from Marcus, driving north to meet with Karesh and Aaron, on their way to the sanctuary of Michael's building, on the north edge of Downtown Washington. They were on their way, she knew that, yet she felt that relaxing would be impossible until Aaron was here, safe among them, safe from whatever darkness James Devlin and his mentor would send after them.

"You are wearing that same expression again, Leonore," Michael said, approaching silently, barefoot as usual, his footsteps uncannily light and his gait smooth. He gestured to the chair beside her and she nodded, allowing him to sit.

"The expression of concern is one I wear more and more, it seems," she said, toying with the stem of her wine glass. "I don't see how you might discern it from any other time I've worn it."

Michael smiled softly. Her petulance was a product of many things, tracing back to her childhood, and he was not about to start trying to curb it now. He knew her well enough to know it wouldn't do any good anyway. "I actually came over to bring more sad news," he said quietly. She looked at him with her cool blue eyes, wet with the emotional strain of worrying after ones you love. "Roland's right hand, the Devlin child, has grown accustomed to his powers. He is far ahead of the game, it would appear, and..." his voice trailed off.

Leonore frowned. Michael was never one to be lost for words, even when those words may cause someone pain or anguish. He simply said words, passed on advice and information, without feeling the need to edit or soften any impact those words may have. "What is it, Michael," she said coolly. "You should simply speak. It's what you do."

Michael looked up at her, nodding thoughtfully. "Yes, and you know me well enough by now, too." He leaned back in his chair and took a breath. "Devlin took the lives of almost three thousand people tonight."

Leonore didn't move, her expression remaining fixed, as it had been all night. She really didn't think that hearing such news could add to a mind already overwhelmed with troubles and woes. Michael let the words sink in. Three thousand lives. Three *thousand*.

"What...? How?" She muttered, finally.

"A convention center. The roof collapsed. There was an event. Everyone in the building perished."

Leonore moved into analytical mode. "Not one person made it out alive? No one just injured? What makes you think that Devlin had anything to do with it?"

Michael's pupils took on a faint amber glow, a glow that appeared only when he was boiling with anger. The look always frightened her and Michael reached out, placing his hand over hers reassuringly. "Because it was a religious event. Three thousand religious figures, from all over the world, from clerks to pastors, to priests." He paused. There was something else. Leonore waited. "And someone was afflicted. I can feel it, although the peak has come and gone. I think he wanted this poor soul to bear witness, before he felt the weight of the building upon him."

Leonore closed her eyes, her head still turned toward him. "Oh, Michael," she said. "I feel this is coming too late in life for me. I am old and tired, and we are dealing with monsters of such power, with such little regard for life. It's like a game to them."

"It is a game to him," Michael said, squeezing her hand gently. "It always has been. And this human, Devlin, has been anointed with arcane power. From the source itself. He will be almost as difficult to overcome as..."

"You don't need to say it," Leonore interrupted. "I know who we are talking about here, what this whole thing is about."

Michael nodded. "And still, there is no real telling how strong Aaron has become, what he has learned about himself, and how he thinks he is best equipped for what he must do, the journey he must undertake."

"You will know soon enough," she said, drawing her hand back and straightening, almost defiantly. "Tonight."

Michael bowed his head and stood slowly. "You should try to rest, at least," he said. "I don't think you will manage it once everyone is here."

She started shaking her head, the same old, stubborn Leonore, and Michael reached out a hand, touching her lightly on the shoulder. "Rest, Leonore."

Immediately, she stifled a yawn, blinking away the tiredness in her eyes. "Yes," she said, finally. "Perhaps just a short nap."

Michael helped her up and led her toward Eric, walking slowly over to guide her to one of the large bedroom suites toward the back of the room. He watched her go, waiting until Eric had shown her through the doors before turning away toward the balcony, his footsteps completely silent as he walked over to the windows. The storm had cleared, leaving behind a crisp and clear night, the sky above appearing to sparkle and glisten in a perfect display of heavenly glory. He stood there, unmoving, for two hours, staring silently out over the city, until a cough from behind him drew his attention away from the scene.

"Michael," Eric said, standing a few feet away. "They are here."

Michael looked past Eric as he stepped aside, to the three figures walking across the polished floor toward him. Marcus, looking relaxed and rather pleased with himself, the soldier, strong and wary, walking protectively beside...there he was. Michael stepped forward, holding out a hand in greeting. "Aaron, it is so good to finally meet you. Welcome."

Chapter Thirty

The box sat just where Gabby had left it, on the side table by the window. She didn't look at it, she watched it, as if it would move, with an aura, a presence all its own. The bright, snow-laden light beyond the glass was gone, replaced by the dull gray sky and muted green of a post storm early morning landscape. The gloom broken only by two far off lights of other properties, somewhere out beyond the farthest tree line to the north. Alex sat, dozing in the armchair opposite. She recalled how he had made it from the bedroom door to the chair with barely a frown when he had surprised them earlier. maybe Gant was right. Maybe he was just lucky, and a really quick healer. Holding a cup of coffee in one hand and her cell phone in the other, she glanced down, clicking on a text message from the night before. It was from Jerry.

Roads too flooded. First snow, now rain. Will be there first thing. Stay warm.

She slipped the phone into her pocket and nodded, knowing that the weather had kept many people from driving anywhere, let alone into the less traveled areas outside of the city, although the weather seemed to be showing signs of clearing at last. Gant approached her from the kitchen and Gabby turned as he stepped down onto the thick woven rug.

"How is he?" she asked, slipping her cell phone into her pocket, looking over at Alex's sleeping form, his chest rising and falling with reassuring consistency.

"He's actually far better off at this stage than I thought he would be," Gant said, his hands pushed deep into his cargo pants pockets. There were spatters of dried blood on his shirt. "He's looking pretty damned good for just over a day. We should get some food into him later today, sooner if he wakes up. I made some red whiskey broth earlier. It's in the pan there, on the stove. If that doesn't make him feel better it'll at least put some hair on his ass."

Gabby chuckled, and then her expression leveled out. She looked back toward the box, lifting her gaze to the window, and the gray, almost featureless landscape beyond.

"For the first time since I joined the Bureau," she said, "I don't know what to do next. All of my training, my knowledge and experience, and I'm stuck. I don't know where to start."

Gant reached down, taking the coffee from her hand and replacing it with a fresh cup. The black liquid steamed furiously. "Well, you know far better than me, so if you don't know..."

"It's like there's just too much to go on," she continued, wrapping both hands around the thick ceramic mug. "Everything I told you, about Alex, the lab, the murders at Alex's apartment. It all seems so simple and straightforward, on the face of it, like I could bullet point it all and stick it on the fridge or something. We all know what happened, and who it happened to, and yet there's this sort of red tape wrapped around everything, and I can't untangle it. I don't even know where to begin."

"You can start by getting some sleep, Gab," Gant said softly. "I've handed you a half dozen fresh cups of coffee over the last few hours and you've barely touched a drop. So, if it's not the coffee keeping you awake, there's no reason not to try and get some rest. You'll be in better shape to help Alex if you do."

"And what about you?" she said, smiling up at the older man. "I don't think you've closed your eyes for a second since we got here. You need sleep too."

"Oh, I slept," Gant replied. "I was just moving around and talking, so you didn't notice."

Gabby laughed, quickly covering her mouth when Alex stirred in the chair, a soft moan escaping his dry lips. "You expect me to fall for that one?"

Gant moved away toward the kitchen. "There are all kinds of things they taught us in the military," he said. "Ways to conserve energy, power nap through long hours of combat operations. Things far too classified to tell a lowly FBI field agent."

She pulled a face and turned back to the window. She could see patches of clear sky over toward the horizon, and was about to tell Gant that there was blue sky out there, when her phone rang, the steady buzz demanding her attention as she drew it from her pocket.

"Jerry," she said, trying to keep her voice low. "Tell me you stopped by my place and picked up a change of clothes for me." She smiled after a moment. "That's great. I'll ask the Chief to put you up for a raise for being such a good partner. I'm sure he'll go for it." Alex stirred again and Gabby turned, looking for Gant, busy concentrating on something on the stove behind the counter. Gabby lowered her voice even further. "Okay, just get here as soon as you can. Thanks."

"I gave him a dose of antibiotics last night," Gant said, stepping beside the chair and frowning down at Alex. "We can dose him again if he develops an infection, but really...well, I think he's good, Gab. Key is to catch it early if it shows, but I think we preempted it pretty well. He should even be up and around some today. We got him pretty well cleaned up."

Gabby pulled the blanket higher up her lap. "There's a bed that's way more comfortable than that chair," Gant said, pushing his point gently.

"Well if you can grab some sleep while humping through the jungle or half way up a tree covered in mosquitoes, I'm sure I can manage in this comfy chair, by the window, with a fire burning close by."

Gabby fell silent, turning to stare off into space, her eyes fixed vacantly on the window and the slowly lightening scene of fields and a misty tree line beyond. "I can put together just about everything, except one thing," she said after a moment. "Alex was working on some top secret project that obviously had a razor sharp deadline. The military are involved. I'd bet my ass on it." She trailed off and Gant watched, her brain crunching information and piecing together clues, and gut feelings and hunches.

"So you would think there is competition," she said softly. "Competition leads to pressure and tension, and tension under pressure leads to conflict. High stakes, billion dollar government contracts for the military. He's a geneticist. Genetics, the military, soldiers. He was working on some kind of highly classified military government project. So maybe others are working on it too, or want to be. He is gifted, a machine when it comes to formulas and codes and data..." She stiffened, sitting up straight before kicking off the blanket and standing quickly to stalk off toward the bedroom.

Gant watched her, standing over Alex as he stirred, blissfully oblivious to the sudden furore around him. A minute later, Gabby reappeared, peering at something in her hand and walking back toward the window, slowly.

"What have you come up with, kiddo," Gant said. "You look like you had a brain fart there for second."

Gabby stepped past him and walked to the window, slowly turning to sit on the narrow ledge, her back to the glass. She held up a small flash drive, her gaze shifting from the domino-sized device to Gant.

"Data," she said, holding it out toward Gant a little more. "This is what he was working on. This is what he almost died to protect. It has to be. It was the only thing he had on him when we saw him, and Alex doesn't do a damned thing without a good reason."

Gant frowned. "What makes you so sure?" he said, putting his Devil's advocate hat on. "He could've just had it on him when he ran into you."

Gabby was shaking her head, already certain of her conclusion. "I'm right," she said, and Gant could see the conviction in her expression. "I can feel it. Whatever is on this drive is at the center of everything."

"Not quite, but you're half-right."

The voice cut the air between them, and Gabby looked over to see Alex, his eyes open, staring at her from beneath a furrowed brow. His eyes were bright and clear, though, and Gabby laughed out loud. Alex was back, he was real, and he was okay. She stood and leaned over him, brushing the loose hair from his forehead. Gant went to the kitchen. She could hear him pouring a glass of water from a pitcher.

"Hey, you," she said, smiling down at her friend. "I thought you were gonna sleep the day away, you lazy ass."

Alex smiled, glancing at the window and the barely breaking day beyond. He looked amazing for someone who had gone through what he had. As she watched him grow more alert with every passing second, she felt a sudden wave of fatigue wash over her, weighing her down like a heavy blanket. After being so stubborn about watching over him until she knew he was out of danger, Gabby now felt the full weight of exhaustion she had been fighting off for so long. Gant, she knew, would rub it in later.

"They are going to come for it," Alex said suddenly, his bright eyes boring straight into Gabby's own. "You're half right," he said again. "About that... but only half right, which makes you half wrong, too."

Gabby leaned back, resting on the window ledge. "Wrong about what, Alex?" she asked. Gant walked over and handed Alex the glass of water.

"Steady now," Gant said as Alex reached out a hand from beneath the blanket to take it. His hand was steady. "Take it slow, okay? You're looking pretty good, Alex, but you've still some healing to do." Alex nodded, taking a few sips from the glass. It tasted like heaven.

"What am I wrong about, Alex?" Gabby repeated.

"The data," Alex said, taking a breath after slowly draining half the glass. "It's not normal data, it's far, far more than that. If I hadn't seen it for myself, I wouldn't believe it either."

Gabby frowned, glancing up at Gant. Was Alex still delirious? Was he making perfect sense, and there was something more to the data on the drive than she had first thought, or was he simply babbling, having picked up key words from her musings before he had woken?

Alex took another sip of water. "I need a computer."

"Well, I can help you out there," Gant said, turning to leave the room.

Alex snorted. "You have a Mainquest DS-11 running the latest Viking OS and Dormatech DNA profiling software?"

Gant said nothing, disappearing down the hallway.

"Alex," Gabby said. "There are times when your... emotional challenges are a good cover for a shitty attitude." She shook her head. "But not today. Not with Gant. He saved your life."

"You've no idea what we are dealing with, Gab," Alex said, his gaze cold and serious. "It's not my life we need to worry about. It's every life. Every life and then some. A little bit of sarcasm isn't going to make the damnedest bit of difference. What will make a difference is getting me in front of a piece of hardware I can actually use, and not a five-year-old three-ninety-nine home laptop from Best Buy."

Gant stepped back into the room. He was holding a laptop.

"Well this one wasn't three-ninety-nine, and I didn't get it from Best Buy."

Alex shot Gabby a 'I told you this was going to be some useless piece of home computing garbage' look and reached up to take the silver laptop. Gant didn't say anything, but stood back, taking a sip of coffee as Alex opened the screen.

"Well, let's see," Alex said, settling the computer on his lap and tapping a key. "Windows '98 perhaps? Or even Vist..."

His words stuck in his throat, Alex watched the screen as the laptop came to life. As the machine's technical specifications were displayed on the screen, he began to nod, a smile forming on his lips that soon turned into a full-face grin. Gabby sat back, enjoying the scene as it unfolded between the two men in front of her.

"Like I said," Gant said. "I didn't get it from Best Buy."

Alex was still grinning. "This is a Zeus 4400. How the hell did you get a Zeus 4400? Even Drexler had to kiss some serious backside to get the 3400 model and he has the only one at the lab."

Gant peered at Alex over the rim of the mug. "I know some people who know some people." He sipped the steaming coffee. "And one life lesson I've learned over the last forty years is that you need the best tools if you want to stay ahead of the game. So there it is."

Alex nodded, staring at the screen. A high definition 'Z' logo rotated against a honeycomb backdrop and Gant chuckled. "Like a kid on Christmas morning."

Abruptly, Alex snapped his head up. "The drive. Where is it?"

Gabby had anticipated the request and reached forward, holding the small device in the air between them. Alex hesitated, just for a moment, before reaching up and taking it with a slight nod.

"The data on that drive," he said, slotting it into one of the USB sockets on the side of the laptop. "It's a DNA code."

Gabby shook her head slightly. "A DNA code? But don't you work with those things day in and day out? You have that giant archive of the things. What's so special about this one?"

Alex smiled. He remembered telling Gabby about the top secret archive, and had almost regretted it in that moment, as she mentioned it so casually in open conversation.

"It's not what it is," he said, his fingers flying over the keyboard, opening programs and popping open windows. "It's who it belongs to."

Gant and Gabby exchanged frowns as the intensity in Alex's voice increased.

"It's okay," she said soothingly. "Whatever it is, we'll take care of it. Maybe you should get some rest. We can talk about all this later."

Alex shook his head, staring at the screen. "No," he said, his voice growing stronger as he sat up a little straighter. "Now. You need to see this now. You have no idea what it is and what's coming. They will come for it."

"Who's going to come for it?" Gabby asked.

"All of them," Alex said. " And you need to know what it is and what it means for everyone."

"Everyone?" Gabby asked, shooting Gant another worried glance. "We are all okay, Alex. You're safe now. Everyone is safe. I'm sure that whatever it is, you can just get it back to the lab and everything will be okay."

Alex was shaking his head more adamantly. His eyes darted across the screen and his fingers tapped keys in a blur as he talked. "No, you don't understand, you don't get it. I don't mean everyone right here; you, me, Gant, and whoever else might've touched this. I mean *everyone,* as in, the *whole world*."

"Ok, Champ," Gant said, taking a step closer. "You got your fancy machine, so tell us what this is all about."

Gabby almost hissed a curse at the older man, but caught herself when she saw how Alex nodded, responding to the request as if it had come from his boss in the midst of some down-to-the-wire project.

"Almost there," Alex said, his eyes wide and unblinking as he immersed himself in his process.

"So," Gabby said, joining in Gant's strategy of encouragement. "This must be some pretty important person we're talking about here. Someone who..."

"I don't even know if it's a person, or... or something else," Alex said, not taking his eyes from the code data now flooding the screen.

Gant and Gabby exchanged another concerned look and Gant straightened. "Ok, so if we don't know if it's a person or not, what are we..."

"This," Alex said, spinning the laptop around on his knees so that gabby and Gant could both see the screen. "We are looking for this."

The screen displayed the same rotating 3D rendering of a DNA strand that Alex had seen in his lab. Gaby and Gant both frowned, and Alex recognized the vague confusion of ignorance on both of their faces. He tapped the flash drive, sticking out of the side of the laptop. "This is a visual representation of the DNA strand that's on this drive. Do you see it flashing? Look closely. Do you see any part of it moving?"

Gabby leaned forward, her eyes fixed on the screen. After a moment, she shook her head slightly. "No, I don't see anything. At least nothing flashing or weird."

"Ok," Alex said, turning the laptop around again. "Just wanted to make sure."

"Just what is it that you're trying to do, son?" Gant asked. "I have a pretty secure network, but I'd really think about it if you're gonna connect to the outside."

"No," Alex said without looking up. "This needs to stay in here, with me. It's not safe out there. No one is safe. I need to find out who this belongs to, and it all starts with this file."

The loud buzz of Gabby's phone interrupted Alex, cutting off the conversation abruptly. She looked down at the phone and hesitated for a moment before answering. "Jerry? No, it's ok, we are all up. Where are you? Yeah, coffee is on." She listened for a few seconds before hanging up, sliding the phone on top of the wooden box on the table. "Jerry is on his way in," she said, "He says he has goodies for us."

Gant snorted, casting a glance toward Alex, staring out through the window. "With all that's going on, that could mean anything from intel to donuts."

Chapter Thirty-One

Major Raymond Keene had never liked Washington DC. After leaving the Army Rangers and going private, he had hoped for a posting someplace where his balls didn't freeze off in the winter and the better part of Spring, too. He looked around the room, the sprawling, open living room of the large modern house they had rented for a month, just for the one-night op. His team was prepping, readying weapons and gear with the calm, practiced rhythm of seasoned, well-trained professionals. He looked at his watch. "Fifteen minutes."

No one acknowledged the announcement, yet they were all keenly aware of their schedule, both individually and as a team. Eight men—two fire teams—plus Keene, all linked by state of the art comms and video equipment. Keene nodded. They would be more than enough, even taking into account the overestimations of their quarry's potential resistance and skill level. He didn't like overkill, yet would rather the odds be in his favor when it came to available manpower, and there would be at least one trained Federal agent among them.

"We have air support available if you need it, Major," Sergeant Heller said, stepping beside him, his appearance that of a regular civilian, his compact assault rifle stowed neatly out of sight beneath his jacket. "Storm just up and blew itself out last night. Skies are clearing throughout the morning."

The Major looked up. "Too late for that now. We'll manage without it. Tell them to stand by. We should be in and out within the hour, long before they manage to get on station, but if they're on the pad and spun up, they can be here in fifteen minutes if necessary."

The sergeant nodded. He turned away, facing the room. "Okay, guys, we're out of here in ten. Final checks, then outside and mount up. Alpha team in the follow vehicle, Bravo in the lead."

The men went about their weapons and equipment checks, making sure their spare magazines were full and safely stowed in mag holders beneath their jackets. Keene led the Sergeant over to the dining room and the large satellite map sprawled across the table. He gestured with a gloved hand. "Your assessment, Sergeant."

Heller leaned on the table and pointed to a group of buildings at the center of what looked like a number of adjoining fields. "The two main buildings are close together, but we have plenty of space between them to get one of the vehicles in behind the back side of the house, here." He slid his finger across the image. "Only one way in," he said, pointing to the main entrance gate, just shy of a mile from the main house and its open courtyard. "So we drive both vehicles right up to the front door. It's fast, and far safer than trying to cross all of this open land from anywhere around the perimeter. They would see us coming and have time to make coffee before we got there."

"And what about this up here?" Keene pointed to a small white rectangle at the top left of the map.

"There's an old gate up there, in the hedgerow. Pedestrian. It's pretty well overgrown, from what I can see. And this looks like an old shed, probably used for storing farm equipment. This track in front leads up to the hedgerow here, about thirty yards from the smaller gate. Looks to be even more overgrown, so I'm guessing no vehicles have gone in or out of there for a long time."

Keene looked thoughtful for a moment. "Put someone up there. If there's so much as a trail leading back to the road, I want it covered. We aren't dealing with numbers, but what we are dealing with are at least one FBI agent, and a decorated ex-special forces soldier who's had a lot of time on his hands."

"Yes, sir. I'll put Hawkes on it. It'll be a good spot to lay up and cover the house from the north. I checked over the rest of the perimeter. There's been no movement in, around, or out of the place save for the main access road."

Keene nodded his approval. "Very good, Sergeant. Let's get going. I want to be in and out and back to base as quickly as possible. Mack has a full English breakfast on the canteen menu today and I don't want to miss it because we couldn't get our ducks in a row around a God damned farm house."

Looking around the room, Keene took a deep breath. He had worked tirelessly putting together the Black Wing team, recruiting only from the best in ex-military, from various branches, and who had seen their fair share of combat. The two newest men, Hamua and Drake, sat close to one another,

282

feeding the last few rounds into their magazines. Both had come highly recommended, were decorated Army Rangers and were recent veterans of back-to-back tours in Afghanistan. Keene prided himself on being an excellent judge of character, his radar sweeping over the men around him, sensing only calm, measured confidence and a heady mix of sharply honed experience and deadly killer instincts. But Drake; there was something slightly off with him that he just couldn't quite put his finger on. Nowhere near enough to sway his decision to bring him on board, but a vague, indistinguishable *something*. He shook his head, dismissing the thought as Heller addressed the men. "Okay, guys, let's get outside and mount up. Ready to go in five. Let's go!"

The men moved in unison, the room clearing in less time than it took Keene to unwrap a piece of gum and put it in his mouth. He nodded, satisfied, and turned from the map table, heading outside toward the two waiting SUVs and lone Dodge Charger bringing up the rear.

Jerry wished every morning drive was so quiet. The nearly empty roads were devoid of the usual morning rush traffic. The light was still gloomy, the sun barely up, pushing away the last remaining gray remnants of the previous night's storm clouds. He drove a little too fast on the wet roads, heading north out of Olney, his large headlights casting bright splashes of light in the puddles on the winding road ahead of the Tahoe. He glanced over at the manilla folder on the passenger seat, feeling pleased with himself for snagging the file page from Eriksen's desk, even if it had been an act of clumsiness that had revealed the page in the first place.

He wasn't exactly sure why this James Devlin guy was important, but, as a known associate of Lincoln Klick—the guy they pulled out of the cult house before delivering him to New York—he obviously had some part to play, and if anyone could figure out what that was, it was Gabby. Her frosty exchange with that cow, Director Cole, had only served to reiterate his notion that Gabby was more than a level above the above-average agents in the Bureau. She always had a way out, an answer, a solution, and he had no idea where she pulled her logic from, most of the time, often wondering if she was just running on pure instinct, along with an uncanny amount of luck.

Glancing over at the passenger seat again, he wondered absently if the box of fresh cronuts sitting on top of the folder would stain the cover. He checked his GPS, confirming his estimate. Ten minutes out. He was dying for a coffee, and Gant's was surprisingly good, if a little strong. He thought that the old soldier would drink gasoline if the coffee ever ran out. He pushed the SUV a little harder, humming along with the song on the radio. Long Tall Sally was apparently built for speed.

Keene climbed into the passenger seat of the lead SUV, one of two identical gray Suburbans, parked nose-to-tail in front of the house, the entire property protected from prying eyes by tall hedgerows and trees. Heller took the wheel and pressed the main button on the remote, opening the gates at the bottom of the inclined driveway. He checked his rearview, returning the nod from the driver in the second vehicle, and pulled away, nosing through the gate and turning onto the road, heading toward Gant's ranch, a few miles away. The three vehicles formed a small convoy as they made their way steadily south. There was very little traffic, and Heller watched every vehicle that passed them on the road, checking the mirrors as they passed by, always alert, and wary of any possible threat.

"Split point approaching," Heller said, and the Charger slowed, falling behind the second SUV, the headlights growing rapidly smaller before they swung away as the vehicle turned off the road.

"Keep a slow pace," Keene said. "Until someone catches up with us, we'll drag to give Jackson some time. How far to the entrance?"

"Three point five," Heller replied, his eyes fixed firmly on the road ahead. "He should be back with us by the time we hit the half mile mark. Hawkes will run the last leg on foot. He'll be in position by the time we hit the house."

Keene felt relaxed, calm in the knowledge that he was surrounded by professionals, all of whom had passed, not only Apex's stringent background checks, but also his own, personal vetting procedures. He knew about as much as it was possible to know about every man under his command, the exception being the newer team members, yet they had still been thoroughly checked and he had the final call on each and every new recruit. He glanced in the rearview mirror, watching Sergeant Hamua, the giant Samoan, as he stared casually out the window as if he were on the way to vacation, not potential combat. Drake sat beside him, the epitome of cool, calm and collected. As he caught the young Corporal's eye, he again felt a fleeting sense of something being not quite right with his newest recruit. He made a mental note to have a deeper chat with him when they got back to the Ark Complex.

"Two point five," Heller said, the SUV crawling along the glistening road at a leisurely twenty-five miles per hour. He reached up, pressing a finger to his earpiece. "Jackson is back on the road, catching up now."

Keene smiled. "Well, don't let it be said that he can't at least drive fast."

"That's why he's the designated driver, Sir," Heller replied, smiling. "Two miles out." Another check in the mirror and Heller nodded, seeing the Charger's headlights slide up behind the second SUV, reforming the small convoy. "There he is," he said, pressing the throat mic. "All units, final checks. ETA, Two minutes."

A flurry of activity in the back seat as the two men there re-checked their weapons and comms gear. The safeties came off with a distinctive *click* and the vehicles rounded a long right bend, bearing down on the entrance gate.

Jerry had to squint through the fine spray, kicked up onto the windshield by the still wet roads, as he drew closer to the entrance to Gant's place. It was easy to miss an old gate to a narrow, single-lane road, set back into the thick bushes and trees that lined the road for miles in both directions. "Come on, where are you?" he whispered, glancing at the GPS, the blue arrow icon of the Tahoe sliding up the road toward the green star on the small map screen. The road had been clear, except for a tractor that had held him up for a half mile, before it had pulled off, the driver waving him past. A car pulled up behind him and flashed its high beams as he slowed, looking for the entrance in the gloom.

"Great," he said, speeding up a little but afraid to miss the entrance. He put his turn signal on just as he rounded the bend, fifty yards from the entrance, the car behind him riding his rear bumper. Suddenly, bright headlights appeared, rounding the corner as a pair of SUVs braked quickly and turned into the entrance, the lead vehicle smashing open the old gate as both trucks sped up the narrow driveway. A third car, a Charger, pulled up to the gate, blocking the entrance. He punched the gas and drove on, speeding past the now parked Charger, looking straight ahead and hoping the driver hadn't seen his turn signal.

"Shit. Shit, shit, shit *SHIT!*" He dialed Gabby's cell on the console display, speeding north, looking for another way on to Gant's property. The sun was finally pushing the last of the storm clouds away from the orange hued horizon to his right.

"Come *on,* boss. Pick up."

Heller gripped the steering wheel as the big SUV rammed through the wooden gate, smashing it to splinters against the old wall. He floored the gas pedal and the Suburban surged forward, the second SUV mere yards behind him. The buildings looked distant, slightly atop a gentle rise, the only light an external lamp, shining brightly above the side door of the main house. He keyed his throat mic. "Jackson, I thought I saw a turn signal from a truck closing on the entrance. Do you see anything unusual?"

Jackson's voice came back, crisp and clear in his earpiece. *"Negative. All traffic moving by."*

Keene looked over. "What did you see, Sergeant?"

"Probably nothing, sir," Heller replied. "I thought, for a second, that one of the vehicles coming toward us had its turn signal on, but I was already looking to make the turn and with all this water around, I doubt the odds are that it was someone looking to drop by the place at this hour."

Keene looked thoughtful for a moment. "Notify Hawkes. If Jackson doesn't see anyone at the main entrance an unwelcome visitor will have to take the same track he did, or run the risk of moving over open ground, in which case Hawkes will take him out anyway."

"Yes, Sir."

Heller gave Hawkes the heads up of a potential inbound on his position, waited for the acknowledgement, and then turned his attention back to the road. Two hundred yards later, both SUVs turned hard right into the open courtyard, the main house in front of them, the large barn doors back and to their left. Team Alpha sped past, turning left between the house and barn to cover the rear of the house and the open ground to the north. Heller braked hard, the doors all opening simultaneously and boots hitting the ground before he'd pulled to a full stop.

Keene and Heller stepped out together, the latter raising his MP7 and quick-walking toward the front door, covering windows as he moved. Hamua reached the door, pressing himself against the wall as Corporal

Drake did likewise on the opposite side of the door. The house was dark and silent. As Keene and Heller approached, Keene's earpiece clicked into life as team 2 confirmed they were in position at the rear. He nodded at Hamua, who reached out, his fingers stretching for the polished brass door knob, every weapon trained on the doorway. His fingers wrapped around the metal handle.

CRACK!

Hamua flew backwards, literally taking off from the ground and flying back, past Keene, to land in a twitching heap on the ground, his eyes staring blankly at the sky and his heart stopped dead in his barrel chest.

* * *

Gabby put her phone back in her pocket and Alex sat up.

"Ok, listen," he said, edging forward on the chair. His hands were gripping the sides of the laptop. Gabby could see the knuckles, stretched white against the dark gray plastic. "I know you're gonna think I'm crazy, but you have to listen."

Gant and Gabby were listening. They were listening to every word. Alex had taken on a new energy since he had awoken, and spoke with an edge that was impossible to ignore.

"Okay," Gabby said, trying to sound calming. "We're listening, Alex. What is it?" She understood completely that whatever Alex had gotten himself all wound up over, was of critical importance to him. If getting it off his chest would make him feel better enough to allow her to help him, then she would just let him get it out now.

"The code, the one on this drive. It's the only one there is. It's the only version. Not a copy, but the only *original* one in existence."

Gant stood back a few feet, not wanting to crowd Alex as he gesticulated on the edge of the chair, trying to emphasize his point. The laptop rested precariously on his knees. Gabby had seen him like this before, usually when he was on the cusp of some big breakthrough, when every thought, every complicated calculation would come to fruition and he would be free of their weight, his mind relieved of some immense burden. She could see him struggling to keep his words from tumbling over one another and he paused, steadying himself. He shook his head and chuckled, letting his head fall forward, resting on the edge of the laptop screen.

"Oh man, you're not going to believe me. You're just not going to believe me." He looked up. "The DNA code on that drive belongs to the Antichrist."

No one said anything for a moment. Both Gabby and Gant stared at Alex, perhaps waiting for him to break into laughter and tell them he was joking, but he didn't. He looked up at Gabby, meeting her gaze, unwavering and deadly serious.

"The Antichrist," Gant repeated, breaking the sudden, awkward silence. "Like, the Biblical prophecy, son of Satan, Antichrist."

"Yes."

Gabby's thoughts were racing. She could hear Gant asking Alex questions, but they were just a distant muffled murmur. As her head turned, she looked at the box on the table. Not just the box, but what was *inside* it.

"Okay," Gabby said, returning her gaze to her friend, sitting bolt upright in the old chair. "How do you know that, Alex?" She was very careful not to word the question; '*Why do you think that?*'

"It showed me," he said, without hesitation. He had calmed considerably, and that somehow deepened Gabby's already substantial concern. It was one thing to wake up in a strange environment, having gone through all the trauma he had experienced, little more than a day after having been shot, and to experience some kind of understandable psychosis, and another thing entirely to be lucid, direct and clear-eyed, just as Alex appeared to her now. It was the Alex she knew, and he didn't play games, or lean toward melodramatics. In his mind, he simply didn't waste time on such things. He looked at her, dead in the eye, and she believed him.

"You require elaboration," he said flatly. Gabby said nothing and Gant sighed softly, unsure of whether to even be in the room. "I wasn't really getting anywhere with Icarus," Alex said. "I had a flight of codes set up to work into the formula protocols I had established after my meeting with Drexler and the others last week. If Drexler hadn't spent so long attempting to trip me up by infiltrating my work with deliberate errors, I probably would've paid more attention to it sooner."

"Drexler did what?" Gabby asked, her tone saturated with incredulity. She really needed to hear that again.

"Drexler had several others working on projects that would give him a good idea of who would be the best candidate to put forward for the Icarus project. I was always his favorite. He probably knows that I know that. He would insert errors into my work, remove or corrupt security tags, reverse engineer some of my smaller project successes to make me think that my process was flawed, or just rename, move or switch out codes I was working with. All at the behest of Charles, I'm sure, and just to see how I would spot the errors and rework them under the assumption that I was at fault. He needed to see both my thought and working processes in error resolution and also forward dynamic problem solving." He shrugged, casually. "It's a logical way to cover all of your bases and see if I was up to the challenge. He just wasn't aware that I knew from the beginning."

"Knew that you had figured out what he was doing?" Gant asked.

"Exactly," Alex replied. He shifted his weight back, relaxing a little into the chair. "I think he knew near the end, but probably after he had recommended me anyway, and I'm sure he used that in order to push my name forward. Doctor Drexler isn't the kind of man to throw his ego around. He's actually quite humble; naive even."

"So, what happened," Gabby prodded, and Alex looked up at her. "With the codes."

"There was an error," he said. "I was frustrated. I thought that Drexler was up to his tricks again. His redundant and pointless tricks, at that point." He paused, looking down for a moment, and then reached up to scratch the back of his neck. Gabby saw the anxiety, just a small glint of it in his movements as he became more fidgety.

"It..." he hesitated. "It was burning me, but I wasn't burnt. I was on fire. My lab was on fire. I..."

"It's okay, Alex," Gabby comforted, moving to stand from her chair.

Alex held up his hand. "No, I'm all right. It was real, Gabby. I wasn't suffering some kind of hallucinogenic meltdown. I saw things, horrible things. It showed me."

"What kind of things?" Gant asked, stepping closer. "Like a dream? A nightmare?"

"It wasn't a nightmare!" Alex yelled, his frustration boiling over in an instant. "It was real. I was in my lab one moment, and then... darkness. Just darkness. And there were... things." He looked up. "They wanted to drag me down there, but something else came and I was back in my lab again."

Gabby and Gant exchanged concerned looks as Alex continued. "So I *know* what this is. You *have* to believe me." He left out the part with the horrifying voice; what it had said to him. He felt less sane even recalling it. "And that wasn't even the worst of it," he went on. "I saw the lab. I was outside, and there were fires, everything was burning."

He recalled the images from his vision and took a deep breath. "And there were these creatures; winged, dark... things. They came down from the sky and just picked people up. The soldiers, everyone. They tore them apart. And the sky..." His eyes almost glazed over and he stared off, looking past Gabby's shoulder. "The sky was on fire. It... it was the end. The end of everything."

Gabby looked at the flash drive, plugged innocently into the side of the computer, just like any other, and then to the box on the side table. "Oh, my God," she whispered. Gant and Alex both looked at her. "We're not safe here."

Chapter Thirty-Two

BEEP BEEP BEEP!

Gant spun around at the sound of an alarm, coming from the other room. Gabby stood and immediately checked the windows, scanning the grass fields outside. Between the kitchen and living room area, there was a small office nook off the hallway. Gant ran to the desk and opened the upper cupboard doors, revealing two monitors, both screens split into four camera views, all from different vantage points around the property. Immediately, the image of two speeding SUVs filled a quadrant on one of the screens. They quickly drove out of shot, and Gant looked down to a view of the courtyard.

Gabby's phone buzzed and she paused, waiting to hear word from Gant, out of sight in the office along the hallway. She snatched it up. "Jerry, don't..." She stopped mid-sentence. Alex sat, frozen on the edge of his seat.

"Okay," Gabby went on. "Don't engage, Jerry. Call it in and get us some backup out here, ASAP, but do *not* engage! Jerry! Jerry? God*dammit*!"

She hung up the phone and shoved it into her pocket, moving to the window and reaching out toward Alex as she crouched down, peering out over the vast tracks of unbroken land to the north east. "Alex, get down out of the chair and move to the kitchen. Stay low if you can."

Alex slipped onto the floor, the blanket bunching around his legs as he slid off the chair, and then moved to the side, kicking his feet free as he began to crawl gingerly across the rug toward the kitchen, the laptop clutched under one arm.

"Gant, talk to me!" Gabby yelled, her eyes scanning the fields and distant tree lines as she peered above the windowsill. She could hear him moving around, farther down the hallway, probably shoring up the front door.

"Get Alex up to the spare room," Gant said, appearing as he stalked down the hallway and into the kitchen area, just as Alex was pushing himself up against the front of the stove, drawing his knees tightly to his chest. "There's a staircase that leads up to the balcony, and another room at the far end," Gant continued, opening cupboard doors and drawing out a pair of semi-automatic handguns. A pump-action shotgun rested on the counter, beside a Darth Vader cookie jar.

Gabby reached down, helping Alex to his feet. "How long?" she asked, watching Alex struggle as he tried to stand.

"Ninety seconds. The front door is wired, so that will either buy us some time or just kick the hornets' nest."

Gabby guided Alex through the door into the back room. It was dim, with a pair of old couches facing one another and a low coffee table between them. Against the far wall, a short hallway led to a narrow staircase to the upper level. Gabby headed for it, pushing Alex ahead of her as they went up. She reached the top of the stairs onto a loft area. It looked as though Gant was in the middle of remodeling, with some of the old wooden flooring torn up and dust sheets and various tools laying around.

"This way," she said, guiding Alex toward an opening at the far end of the room. It led to a balcony walkway that linked the two ends of the main house. She looked down into the main living room, separated from the hallway and kitchen by a supporting wall. As she moved, she had a birds eye view of the room, and all of Gant's collectibles, scattered around the room on side tables and shelves. There were books—*lots* of books—old artillery shell casings, maps and glass cases with medals, and a few dusty wooden boxes on top of the book cases. She paused. *The box!*

"Alex, head into that room and hide. Get under a bed if you have to. I'll be right there. Go!"

Gabby watched him back away—he was moving pretty well—and then turn to walk quickly toward the far room. She heard a crack from somewhere downstairs, and the lights suddenly went out. Moving fast, Gabby ran back down the stairs to the lower level. Gant was just heaving a duffel bag onto his shoulder in the kitchen when she burst into the room, turning toward the window. The box was still on the side table where she had left it, and she ran over to it. As she reached for the smooth wooden box, a shadow moved across the table and she looked up. A man in a plaid shirt and ball cap was standing outside, looking at her through the window. She thought he might have been a neighbor, he was dressed so casually, and then he swung the sub machine gun up and she saw the open end of the barrel, pointing directly at her face.

"Down!" Gant yelled from behind her, but she was already moving, dropping away, swiping the box from the table as she fell. Gunfire erupted, and the window exploded, showering her with glass and wood splinters as she lay on the rug, covering her head with her arms. A strong hand grasped her arm and she looked up to see Gant, reaching down to pull her to her feet. He wore a gas mask, pushed up onto the top of his head.

"Where's Alex?" he asked, scanning the field of view outside the shattered window before pulling the chair over onto it's side and kneeling down to place something beneath it.

"Upstairs, the spare room," she said, looking at the man with the plaid shirt, laying on the ground outside, his chest riddled with the red blooms of half a dozen bullet holes.

"Good," Gant said, standing and backing away from the chair. "Let's get up there. There's only one way up, but two ways down."

He pulled her away from the window and turned as a smoke grenade came flying inside, hitting the rug and hissing acrid, grey smoke into the room.

Jerry almost missed the small side road, braking hard and yanking on the steering wheel as the big SUV leaned and shuddered, struggling to make the turn. The track was seldom used and so narrow that branches and twigs whipped at the windshield and scratched body of the vehicle as it pushed farther from the main road. He eventually came upon a small clearing and pulled to a stop, leaping from the driver's seat and running to the back of the vehicle, the tailgate already opening.

A minute later, armed with an AR-15 assault rifle, he secured the Tahoe and ran off, following the track as it narrowed to a rough foot trail that skirted the open field of Gant's property to the north and north west. He cursed at the spare magazines, clattering noisily in his pockets as he moved forward. There just wasn't the time to move more slowly, despite the risks, and he scanned every bush and shadow intently with each step.

After a frustrating twenty yards, he removed several of the magazines and dropped them into the undergrowth. With two spares, one in each jacket pocket, he was about to move and looked down. Beside the small clump of thick grass was the distinct impression of a boot print, pushed deep into the sodden earth, made muddy after the night's rain. Moving forward slowly, he saw another, and then more, pressed into the ground at random points along the trail. Whoever had left them had made little effort to disguise their tracks, but Jerry held the image of those SUVs, charging through the gate and backed up by the lone car, left by the entrance as cover. These were professionals, regardless of a set of careless tracks, no doubt left by someone who simply wasn't expecting any company in this, an obviously less traveled, area.

He moved on, raising the rifle and giving himself a mental pat on the back for wearing his tactical boots instead of the standard issue dress shoes he, and every other agent, wore on a daily basis. Slipping between two small trees, he hunkered down by the old wooden fence that bordered the property. He could see the house, its misty visage visible across the open field. To the right he could make out another building, a shed or garage of some kind, close to the hedgerow a couple hundred yards away. If he was going to position anyone to cover the house, that's where he would be. A deep breath and a 'what the hell am I getting myself into' later, Jerry moved away, heading along the narrow trail toward the distant shed, and his welcoming committee.

Alex moved into the front loft room, crouch-walking to the window in the far wall. He could see a corner of the courtyard, and most of the driveway that led down to the main road, but no vehicles. As he peered over the windowsill, he caught movement below. Inching up, he looked down, onto the figure of a man, creeping slowly along the front of the house. He flinched as gunfire erupted from somewhere downstairs. Moments later, the man outside smashed the window and climbed through. He was inside the house, directly below him.

"Come on, Gabby," he whispered, clutching his heavily bandaged shoulder, his right arm in a well-made sling that held it tightly to his torso. He looked around the room. Beside the bed, a large closet and nine-drawer dresser, the only other thing of note was an old armchair in the far corner. An even older-looking stuffed bulldog sat stoically on the worn seat cushion. It stared at him questioningly, with black button eyes that somehow put Alex on edge even more. "And you're not helping, either," Alex said, as the floorboards outside the door creaked and the door swung open.

Keene cursed himself for the few seconds it took him to get over the shock of seeing Hamua sail past him in the air, killed by a simple, but very effective, improvised defense device. God knows how much power had been flowing through the door knob when the big Samoan had grabbed it, but it had been more than enough, killing the soldier before he had left the ground, and hurling him fifteen feet through the air. He moved to the wall, standing beside Heller. Drake pulled a frag grenade from his belt, but Keene held up his hand. "Don't waste it," he said. "They aren't in this part of the house by now. Find another way in. Front window."

Rat-at-at-at-at-at!

Gunfire from the other side of the building gave Keene pause, and he touched his earpiece as the second team confirmed contact on the north side of the house. Drake disappeared around the corner at the front and Heller knelt, scanning the open ground through the sights of his rifle.

"The other doors could be wired, too," Heller said. He pressed his throat mic. "Biggs, window ingress only. The doors are BT'd. Check for wires." He relayed the same message to Drake before turning to Keene.

"Follow Drake," Keene said. "I'll join up with Team 2. I don't want to give them a chance to..." He cut off, putting his hand to his ear as a radio message came through. His expression darkened. "Understood," he said. "Proceed with caution, Sergeant." He looked at Heller. "Madsen is dead."

Heller's face stiffened, but he said nothing. Keene knew that he had to get a hold of the mission before it fell apart any further. He could see Heller, mentally chewing over his mission plan, and his decision to make a fast approach instead of a stealthier, more drawn out alternative.

"All right," Keene said, drawing his sidearm. "It was a good plan, Sergeant, but it's going to shit, so let's see if we can't put it back together." He heard glass break as Drake made his way into the house via the window around the corner. He listened as Team 2 reported deployment of a smoke grenade at the north side of the house. "Go with Drake, and keep an eye on him. Force them upstairs if you can't take out the vet. I'd rather not have the blood of a Federal agent on our hands, but do what you have to do. And move with gas precautions, I won't put it past this bastard to try anything at this point."

Heller nodded, "Yes, Sir," and ran off, pulling his gas mask from inside his jacket and pulling it over the top of his head before disappearing around the corner and climbing through the window after Drake. Keene turned and trotted down the side of the house. He activated his throat mic. "Team 2, Gas protocols. Be advised, I'm coming around from the south."

"*Roger that, Sir,*" Biggs replied. "*We're about to breach through the window. Deakins is hanging back for you. Confirm gas protocols.*"

Keene turned the corner and saw Biggs disappear through the window, and then Madsen's body on the ground. He was laying flat on his back, his arms tucked neatly at his sides, as if he had been arranged that way. Looking up, he saw Deakins, kneeling on the grass, a few feet from the window, the menacing black gas mask already in place over his face. He turned and acknowledged the Major, before standing and moving to the window, about to follow Biggs.

The explosion vaporized Biggs and sent the two halves of Deakins' body flying out into the field. It blew out what was left of the window frame, as well as a good portion of the lower wall, and shoved Madsen's body across the rough grass. Gant's knee jerk booby trap had consisted of a high-yield block of C4 attached to a simple pressure switch. He had wedged the device—concealed beneath a simple napkin—under the edge of the overturned chair by the window, barely balancing on the sensitive switch, and knowing that the chair could've shifted any second after he had set it. When Biggs had climbed through the window, he had barely touched the chair as he moved in, not even wanting to use it for support. It had shifted just enough, and detonated the charge.

Keene was knocked back, twisting away and shielding his eyes from the flying dust and debris. Flattening himself on the ground, he looked back at the house and the now gaping hole in the wall. He touched his throat mic. "Team 2, report, over." He knew there would be no response. In the space of five minutes, his team had been decimated and Heller's plan had been blown to hell. Gritting his teeth, Keene let the others know they were on their own, weapons free. "Team 1, Hail Mary. I repeat, Hail Mary."

Chapter Thirty-Three

Gant pushed Gabby toward the stairs, her arm covering her nose and mouth as the smoke seeped quickly through the door from the other room, driven by a breeze that moved unhindered through the house, now that more than one window had been shattered. As he reached the bottom of the stairs, he caught movement to his right, at the far end of the hallway that led to the front living room. He turned just as Drake fired a burst down the narrow corridor. Gant reeled, taking two hits; one a grazing wound across the front of his thigh, and the other striking him in the buttock, knocking him off balance as he stepped up onto the first step of the narrow staircase. He returned fire, emptying half of the clip in his handgun as he moved up, trying to ignore the searing pain in his backside.

The rattling thud of a flash bang grenade hitting the carpeted stairs just behind him gave him the extra incentive he needed to dive up onto the landing with a grimace as the device went off, a few feet below the top step. Bullets ripped into the wall above his hip as someone raked the stairs from below, and Gabby reached back to drag him away from the top step, firing down sporadically as Gant struggled to a kneeling position by the wall. He pulled what looked like a TV remote from his jacket and entered a code on the keypad. A few seconds later, a strange, stuttering, hissing sound filled the room around them, quickly followed by the eruption of fire sprinklers as they showered every surface with cold water from a multitude of nozzles positioned all over the house.

"Go," he said, breathlessly, becoming quickly soaked. "Get to that front room. Go for the closet. Trust me, and here, take this." He held out a non-explosive shock grenade—a canister of high-pressure air and powder that caused a powerful, disorienting pressure shockwave—pulled from the utility belt he'd strapped around his waist in the kitchen. "Drop this into the living room hallway. It'll give them something to think about," he whispered. "And then get into that room." He held up a hand to silence her protests as she moved to speak. "I'll be right behind you, don't worry. We need to get Alex out of here, and you *need* to keep that box and the data safe. Those are your priorities now."

Gabby nodded, checking her pocket for the small bulge of the flash drive. She took the grenade and turned, heading along the balcony that ran along the wall above the open living room below. When she got half way along, she stopped, crouching beneath the only window, looking out over a porch roof and grass fields, stretching away to the north. She pulled the pin and bobbed her head over the railing, peeking down into the living room and the entrance to the hallway that led to the stairs at the back end of the house. The banister shattered in a shower of splinters as Heller shot upwards from the room below. Gabby dropped the shock grenade through the wooden bars, before scrambling away, holding the box like a football, toward the door at the far end of the balcony. Gant watched her go and then pulled a different grenade from his belt, an incendiary, and tossed it down the stairs, before turning to hobble slowly after Gabby.

Keene felt the shockwave of the first flash bang even as he climbed over the rubble of the destroyed window in the back wall. He surveyed the room—the smoke clearing—and scanned the floor for trip wires and potential pressure pads. The rug had been blown away from the floor and was crumpled in a heap against the low counter that separated the room from the raised kitchen area. The doorway that led to the stairs was to his left and he crossed to it, gun raised as the stilted, chattering sound of gunfire echoed through from the next room. He paused at the sudden sound of fire sprinklers hissing to life, and frowned as the air was filled with a mist of cold liquid, quickly saturating his jacket and plastering his dark hair to his forehead.

Peering around the corner, he could see the bottom of the flight of stairs, heading away up to the right. Heller was directing Drake toward the stairs as he covered him from somewhere out of sight along the hallway. Drake came into view, swinging his weapon toward the Major before turning back to the stairs and firing upwards. Return fire snapped from somewhere above and Drake took cover, ducking back to stand just in front of the Major. Keene looked at the rivulets of liquid running down the back of Drake's neck and frowned. There was something about the way the liquid clung to his skin, like more of a sheen, somehow. There was just something... he reached up, running his fingers across his cheek and then rubbing the fingertips together.

After another burst of automatic fire from somewhere down the hallway, Drake moved forward, checking the hall before stepping up onto the first step, the boards creaking in protest under his weight. A moment later, a *thud* and the sound of quick movement down the hallway made Drake pause, tensing on the steps before the dark red canister of an incendiary grenade came sailing over the top step to land squarely between his feet.

Keene, still looking at his fingers, realized too late. He moved before he could think, grabbing Drake's jacket and yanking the young soldier backwards, away from the stairs, and thrusting him back toward the doorway to the kitchen.

"Firetrap! Out, *Now!*"

Two explosions in quick succession rocked the downstairs, the first, from somewhere along the hallway, close to the front living room, knocked Heller from his feet, momentarily stunning him. The second, less than five feet from Keene's right boot, exploded with a bright flash, igniting the liquid now saturating the carpet, walls, floors and all of Major Raymond Keene. He was engulfed in roaring flames from head to toe inside just a few seconds. Heller appeared, wheeling down the hallway, flapping his arms futilely as the flames engulfed him. Keene staggered back into the wall and slid down to the floor, his last thought an image of his son, killed in action in Iraq only this past month. And now, he raced to see him once again.

Gant was backing slowly away along the balcony, blood seeping down his leg. The fire spread across the floors and walls like a predatory creature, searching for its next prey, and within seconds was rolling across the carpet and wall, a few feet away from his boots. Gant turned and made for the door. He was limping badly, the pain in his thigh and backside a white hot spear that spread like lightning down his leg and into his back, almost crippling him back to the floor, half way along the balcony. The railing burst into flame beside him and he fell sideways against the window, turning to look at the wall of fire surging toward him. The entire back half of the house was already aflame, and soon it would consume the entire building. The searing heat hit him like a furnace blast and as the edge of the fire closed in, he turned to the window, and a final look out over the visage of rolling fields, a bright shaft of morning sunlight washing over perfect grass.

Gabby's face appeared around the door, and Alex let out an audible sigh of relief, sliding down the wall to sit heavily on the wooden floorboards. Closing the door behind her, she moved quickly toward Alex, reaching down, pulling him to his feet as he grimaced in pain.

"Where's Gant?" he asked, Gabby guiding him around the bed. She heard the sound of breaking glass, outside the room on the balcony, followed by a slowly growing sound of something big and growling and alive, and it was right outside the door. She looked down to see a thin veil of smoke wafting through the crack above the carpet.

"Right behind me," she said, walking quickly to the large closet. Pulling the doors open she saw only a row of neatly hung clothes, the hangers evenly spaced on a single rail. She reached in, pushing the clothes apart and gasped. Alex leaned against the end of the bed, tired. "Gab, what are you doing? We need to get out of here."

Gabby paused, staring into the closet. The floor was an open hole, with a ladder leading down, past the ground floor and beyond, into a deeper, gloomier shaft.

"Come on, we need to go," she said, turning to Alex. "The whole place is going to…"

CRASH!

The bedroom door exploded inwards, flying off its hinges and hitting Alex, knocking him to the floor before crashing into the far wall, beside the window. The laptop spilled from his hands, skittering out of sight under the bed. Gabby instinctively raised her gun toward the now open doorway. The figure of a man stood there, his entire form smoking and charred from the flames as the door frame burned around him. Alex could see his clothes, blackened and tattered, disintegrating as he stood there. At first he remained still, eyes closed, his arms hanging loosely at his sides, blocking the doorway as the fire from outside began to creep and flicker into the room.

"What the…" Alex whispered, struggling to lean up on his elbow on the floor beside the bed. His head was bleeding at the temple, but he didn't seem to notice. For a few moments, there was an uneasy silence as Gabby stood, eyes fixed on the unmoving figure. Alex moved slowly back, away from the door. He was about to climb to his feet when the figure opened his mouth in a twisted, grimacing smile, revealing rows of stunted, pointed teeth. His eyes opened, glistening orbs of solid black, set against the charred and reddened mask of burnt flesh.

"Holy shit," Alex whispered, as the figure abruptly strode forward toward him. Gabby raised her gun and fired a trio of well-aimed shots at the advancing figure, striking him in the neck and chest and knocking him sideways into the wall. She raced around the bed, gun pointing at the lurching figure, struggling to right himself against the wall, and heaved Alex to his feet. Before she could drag him away, the man stood, facing them. He laughed, the pointed teeth glistening between cracked and bloody lips. Gabby raised her gun again but the creature sprung forward, knocking it from her grasp and swatting her aside, sending her tumbling over the footboard of the bed and into the wall.

"Too easy," the creature hissed, moving menacingly toward Alex, now shuffling backwards along the side of the bed. "When the last of your hope is gone, he will rise."

Alex saw Gabby, struggling by the wall, her head bowed and turned away. Her gun was on the floor by the closet, too far to reach in time. He looked up and saw the creature closing in, reaching toward him with bloodied hands, the fingers gnarled and twisted into wicked-looking claws. Alex cried out as the creature gripped him tightly by the face, a deep, echoing laugh rumbling within its throat.

"You have come so far," he hissed, leaning in close. Alex tried to jerk away, the stench of burning flesh filling his nostrils. "You are so close, *so close!*" He brushed a thumb across Alex's cheek, almost tenderly, and Alex tensed. "Ah, yesss," he mocked. "So beautiful. So much *fear*. Would you like me to end it for you? Is it all too much for your weak heart? Perhaps you would like that, to be released from this cesspit of a life. That is why I am here, Alexander, to relieve you of this dull and meaningless existence." He chuckled, caressing Alex's face with blackened hands, and then, as if some kind of switch had been thrown, his expression suddenly changed. The smug, smirking grin melted away and he looked up toward the ceiling, as if the sound of some high flying aircraft had caught his attention. He turned his head to one side, looking away. Alex followed his gaze with his eyes to where Gabby was leaning, crouched against the wall beside the open doorway. As he watched, the room began to darken around them, as if black storm clouds had suddenly settled overhead, blocking the sun and casting a heavy, sinister shadow over the house, sucking the light and color from the room.

Gabby stirred, lifting a hand to place it on the wall beside her resting head, and slowly turned her face to look at them. The color drained from Alex's face as an icy ball of terror bloomed in his gut. He felt the grip on his face suddenly loosen as the claw hands slid away.

"No," the creature said. "You cannot be here."

Gabby was no longer Gabby. Outwardly she looked the same, but in a way that Alex couldn't put into words, she also looked very different. But it was something else that drew the fear out of hiding and caused the breath to catch in his throat. Her eyes; they shone with an ethereal aura, her pupils like bright stars that glistened eerily in the now gloomy room.

"Gabby?" Alex said, his voice trailing off as she looked to him, cocking her head to one side like a vulture, trying to decide if he was prey or not. After a moment, she looked away, turning her attention to the burned man, now backing toward the corner, his expression a mixture of confusion and disbelief.

"You... you can't be here," he said, pointing an accusatory finger across the room.

Gabby stood slowly, the movement smooth and effortless, and took a step forward, her form somehow appearing more imposing, taller than before.

"Hello, Arioch." She paused to look down at her hands, flexing the fingers, clenching and unclenching them into fists, testing them as if she was using them for the first time. She shrugged, as if settling into a new overcoat, stretching her neck to one side, and looked up. "You have broken your vow," she said, her voice smooth and even. "The line that cannot be crossed has been crossed." She tilted her head slightly. "You should know better."

The creature blanched at the sound of his name, his shoulders dropping and his posture straightening slightly. "Do you remember hat happened last time?"

Gabby's expression remained a mask of cool indifference. "That was different," she said. "You changed the rules."

"She *chose* to come with me," the creature said. "And you were powerless to save her. You lost, and if it was because I changed the rules, why didn't you fight for her?"

"Even I am unable to save a soul that does not want to be saved, but you, you took that woman's life on a promise disguised as a lie."

"She wasn't worth saving," the creature sneered, waving a gnarled hand dismissively as a crooked smile cracking his charred features. "All's fair in love and war."

Alex watched as Gabby stood, swaying slightly, looking away from him toward the creature in the far corner. The room was becoming so gloomy that he could barely make out the creature, drowned in shadow, it's eyes glowing a soft red hue.

"And who are you to tell me what is best for these... creatures?" it said. "Who are you to tell any of us what is best, what is just? There is no right here, no claim, not even by you, *Gabriel*."

"Why can you not just leave them to fight their wars and battles alone?" she said, "You do not need to give yourself to this cause. It will be the end of you, whether by my hand or your own."

The creature looked up. "Cause? You think that I am here for some kind of cause?" He laughed, the low chuckle rattling in his chest. "You are all too arrogant to see your own hypocrisy. Their world is coming to an end, and the amusing thing is, that they haven't even needed any help in securing their own destruction. Our work has been so much easier than even we dared hope. They discard one another so casually as they search for a way to live forever, and are blind to the fact that it's just pushing them closer to the brink of extinction."

Gabby lowered herself to the floor, kneeling close to him. "Despite the tragedy of man's many failures, they are all worthy of the chance to endure, to succeed, to live. Neither you nor I are worthy of trying to change that. And if they are to meet their end by their own hand, then they do not need your help to ensure it, any more than they would receive ours to avert it."

Alex watched in dumfounded silence at the conversation unfolding before him. The house was shifting and creaking as the fire took hold outside, and he wondered how long it would be until the whole place came down around them. The creature shifted uneasily, his black eyes never leaving Gabby's face. Alex could sense Gabby's tension. She appeared outwardly relaxed, kneeling almost casually beside the man as the fire raged through the doorway behind her, but she was alert, ready for the slightest move.

"Why do you love them so much?" the creature asked, its voice low and cracking. "Why, with all of the wickedness in their hearts, do you continue to stand by them, defending them, when all they do is seek their own downfall and to disprove your very existence? It is *you* who should withdraw, *you* who should give up *your* cause, and let them go the way they will inevitably go."

He smirked then, leaning back against the wall as she stood. "You know it's going to happen. They are doomed. Why should you help them? They will never change. There is evil in the hearts of men, Gabriel, and there has been since the dawn of time. It is just who they are meant to be, and nothing either you or I do will change that."

And then Alex saw them. At first he thought it was a trick of the light as tendrils of smoke wafted about the room from the encroaching fire outside the door, as she stepped forward, her body moving through the smoke, he made out the vague shapes of two large wings, appearing to move and flex in the air behind and above Gabby, as if she were some kind of...

"I saw your wings," he whispered suddenly, recalling the strange dream of dead streets and storms and the mysterious winged figure who had pulled him from the shadows.

Gabby did not acknowledge the comment, instead moving forward slowly, toward the cornered creature, still staring at her, a look of curious confusion on its burned and bloody face. He felt those red eyes upon him then, and gazed into the shadows as the creature appeared, leaning forward and glaring at him.

"Go into the closet, Alex," he said, his voice suddenly smooth and reassuring. "It's your way out, just step inside and you will be free. Go, you can go now." He made a shooing gesture with his hand and Alex looked toward the closet, the door hanging half open, blocking his view of the interior.

"This one is different," Gabby said, her attention still fixed upon the now leering creature. "He will not be swayed so easily."

The creature chuckled. "Are you serious? There is more doubt and guilt in this one than that fawning woman you failed to save all those years ago. Oh no, he's ripe for the taking."

Alex climbed slowly to his feet and reached out for the door, slowly pulling it open wider.

"Alex," Gabby said, her voice impossibly clear and strong. "Alex, don't listen to him. He wants only to harm you, to harm all that you know and love. Don't go in there."

"You see, Alex? She wants you to stay here. She doesn't want you to get away. She would see you trapped here and burnt to a cinder. You don't have much time!"

Alex could smell something strange just then, like the humid, heavy scent of a rain forest, mixed with the biting, bitter taste of smoke and ashes.

"You don't have to go that way, Alex," Gabby said, but Alex didn't turn around. Instead, he reached out and pulled open both doors, revealing the open closet and the hanging clothes, pushed aside to revel the gaping shaft in the floor.

"I can tell you where to find him, Alex," the creature said, and Alex paused, staring into the open closet. "I can help you find your father. He needs you, Alex. He's so close. This time you can help him. This time you will be there for him."

Alex closed his eyes as a wave of warm, heavy air washed over him. The sound of gusting wind and rustling leaves came to him, and then something else. He opened his eyes. There before him, through the opening of the closet, he saw a jungle landscape, thick with lush, green foliage and a multitude of tangled vines hanging from the trees. Dappled sunlight played over giant palm leaves and patches of thick, knee-high grass, and a trio of exotic birds flew by, their song cutting sharply through the moist air.

The scene appeared to grow toward him, stretching around him, enveloping him, and he heard the other sounds then, growing louder until they drowned out the serene noises of the tropical scene around him. The distant, echoing rattle of gunfire grew nearer, until it seemed to be all around him, and he flinched as the first explosion uprooted a tree to his right, showering him with leaves and clumps of soil.

"Alex!" He knew the voice as soon as he heard it, drifting toward him through the undergrowth and broken by gunfire. "Alex, help me!"

He saw the arm, bloodied and pale, waving above the grass. On the forearm was a tattoo. It had always fascinated Alex as a child. A dagger, wrapped in barbed wire, piercing a heart.

"Dad!" Alex cried out, taking a step forward, his hand gripping the edge of the helicopter doorway as he stared through the bushes and trees. "Come on, Dad!"

Gabby had turned to watch Alex move toward the open closet, the escape shaft a gaping hole in the floor that led straight down, thirty feet to the tunnel floor below. Alex took a step, placing one foot inside, his toes hanging over the edge of the open shaft. He gripped the upper edge of the opening and reached forward with his other hand, the sling falling away from his injured arm.

"He is so close," Arioch said, "And he will go gladly, willingly." He looked up at Gabby and she turned to look down, meeting his gaze. "And you are powerless to stop him, just as you were with her."

Alex could feel the breeze, hot and humid, blowing across the tall grass, as he hung onto the helicopter's door frame, the rotors turning somewhere out of sight overhead. He edged his foot forward more, toes hanging over the edge of the door.

"Help me, Alex!" His father cried, barely visible amongst the grass. "I'm right here! Help me!"

Again he edged forward, feeling the lip of the doorway pressing into the arch of his foot as he moved closer to stepping out.

"Don't do it!"

He was startled by the loud voice in his ear and turned to see Gabby, dressed in a flight suit and manning the heavy caliber machine gun that hung in the doorway. The helmet looked a little too big for her.

"Alex, don't do it! You won't make it!"

The noise of the wind was a series of blustering gusts, buffeting his hair and pressing his shirt against his chest, already clammy with sweat. He stared at Gabby, shaking his head. "What are you doing here?"

"Jump, Alex!" his father cried out, his hand stretching, claw-like toward the sky. "I need you!"

He turned to the door again, suddenly hesitant, confused.

"Alex, listen to me," Gabby said from beside him. "This isn't real! You are not here! Don't do it, Alex. If you jump you will die!"

He looked out and saw his father suddenly appear, pushing himself up, his torso visible above the grass. His face was bloody and Alex could see bullet wounds across his chest.

"Alex, son! I need your help! Jump! Do it!"

He hesitated, feeling the pull of fear tugging at his back, fighting with the urge to run to help his stricken father, bleeding and dying out there, amongst the grass and the rain.

He turned to look at Gabby, hands still on the machine gun, just staring back at him from beneath the heavy crew helmet visor. "I can't leave him!" he shouted, the drone of the helicopter growing louder as the unseen rotor blades began to wind up, spinning faster above his head. "He needs me!"

"This isn't *real* Alex! Don't jump, please! Think about it! How am I here? How are *you* here! This isn't happening! Is isn't real!"

"Alex!" He turned to the door and gasped as he came face to face with his father, standing by the door, one hand gripping his ankle. "I told you to help me! Now get your ass out here, or there will be *hell* to pay!"

Suddenly, an explosion shook the ground and a fiery tree branch fell onto the side of the chopper, showering them all with glowing embers and flaming leaves as the helicopter bucked under the impact.

"Alex, get back!" Gabby cried, still holding on to the door gun. He wondered why she wasn't helping him. She was just sitting there, an imploring look on her face.

Another flaming branch, this time looking more like a tree trunk than a branch, came crashing down behind him. A wave of heat gusted through the open bay of the Huey and Alex cried out as the skin on his back began to blister.

"Come with me, *now!*" Alex's father screamed, his grip tightening on his ankle, tugging it toward the edge of the edge of the bay. Alex softened his grip on the edge of the door and edged forward, his foot dangling in the open air.

As he let go of the door, he saw his father smile, except it wasn't his father anymore. His teeth were rows of pointed fangs and his face was ashen grey. His eyes stared, black as onyx as he pulled Alex's foot out of the door toward him. Alex began to fall forward, the air filled with the cracking, roaring cacophony of the fire that raged all around the helicopter.

"NO!"

A hand grabbed the back of Alex's shirt as he heard Gabby's last, desperate plea. Suddenly yanked backwards, his ankle was torn from his father's clawed grip, and the noise around him grew louder as he fell, landing heavily on the floor... of the bedroom in Gant's house, the jungle visage disappeared, replaced by burning walls and a room that was collapsing all around him. He raised his arms to protect his face as half of the wall gave way to a stack of flaming roof beams, crashing and tumbling into the room around him.

Chapter Thirty-Four

Gabriel watched as Alex stepped into the open shaft inside the closet. She could hear the distant, sinister whispers of Arioch's seductive influence as he pushed the illusion into Alex's mind, filling him with the doubt and temptation he needed to make him take that fatal step into the void. At the last moment, she turned away from Arioch, hurling herself over the bed toward Alex as he took that final step. She saw his hand slip away from the edge of the closet door opening and watched as he body moved forward, his foot stepping out over the open, yawning shaft that dropped away to darkness below.

She reached out, her hand grasping his shirt as he began to fall forward, and jerked him back from the edge before he could fall into the opening.

"No!" Arioch leapt to his feet, brushing away a burning, foot-thick beam and striding forward as Gabriel and Alex lay a heap in front of the open closet, his arms crossed in front of his face. Arioch leapt over the bed with a scream, raising his fist and slamming it downward, aiming the blow at Gabriel's upturned face.

She twisted toward him, punching upward, and smashed her knuckles into Arioch's own clenched fist, shattering the bones in his hand and arm. He had no time to react, falling to his knees beside Gabriel, his ruined hand flopping sickeningly, eyes wide with horror. Gabriel reached up, instantly grabbing Arioch by the throat and pulling him up and over her, slamming his head into the floor. She was on her knees in an instant, turning him over onto his back and pinning him to the floor, her hand pushing hard down onto his chest.

Alex was laying a few feet away, in front of the open closet, a heavy wood roof beam laying across the top of it, burning steadily, the flames reaching up toward the rapidly disintegrating ceiling. The house was finally coming apart, the room now little more than a crumbling shell as the walls began to give way and the ceiling began to crumble the floor in clumps of burning wood and drywall.

"Alex!" Gabriel yelled, her palm pinning Arioch to the floor. "Get down the ladder! Get out, now!"

He stirred, peering between his forearms, straight into the glowing eyes of his friend, who was perhaps no longer his friend at all. His face betrayed his absolute fear and Gabriel softened her tone as she spoke again, the words calming, reassuring. "Alex, we're out of time. You need to get out. Go, now, please."

Arioch cried out, a mixture of frustration and agony, twisting and writhing beneath the weight of Gabriel's hand. She leaned harder, the sound of his cracking ribs blending with the crackling of the fire all around them like some macabre duet. He cried out again, gripping Gabriel's wrist with his one good hand, but his thrashing stilled and he lay there, staring up at her imploringly as she waited for Alex to move. He did, looking right and seeing Gabby's handgun a few feet away by the closet door. And just to the left, on the floor beside the bed and a pile of burning debris, was Gant's laptop. Rolling to his knees, Alex knocked the debris away in a shower of sparks and smoke. Gabriel watched as he climbed gingerly to his feet and scooped up the laptop, turning toward the closet, creaking beneath the weight of the burning beam that was partially blocking the open doorway.

"You cannot take him!" Arioch screamed, and Gabriel turned to look down at him, her expression flat and impassive. "You dare to accuse me of breaking my vow!"

"In defense of this innocent soul, I contest thee," she said, her voice strong and full of power. Alex paused, turning to look over his shoulder at her hunched figure. The closet cracked, shifting under the weight of the beam, and Alex turned back, ducking inside and stepping across the shaft and onto the first rung of the metal ladder.

Gabriel could sense that Alex had made it into the shaft and was making his way down, each step taking him closer to safety. She glared down at Arioch, his face a twisted mask of agony and rage. "I know you had little choice," she said. "But you should not have come here. My duty is not only one of delivering messages." She raised her free hand above her head, fingers relaxed as she held it there, in the air above the demon's face. The light in her eyes intensified for a moment. "It is to defend His children and cast out the evil that seeks to claim their souls with temptation and deception."

"Wait, no," Arioch protested feebly, his expression suddenly softening, the blackness in his eyes clearing to a crisp pale blue. "Don't send me back this way."

"You are the deliverer of His revenge," she continued, ignoring his plea. "For pursuing the prophecy of light against His one true son."

"Gabriel," he whispered, his voice broken and croaking with fear. "Oh, highest messenger and strength of God. Oh, mighty one, bringer of justice, forgive my trespass. Allow me to leave this vessel and withdraw. I shall never return."

Gabriel closed her eyes and the room fell silent then, the fires suddenly slowing to a stop as if time had been swept from the room by an invisible hand, the raging wind dissipating to stillness, the clumps of smoke hanging in the air like clouds of blackened cotton candy. Even the sounds of the still raging fire seemed to fade to subtle background noise.

"Ecce dabit voci suae vocem virtutis, tribuite virtutem deo." She said, closing her eyes and making the sign of the cross in the air above his face.

"Please, Gabriel," Arioch pleaded, a note of panic in his voice. "Don't send me back this way. I beg of..."

"Ergo draco maledicte et omnis legio diabolica adjuramus te." Gabriel spoke smoothly, the latin phrases falling from her lips as wine from a glass as Arioch began to struggle once more, thrashing and twisting in vain beneath the immovable strength of Gabriel's hand.

"Gabriel, please! I beg you!"

"Ab insidiis diaboli, libera nos, Domine," Gabriel continued, her hand poised in the air, her fore and middle fingers together as she repeated the sign of the cross, passing on the power of her spoken ritual. She opened her eyes and looked down. "Benedictus deus. Gloria patri," she said. "Blessed be God. Glory be to the Father."

"Gabriel!"

She thrust her hand down, her two fingers spearing his chest. Arioch arched his back, a scream frozen in his throat as his eyes widened, mouth open in a silent cry for mercy as his flesh began to crack, revealing an orange hued light from within, like the lava-filled crevices of an erupting volcano. The cracks spread across his features, engulfing his body until it resembled a carcass of cracking, glowing embers, pulled from a fire, his eyes two glowing orange orbs and his body frozen in a twisted portrait of torment on the floor. Gabriel drew away, standing over the now lifeless body as the glow peaked, and then began to subside, fading to dull orange and then red. What was left was nothing more than a charred and blackened husk of a man's form, crumbling to the carpet in a pile of black soot and ash.

The firestorm returned as suddenly as it had stopped, roaring back to life as roaring flames and searing wind. The last remnants of the outer wall began to shift and collapse, dropping away to the grass below. Gabby stood for a moment and then blinked, startled back to the present, and back to her normal, suddenly overheated self. A loud *crack!* made her turn toward the closet and she leapt forward, reaching down to scoop up Gant's box and disappearing through the door and down into the open shaft as the heavy beam finally crushed through the top of the closet and fell, barring the shaft entrance and sending clouds of charred wood and embers down to the floor below.

Jerry stopped as the unmistakable sound of gunfire echoed across the open land from the house, a few hundred yards to the south. He knelt instinctively in the icy mud, and instantly regretted it as the frigid moisture soaked through his pant leg at the knee. Looking out through the hedgerow across the field, he listened as the muffled sound of an explosion followed a moment later.

"Goddammit, boss," he whispered, his breath billowing from his lips in a cloud of steam. "There's no fucking cavalry this time."

The distant sound of combat rumbled and clattered in the early morning air and he moved onward, keeping his crouched walk low, beneath the top of the hedgerow and bushes. The grass was long to the side of the narrow trail, and he kept his eyes darting forward and to the ground, still following the random boot prints in the mud. He was coming up on the shed-like building—a little less than fifty yards away now—set back around twenty-five yards from the tree line. The hedgerow started to curve around to the left, the thick bushes pushing in on his right, making the already narrow path even harder to navigate. The explosions and gunfire from the main house had died down, and Jerry crouched to scan open land through the hedge with a pair of small field glasses. He could see one wall of the house completely blown out, and what looked like a body, laying amongst the debris. There was no one outside that he could see, and...

Snick.

Jerry froze at the small sound, from somewhere farther along the hedgerow, and stowed the binoculars before picking up the rifle and turning moving on along the trail. A particularly large bush blocked his path and he cursed beneath his breath at the thought of giving away his approach. Searching for a way around, he spotted a small gap in the underbrush and moved toward it, entering the thick foliage in a low crouch as he searched for a way around the bushes encroaching on the trail.

It wasn't long before he came across the source of the sound. Moving silently through the bushes he coming up on a pair of squirrels, skittering about in the underbrush. He was about to move back onto the trail when he caught a glimpse of something up ahead, barely out of sight, beside a section of old fencing, overgrown and festooned with mildew and moss. Carefully slinging the rifle, he drew his handgun, moving forward slowly, picking his steps with deliberate caution. Away to his left, across the steadily brightening fields, he saw that the house was on fire, belching black and grey smoke into the early morning air. His stomach sank as he thought about who could have gotten out, and who had not.

He forced himself to refocus, steadying his aim and moving forward again. Thirty-five yards from the fence, there was little in the way of obstacles, and yet he moved as if every step was a potential twig-breaker or giveaway, watching for wires and leaves; anything that would warn someone of his presence. What he didn't see was the small grey rock, about the size of a packet of cigarettes, laying half-hidden beneath a clump of grass and smeared with mud. A rock with a laser trip beam that Jerry broke when he walked by it.

Hawkes lay prone, with only a thin shooting mat between him and the cold earth. He had been in position and set up since the teams had gotten into position around the house, his rifle scope trained on the corners, walls and windows on the north side of the building. His focus now was on the remnants of the structure, watching it burn to a blackened husk with magnified clarity. The only thing keeping his raging frustration at bay was years of training and well-honed discipline. Inside, he wanted to blow someone's head off, and he tracked his crosshairs from window to window, searching for a target, pausing only on the gaping hole in the wall that had been blown out by a grenade or some kind of tripped explosive.

The remains of Deakins' body were visible on the grass, his head and torso resting a few feet away from his legs, which were surprisingly intact-looking. No one besides Johnson had answered his radio calls, and he was under strict instructions to remain at the gate until the mission was over. Assuming that only Johnson and himself were what remained of the entire unit, he thought that might qualify as mission: over.

Beep.

He looked down at the small, hand-held device beside him. A red light was flashing on a small display, indicating an intruder, some thirty or so yards down the trail. One of his trip warnings. Heller had considered the chances of someone making it out here to his spot to be remote. Prudence dictated, however, that he prepare for potential visitors, whatever the level of his positional security, and he had set a trio of early warning devices to alert him of any approaching threat. According to unit B, that threat was indeed approaching. He flicked a button to silence the device and rolled to the side, crawling backwards until he had crossed the trail and disappeared up into the undergrowth a few seconds later.

Jerry rounded the bend, keeping low as he moved forward, rifle raised, the trail in sharp focus through the red dot sight. He saw the shooting mat and the scoped rifle, laying at an angle on its bipod, the barrel barely poking through the rungs in the fence and aimed at the house. Dropping to a knee, he held his breath, listening for signs of anyone close by, sweeping the small clearing with the rifle. He knew he'd been made. The cold steel of Hawkes' Beretta pressed firmly into his neck, just below his right ear. Jerry let out his breath, the silent curse escaping his lips only as a warm cloud in the still morning air.

"Drop it, agent man," Hawkes said. "Slow and steady, and you get to go home walking and talking today."

Jerry straightened, slowly raising his hands and lifting the rifle away from his body, watching it disappear as Hawkes took it, the handgun's barrel still pressed into his neck.

"Who else is with you?" Hawkes asked, stepping back and holstering his sidearm. He checked the rifle and looked around. "They wouldn't send you to me all by your lonesome, would they?"

"You are acting outside the law and interfering with a Federal investigation," Jerry said, kneeling in the mud and staring straight ahead. "Your mission is over. Surrender your weapons and lay on the ground."

Hawkes chuckled. "Whatever you say, agent man. Hands behind your head, and lace your fingers."

Jerry complied and Hawkes slung the rifle, stepping up behind him and grasping his fingers to hold them there as he reached for a plasti-cuff on his utility belt. The sounds of the house, crumpling and collapsing as it succumbed to the fire, echoed across the fields toward them. As Hawkes reached forward to slip one plastic loop of the cuffs over his hand, Jerry slid one leg back, between Hawkes' two feet, and pivoted, turning toward him and dropping down, dragging Hawkes forward and off balance. Jerry pulled one hand free and reached up, grabbing Hawkes' arm, as the mercenary released the cuff and jerked a hand away, reaching down and across toward his holster.

Jerry fell back with one of Hawkes' booted feet trapped under one arm, and grabbed the other ankle, pulling on Hawkes' arm. He kicked up, catching the mercenary in the butt and pushing with his shin, tossing him over, head first, to the ground above his head. He heard Hawkes grunt as he fell forward, tucking his head and trying to roll out of the throw. Jerry twisted in the dirt and was on his knees in a second, shuffling quickly toward the sprawling soldier. He noticed Hawkes' gun, still in its holster, and moved in, not seeing the push dagger Hawkes had drawn from the small sheath on his belt as he had rolled.

The blade sliced upward as Hawkes turned on the ground, instinctively striking as he sensed the FBI agent moving in. As Jerry reached out toward the scrambling soldier, he felt the dull impact on his forearm as Hawkes struck him with his fist, narrowly missing with the small blade. As they scrambled, Jerry catching Hawkes' wrist and the soldier spinning around to face the agent, the house came down in the distance, collapsing in on itself and leaving half-demolished walls around a huge, pyre-like fire with blackened wood beams jutting out of the flames like the burnt ribs of some giant, fallen beast.

They rolled, a tangled mess of struggling arms and legs, Hawkes kicking into the mud as he tried to push Jerry backwards to pin him against the fence. Jerry struggled to maintain control over Hawkes' knife hand and fight him off as the mercenary used the distraction to begin to maneuver the Federal agent down into the ground, gradually gaining more and more control over the engagement, moving to Jerry's side and working hard to free his knife hand. The faint sound of an engine firing up somewhere close by distracted Jerry long enough for Hawkes to aim a crushing knee into his ribs. Jerry crumpled—three of his ribs breaking under the impact—and twisted on the ground as Hawkes sank his knee into his side again and then reared up over him, pulling the dagger out of Jerry's loosening grip and aiming a punch down into Jerry's face, turning his head to one side and opening a gash over the agent's left eye.

"You mother fucker," Hawkes spat. "I was just gonna break a couple of things and leave you here." He stood, towering over the stricken agent, breathing hard, his brown glistening with sweat. "But now I may as well have a little fun before I go."

He stepped back slightly, and stood on Jerry's ankle, pinning it painfully into the ground, grinning wickedly. "Hey, sorry about those ribs there, friend. Those bitches take forever to heal, too."

Jerry winced with every breath, the white hot pain stabbing him with every movement. "Drop your weapons," he said, the words short and sharp, in between painful gasps of breath. "You're under...arrest."

Hawkes laughed, his shoulders heaving as he grinned down at Jerry, his fists resting on his hips. "Boy, you got some set of balls on you for a pussy agent man, I'll give you that." The laugh subsided to a chuckle and he leaned forward, bending over Jerry, waving the knife in front of him. "But I still gotta pull me out a few of them ribs."

CRASH!

The sound of splintering wood and buckling metal shattered the calm as the doors to the shed burst outward. An old Bronco exploded from the small building, spitting up dirt and grass as the big tires drove the heavy truck toward the fence. Hawkes' head snapped around and Jerry drew a knee up, kicking out with everything he had, striking Hawkes in the stomach and sending him flying backwards to the ground. Jerry cried out in pain and rolled onto his side, lifting his head to see Hawkes scramble to his feet, just as the Bronco smashed through the old fence and into the startled soldier. Jerry watched the truck continue into the bushes, finally coming to a stop, it's brake lights glowing and tailpipe chugging out a steady stream of grey mist.

Collapsing onto his back, he rested his head in the mud and stared up at a patch of perfectly blue sky, finally allowing himself to breathe. Footsteps approached, stopping by his feet. He didn't look down, instead keeping his eyes fixed on the sky above.

"Good morning, Jerry."

"Morning, boss."

Gabby knelt beside her injured partner as Alex walked up, stopping beside her. Jerry glanced down, his hands gripping his torso protectively. "I hope that whatever you have in that damned box is worth all of this shit, Alex," he said, catching short gasps between every few words.

"Shut up," Gabby said, examining him carefully. "Let's get you out of here."

Chapter Thirty-Five

The black Ford sedan pulled up to the curb, its front passenger door opening before it had come to a stop. The agent got out and quickly moved to the back door, pulling it open and looking up and down the sidewalk with practiced routine. Director Cole stepped out, tugging the hem of her suit jacket as she strode purposefully toward the front entrance of the Akron Hotel. A doorman ushered her inside—along with the agent who had seen her from the car—and they moved across the marble-floored lobby toward the concierge desk. They made it half way when a thin, gaunt man approached, flanked by two burly security guards.

"Director Cole? My name is Hammond. I'll be taking you up to see Mister Devlin. Your chaperone is more than welcome to wait down here in the lounge. If you'll follow me, please."

Cole turned to her agent and nodded, watching as he turned to walk toward a lounge area across the lobby, tailed by the two guards, both in dark suits and carrying poorly concealed sub machine guns under their jackets. She turned away to follow Hammond toward the elevators. He inserted a card key and gestured for Cole to enter before stepping inside and punching a code on the small keypad that took the place of a regular floor button panel.

"This will take us directly to Mister Devlin's suite," Hammond explained, as the elevator rose, quickly ascending to the top floor a few moments later. The door slid open and Hammond gestured for Cole to step out ahead of him. He remained in the elevator and the door closed, leaving Cole alone, standing in one corner of an enormous living area, the entire wall to her left one long window, giving an impressive panoramic view of the city. A fire was burning eagerly in an immense, black marble fireplace, set in the far wall to the right. She took a step forward, uncertain of whether to announce her presence or take a seat on one of the leather couches in front of her.

"Do you believe in chance?" a voice said, echoing across the room from somewhere in the far corner.

Cole turned her head, frowning at the glimpse of someone walking behind a row of columns on the far side of the room that acted as a sort of partition between the living area and the large, conference-size table beyond.

"I believe in it when it suits me," she said, walking forward, the clicking of her heels on the polished floor dampened as she stepped onto the rug by the couches. "But I would never trust anything to it."

James appeared and walked slowly toward her, two crystal tumblers in his hands, each containing warm amber liquid. She watched him as he walked, coming to a stop in front of her, holding out one of the tumblers.

"Elijah Craig, single barrel bourbon, if I'm not mistaken," he said. Cole reached out and took the glass, hiding her surprise at his knowledge of her favorite drink. She nodded a toast and raised the glass to her lips. James saw the hint of a smile before Cole could choke it off. "Please, " he said, turning to take a seat on the couch. "Make yourself comfortable, and I'll tell you why I'm in your city."

Cole sat, placing the tumbler on the glass coffee table that separated the two couches. "Would you be surprised to know that's not why I came here?"

"I know why you came here, Director Cole."

"Really? And why is that?" She said, scanning the room.

James sat regarding his bourbon. "Because you're a predator, and you smell blood in the water." He sat back, crossing his legs casually, and Cole noticed the hovering figures of two suited men, both keeping a respectful distance beyond the columns, close to the windows on the far side of the room.

"And what about chance?" James said. "We all play out those scenarios in our head," James went on. "If I'd have done this, would that have happened, or if I hadn't done that, would I be here now?"

"And what about you?" She asked. "Do you feel that you are where you are today because of chance, or is everything predetermined, set in stone, no matter what decisions we make?"

"Predetermination is just a fancy word used by the people of this world who lack the drive to make something different of their lives, but it's really the more boring option, don't you think? It doesn't matter what I do, I am always meant to do it. There's really no escaping that, is there?" He shifted in his seat. "No, that's far too claustrophobic for me. Too...smothering. I believe that we make our own destinies and forge our own futures with courageous risk-taking and the hard work of critical decision-making."

James sat forward, gesturing toward Cole with the tumbler. "If you didn't think the same way, you wouldn't have given yourself to the chance that this meeting wasn't simply my way of eliminating a potential thorn in our side."

Cole appeared unfazed, as if having considered every scenario, including that one. "I believe that you came to my city for a reason, and while that reason has something to do with me, I don't believe that it's just to get rid of me. You wouldn't have wasted the time getting the bourbon if it was. I'm important to you, somehow, just as I thought you were important to me, and I would just take you in right now if I felt I would gain more from that than staying and hearing what you have to say."

James nodded. "That's a bold statement, coming from a director of the FBI."

"I'm not being bold," Cole said, her tone taking on a more serious tone. "You are here because of your ties to Lincoln Klick. I am at a disadvantage only because, at the moment, I don't know exactly what those ties are." She sat forward. "I would have asked him myself if you hadn't had him killed before he could tell us anything about the real reasons behind you coming here and why, frankly, that should matter at all."

"What makes you think we are in the business of killing people?"

The question was asked by someone out of sight, somewhere at the far end of the room, beyond the columns and the large table by the window. Cole sat forward, staring across the room as James casually sipped his drink, his eyes never leaving the FBI Director.

"I think," Cole said, raising her voice so that the mystery guest could hear. "That you aren't in the business of killing people. I think that you kill people that get in the way of your business." She was reaching, drawing on years of experience being inside interrogation rooms with hundreds of unwilling conversationalists.

James smiled, as much at Cole's deflection of the question as the question itself, and the two men by the far window suddenly moved. Someone stood up from one of the chairs around the large table, partially obscured by the thick columns. A man appeared, walking around the corner toward them. He walked slowly, buttoning up his jacket, with the gait of unhurried confidence. As he approached, stepping onto the rug, he smiled and held out his hand toward Cole.

"Hello, Director Cole," the man said. "I've been wanting to meet you for quite some time. I am an admirer of your work. Especially that messy affair in Turkey in '03."

Cole stood, trying hard to appear unfazed at the last comment. If nothing else, she was being reminded that these people had at least done their homework on her.

"I don't believe I've had the pleasure," she said, taking his hand.

"Black," the man said. "Roland Black, and I think I can help give you something you want, something you've always wanted, and have been working hard your whole life to get."

Cole regarded him for a moment. "And what's that?"

"The FBI, Director Cole. The FBI."

*   *   *

Father Peter Benson, the sole survivor of the convention center disaster, squinted as he walked out through the automatic doors and left the bustling lobby of the Holy Trinity hospital, his discharge papers crumpled in his hand. The sky was a total contrast to the malevolent, stormy grey of the night before and he looked up, shielding his eyes against the bright winter sun. Stepping to the curb, he saw a cigarette butt, crooked and still smoking on the edge of a trash can. He picked it up, resting it between his lips as he shook his overcoat and hung it over his arm. His hair was dirty and mussed, and he needed a shower. Yeah, a nice, hot shower.

Stepping off the sidewalk and into the street, a speeding yellow cab came to a screeching halt, two feet from his legs.

"What the hell are you...?" The cab driver was out of the cab in a second, holding onto the open door and waving his hand at Father Benson with abject frustration. "Oh, I'm sorry, Father, but you should be careful, you know?" Benson climbed in the back as the cab driver settled into the driver's seat, turning to face the young priest. "If it had been anyone else but me, you could've been truly crushed right then. I'm just saying. I mean, I know you got the big man upstairs probably looking out for you, but you need all the help you can get down here, too, right?"

Benson nodded. "The Grange Hotel, on Willow."

Turning back to the wheel, the driver punched the meter and pulled sharply into traffic, to the sounds of protesting horns. "Grange Hotel, out by the airport, right?"

Benson looked out the window at the cars and people, the city all around him, and he felt a sense of helplessness. He wanted to save them all, desperately.

"So many," he said to himself.

"You want to go straight to the hotel?" the driver asked, as he swerved across two lanes, cutting off a cement truck. "I know a great pancake place, if you're hungry. Best in the city, trust me."

"No," Benson said, not taking his eyes from the window. "Take me to the hotel."

"Sure, no problem. Hey, you're probably a busy guy, I know. You're trying to save the world, right? Save all of us sinners from the Devil? I know, I know. I don't envy you, Father. It's a tough job. Maybe impossible. I mean, how are you gonna save all of us, ya know?"

Benson watched the city slipping by, the hard, grey concrete in sharp contrast with the overwhelming beauty of the sky above the rooftops. The driver was right. It was an impossible job. He looked down at his hand, rubbing his palm with his fingers. The black stain had gone, disappeared from his body by the time he had been admitted to the hospital, but he felt its mark, forever etched in his soul. It would drive him on his mission, and the work he had ahead of him was daunting.

"One soul at a time."

END of PART ONE

Printed in Great Britain
by Amazon

21727990R00185